TRUE

TO THE

HIGHLANDER

Also by Barbara Longley

Love from the Heartland series, set in Perfect, Indiana

Far from Perfect

The Difference a Day Makes

A Change of Heart

TRUE TO THE HIGHLANDER

A Novel of Loch Moigh

Barbara Longley

Published by Montlake Romance, Seattle

www.apub.com

ISBN-13: 9781477817445
ISBN-10: 1477817441

Cover design by becker&mayer, LLC
Cover illustration by Dana Ashton France

Library of Congress Control Number: 2013916302

Printed in the United States of America

This book is dedicated to dreamers everywhere. To those of you who are able to suspend disbelief and consider the possibilities, dream on.

CHAPTER ONE

New York, Present Day

Alethia Goodsky gave all things supernatural a wide berth—and Madame Giselle reeked of magic. The old fortune-teller often followed her around the fairgrounds, popping up whenever Alethia took her breaks—always watching. She couldn't help but feel uneasy around the woman. Fixing a wary eye on the fortune-teller's green-and-white-striped tent, she contemplated the two paths before her. The longer route to the parking lot meant an uphill trek all the way around the New York Renaissance Festival fairgrounds, in her gown no less. The shorter path cut the distance in half, but she'd have to pass within a foot of Madame Giselle's door.

A gust of wind whipped a cloud of dust into her face, stinging her eyes. She gagged on the sour smell of garbage carried by the breeze. Exhaustion tugged her toward the shorter route. As much as she loved her job at the Renaissance festival, weeks of working around the clock had taken their toll.

Shifting the strap of the canvas duffel biting into her shoulder, Alethia started down the hill, her violin case bumping against her hip with each step. Near the tent's entrance, she clutched the skirt of her Renaissance gown and tiptoed past.

The sound of muffled sobs brought her to a halt. *Crying?*

Torn, she listened for a moment before compassion won out over common sense. Moving the tent flap aside, she peered in. "Hello, is everything all right in here?"

"No, it's not." Madame Giselle had changed out of her gypsy costume and into gabardine slacks, a cashmere sweater and a suede blazer. Riffling through her designer handbag, she resembled nothing more sinister than someone's upper-class grandmother. She pulled out a linen handkerchief and turned to face Alethia. "I'm glad you stopped by. Come in."

Alethia really didn't want to go into that tent, but she'd been the fool who'd lifted the flap, and disrespecting an elder went against the grain. She took a tentative step forward. "What's the matter?"

"Oh." Giselle blew her nose into the fancy hanky. "Someone I care about is in grave danger. I'd do anything to help." She turned red, puffy eyes toward Alethia. "Wouldn't you if it were someone in your family?"

"Yes, ma'am, I would."

"I thought as much." Giselle's eyes lit up through her teary smile. Dark eyes shining with acuity and something deeper fixed on Alethia. "You grew up on your father's reservation, didn't you, near the Canadian border?"

"How could you possibly know that?" The familiar prickle of unease she felt around Giselle cat-pawed its way up Alethia's spine.

"Not all of what I do is for show." Giselle arched an eyebrow. "You better than anyone should understand."

"I don't know what you mean." Heat rose to Alethia's cheeks at the lie.

"Come now, you can be honest with me. You have . . . certain gifts, do you not?"

Gifts? That's not the word she'd use to describe her abilities. Alethia could read other people's energy and always knew whether someone was lying or telling the truth. She'd read everything she could about

ESP. Her talent wasn't all that unique. Still, on top of being biracial, her so-called *gift* made it even more difficult to fit in. "I don't—"

"There are depths to you not yet tapped," Giselle added as if speaking to herself. "You'd be able to survive anywhere." Her eyes narrowed. "You have plans for the future, a carefully laid path already in the works?"

She didn't know about the tapping depths part, but her plans at least felt like safe territory. Alethia nodded. "I graduate from Juilliard next spring, and I already have a job lined up in Los Angeles." Pride rippled through her. "I'll be playing in a Hollywood orchestra that does soundtracks for movies."

"Sounds lovely." Giselle smiled back. "Why don't you sit? That pack looks heavy."

"I can't stay. My ride is waiting." Alethia stepped back, and the air in the tent became charged with an unfamiliar tension. *Magic.* Giselle's image blurred and shifted as if it had been superimposed over another's, more ethereal and insubstantial. Alethia's heart beat inside her chest like a fly trapped in a glass jar.

She blinked, and the ordinary grandmother in gabardine came back into focus. *Not possible. It's exhaustion, that's all.* Alethia took a deep breath and let it out slowly.

"Stay for a moment." Giselle pointed toward a rickety chair set close to an equally shabby table. "I thought of you while packing my things."

Alethia frowned as her legs carried her toward the chair. She didn't want to sit, much less stay, but she couldn't seem to turn herself around to march out that door. "You thought about me?"

"Oh yes. I've been thinking about you for a very long time."

"A *long* time? This is the first festival we've ever worked together, and we've never even had a conversation. How—"

"Time is relative, Alethia, and completely malleable for one such as myself."

What the hell does that mean? Despite her desire to bolt, Alethia stayed planted where she was. Giselle mumbled to herself while she rummaged through a plastic bin full of her fortune-telling paraphernalia. Alethia shuddered as she listened.

"Ah, here it is." Giselle turned back with a pendant on a gold chain dangling from her hands. The charm was an animal effigy made of Celtic knots with a green stone mounted in the middle. "You've been so kind, stopping by to cheer me up even though I'm a stranger to you. I want you to have this." She slipped the pendant around Alethia's neck.

Alethia traced the intricate design with her finger. The knots formed the image of a crane. Among her father's people, the Anishinaabe, she belonged to the Crane clan. "It's beautiful, but I can't keep this." She lifted the chain over her head to return it. "It must be worth a fortune."

"It's yours." Giselle caught her hands and pushed the pendant back down around Alethia's neck. "This was crafted in the Highlands of Scotland eons ago. It is fitting that you should have it. Don't you think?"

Her mother had been Scottish, a MacConnell, but how could Giselle know so much about her life? The gold chain came to rest with unnatural warmth against Alethia's skin. Every instinct she had screamed at her to get the hell out of there. Now. "Thanks. Can I pay you for the necklace? I didn't really do anything to deserve it."

"Ah, but you will." Giselle laughed. "I don't want your money. The pendant is a gift."

Alethia grabbed her things from the ground, relieved to find that her body finally obeyed her mind. "I hope everything turns out all right with your relative."

"I am certain it will. Go, child. Your destiny awaits."

Giselle had obviously played the role of the gypsy fortune-teller far too long. Alethia's future had nothing to do with destiny and everything to do with hard work, determination and careful planning.

Alethia took a step toward the tent's exit, and every hair on her body stood on end. An eerie electrical charge filled the tent, along with the distinctive scent of ozone. All the familiar sounds associated with the closing fair faded. A loud *clap* made her ears pop, and everything flattened in an impossible two-dimensional way.

Pulled by a powerful current, she lurched forward. It took all of her strength to hold on to her things, and she fought to remain upright against the invisible force pressing in on her from all sides. A blur of light and color flashed by in microsecond increments. Nausea and pressure made it hard to breathe. She gasped for air, and pain ripped through her. God, she was being torn apart. *I'm going to die. I don't want to die!*

Blackness edged its way in around her as she struggled to remain conscious. No use. The vortex pulled her under.

Northern Scotland, 1423 AD

Malcolm leaned forward in his saddle and glared down at the well-dressed stranger asleep on the ground. On *MacKintosh* ground. With an important missive to deliver into his father's hands, he had no time for problems not his own. "What devilry is this?"

"She looks far more angel than devil," his cousin Robley remarked. "Who could she be?"

"She's no' *Sassenach.* 'Tis certain. Her complexion is far too dark. Mayhap she's Italian or Basque." Malcolm glanced at the tree line.

"Aye, no' English, for certes. Mayhap she's fae. She's lovely to look upon," Angus murmured. "Enchanting." He cleared his throat, and his face turned as red as his hair.

"Nay. The fae are always fair skinned," Galen argued. "'Tis why they're called *fairies.*"

His men grunted as they contemplated the possibilities, and Malcolm kept a wary eye on the edge of the forest. The lass wore clothing and jewels proclaiming her nobility. Where were her servants and escort? Something was amiss, and it turned his foul mood to pitch. No doubt this sleeping apparition was some new mischief conspired by fate to beleaguer him further. Between the Comyn clan's never-ending treachery, the greedy, ruthless rule of their regent, and his parents' expectation that he make an advantageous marriage, 'twas a wonder he slept at night.

Was peace too much to yearn for? He scowled at the sleeping woman—another complication he didn't need or want. His gelding stretched its neck to nose the curiosity on the ground, and a delicate hand rose to bat the disturbance away. The lass sat up and looked around in sleepy-eyed confusion, leaping to her feet when she saw him and his men in a circle around her.

"Who are you, lady? From whence do you come?" Malcolm demanded.

At his words, she turned to stare owl-eyed up at him. "Holy. Crap."

The corner of his mouth twitched up. "Where are your guardsmen and servants?"

Her spine straightened, and her chin lifted. "They're . . . in the woods."

Malcolm studied her. She had eyes the color of the sea on a stormy day. Hair the lustrous shade of fine sable hung in a braid down past her waist. He lost himself in fantasies of that glorious hair free and cascading down around her shoulders. She was a vision.

Malcolm gave himself a firm shake. Her looks mattered not in the least. "Aye? What might they be doing in *my* woods?"

Her eyes flew to the forest. "Um . . . tending to . . . things."

His men chuckled. She was a terrible liar, clearly alone and abandoned by the side of the road. This could only mean one thing. Trouble, and more trouble he did not need. "What sort of *things*?"

"Very important things," Alethia muttered. Definitely the alpha male in this barbarian six-pack, the brute confronting her radiated arrogance and authority. Sun-kissed golden hair fell to his shoulders, and a few days' growth of thick russet beard stubbled his strong jaw. He wore nothing but a swath of wool in muted plaid draped around his body and soft leather boots that reached mid-calf.

Where the hell was she, some kind of *Braveheart* parallel universe? *What did that old witch do to me?* Giselle's words echoed inside her head. *"Time is relative, Alethia, and completely malleable for one such as myself." Oh my God. Did she send me back in time?* Was such a thing even possible? Her head rang from the pounding of her heart, and her mouth went dry. None of this was possible, and any minute she'd wake up and find everything back to normal.

The leader scowled down at her, his wide, generous mouth drawn into a straight line that screamed *annoyed*. Well, she wasn't all that happy herself.

Sparing a glance for the rest of his crew, she couldn't help noticing the large swords slung over their backs and all the daggers tucked into belts and boots. She sucked in her breath and stood a little straighter. The Anishinaabe had always been a peace-loving people but also fearless when the need arose. Intending to be brave now, or at least appear to be, she clasped her trembling hands together in front of her. "Now, if you don't mind, please move aside," she said, clearing her throat, hoping that would get rid of the telltale quiver, "and I'll be on my way."

One of the men nudged his horse forward. As dark as the leader was fair, this one gave off a bad vibe. As frightened as she was, she could still sense his malicious nature.

"Let me take her off your hands, Malcolm. She's a foreigner and without protection. That makes her fair game."

"No!" A surge of adrenaline hit her bloodstream, and she searched for a gap in the wall of horses and men. How far would her trembling legs carry her? "I'm responsible for myself and not *game* of any kind."

"She is on my land, Hugh," the one called Malcolm replied. "That makes her my responsibility."

"My people are waiting for me to join them," she bluffed, "and they're heavily armed."

Malcolm snorted and scooped her up off the ground like a sack of grain. Placing her in front of him, he nudged his horse down the road. His chortling men fell in line behind him.

"Put me down! I have no intention of going anywhere with you." She tried to pry herself out of his hold.

"And I have no intention of leaving you alone in the wilderness." Malcolm's arm tightened around her waist.

She blinked back the tears of fear and frustration and struggled to get out of his hold. It was useless. He probably weighed more than twice what she did, and every inch of him was granite. She glanced back at her violin and duffel bag. The only links to her life lay by the side of the road, growing smaller by the second. "My things. At least let me get my—"

"Nay, we travel in haste. I'll no' burden our mounts with any *more* useless baggage."

Damn the tear trickling down her cheek. "I didn't ask you to take me anywhere. I didn't ask for any of this."

Don't panic. Think. Swiping her eyes, she took several deep breaths to calm herself. Her mind raced for a way out of this mess. Thank heavens her friends had insisted she take self-defense classes after one of their classmates had been mugged.

She forced herself to relax into his hold. His grip eased. Reaching back, Alethia placed her hands on either side of his neck below his ears. Using the pads of her thumbs, she found his pulse points and applied pressure. Within seconds his body slackened. Shoving his arm from around her waist, she slid off the horse and hit the ground running. Her captor fell with a loud thump behind her.

Alethia snatched up her belongings and ran for the forest bordering the rutted dirt road they traveled. Thundering hooves ate up the ground behind her. She dashed into some brush and glanced over her shoulder. *Damn.* The dark one was after her, the one who saw her as game. Frantic, Alethia searched for a place to hide.

Malcolm awoke on the ground to find the eyes of his cousins staring down at him. "What the devil happened?"

"The lass, she . . . ah . . . ," Liam stammered.

Robley reached out his hand and grinned. "The wee sorceress put you to sleep. I've never seen the like."

Malcolm took the proffered help and hoisted himself from the ground. "Where is Hugh?"

"He went after her," Angus replied.

"God's blood!" He glared at each of his men until they squirmed. "I dinna keep Hugh close because I desire his company. You know my thoughts, yet you let him go after the lass with no thought to her safety?" He leaped onto his gelding's back. "Liam, you're in charge. Ride ahead and make camp by the burn. I'm going after Hugh and the lass."

The last thing he remembered, her soft hands had brushed his neck. The next thing he knew, he awoke flat on his back in the dirt. He gave sorcery no credence and knew her actions had been physical in nature. Still, what had she done to him, and how dare she?

Hugh had left an easy trail to follow, but there were no signs of the woman. Malcolm overtook him, bringing his mount around to cut him off. "Return to the men, Hugh," Malcolm commanded. "They've ridden ahead to make camp."

"She means naught to you. Leave her to me."

"Nay. She will remain in my care until I can return her to the protection of her family."

"Mayhap she's a spy, left in our path for a purpose."

"Mayhap you are as well." Malcolm's grip tightened on the reins, and his gelding danced with tension beneath him. "The MacKintosh have naught to hide. We are, and always have been, loyal to king and country."

"To king and country?" Hugh smirked. "What of our regent, the duke of Albany?"

"What of him? What are you suggesting?" Malcolm suspected Hugh was a spy, but had no proof. Most likely he'd joined their garrison for the sole purpose of selling information to the treacherous Red Comyn, who had their regent's ear. If it came to it, Malcolm would not regret running Hugh through with his claymore. A Fraser, Hugh had fostered with the MacKintosh. As a youth, he'd been sullen, cruel, and spiteful. As a man, he'd grown even more perverse.

Hugh had come to Moigh Hall a fortnight ago seeking a place in their garrison. If the decision had been his, Malcolm would have sent him on his way.

Drawing his sword, Malcolm edged closer. "Do you challenge my authority or my loyalties? If so, draw your weapon. Let us settle the matter forthwith."

Hugh glared at him. "I'll rejoin the rest of the men if that is your command."

"It is." Malcolm watched to ensure Hugh didn't double back, and then he started his search for the woman. He returned to the point where the chase had begun, dismounted and examined the forest floor. A tree-covered hollow caught his eye. The earth and the brush around it had been disturbed. She'd hidden there until Hugh had passed. Canny lass.

He picked up her trail, and it wasn't long before he caught sight of her, doubled over and gasping for breath. Her paltry bundles lay on the ground beside her. Malcolm secured his horse and stepped through the brush separating them. She whipped around, eyes darting, most likely searching for another escape route. He stood still before her, keeping both hands in plain sight. "I mean you no harm."

She straightened and glared him down. Her bravado amused him, made him want to laugh, though he wouldn't. To do so would be a grave insult to her bravery.

"You have no right to interfere with me, and you have no idea what I've been through today." Letting out a shaky huff of air, she lifted her belongings from the ground, gave him her back and walked away.

Malcolm let her get as far as the end of her braid.

She made a growling noise and let her burdens slip from her hands. Grabbing his wrist with one hand, she turned and latched onto his little finger with the other. Bending it back with considerable might, she forced him down.

"Ahhh, by the saints." Pain and confusion brought him to his knees. He recovered his wits enough to keep hold of her braid, yanking her to the ground with him. When she reached back with one hand to free her hair, he grabbed her arm and bent it up behind her back, gratified when he heard the sharp intake of her breath.

Had he thought her delicate? Nay, he'd misjudged her. She was a wildcat. A cornered wildcat. He tried to raise his hand out of her reach. "Foolish woman, a broken finger is naught to me."

"Fine, I'll break it then." Keeping her tenacious hold, she increased the pressure. "If you mean me no harm, then let me go."

"Nay."

"Let. Go."

"You first." The rise and fall of her breasts against his chest stirred his blood to a boil. His gaze roamed over her face, settling on the fullness of her lips pursed into a determined pucker. An idea formed in his mind. Raising his eyes to hers, he grinned.

Her eyes widened, then narrowed. "Oh no."

He covered her lips with his. She gasped, and he took advantage, deepening the kiss and drawing her closer. She sucked his lower lip into her mouth, and desire surged through his body in a rush so strong, 'twould have brought him to his knees had he not already been on them.

Then she bit him. *Damnation!*

Never had he been in a more absurd predicament. How the devil had one tiny female managed to best him? Judging by the pain, she had no intention of letting go. So be it. Neither would he. Malcolm bent her arm up behind her a bit more in retaliation for the insult to his pride. She yelped through her clenched teeth, and a twinge of guilt forced him to loosen his hold.

Stalemate.

By God, 'twas a good thing none of his men were here to witness this indignity. She was like no other lady he'd ever met, and he could scarce believe her audacity. What would the earl think if he saw his only heir in such a ridiculous fix?

A rumble began deep in his chest, erupting in loud, raucous laughter that shocked the tiny warrior. He fell backward, taking her with him until he lay flat on his back with her on top. Miracle of miracles, she let go of his lip and his finger as she tried to wriggle away. He encircled her waist with his arms and trapped her legs between his. Placing her palms on the ground, she raised herself up and stared down at him as though he'd completely lost his wits.

No doubt he had.

It would not take this braw lass long to attempt escape again. He rolled them over and straddled her. Malcolm took a leather thong out of his sporran and bound her wrists. "You have naught to fear," he told her in a soothing tone. "Though I doubt you lend any credence to my words, I mean only to offer you aid."

"Right." She lifted her tied wrists, her eyes flashing. "How is this supposed to *aid* me?"

"Ah, lass," he said, hefting her off the ground, "in less than a day, you've rendered me senseless, brought me to my knees and drawn blood." He winked at her. "The binding is to aid me."

She huffed, and then her expressions shifted. "I did do all that, didn't I? My uncles and cousins would be proud."

She surprised him at every turn, and her bemused expression had him laughing out loud again. "If you're any indication, they must be a bloodthirsty lot."

"They are." She glared as if challenging him to disagree.

He held her with one arm while retrieving his mount. Still chuckling, he placed her astride his horse, careful to keep the reins out of her reach. Malcolm gathered her things, secured the smaller case behind his saddle and dumped the larger sack on her lap. Even with her hands bound 'twould be best to keep them occupied. He swung up behind her and turned his mount toward the road.

"Where are you taking me?"

"To a place of safety."

"Where are we now?"

"We're on MacKintosh land."

"MacKintosh. Is that Irish or Scottish?"

Malcolm frowned at her odd questions. Mayhap she'd been set upon by brigands and had suffered a blow to the head. "You're in Scotland. Wheesht now, lest any *more* trouble lurking about the forest should find me."

She gasped and placed her bound hands on her pack in a possessive gesture. There was no mistaking the signs she was exhausted, near tears and trying hard not to show it. He always traveled light out of deference for the horses, and with the earl of Douglas's missive to deliver, the need for haste was great.

How had she happened to be alone on that particular stretch of road at the very moment he traveled by? Who was she? What would his family and clan make of her? Each question raised another until his head throbbed.

Tomorrow was soon enough to demand answers, and his father would insist on questioning her himself. For now, he would leave her be.

CHAPTER TWO

The sun had set, and even though the woman shivered from the chill night air, she continued to lean as far from him in the saddle as possible. Malcolm removed the wool from his shoulder and draped it over her small frame. She flung it back in his face.

Several times she slipped into sleep, jerking upright when her body began to slide off his horse. Her stubborn refusal to take the succor he offered frustrated him. He left her to struggle—until he could no longer bear her discomfort.

Malcolm waited for her to fall asleep again, and then he drew her back. Holding her steady, he wrapped her in the wool of his plaid. The fullness of her breasts resting on his forearm sent his pulse racing. Her hair smelled like sunshine and wildflowers. Pulling her snug against his body, he cradled her head against one shoulder and inhaled her sweet feminine scent, taking it deep into his lungs. Sighing, she settled herself without waking. He reveled in the feel of her in his arms and let his horse plod along at a snail's pace.

The scent of roasting meat and the warm glow of the campfire throwing shadows against the pines led Malcolm to the campsite. He gave a soft whistle, and the youngest of their party hastened to him.

"Galen, take her." Malcolm eased the woman into the other man's arms before dismounting. He prepared a place for her to sleep, and Galen laid her down on the thick sheepskin, covering her in wool. Malcolm gestured toward the others, and they walked away, careful not to disturb her.

Taking a seat by the fire, Malcolm was relieved to see Hugh already wrapped in his plaid for the night some distance away. His men sent curious glances his way as he rubbed the dried blood from his injury.

"What happened to your lip?" Robley handed him a large piece of roasted venison.

"She bit me." Recalling their absurd battle, he laughed. His men looked at him in shock, causing him to laugh all the more. "Aye, 'tis truth." Malcolm saw no need to elaborate and settled into his meal.

"How did your lip happen to be between her teeth?" Robley asked, his smile full of mischief.

"I kissed her."

"You kissed her?" Liam glanced toward the sleeping form of their mysterious guest. "As she fled?"

Malcolm leaned forward and signaled for them to do likewise. He chuckled again, and in quiet tones he told them the story in full, embellishing nothing. Finally, he explained, "I hoped the kiss would startle her into loosening her hold." He rubbed his injured lower lip. "I underestimated my opponent. Let that be a lesson for us all." He grinned as they mulled it over.

"She's no' even as big around as one of your thighs," Angus murmured. "'Tis hardly credible."

"She had you on your knees?" Robley snorted. "I'd have paid a small fortune to have witnessed the feat."

"'Twould be worth a small fortune to know who she is and how she happened to be alone on our road," Liam added. The others nodded.

Malcolm sent Angus and Galen off to their rest and asked his cousins to stay. Staring into the fire, he picked up a stick and idly drew circles in the dirt while reflecting upon all that had occurred.

"What are your thoughts, Malcolm?" Liam asked.

"Until we know who the lass is and where she belongs, 'twould be wise to keep an eye on her." Malcolm looked from Liam to Robley. "Spread the word amongst those we trust that she's under my protection. You know my concerns regarding Hugh, and 'tis likely she has trouble following close upon her heels."

Malcolm shook his head. "She speaks the words of the *Sassenach*, but not in a way we've ever heard them spoken. Her accent is unfamiliar. The gown she wears is rich. She's a gently bred lady for certes. Her hands are soft and without callus." He frowned. "Except for the tips of her fingers on one hand. 'Tis curious."

"Curious indeed," Liam teased. "You examined the tips of her fingers?"

"Aye," Malcolm grinned sheepishly, "while I bound her wrists to keep her from injuring me further. Robley, you and I will guard her tonight." Malcolm threw the stick onto the dying fire and stood to stretch his weary muscles. "Liam, you have first watch. Wake Galen for the second. We've a hard ride ahead of us if we wish to make Moigh Hall by Sext. Let us get some rest."

Alethia woke at dawn to find herself wedged between the massive backs of two men. They were like walls radiating heat and smelling of horse, wood smoke and sweat. One of them belonged to Malcolm, the Alpha-Jerk.

Her wrists were still bound. Not a good sign. Her throat closed up, making it hard to breathe. Who were these men, and what did they intend to do with her? *What the hell am I supposed to do, and how the hell am I going to get back home?* Stuffing her panic back into the jack-in-the-box from which it sprang, she forced herself to calm down. She needed a plan.

Alethia fished the pendant out from under her chemise. Giselle had used the necklace to send her here, so there had to be a way to use it to get back. She studied the knotted effigy and wondered how to make it work. Holding the charm tight, she closed her eyes and clicked her heels together three times, muttering, "I want to go home. I want to go home. I want to go home." Her body tensed, and she waited for something to happen. Nothing did.

Maybe if she replayed everything Giselle had said, she might find a clue. Someone was in danger. Who? Giselle would do anything to help them, and Alethia had untapped gifts and could survive anywhere.

If Giselle would do anything to help, then why wasn't *she* the one wedged in the middle of this barbarian sandwich? *Why me?*

Alethia glanced at Malcolm's back, and their battle from the previous day flashed through her mind. When he'd sat astride her on the ground, she'd felt his heat clear through her gown. The intimacy had been unsettling, his kiss even more so. He was huge and physically powerful, and the way he smelled might as well be labeled *eau de testosterone.*

She needed to get away. Alethia studied the knot on the leather cord binding her wrists. Bringing it to her teeth, she started to work it loose. Once her hands were free, she'd wiggle out from between the two men, grab her stuff and try to find the road. It had been rutted and worn, signs it was well traveled. Another group would happen along soon, and hopefully there'd be women in the party.

The knot slipped from between her teeth as she pulled. Her hands jerked forward, hitting Malcolm between the shoulder blades. She froze, held her breath and waited. When he didn't move, she let her breath out slowly, brought the knot back to her mouth and resumed tugging.

Malcolm twisted around and stared down at her. Eyes the most vivid blue she'd ever seen fixed on the leather between her teeth. *Busted.* Alethia struggled to sit up, managing to at last, and held out her bound wrists. "Don't you think this is a tad unnecessary? I know I do."

"I canna say." He rubbed his injured lower lip and arched an eyebrow. "*Can* you keep your hands from me?"

Alethia saw the twinkle of amusement in his eyes, and her face grew hot. She didn't see anything funny about her predicament. She turned away to stare into the forest, biting her lip to keep from tearing up. This pretending to be brave business was hard work.

He rose, pulling her up with him, and cut the leather binding her wrists with a small dagger he pulled from his belt. Malcolm walked over to her violin and duffel and hoisted them to his shoulder. "I'll hold onto these whilst you make your morning ablutions. The burn leads to a small falls offering privacy."

"What's a burn?" She rubbed her wrists and noticed Malcolm's companions watching their exchange with avid interest.

"The wee river." Malcolm jutted his chin toward the stream bordering the campsite. "What do you call such?"

"A stream," Alethia muttered before she fled the camp and followed the burn into the forest. She took care of her body's immediate needs in the brush, then found the place Malcolm had mentioned. If she hadn't been so upset, she would've loved the small waterfall surrounded by thick pines, hemlock and juniper. The sound of the rushing water soothed her tattered nerves, and the fresh, tangy scent reminded her of home. Her heart ached with longing. She had to find a way to get back where she belonged, but how? How does one travel through time?

Alethia searched the shadows to make sure she was alone, took a drink, and then stripped for a hasty shower. Stepping under the falls, she gasped as the ice-cold water sluiced over her body. Once she was done washing, she moved to stand on the moss-covered boulder where she'd laid her clothes. Swiping the water from her skin with the palms of her hands, she heard a twig snap. She snatched her chemise from the ground and tugged it over her head, tying the strings in front with trembling fingers.

Hugh stepped out from the brush. "I do beg your pardon, my lady. I did not realize anyone was here."

Deceitfulness pulsed off him like a strobe light. The lecherous perv had probably watched her bathe. Adrenaline surged through her body, sending her heart racing. "No harm done." Every instinct she had screamed fight or flight. Mostly flight.

"'Tis clear some misfortune has befallen you. You're far from home and your kinfolk." Hugh blocked the path back to camp. "'Tis no' safe for a woman to travel alone and unprotected. Might I offer my services?" He brought his right hand up to cover his heart, while his eyes raked over her with a lascivious glint. "I'd be more than willing to act as your protector until such time that you can be restored to the loving bosom of your family."

Hugh's once-over made her want to bathe all over again, and he oozed malevolence. She grabbed her gown and struggled into it, doing up the laces as quickly as she could. "Thank you for the offer. I'll certainly give it some thought." *Not on your life!* But she couldn't say that. He had the upper hand and knew it. Best not provoke him in any way.

"If I might be so bold, who do you belong to? Will there be a ransom offered for your safe return, I wonder?"

Stepping into her leather slippers, she searched for a deer path along the banks of the stream. Wait. Given her earlier dash for freedom, he probably hoped she'd head deeper into the forest. Best to work her way back toward camp. "I belong to myself. There's no ransom."

Hugh chuckled low in his throat. "A lady of gentle breeding, obviously of noble birth, and you claim to belong only to yourself? How delightfully mysterious. *No one* searches for you, my lady?"

Alethia sucked in a breath as she realized her mistake. If she had no one, belonged nowhere, he'd have no reason *not* to harm her. "I mean—"

"I understand your meaning well enough. No doubt you are fleeing from someone. Poor lass. Did your father marry you off to some wealthy old goat you find repugnant?"

She kept her mouth clamped shut and fought for calm.

"Ah, well, 'tis only a matter of time before I uncover the truth. In the meantime, I do hope you will accept my offer of protection."

His eyes went from the gold chain around her neck, down her gown and back to the pendant, like he was tallying their worth in his head. Alethia cringed inwardly. He was the last person she'd turn to for anything. "Like I said, I'll certainly give your kind offer all the consideration it deserves." She pushed through the brush to pass him and hurried back to camp. How the hell was she going to get out of this mess?

Malcolm watched the woman return to camp. Her cheeks had turned a dusky rose, and her silken tresses fell around her shoulders in damp, shiny ripples. The sight mesmerized him. Likewise, his men were transfixed. Then he caught sight of the fear in her eyes. "Make ready for travel." He barked the order, breaking the spell.

Out of the corner of his eye, Malcolm watched Hugh slink back into camp. The notion he might've been nearby while the lady washed at the falls sent a chill down Malcolm's spine. Something had happened, of that he was certain. He should've had one of the lads follow at a distance. Nay. He should've seen to her safety himself.

"Robley." He looked over his shoulder at his cousin and gestured toward the woman. "See that she's fed. Liam, ride back a league and make certain we aren't being followed." Malcolm tied her small case to the back of his saddle. "Angus, go on ahead to see we aren't riding into an ambush. We'll meet where the road splits to Inverness."

"Aye, Malcolm." Angus spurred his horse into a gallop as he left. Liam's eyes swung from Hugh to the lass and back to Malcolm. With a slight nod, he signaled that he'd noticed her fear and shared Malcolm's suspicions. Then he rode out of camp in the opposite direction.

Robley smiled and handed her a piece of jerky and an oatcake. "Have you a name, my lady?"

"Of course I do. Thank you for asking. I am Lady Alethia Goodsky."

"Sky, like the heavens above? 'Tis a lovely name. I'm called Robley, and the youngster over there is Galen. Angus and Liam are the two who left to see that our way is safe. That's Hugh," he said, pointing across camp, "and the last is my cousin Malcolm."

Malcolm frowned. "Aleth" was the Greek word for truth. His thoughts flew back to the summer he was ten and three. He and his cousins had gone to a fair in Inverness, determined to find some mischief. They all feared an old fortune-teller who plied her trade there. On a dare, he'd agreed to have her tell his fortune. Could this foreigner be the "truth" the old woman had referred to as *her*?

He turned to study Alethia. Had she been left in his path, certain to be found by him? Shaking his head, he dismissed the notion and went back to readying his gear. 'Twas coincidence and silly superstition, nothing more, and he prided himself on being a modern-thinking man.

Swinging up into the saddle, Malcolm continued to give orders. "Galen, carry the lady's larger pack. Hugh, take the lead, and Robley, you take up the rear." Malcolm scooped Alethia up and set her astride in front of him.

"Hey," she protested as part of her oatcake broke off and fell to the ground. "If it's all the same to you, I'd rather ride with Robley."

Robley threw his head back and laughed. Galen grinned.

"It is no' *all the same* to me. Let us be off," he commanded. Malcolm waited until Hugh was out of range and leaned close to whisper. "What happened in the wood?"

"You pulled my braid. I bit your lip," she whispered back. "Did you forget already?"

"How could I?" He snorted and rubbed his injured lip. "I meant this morn."

"I believe Hugh hid in the forest and watched me bathe, but I can't prove it."

"Why did you no' call out?"

"I didn't know he was there until he stepped out of hiding, and he did nothing to harm me. Besides, who should I have called? You?" Alethia twisted around to frown at him. "You used brute force and tied my wrists."

"'Tis different."

"Since I don't know any of you, I don't see a difference." She shrugged. "If I had called out, I might've ended up in more trouble than I was already in."

"MacKintosh men dinna harm women." Her words stung his sense of honor and his pride. "We protect and cherish them."

"Ha! After you tie them up and haul them off against their will, do you mean?"

"You have a sharp tongue."

"Oh yeah? Well, you smell like your horse."

Malcolm wanted to tear his hair and laugh all at the same time. He was beginning to understand why she'd been left behind.

They'd ridden for hours since their all-too-brief break. The muscles in Alethia's thighs screamed for mercy, and she'd lost all feeling in her butt ages ago. Probably a good thing.

How much longer would she have to spend on the back of a smelly horse sitting way too close to Alpha-Jerk? Just as that thought filled her head, they came to a stop on the crest of a hill. Below them, a village nestled on the shore of a lake. In the middle of the lake sat an island with a formidable castle built on the edge of a cliff. Alethia stared openmouthed.

Fields of ripening crops turned the surrounding valley into a patchwork quilt of greens and golds. Horned, shaggy cattle dotted the hills, joined by sheep, stout ponies, and larger horses like the ones they rode.

"*Lock Moigh!*" Malcolm shouted at the top of lungs.

She flinched and covered her ears, just as his men echoed the shout, and two warning blasts from a horn in the village rent the air. A dozen warriors on horseback streaked out from between the cottages, swords drawn, heading at breakneck speed straight for them. *No!*

She cringed at the sound of swords being pulled from their scabbards around her, and a bloodcurdling shout pierced the air. A battle cry? Malcolm kicked his horse into a dead run down the hill to meet the enemy. Her gut turned over, and her heart made a leap for safety up her throat. Clinging to the horse's mane for all she was worth, Alethia shut her eyes tight.

I'm gonna die!

CHAPTER THREE

Alethia intended to meet her death bravely with her eyes wide open like her ancestors would've done, but try as she might, neither eyelid would budge. No doubt Malcolm's enemies would run their swords right through her to get to him. And if by some miracle they both survived, she planned to kill him herself with her bare hands.

Swords clashed and men shouted as they came together. She held her breath and waited for the blow that would end her pitifully short life. Laughter penetrated the cloud of fear surrounding her.

Laughter?

Alethia opened her eyes. The swordplay ended in friendly greetings and backslapping. All the fear and anxiety coursing through her morphed into red-hot anger. She wanted off the damn horse, and she wanted to be far, far away from the barbarian who had so carelessly caused the near explosion of her heart in her chest. Now.

Malcolm slid his claymore back into its scabbard and put his arm around her waist. She flung it off, swung her leg over the saddle and slid off the horse, collapsing to the ground in an undignified heap of velvet and silk brocade. Forcing herself to stand, she formed a fist and slugged Alpha-Jerk in the thigh with all the might she could muster. "You could've put me down *before* you charged down the hill, you moron!"

She walked away on shaky legs, falling to her knees in the grass a short distance away. She couldn't catch her breath, and stars danced before her eyes. Twice now she'd believed she was going to die, and that was two times too many in her opinion. Her mind reeled with everything that had happened. This was not a safe place to be, and more than anything, she wanted to go home.

Baffled, Malcolm rubbed his thigh and watched Lady Alethia fall to her knees in the grass.

"Our guest believed you were riding into battle using her as your shield." Liam rode up beside him. "She does no' know this is our home and must have been frightened out of her wits."

"She's under my protection." Malcolm frowned. "Why would I make the vow and then put her life at risk?"

Liam grinned. "Have you told her she has your protection?"

"Shite. I offered my aid as I would to any wayfaring soul, but no' my protection specifically. Best do so now." Malcolm dismounted and went after her. When she saw him coming, she rose from the ground and headed in the opposite direction. He quickened his pace and caught up, placing a hand on her shoulder to turn her around.

She shook him off and moved out of his reach. "Go away, and leave me alone."

He stepped in front of her, only to have her turn her back to him again. Their odd little dance continued until he was filled with helpless frustration. "Hold still, ye wee termagant. You were no' in any danger."

She spun around to face him, her eyes wide. "There were swords drawn, and . . . and battle cries shouted. How was I supposed to know I wasn't in danger?"

"As long as you are on MacKintosh land, you are under my protection." Malcolm's gut twisted. She made an incredulous sound, but at least the hurt he'd glimpsed in her eyes turned to something more akin to fury. Fury he could deal with. "You will trust me in the future."

"Don't hold your breath." She snorted. "Aren't you the same guy who carried me off and left my violin behind? Do you have any idea what would happen to my instrument if it rained? You have no idea what it means to me," she said, her voice breaking.

"I know nothing of this *Guy* fellow and even less of violins. I intended to have someone return to fetch your belongings once we reached home."

"And I was supposed to know this how?" She crossed her arms in front of her and shot arrows at him with her eyes. "You tied my hands—not exactly a trust-inspiring gesture."

"You used them to put me to sleep. I had no choice." Malcolm took a small step closer.

"You pulled my hair." Alethia threw her hands up in the air. "Who *does* that?"

"My finger still pains me from the injury you inflicted." Another step. "So does my lip."

"What did you expect me to do? You *kissed* me."

"I might kiss you again just to stop your tongue from wagging."

Alethia gasped and blinked several times. "Because you want your upper lip to have a matching set of teeth marks?"

Malcolm bit the inside of his cheek to keep from laughing. "You dinna fear me at all, do you, lass?" Her brow creased as she stared up at him. Malcolm felt as if she were reading his soul and wondered what she saw there.

"No. I guess I don't." She said the words as if they surprised her. "You told the truth when you said you don't mean me any harm, and you meant what you said about how the MacKintosh treat women." Alethia shook her head. "But that doesn't mean I trust you."

"Your lack of fear will suffice for now." Malcolm drew her into his arms and kissed her, pulling back quickly enough to avoid getting bitten.

She shoved him away with both hands. "*Why* do you keep *doing* that?"

Her cheeks colored, and his breath caught in his throat. She was like the wild roses growing in the dales, lovely and thorny all at once. "Because it pleases me."

She huffed, gave him her back and hurried off toward the group getting ready to cross the loch. "Well, it doesn't please *me*," she shouted.

Malcolm watched the sway of her hips and her braid bouncing back and forth as she moved. He threw his head back and laughed. By the saints, their exchange exhilarated him in ways he'd never before experienced. Goading Lady Alethia could well become his favorite pastime. Sharp teeth and a sharp wit—a rare lass indeed.

"Robley, Liam, to my father." Malcolm set Alethia's belongings on the trestle table in the great hall and placed a hand on her shoulder. "Stay here until I send someone to fetch you."

"Where else would I go?"

Malcolm didn't like the forlorn tone in her voice. He watched as her eyes roamed around the hall like she'd never before seen the like. Mayhap people lived differently where she came from. Curiosity had been eating away at him since he first laid eyes on her, but now was not the time for questions. His father waited.

With his cousins at his heels, he took the narrow stone stairs two at a time. Knocking at his father's solar door, Malcolm paused briefly before entering. William rose from the table where he sat with his brother, Malcolm's uncle Robert.

"Son, nephews, 'tis good to have you home safe." He gave Malcolm a brief embrace and gestured for them to sit. "What news from old Archibald?"

Malcolm pulled a neatly folded vellum packet from his sporran before taking a seat and accepting an ale from Robley. The packet was sealed with wax imprinted with the Douglas crest. "The rumors are true. Our James is to wed a *Sassenach*, Joan Beaufort, the daughter of the earl of Somerset. Since our king is marrying into English aristocracy, they are finally amenable to negotiating his freedom.

"Archibald has been arranging James's ransom in secret. He's forming a contingency of Scottish nobles to finalize the treaty." Malcolm pushed the sealed vellum across the table to his father. "This missive gives the details. The earl of Douglas wishes you to join the delegation traveling to London within the month. He'll send word when all is in place."

His father opened the vellum and read it through.

"Will you join them?" Malcolm asked.

"I will." He handed the missive to his brother. "Robert, I want you to accompany me."

"Who will act as steward in my absence?" Robert asked.

"Your lads have trained at your knee since they were bairns. 'Tis time they had the chance to prove their mettle." He grinned at Liam and Robley. "Malcolm, you will act in my stead while I'm away. Nephews, I'll depend upon you both to take up your father's responsibilities. For eighteen years our king has been imprisoned by the *Sassenach*. For eighteen years we've been under the ruthless thumb of our self-appointed regent, the duke of Albany. 'Tis high time our king came home to rule."

"Aye, and the Comyn clan will at last be exposed for the traitorous lot they've always been." Malcolm grinned. "Speaking of Comyns, have you discovered any more of their men lurking about in our absence, Father?"

"Nay, not since we increased the number of our garrison billeting in the village."

"Good. Will you take Mother with you to London?" Malcolm asked.

"Nay, the unrest in Britain since King Henry's death is reason enough to leave her here. The palace must be rife with intrigue and treachery. His heir, the young Henry, is no' yet fully weaned from the teat. Were it not for James and the future of Scotland, I'd have no wish to go myself." He shook his head. "Besides, as you know, your mother has no love for that cesspool and even less for travel." His father fixed him with a pointed look. "What of the earl of Douglas's niece?"

"She will not suit," Malcolm answered tersely.

"I grow impatient for grandchildren, and you need heirs, Malcolm. I agreed to let you choose your own bride with the understanding 'twould be done in a timely manner." His father scrutinized him. "What happened to your lip?"

"Uncle William," Robley said, grinning from ear to ear, "you must ask Malcolm what we found by the side of the road on our journey home."

"What has that to do with my finding a wife?" Malcolm shot his cousin a dark look.

Alethia studied the great hall in amazement. A fireplace massive enough to roast a whole hog filled one end of the room, and the opposite wall boasted another hearth just as large. The acoustics in this place must be outstanding. Exquisite tapestries depicting hunting scenes in rich crimsons, golds, blues and greens adorned the walls, along with weaponry of all sorts and shields bearing two distinct crests. Being torn from her life was frightening and horrific, but to see something like this castle, to exist in this time after years and years of fascination with everything having to do with this historical era—it truly filled her with awe. She'd treasure this memory for the rest of her life once she got home, and she *would* get home.

The sudden sting behind her eyes brought her back to more practical matters. What was Malcolm's position in the scheme of things? His arrogance and the way he strode through the bailey, the deferential greetings he'd received and how he went so freely up the stairs leading to the castle's private chambers could only mean one thing—Alpha-Jerk had to be family. "Figures."

Eager to test the hall's acoustics, Alethia retrieved her violin case and looked around for the most advantageous place to play. Reverently, she placed the case on the trestle table and undid the latches. One look at the eighteenth-century German violin, with its reddish brown varnish and inlaid rosewood edging, and the link to her real life snapped back into place. Once she held the instrument in her hands, everything inside her settled. Her violin, the last gift she'd ever received from her father, always brought her comfort.

Stomping her foot, she listened for reverberation, repeating the process as she walked around the room until she'd chosen a spot before the dais. She tightened and rosined the bow, and struck the tuning fork against the edge of the table, tuning her instrument with practiced precision.

Closing her eyes, she called forth the score of Vivaldi's *Four Seasons* and put bow to string, pouring her heart into the music.

"La primavera," Allegro, Largo, Allegro: Scenes from her life played like a movie behind her closed eyes. She remembered the day her father had given her the violin. She'd been five years old. He'd stopped at an estate sale in Duluth, Minnesota, on his way home from a tribal conference, and he'd picked the instrument up for next to nothing. They'd found out later the instrument was worth a tidy fortune. Alethia had an ear for music, a natural talent, and a love for the violin her father had given her.

"L'estate," Allegro non molto, Adagio, Presto: Being accepted into Juilliard meant everything to her. She'd earned a solo part in the spring concert, and she'd worked hard to live up to the honor. Her heart swelled as images of her family played through her mind. Blue jeans, beaded medicine bags and key chains, long black braids, brown skin and eyes the color of the rich black earth shone with pride among the sea of sameness making up the rest of the audience that day.

"L'autunno," Allegro, Adagio molto, Allegro: Would she ever see her family again? What of her dreams, her plans for the future? Profoundly deaf since birth, what would Gran do now that her eyesight was failing? More than anything, she wanted to be there for her grandmother the same way Gran had been there for her when she'd lost her parents.

"L'inverno," Allegro non molto, Largo, Allegro: Her memories became part of the music as she wove them into each note. She'd been correct about the acoustics. Never had her violin's sweet tones been so profoundly accentuated. Her head remained bowed long past the last note.

Someone coughed, and Alethia looked up. She'd been alone and completely absorbed in the music when she began playing. Now the eyes of at least thirty people stared at her.

Malcolm had never heard such music before, and he was a well-traveled man. When Alethia began to play, the sound drew everyone near enough to hear it. Malcolm's father, his mother and sister were there, along with his cousins, uncle and aunt, and a number of their clan who had been caught up by the magic. They had come on silent feet so as not to break the spell.

Little did she know she'd just secured a place for herself in clan MacKintosh. His people loved a good story, good music, and a great mystery to chew on during the long winter months. Here were all three of those elements embodied in one bonnie lass.

Malcolm located Beth, the servant he'd chosen to care for their guest, and went to give her further instructions. "Has the chamber been made ready?"

"Aye, and a bath has been prepared, just like ye asked." Beth curtsied as she answered.

"See Lady Alethia to her chamber. You are to look after her every need."

"Aye, milord. I'm pleased to serve the lady." She smiled and curtsied again before hurrying off to carry out his instructions.

Even though theirs was a modern keep with a bathing room, he'd arranged for a bath to be brought to Alethia's chamber. She must be weary from traveling. Surely she would appreciate the thoughtfulness of his gesture.

All Malcolm wanted now was a bath and a shave before supping with family and clan. Anticipation filled him. What did his family make of their mysterious visitor? He guessed her to be around the same age as his younger sister. Would they become confidants the way young women often did? Mayhap their guest would reveal more to Elaine than she would to him or his father. Time would tell.

He caught up to his father and placed a hand on his shoulder. "Father, she's the lass we found on our way home."

"She was alone, did you say?" His father frowned.

"Aye. There are questions begging answers. I had hoped you would find time to speak with her this eve."

"Unless she was being followed, it can wait. Did you find evidence of brigands?"

"Nay, but—"

"We have more important things to attend to, aye? This night we'll feast with our clan and share the good news of our king's return." William slapped Malcolm on the back. "Let the lass settle in. Then we'll have our talk. She's hardly a threat, lad."

Torn, Malcolm watched his father stride off toward his mother. Waiting had never been one of his strengths.

Left alone for the time being, Alethia surveyed the chamber she'd been given. Though small, she knew she was being treated as an honored guest rather than a nobody lucky to secure floor space in the great hall. She needed to tread carefully if she was to hold on to that status.

Laying a hand flat on the cold stone wall, she tried to absorb the reality she'd been thrust into. A real castle complete with lords and their ladies! She'd always studied everything she could about the Renaissance period. That's why she worked at Renaissance fairs all over New York and neighboring states. Now she found herself in the past, maybe even in the Renaissance period. How was this possible?

A copper tub full of steaming water sat before a small hearth. Pegs were mounted right into the stone on one wall, and a wooden trunk had been placed underneath. The bed took up most of the small space. She went to check it out, thrilled to find it held a feather mattress covered in linen and thick woolen blankets. One tall, narrow window graced the outside wall. The shutter had been left open, letting in the daylight and fresh air.

She emptied her duffel onto the bed and took inventory. She had one other gown besides the one she wore, plus another chemise. Assessing her supply of soap, toothpaste, deodorant, shampoo and conditioner, she mentally calculated how long they'd last. A small bag of Ocean Spray Craisins and an apple she'd forgotten about were stuffed into the bottom. She snatched up the full box of tampons and hugged it to her chest. "Score!"

Anything futuristic, like her laptop and cell phone, she wrapped in her street clothes and stuffed back into the canvas duffel. No one discovering the items would have any idea what they'd stumbled onto, but she didn't want to have to explain. If she told her hosts she'd been sent back in time . . . A shudder wracked her at the thought of where such a revelation might lead. For now, she'd hide her electronic gadgets at the bottom of the trunk. Her beads and sewing supplies would be fine on top. She wrapped them in the yard of tanned deer hide she carried with her for beading projects. Everything else, sheet music, her purse and a few books, would go into the middle.

Alethia undressed and sank into the hot water, sending thoughts of gratitude to the kind soul who'd arranged for the bath. Once she was done washing, she stood up and reached for the large piece of cloth draped over the one chair in the room, dried off and dressed in the cleanest of her two gowns.

Alethia smoothed the wrinkles from the garnet-hued fabric. She'd beaded the bodice with black onyx around the squared neckline and along the tops of the removable sleeves. She loved creating her costumes for the Renaissance fairs. Next to music, sewing and beading were her favorite pastimes. Her grandmother and aunties had taught her everything they knew. Running her fingers lovingly over the intricate beadwork, she felt connected to all the generations of Goodsky women preceding her.

She'd just sat down before the hearth to begin working a comb through her wet tangles when someone knocked on the door. She crossed the chamber and opened it a crack, keeping her foot firm against the base.

Beth, the young woman who had led her to the room, smiled and curtsied. "There's to be a feast this eve, milady, and I'm to help ye make yerself ready."

"Oh, thanks." The tension she'd been holding eased, and Alethia stepped back. "I can manage."

"Och, for certes ye can, but the young lord gave his orders, and I'll no' be slacking on me duties." Beth hustled her over to the chair and gently pushed her down by the shoulders. "Since ye've already dressed, I'll tend to yer hair." She snatched up the linen and began a vigorous squeezing and rubbing of Alethia's scalp. "'Tis an honor to be chosen to look after ye. All the other maids are pea-green with envy. I'll no' be lettin' the lord down, or it's back to the kitchen with me."

"You don't like working in the kitchen?"

"Nay, milady. Cook is as prickly as a thistle stalk."

"Oh." Alethia couldn't help but smile as Beth chattered on. She had to hold her hand up by her nose more than once as her hair was arranged in an elaborate braided coronet around her head. Judging by her body odor, Beth rarely bathed.

"Ye've the loveliest hair, milady."

"I use a special soap. I'd be happy to share it with you." She turned to gauge the younger woman's reaction, catching the doubtful look in her eyes.

"We'd best be on our way. They'll be waitin' to serve until ye take yer place upon the dais."

She'd be sitting with the laird and his family? Her gown had marked her as nobility. Still, they had no idea what her rank was, and nobility didn't guarantee a place on the dais. Because of the family's assumptions, she would be treated well, at least until the truth came out.

That thought sent her heart fluttering. What would she say when someone finally got around to asking questions? *Oh, and by the way, I come to you live from the twenty-first century. Ta-da!* Nope, that little tidbit she'd keep to herself. No way did she want to be associated with sorcery or witchcraft.

Beth hustled her down the narrow stairs to the great hall. It seemed to Alethia the entire clan had gathered, or at least all those who lived on the island. Besides the long table she'd noticed earlier, another had been created by placing planks on top of barrels. She squelched the urge to run for the hills and squared her shoulders. Her eyes were drawn to the dais, where she found Malcolm's intense gaze fixed on her. He'd bathed, shaved and changed into a clean linen shirt with billowing sleeves and a kilt in brilliant crimson, dark green and white. He wore his hair tied back at the nape of his neck. Lord, he cleaned up *real* nice. She lost her breath and the ability to move. Beth nudged her forward. One side of Alpha-Jerk's mouth quirked up.

Eight people sat at the high table, and Malcolm bore a striking resemblance to the middle-aged man in the seat of highest honor. Must be the lord of the castle, and his lady was seated to his right. Another middle-aged couple flanked the lord's left, followed by a lovely young woman who might be around her age. Liam and Robley were next to Malcolm. There were two empty chairs. One between Malcolm and his cousins and another at the very end near the young woman. She set out for the open spot next to the very safe-looking woman.

Malcolm stood. "Father, Mother, this is Lady Alethia Goodsky. My lady, this is my father, the earl of Fife, and my mother, Lady Lydia. You already know Liam and Robley, and these are their parents, my Uncle Robert and his lady wife, Rosemary. My younger sister Elaine is seated to Rosemary's left." He gestured to the empty seat next to his. "Come. You must be hungry, aye?"

Drat. So much for her plan to sit next to Elaine. Alethia executed a perfect curtsy, courtesy of many months of practice at all the fake courts in every fair she'd ever worked. "I thank you for your kind hospitality."

"We all enjoyed your music earlier today, lass." The earl's eyes twinkled with warmth. "'Tis my wish that we might hear you play again this eve, if that is agreeable to you."

"It would be my pleasure."

"We'll have someone fetch your instrument." The earl gestured to the seat next to Malcolm. "Come, sit. 'Tis high time we ate."

Alethia exchanged a shy smile with Malcolm's sister and made her way to the chair Malcolm had pulled out for her. Her knee brushed against his thigh as she settled herself, and a current of electricity raced through her body.

"Let us bow our heads and give thanks for the food we are about to receive." The earl's voice reverberated throughout the hall. "Join hands."

Oh great. Just what she needed. Everyone made the sign of the cross, and Alethia imitated their movements. Malcolm took one hand, and Liam clasped the other. Odd, the hand Malcolm held was the only one she felt. All the while the earl droned on in Latin, the feel of Malcolm's strong, callused warmth sent all kinds of sensations pulsing through her. *Whoa. Not good.* Finally grace ended, and she tugged her hand back.

Malcolm glanced her way, his eyes twinkling. He reached for her hand again and held on tight. "I'm no' yet done giving thanks."

"You don't need my hand to continue," she whispered, heat rising to her cheeks.

"Ah, but I do. Your gentle nature, my lady," Malcolm said, rubbing the bruise on his lower lip with their clasped hands, "fills me with the reverence." He brought their twined fingers to rest on his thigh.

Gulp. Her face turned to flame, and she tried her best to free herself. "For a moment there, while you made the introductions," she said, managing to pull her hand free, "I almost gave you credit for being well mannered."

He threw his head back and laughed, Robley and Liam joining in.

She seethed.

"Would you share my trencher, Lady Alethia?" Robley asked, gesturing toward the flattened slab of day-old bread they would use to hold their meal.

She graced him with her sweetest smile. "Gladly."

Servants came with platters of food, and everyone began to serve themselves. Robley offered her pieces of lamb, root vegetables, and dark bread. How clean could their kitchen be? For that matter, how clean was the cook? If Beth was any indication, not very. Which was the greater risk: eating questionable food, or insulting her hosts? She took a tentative bite, surprised to find the meat tender and tasty. She hadn't eaten a decent meal in two days, and she decided this meal was definitely worth the risk. Conversations buzzed all around her. She let her attention drift to the people sitting below the dais.

A disturbance toward the end of the long trestle table caught her attention. Something caused a ripple of movement among the diners farthest from the dais, where the villagers and crofters sat. People turned in their places, handing bits of bread, meat or vegetable to something small behind them. A dog?

No, not a hound. A small boy tugged on shirtsleeves until given a bite to eat, moving on to the next person once he'd taken the offered morsel. Dressed in rags with his hair a matted tangle, he seemed to be equal parts dirt and child. A quarrel broke out between two rough-looking men sitting directly behind the little beggar. One of them shouted and pounded his pewter mug on the table. The boy didn't react in any way. *He's deaf.*

Unable to look away, she gripped the edge of the table. As if he could feel her stare, he lifted his eyes to hers with a solemn expression at odds with his age. Her heart went out to him, and she couldn't help but sense his loneliness and isolation. She wanted to wrap him in her arms, care for him and teach him to talk with his hands. Like her, he found himself in a frightening world impossible to navigate.

Alethia paced the small confines of her room until she was certain everyone in the castle had gone to bed. The flame from a single candle burning on the mantel flickered with each pass she made. The deaf child hadn't seemed to belong to anyone. None of the adults had paid him any attention other than to give him food. She couldn't bear the thought of his being alone and frightened. *Someone should look after him, and it might as well be me.*

Taking a blanket from her bed, she folded it into thirds and laid it on the wood-planked floor near the hearth. It would have to do for the boy's bed until she could come up with something better. She crossed the room, lifted the bar securing her door and peered into the corridor. The glow of firelight spilled up from the great hall. She made her way to the stairs and crept down.

The extra tables set up for the feast had been left standing. Dogs sniffed through the rushes for hidden morsels, and the snores and grunts from the sleeping revelers reverberated through the room. Burning logs in both hearths cast the cavernous chamber into golden light and dark shadow. Picking her way through the sleepers and the hounds, she searched for the little beggar boy.

Beginning with the places with the most light, she worked her way outward toward the darker corners. A hand shot out from the shadows to grab her, and a man's arm snaked around her waist, dragging her back against his hard chest.

"Looking for me?" Hugh whispered into her ear, dragging her deeper into the darkness. "I'm glad you've sought me out, my lady. Shall I take this to mean you've decided to accept my offer of *protection*?"

"No." Her heart pounded, and her mouth went dry. She removed his arm from around her waist and stepped out of his reach. His words were slightly slurred, and the sour scent of too much wine emanated from him. Great. "I've decided I don't need or want your protection. Thank you just the same."

His brow furrowed for a moment, before her words registered fully. His expression darkened to rage. He grabbed her wrist and dragged her against him. "Ungrateful bitch. I'm the son of an earl. D'ye know that? D'ye think yourself above me—you a foreigner to our land, without so much as one guard in attendance? I begin to suspect you're naught but a whore after all, masquerading as a lady. There's a penalty to pay for such a deception, and I intend to be the one to collect." He spun her around and pressed her against the wall, covering her mouth with his with brutal force.

Twisting and turning, she struggled to get free. Her movements only served to incite him even more. If she could only get free enough to shout, surely someone in the great hall would wake. Panic wouldn't save her. *Think!* She gagged on the bile rising in her throat. He caught her wrists and held them above her head with one hand. With the other, he started to pull her skirt up her legs. *No!*

Letting her body go completely slack, she forced him to support her weight and sank down along the wall until he leaned over to follow. He cursed her as he broke contact to keep his balance. She shrieked, tucked her chin and sprang up as hard as she could. Her skull slammed into his nose with a satisfying crunch.

"Ah, you bitch!" Hugh staggered back, blood spurting down his face.

She lunged away from the wall and shoved him, hooking a heel behind his feet. He fell backward, and she ran—right into the arms of another man.

From one nightmare straight into another! Screaming and twisting she fought to free herself.

"Cease your caterwauling. Be still."

Malcolm's command penetrated her fear, and a rush of relief

washed through her. Alethia sagged against him and sucked in huge gulps of air.

"What the devil goes on here?" he demanded.

Hugh rose from the floor, blood seeping through his fingers. "She came to the great hall seeking my attentions. I obliged, and the bitch turned on me."

Alethia straightened, every muscle in her body tensed for another battle. "I never did any such thing, you lying sack of—"

"Wheesht, woman."

"But I—"

"You've no business below stairs at this hour, Lady Alethia." Malcolm gripped her arm above the elbow and sent her a look sharp enough to cut glass. He turned to Hugh. "Judging by your injury, it would appear the lady has had a change of heart."

"Wait a minute." She jerked her arm out of his hold. "I did *not* come here looking for this dirtbag."

"As you say." Hugh bowed toward her. "Mayhap I mistook your intent, my lady. Please forgive me. Until we meet again . . ." His tone dripped malice, and the promise of retribution hung in the air.

"Hie yourself to the barracks, Hugh. You've no reason to be here."

She waited until the rat bastard left the hall and turned to Malcolm. "You believe him?" She couldn't keep the quaver from her voice.

"What other plausible reason could you have to be here at this hour?" His angry tone stung. "If you did no' arrange a tryst with Hugh, then who did you intend to meet?"

Stunned by the accusation, she bit back the burning retort she longed to throw in his face. Anger surged, and her hands fisted. Fine. If that's what he chose to believe, let him. What difference did it make to her anyway? Tomorrow she'd figure out how to make the stupid pendant work, and she'd find a way to go home where she belonged.

"I will accompany you to your chamber." Malcolm gripped her by the wrist and tugged her toward the stairs.

Head held high, she managed to keep up with him as he pulled her down the corridor. She refused to utter a word as he swung her door open and pushed her none too gently over the threshold.

"Stay put," he snapped, slamming the door shut.

She pressed her forehead against the wood and listened to the sound of his retreating footsteps. "You're such an ass." She crossed the room on shaky legs, threw herself face down on the bed and pressed her face into the pillow. All the events from the past two days caught up with her. Overwhelmed with helplessness, frustration and fear, she gave in and cried herself to sleep.

CHAPTER FOUR

Something had to give, because Alethia was tired of feeling like a *manidoo-waabooz*, a rabbit bolting for her hole every time a shadow crossed her path. Besides, she hadn't had a full bath in almost a week, and the scant buckets of water Beth brought every day weren't getting the job done.

Since the incident in the hall with Hugh, she'd made every effort to avoid Malcolm on her brief forays to search for the little deaf boy. She'd also tried everything she could think of to make the magic that had landed her here somehow work in reverse. Neither effort had paid off. Alpha-Jerk seemed to pop up wherever she went, hovering and staring at her with his mouth a straight line of displeasure. And . . . she was still here, firmly planted in whatever time frame this proved to be.

The only bright spot on her otherwise bleak horizon was that she hadn't caught sight of Hugh since his attempt to molest her. Maybe he'd been sent away. One could hope.

On that hopeful note, she snatched her basket of soap and shampoo from the mantel, worrying about how long her supplies would last. She'd use them sparingly. Pausing to listen for anyone stirring in the corridor, she slipped out of her room. Alethia headed down the back stairway, darting past the kitchen, which was already bustling with activity, and slipped through the door leading out to the herb garden. There she paused to catch her breath, scanning the area to make sure no one saw her leaving the castle.

The eastern horizon barely held the hint of pink, and she kept to the shadows as she went, looking back all the time to assure herself that no one followed. After bathing and breakfast she'd search for Malcolm's sister and beg for a weapon of some sort. If Hugh or anyone else tried to trap her in a dark corner, she'd be more than able to defend herself.

Setting her rush basket on a flat rock, she searched the shore for the best place to enter. After one more look to make sure she was alone, she stripped down to her undies and waded in. The frigid water raised goose bumps on her skin, but Lord it felt good to wash her hair. Her breath sent a cloud of steam to mingle with the fog hovering above the lake's surface, and her shivers sent circles rippling outward.

The sun inched its way above the horizon. She intended to be safe inside the castle before too many people were up and about. One more quick rinse, and then she swam around the rocky outcrop toward shore. Her stomach dropped, and dread stole all the breath from her lungs. Hugh stood on the beach, her clothing in his arms and a cruel smile on his bruised and swollen face. Damn. Had he followed her here? She'd been so careful.

All the stress and fear she'd been living under for the past week erupted. "I would rather die of hypothermia than get out of this water for you, you knuckle-dragging, scum-sucking, waste of space!"

"You must come out eventually." He moved closer to the water's edge, his wicked smile growing larger. "When you do, you will pay dearly for breaking my nose."

"I'll break something else if you don't leave me alone, you rat-bastard perv!" Her muscles were beginning to cramp from the cold, and she couldn't control her shivering. Hypothermia was a very real possibility. She searched for an out and prayed someone would hear her shouts and come to investigate.

Malcolm walked back toward the keep from the lists. He'd worked up an appetite and a good sweat and looked forward to breaking his fast before bathing and seeing to the rest of his daily tasks, including seeing to Lady Alethia's whereabouts.

Their odd guest once again occupied his thoughts. The more she avoided him, the more obsessed with her he became. Whom had she gone down to the great hall to meet? It had rankled and nagged at him, until he could no longer think straight. Directly after breaking his fast, he'd search her out and demand the truth. Everything would return to normal, and he'd be able to get her out of his system once and for all. *Not bloody likely.*

The image of her as she'd first walked out of the forest with her silken sable hair falling freely about her shoulders flashed before him. Her exotic beauty haunted his dreams and left him restless and wanting. The sooner he discovered exactly who she was and from whence she came, the sooner he could see her safely returned. And *then* his life would return to normal.

Shouts broke through his thoughts. He recognized Alethia's voice, and she was in trouble. He ran toward the sound with his heart in his throat. Crashing through the brush with his dirk drawn, he came upon a sight that turned his blood to ice. Hugh held her clothing in his arms, while she hid her nakedness in the loch. Her eyes were wide with fright.

"What do you mean to do here, Hugh?"

"I mean to have a bit of sport with the lass. Leave me to it." Hugh's eyes slid to Malcolm for a second before returning to Alethia shivering in the ice-cold water. "You're welcome to her when I'm through."

The thought of Hugh's filthy hands touching her turned Malcolm's vision red. He shoved him around by the shoulder, his fist connecting with the blackguard's face before he even knew he meant to strike.

Hugh cried out and staggered back, dropping Alethia's garments to the ground. "Damnation!" Touching his split lip with the back of his hand, he glared at Malcolm.

Malcolm took a step toward him. "This is your idea of sport, is it? Terrorizing a defenseless woman? You have until Terce to gather your things and be gone. Your life is forfeit if I find you here after that."

"You'll pay for this. You'll both pay." Hugh's face twisted with hatred.

"Harken well." Malcolm shoved him back. "If you *ever* lay a hand on her," he said, shoving again, "'twill be the last thing you do." The last push sent the blackguard sprawling in the dirt.

Hugh scrambled up and fled. Malcolm watched until he was well away before facing Alethia. Only her head showed above the surface, and she shivered uncontrollably. He grabbed her garments from the ground and placed them near the shore, taking several steps away before turning his back to her. "'Tis safe to come out. I'll keep watch."

He heard her splash out of the water and pull on her garments. Sobs broke from her in great gasps.

"I . . . I . . . w-want to g-go h-home," she cried. "I. Want. To. Go. Home. I w-want m-my g-gran, hot showers, a washer and dryer . . . m-my hair dryer . . . and f-freakin' electrical outlets, dammit. Central heat, b-blue jeans and . . . and . . . s-sweatshirts." Her voice trailed off as she sniffed and hiccupped.

Her words made no sense. Had she lost her wits from all the strain? Certain she'd clothed herself, Malcolm sheathed his dirk and approached. Water dripped from her hair down the front of her gown. Her teeth chattered, and her lips were tinged blue.

Her distress twisted him up inside. "Where is your home, lass?"

"S-so far away I d-don't know h-how I'll ever g-get b-back," she sobbed.

"Nonetheless, where might that be?" Taking his plaid from over his shoulder, he wrapped her in it and rubbed her back and arms vigorously.

"A-across the ocean."

Could she be any more evasive? Now was not the time to press for answers, not while she was still so upset. "Hugh will no' trouble you any longer. I swear, you have my—"

"D-don't say it. Don't say I have your p-protection, because I've f-felt everything but protected ever since I l-landed here." She swiped at her tears with a corner of his plaid. "You took Hugh's side the night he t-tried to rape me."

"Nay. I took no one's side." Malcolm's jaw clenched, and he fought to gain control over his emotions. "If not Hugh, whose company did you seek that night, lass?"

She shrugged his wool off her shoulders and stepped out of his reach. "I was looking for the deaf child who begged for food during the feast." Her head came up a defiant notch, and her anger lashed at him. "I have experience with the deaf and hard of hearing. I thought maybe I could look after him. H-he's all alone."

Her own life had been turned upside down, and yet she thought to help another. Guilt laid him low. "Why did you no' come to me about the lad?"

"Come to you? You haven't exactly . . . You've done nothing but castigate, scold, and make your disapproval clear." She bit her lip and studied the ground. "Why would I come to you for anything?"

Malcolm placed a finger under her chin and raised her face to his. "Your words ring true. 'Tis clear I've given you no reason to trust me. Is that no' the way of it?" God's blood, but her tiny nod made him feel like an arse. In that moment he realized something else.

Her sharp tongue and bravado were naught but bluster to hide how terrified she truly was. Malcolm wanted to snatch her up in his arms and hold her fast. Instead, he raked his fingers through his hair. "I am the worst kind of churl."

"That's not entirely true." She glanced up at him through her thick lashes. "You've given me a roof over my head and food to eat, and I'm grateful for both. It's not your fault I ended up on your land."

He wasn't so certain about that. Surely she'd been left in his path for a reason. Malcolm stared out over the loch, pondering how best to rectify the situation. "You must allow me to make amends. Let us begin anew."

She took a deep breath and let it out slowly. "OK. Thanks for rescuing me from that creep."

"Creep?" He shook his head. "Your speech confuses me, lass. Though it sounds English, 'tis not wholly the same at all. What do you mean by oh-kay?"

"Where I come from, the word *creep* is sometimes used to describe someone whose intentions are predatory." She wrung some of the water from her hair and took another deep, shuddering breath. "*OK* just means all right, and your speech sometimes confuses me as well."

"Oh-kay." He tried the word, letting its strangeness roll over his tongue. Alethia deserved his compassion, and all he'd done was add to her misery. It fell to him to set things right, but how? Malcolm squared his shoulders, his mind racing to find common ground. "I have two sisters. One is older, and the other younger. Helen, the oldest, is married and lives with her husband two days' journey from our keep, and you've met Elaine. Perhaps if you spent some time with my mother and sister, you might feel more comfortable."

"Oh yes. That would be nice." Her expression brightened. "I don't have any siblings, but I do have about twenty cousins, and most of them are boys."

She smiled up at him, and Malcolm's knees went weak. "Come, you are chilled to the bone." He took her arm and started her back toward the bailey. "Why were you in the loch?"

"I wanted a bath."

"We have a bathing room in the keep. There are lads whose job it is to keep a constant supply of warm water available."

"How was I supposed to know?"

"Beth did no' tell you?"

"No." She snorted. "I don't think personal hygiene is at the top of her list of priorities, and it was just by accident that I found the . . . the . . ."

"Garderobe?" Malcolm found her modesty enchanting. Another question had nagged at him since the day he'd found her, and now seemed like a good time to satisfy his curiosity. "What did you do the day you put me to sleep?"

"Oh. That. I cut off the blood supply to your brain, and you fainted." She stopped walking and placed her fingertips on his neck, feeling along under his jaw. "Here, feel the pulse?"

Malcolm took her hands in his. They were close to the keep, and he was conscious of his people's watchful eyes. "Come, we must seek my father. He'll have questions."

She tugged her hands free. "I can't see your father looking like this. I'm a mess."

Malcolm took in her wet tangles and sand-covered gown. "He will no' concern himself with your appearance."

"Maybe not, but it does concern me." She frowned.

"Hie yourself to your chamber, then, and make yourself presentable. I'll send Beth to you anon."

"I have nothing to wear," she argued. "I only have two gowns, and they're both a mess."

"I'll have my sister lend you one of hers."

"She's a lot taller than I am. Let's wait until I can clean one of mine." She glanced up at him. "Like maybe tomorrow or the day after."

Malcolm placed his hands on her shoulders and turned her to face him. "Lady Alethia, do you *mean* to vex me?"

"No." She frowned. "It's a natural talent."

Alethia flopped back on the bed and covered her eyes with her hands. The laird would have questions, all right, and she needed time to come up with answers. Telling them she'd been sent back through time from the twenty-first century? Not a good idea. It sounded like an invitation to be the guest of honor at a bonfire complete with a stake and accusations of witchcraft.

If she wanted to keep the private room and the special treatment, she had to present herself as nobility. Fortunately, it wouldn't require outright lying, just a little bit of truth-twisting and era-blending. That she could manage. She got up and worked herself out of her damp gown.

Beth bounded through the door. "I've brought ye a clean gown, milady. We must make haste. The laird awaits." She draped the rose-colored wool over the bed and led Alethia to the chair to work the tangles out of her hair. Reaching for the comb on the mantel, Beth chattered on. "I'm to show ye the bathin' room, though to my way o' thinkin' 'tis unhealthy to submerse a body in warm water."

"Oh? I've always believed the opposite. Is the laird's family often ill?"

"Nay. The family never takes sick."

"They all bathe regularly." If she did nothing else while here, she'd get her unwashed friend into a tub. "Where I come from, we believe that a hot bath and cleanliness keep illness away."

"Aye? I've never heard such a thing." She resumed her ministrations. "Ye have the shiniest hair, milady."

"Like I said before, I'd be happy to share my secrets. The scented soap I use is called Caress." She glanced at Beth to gauge her reaction.

"I wash my hair with a secret blend of herbs that make it shine. It's called Herbal Essence. Do you have a special man in your life?"

"Nay. Though I wish more than anything for a certain lad in the garrison to take notice." Beth sighed as she fetched the fresh gown and helped her into it, tugging the sumptuous wool over her damp chemise.

"Have you ever noticed how the flowers with the sweetest scent draw the most bees?" For the first time since meeting her, Beth went silent as she laced up the gown. Alethia hoped she was considering her words. "The offer stands. You're welcome to borrow my soap."

"Come, milady. I'm to take ye to the laird's study."

Lifting the overlong hem, she followed her down the maze of corridors. Beth ushered her through a heavy oak door, where she found Malcolm and his father waiting. She curtsied.

"Please, sit. My son tells me you've had a trying morn." The laird smiled kindly.

"Very trying, yes." She took the seat at the table opposite him. Parchment, ledgers, inkwells and quills covered the surface.

"Hugh will trouble you no more. Rest easy." The earl leaned back in his chair and studied her. "How is it that you found yourself on our land and alone?"

"I don't know." Folding her hands in her lap to keep them from shaking, she forged on. "I was attending a fair in my own country. I went into a fortune-teller's tent because I heard crying, and once I was inside, I couldn't get away from her."

She glanced up at Malcolm, who stood next to his father. "She calls herself Madame Giselle, but I don't think that's her real name." She noticed a brief look of shock cross his face. "Being with her is the last thing I remember before your son found me."

"Did she offer you anything to eat or drink while you were with her?" Malcolm asked.

"Why do you ask?"

Malcolm shrugged a shoulder. “Mayhap she slipped you some kind of sleeping potion.”

Good one. Why hadn’t she thought of that while concocting her story? “Come to think of it, yes,” she lied. “She offered me a goblet of spiced wine, and I did drink all of it.”

A knowing look passed between father and son.

“I don’t know how you wish to be addressed,” she said, turning to Malcolm’s father. Though slightly shorter than his son, he appeared to be every bit as powerful. Their resemblance was striking. His hair, now streaked with silver, had once been the same tawny gold as Malcolm’s. The older man’s eyes were the same brilliant blue.

“My given name is William. It is the custom here to address me as Laird. You say you were in your own country when this happened. What country might that be, lass?”

“I’m from a land far away across the Atlantic Ocean.”

“The Continent.” Malcolm nodded.

“Well, *a* continent, but not the one you’re thinking. My land is not commonly known, though there have been Europeans who’ve traveled to our shores. Not long before William the Conqueror came to England, Norwegians came to my land. Erik the Red, and then later his son, Lief. Have you heard the tales?”

“Aye, we’ve heard rumblings of faraway lands, but we gave it no credence. Did the Norse conquer your land as William did England?” Malcolm asked.

“Hardly.” She snorted. “They were few against many, and our men are excellent warriors.” She boasted her way down the murky road of embellishment.

Malcolm’s eyes lit with interest. “Your land must lie near the edge. Have you seen it?”

“The edge?” Her brow rose in question.

“Aye, the edge of the world.”

“Um . . . no.”

"How is it you speak English?" William asked.

"Priests. They seem to find their way to all corners of the world." *Lord, forgive me for my sins.* The more details she could give them, the more believable her story would seem. "If you have something for me to write on, I could draw you a map, a rough one anyway."

Malcolm went across the room and returned with a rolled piece of parchment, a quill and an inkwell. He set them down before her and gathered stones to keep the parchment flat. Alethia picked the quill up uncertainly and dipped it into the ink. Her first try at drawing made a big blob of black on the parchment. The second time went better, and soon she was tracing a rough outline of the continents they would already know.

"Could you tell me the date?" She looked up from her task. "And the year?" If they thought her request odd, they gave no hint. She'd been too afraid to ask before—afraid and overwhelmed with everything that had happened.

"'Tis early autumn, in the year of our Lord 1423."

Her mouth went dry, and the quill slipped through her fingers.

"I take it some time has passed since you visited the fair?" Malcolm asked.

She swallowed. "You could say that."

"Continue." William gestured toward her map.

She retrieved the quill and leaned over her drawing. "This is Scotland and Britain." Both men leaned forward to watch with interest as she labeled each continent. "Here is Ireland, Europe, the Orient, and Africa. This island is called Iceland. This one is Greenland, and here is my continent." She sketched North America with the Great Lakes in the center. "Here in the center we have five very large fresh-water lakes. On the tip of this one is where my homeland starts. It's called Minnesota." She moved to the side of the parchment and drew a separate outline of her state. This is the Red River, here is the

Minnesota River, this one is the Mississippi, and here's the St. Croix." She labeled each one.

"Our land is north of the Minnesota River and bordered by the other two." Satisfied with her rendition, she sat back. For the first time she noticed the stunned expressions worn by father and son. "My people also have clans, though they aren't like yours." She continued, warming to the subject. "Our communities are made up of members of all the different clans. In my culture, clan identity has to do with one's role in society."

"How so?" Malcolm asked.

"Well, for instance, we have the leadership and warrior clans. There are clans for hunting, learning, medicine, and just about everything. Each village must have members from a variety of clans to be whole. Our villages are each governed by a council of elders who are led by a chieftain. All the villages are governed by a greater council led by our president."

"A president?" William asked.

"The closest I could come to it in your culture is a king."

"What is your clan, Alethia?" Malcolm asked.

"I am *Chejauk*, the Crane, which is one of the leadership clans. My father was our president until his death."

The laird's head came up with sudden interest. "How did he die?"

"He and my mother both perished when their, um . . . *keep* caught fire."

Malcolm and his father exchanged another look.

"Where were you at the time, lass?" William's voice took on a grave tone.

"I was staying with my uncle's family. I have cousins about my age, and I often stayed with them. I'm an only child."

"This is enough for now. You may take your leave," William said.

She rose. "I would like to earn my keep while I'm here. I have talents you might find useful."

"Besides the making of extraordinary music?" William smiled.

She nodded. "I'm able to commit to memory anything I study, and I can tell whether a person is lying or telling the truth."

"It seems you are an aptly named young woman, Alethia. I shall put you to work on the morrow. 'Tis the day I hold court for our people."

"She does no' speak our language," Malcolm pointed out. "And most of our villagers dinna speak English." He turned to her. "Gàidhlig is our native language. Our crofters and villagers have no use for the *Sassenach* words."

"Gaelic? Well, it doesn't matter." Alethia shook her head. "It's not the words I listen to."

"'Tis settled. I will expect you in the great hall at first light."

"There is one more thing, Laird." She gripped the back of the chair she'd been sitting in. "The young deaf boy who stays in the great hall at night—who does he belong to?"

"The lad is an orphan." William continued to study her map. "His mother married outside our clan. Her husband disappeared while she was with child, and she returned to live here with her widowed mother. A few years past, both mother and child took ill. The lad's mother died, and the fever took his hearing. He lived with his grandmother until she passed, and now he stays in the great hall."

Her heart broke for the little boy. He'd already suffered so much loss, and he couldn't be more than four or five years old. "I would like to take care of him, if it would be all right. I can teach him to communicate. My people have a language for the deaf."

"I have no objections to your caring for the lad." William rolled her map up and set it aside. "Will you play for us this eve, lass?"

"Of course."

"One more thing, Alethia." Malcolm glanced from his father to her. "For the time being, you are to remain within the curtain wall."

"Why?" Her heart leaped to her throat. Did they intend to imprison her? How would she find her way home if she couldn't leave the island?

"Until we are certain Hugh has no allies here to cause you harm, 'twould be wise to remain where there are guards we trust close at hand. Hugh is a vengeful man."

"Oh." Relief washed through her. "OK."

After she'd closed the door behind her, Malcolm began to pace. "She is the daughter of a king."

"So it would seem, and likely the victim of treachery many times over." His father leaned back in his chair. "'Tis possible her parents were murdered in their beds and their keep burned down around them to hide the evidence. Lady Alethia's guardians may have sent her away to keep her safe. We did the same with our King James after his uncle murdered his older brother. 'Tis just as likely an enemy banished her. She is of age. Mayhap a marriage had been arranged that displeased one faction or the other."

"Aye, 'tis possible." Malcolm continued to pace. "But—"

"Sit, Malcolm." His father gestured toward the chair. "You're wearing a groove into my floor with your pacing."

"There's something odd about all of this." Malcolm took a seat and looked to his father. "The fortune-teller she spoke of, I know her."

"You believe Alethia was sent here to us specifically?"

"Aye."

"For what purpose, Malcolm?"

"That I canna say, but I intend to find out."

CHAPTER FIVE

For as long as he could remember, Malcolm had taken his place by his father's side as disputes between their clansmen were heard and settled. Neither needed a truth-sayer to judge fairly. Alethia's talents would be of use when dealing with outsiders, aye. But he saw no need of her talents now, other than indulging her need to prove herself. He shifted his stance to stand behind her as each of the men presented their side.

She leaned toward his father and whispered what they both already knew. "Both believe they are telling the truth, Laird."

Keeping half an ear on the proceedings, the better part of Malcolm's thoughts dwelt upon the revelations from the day before. What once he thought a flight of fancy no longer seemed fanciful at all. Alethia had been left by the side of the road for him to find. How else to explain her presence on their path the very day they passed? How else to explain Giselle's hand in sending her to him?

It hardly seemed credible. Madame Giselle had been ancient a decade ago. Was it possible she still lived? The words the old woman had spoken bounced around in his head. *Truth will save you. Keep her close by your side.* Was Alethia's presence the harbinger of some coming danger? Mayhap her life was in danger as well.

One thing was certain—he could not allow her to place herself in harm's way for his sake. He'd take extra measures to ensure her safety and his. He'd train harder in the lists and assign himself extra guards in battle, should the need arise. He placed a hand on her shoulder, and she graced him with a shy smile. Every protective instinct within him surged. Aye, no matter the cost, he'd keep her safe.

A single horn blast sounded from the village on the mainland. Court came to an unexpected end. More curious to see who had arrived than in having their disputes settled, his people followed the lure of the horn, eager to hear any news the visitors might bring.

Alethia rose to follow, and Malcolm held her back. "Nay, Lady Alethia. I'm taking you to my mother's solar."

"But—"

"Do as my son bids, lass." William clapped Malcolm on the shoulder. "I'll greet the ferry as it lands."

"What does the horn mean?" she asked, her gaze trailing after his father.

"One tone tells us someone of importance has arrived. Two means our own have returned, and three blasts means danger." Malcolm guided her toward the stairs. "No matter the number, you will remain inside." She rolled her eyes. "'Tis for your own safety." He raised one brow and gave her a stern look. "One more thing—should you need anything, anything at all, you are to come to me." They reached the solar door. Malcolm knocked and waited for his mother to bid him enter.

Ushering her through the door, he nodded his greeting. "I've brought Lady Alethia to join you."

His mother smiled. "We are most happy to receive her."

Content that she was in good hands, Malcolm bowed his farewell and headed for the ferry landing after his father.

"Have you some handiwork?" Lydia asked. "We are pleased you have joined us. We had hoped you would for the past se'nnight."

She surveyed her surroundings and the three women, all working on various projects. "I didn't know."

"Our apologies, Lady Alethia," Elaine said.

"It seemed you preferred to stay in your chamber, and we didn't wish to intrude," Rosemary added.

More like hiding out in her rabbit hole, but they didn't need to know that. "I'm happy to be here now." The square room faced south, with three tall windows letting in plenty of daylight. A wooden bench ran along the wall under the windows. She walked over to study the glass panes.

"My son is responsible for making our keep one of the most modern in Scotia," Lydia remarked with pride. "He has traveled extensively and brought back many innovations from faraway places."

"Oh." Alethia reached out to touch an air bubble captured in the greenish rippled glass. She turned back to study the rest of the room. A cozy hearth took up one wall, and cushioned seats were arranged around it. Elaine sat before a wooden frame holding a tapestry in progress. Rosemary and Lydia both embroidered. "Would you mind if I practiced my music here? I'm working on a few pieces I think might be good for dancing."

"That would be pleasant indeed." Rosemary's eyes lit up. "Mayhap we can persuade one of my sons to accompany you with the bodhran and pipes."

"You'd think after a week I'd know my way around, but I don't think I can find the way to my room and back again."

Elaine rose from her place. "I'll take you. 'Twould be good to stretch my legs." Taking Alethia by the arm, she led her back into the labyrinth of halls to her chamber. "'Tis grand to have another young woman in the keep. I do hope we will become close friends." Elaine gave her arm a squeeze. Elaine radiated goodness. Her soft brown hair resembled Lydia's, and her eyes were the same brilliant blue as Malcolm's.

She liked her immediately. "I hope so too. I could use a friend."

"I am sorry that none thought to bring you to the solar before today."

"It's all right." They'd reached her door, and Alethia opened it.

Elaine gasped as she entered. "What have you done?" She laughed as she picked up one of the rush baskets Alethia had made to pass the time.

"I was bored. No one to talk to and only my own company to keep."

"Again, I apologize for what must seem to you a lack of hospitality on our part."

"No, it's my fault." Alethia shook her head. "I didn't ask, and I have stayed hidden away in this chamber. How could you have known?" She picked up one of the baskets and turned it around in her hands. "I can do better with black ash. If you like them, take one."

"Truly?" Elaine chose a round container with a lid. "They are so finely made. I would no' have thought common floor rushes could be turned into such works of art."

Alethia opened the trunk and fished around for sheet music. "I'm glad you like them." She picked up the basket holding her peasant blouse. She'd cut it down to fit the deaf child, and only the hemming remained to be done. Stashing the sheet music with the sewing, she lifted her violin case from the peg and turned to go. "Do you know how I could get my hands on a piece of wool to make a garment for a little boy? I've tried to speak to the weavers myself, but none of them understand English."

"For a boy?" Elaine gave her a questioning look. "To clothe the lad, a *feileadh breacan* do you mean?"

"Is that what you call a kilt in your native language? It's what the men wear, right? Your father gave me permission to care for the deaf boy who stays in the hall at night."

"Aye, though I've no' heard it called thus before. Leave it to me," she said, crossing to the door.

"Will you teach me to speak your language, Elaine?"

"Of course. We can begin your lessons anon." Holding the door to her chamber, Elaine told her, "*dorus*," and pointing to her bed she continued, "*leabaigh*. Wait here, and I'll come back for you."

Alethia paced and checked things off her mental to-do list while waiting for Elaine's return. Once she had something clean to put on the child, he'd need a bath and a haircut. She shuddered at the thought of what vermin might be living in his matted hair.

She knew what it meant to be orphaned and to lose the people who were the center of your universe. What would've happened to her if she hadn't had such a large extended family? It wasn't in her nature to stand by and let this deaf child fend for himself. He'd been reduced to begging, isolated and unable to communicate, and she could not turn her back on him.

"'Tis done. Let us return to the solar," Elaine said from the corridor.

Spending the morning in the women's solar had been a joy. Alethia hadn't realized how lonely she'd been until she had company again. Reciting all the words Elaine had taught her, she made her way back to her room, surprised to find the door open.

"Milady, I've been waitin' for ye." Beth sat in the chair by the hearth, a pile of mending in her lap. "I brought the wee basket with your soaps back. One of the lads found it by the loch."

"Oh." Two bolts of cloth lay on her bed. One was a muted plaid like the kilts Malcolm and his men had worn the day they'd found her, and the other a fine linen. "Where did these come from? All I asked for was a bit of wool to make a child's garment." She ran the linen through her fingers, savoring the texture. Visions of a new gown and chemise more in the billowing style worn by the MacKintosh women formed in her mind.

"Lady Elaine asked one of our weavers for them." Beth rose from the chair, setting her mending aside. "Their youngest lad has taken ill with *a'ghearrach*."

Alethia gave her a puzzled look.

"Och. I dinna ken the word. Whatever the lad eats or drinks runs right through him. He suffers cramps. Lady Elaine has been visiting the family and helping as much as she can, but he's very ill."

He had dysentery. She thought of her emergency supplies. "There's no healer in your village?"

"Nay. No' for a year past."

"I'm not a healer, but my grandfather was. I might have something that will help, and I have a book of remedies. It wouldn't hurt to try."

"Och, the family would welcome any help, milady."

Alethia moved the basket containing her bath supplies to the top of the mantel. "Have you given any thought to my offer?"

"What offer would ye be talkin' about?" Beth's brow furrowed.

"To use my scented soaps. In exchange, I have a favor to ask."

"Aye?"

"I need a child's bed. I'm going to take care of the deaf boy who stays in the great hall." She could see the battle waging inside Beth. "You do want to be noticed, don't you?"

"Humph. I'll return by None. I'll get what ye ask, and I'll try the other. Once. If, as ye say, a bath and fine scented soap will gain my lad's affections . . ." She shook her head, her eyes full of doubt.

"Oh, I promise it will. Go now. I have things to prepare for the weaver's son." She walked with her to the door. "I'll see you back here at None." *Whenever that is.* Alethia went to her trunk to fetch her book of Native American herbology.

For a moment, she was lost as she traced her grandmother's

writing on the inside cover. *For every illness known to man, the Creator has provided a cure. Look to nature, my darling Alethia. Love, Gran.* Gran had added her own notes on many of the pages, things she'd learned over the span of her life.

She always brought the book with her when she worked the Renaissance fairs. Most of them were held in rural areas, and she liked to get away from the crowds whenever she could. Hiking through fields and woods reminded her of endless summers in the bush country near the Canadian border, hunting, gathering and trapping with her uncles and cousins. She loved identifying medicinal plants used by her people throughout their history.

Alethia's eyes filled with tears as memories poured through her, and once again the need to find a way home overwhelmed her. Nothing she could do about it right now, though, and someone here needed her help. Giving herself a shake, she looked up cures for dysentery. Wild indigo and barberry, did they grow here? It wouldn't hurt to throw in some of her dried cranberries. They were known to inhibit bacteria.

The pages were brown, thick and textured. The pictures appeared to be hand drawn with black ink. Her book would pass for the period. Once the boy's family saw the pictures of the plants she needed, and if they grew here, they'd be able to find them.

She dug through her first-aid kit, taking out a few Imodium A-D tablets, essential for working and eating at fairs week after week. It wouldn't cure him, but it might control the symptoms until the medicine he needed could be made. Alethia placed her things in a basket. In the meantime, she'd cut the plaid for the child's kilt and finish the moccasins she'd started for him.

She was punching new holes in a leather belt pulled from a pair of her jeans when her door opened. Two men carried a child-sized pine bed frame into her room and set it in the corner to the left of the hearth. Beth followed with a feather mattress and linens.

"This is perfect." She ran her hand over the polished headboard. "I wasn't expecting anything so fine." She turned to Beth, who fussed at the two men. "Thank you." She nodded to them as they left. "Beth, where did this come from?"

"From the nursery, and the young lord weren't too pleased about it neither."

"Do you mean the castle nursery? Malcolm knows about the bed?"

"Och, aye. I couldna take it without askin' first, now could I? He awaits ye in the great hall."

"Malcolm?"

"Aye. I'm to send ye down. He was muttering somethin' fierce when I left."

"Oh." She frowned. "Well, let's go. I have what I need for the weaver's son." She picked up her basket and walked to the door. Beth didn't follow. "Aren't you coming?"

"I'll stay here and make the lad's bed ready. I'll be there once ye've finished having your talk with the young lord."

"Coward."

Beth's laughter followed Alethia down the corridor. Why would he be angry? Straightening her spine, she crossed the great hall to where he stood, an imposing figure with one foot on the hearth and his face set like stone. "You asked to see me?"

He turned to scowl at her. "Did I no' tell you this morn should you need anything, anything at all, you are to come to me?"

"Yes." She met his frown with one of her own. "But I didn't think you meant it in a literal sense."

He took his foot off the hearth and stepped toward her. "Had you come to me about the wee bed, I would have seen to it."

"Why?"

"You're my responsibility."

"Because you found me by the side of the road? Is that what makes me your responsibility?"

"Nay. 'Tis because I choose to accept you as such."

"I don't want to be anyone's responsibility. I want to earn my keep and take care of myself."

"Whether you will it or no', 'tis the way of things, and you'd best make peace with it."

"Let's see if I have this straight." She looked away from him. "I can't go beyond the curtain wall, I can't fend for myself or see to my own needs, and you'd prefer it if I'd spend all my time in your mother's solar. Have I covered everything?"

"Aye." He looked pleased that she understood him so well.

Her heart dropped to her stomach. "Am I a prisoner here?"

"Nay, I wish only to keep you out of harm's way."

Overbearing, controlling alpha male. An ember started a slow burn inside her. "Maybe there's a vacant cottage nearby the boy and I could move into."

"You'll no' be moving anywhere." He placed his hands on her shoulders and gave her a little shake. "You'll stay right here."

"If I'm not a prisoner, why do I have to stay here?"

"Because you're my . . . my . . ." He raked a hand through his hair.

"*Responsibility*." Of course. All her anger dissipated. He and his father were responsible for everyone's well-being, and she was just one more burden for him to carry. The last thing she wanted was to be anyone's burden. "I'm sorry, Malcolm." He appeared pleased with her apology, and she almost didn't have the heart to clear up his misconception.

"I accept your apology, Alethia. Next time you will come to me."

"What I mean is . . ." The doors to the great hall were thrown wide, and a half dozen men flanked by Liam and Robley strode into the room.

Malcolm took her by the elbow. "These are the earl of Douglas's men. The one in the center is his second eldest."

The man he'd pointed out approached and punched Malcolm in the shoulder before they grasped each other's forearms briefly.

"Welcome, James, 'tis good to see you again," Malcolm said.

"Aye, and you. Who is this lovely lass by your side?" James took her hand in his. Bowing, he brushed a kiss across the sensitive skin on the back of her knuckles. "Could she be the treasure you found by the side of the road? Your cousins have spoken of naught else since we boarded the ferry."

James matched Malcolm in height and was every bit as fit. His frank appraisal made her uncomfortable. Lust radiated from him in waves. She snatched her hand away, feeling like a mouse in a hawk's supper dish. "I'm sure you misunderstood. I am not his treasure. I'm his *responsibility*."

James laughed and looked her over from head to toe. "Och, well, if he does no' see you for the treasure you are, leave Moigh Hall and come to London with me."

The precariousness of her situation pressed in on her. Her whole life she'd been surrounded by a loving and protective extended family. Here she had no one, and most considered women on par with their cattle. She inched closer to Malcolm.

Malcolm sensed Alethia's discomfort. That she stepped closer to him was telling. Whether she realized it or not, he had her trust. That pleased him almost as much as her apology had.

One glance to his cousins brought them to flank her on either side. "Lady Alethia, this is James. James, this is Lady Alethia. She will no' be going anywhere with you." He flashed James a hard look. "Will we see you and your men in the lists on the morrow?"

James laughed and took a step back. "Aye, at dawn. Come," he commanded the men behind him. "We have traveled far and wish to refresh ourselves before talking with the earl." He bowed slightly and led his men toward the stairs, where a servant awaited.

Malcolm turned to Alethia. "Did you sense something that gave you cause to mistrust him?"

"No. He doesn't mean me any harm. His interest made me uncomfortable, that's all."

"Milady." Beth crossed the great hall. "Would ye be wanting to go see the weaver's son now?"

"Go." Malcolm gestured toward the doors. "They live within the curtain wall, and we must see to our guests. Remember well my words. You will come to me should you need anything."

Alethia had managed to get the Imodium A-D down the boy's throat, and with Beth's help, she communicated as best she could with the family. Satisfied that someone would find the plants she needed, she walked with Beth back to the keep. "Do you know where I'd find the deaf boy? He's always hanging around the keep in the mornings because there's food out for any who want it, but I don't know where to find him during the day."

"Aye. We keep a few horses here on the island. The lad does well with the animals, and the stable master is kind to him. He gives him work to do, so the lad feels useful."

"Where is the stable?"

"I'll take ye."

"Would you get a bath ready for him? Maybe you'd like to take one too," she asked hopefully. "I'm sure the Douglas men have finished with the bathing room by now."

"Och, ye think I'll be takin' me bath with the lad in the room?"

"There's a screen we can place between you." She crooked her arm through Beth's and smiled. "The garments I've made for him are folded on top of the trunk in my chamber, and the basket with my soaps is on the mantel above the hearth. I'll meet you there."

Beth left her at the entrance of the stable. Smells of horses, sweet hay, and leather wafted over Alethia. Clean straw carpeted the dirt floor of the stone-and-timber structure. A still kind of peace hung over the place. No wonder the boy liked it here.

The aisle between the stalls led her to a room in the rear where saddles and bridles were stored. A wide window with shutters thrown open faced south to take advantage of the daylight. The child sat on an overturned half-barrel. He worked at rubbing oil into a bridle. An older man tended to a saddle across the room.

"Hello," she called. "Do you speak English?"

"A bit, milady. Harold be my name." He lifted his gaze to her. "Would ye be wanting a palfrey?"

"No. I've come for the boy." Every day since she'd first seen him, Alethia had found him in the great hall whenever there was food left out. She was eager to begin teaching him signs, but she'd been hesitant to approach him until all was ready.

She caught his attention and signed a greeting, then held out her hand, a universal gesture. The child looked at the stable master, who nodded his assent. The child brought the bridle over to Harold and then came to her. Putting his hand in hers, he regarded her curiously. She gave him a reassuring smile, thanked the stable master and led him to the keep and his waiting bath.

Beth had everything ready by the time they arrived. Alethia took a seat on the wooden bench and positioned the boy between her knees. He rested a hand on each of her knees, while she checked his hairline behind the ears. As she feared, his matted hair was filled with nits and lice.

She'd taken off her gown and bound her own hair, covering it with a makeshift bandana. After his bath, she'd have Beth prepare one for her. She didn't want to come away with any tiny hitchhikers herself.

She took the scissors from her basket and cut his hair close to his scalp, careful not to nick him. Once done, she gave his shoulders a squeeze and pointed to the tub filled for him. His eyes grew large with alarm. "Before you bathe, could you please do something with this hair, Beth? It's full of lice."

Without a word, Beth scooped up the pile and threw it into the fire under the cauldron heating the water. A bitter, acrid stench filled the room.

"I could've done that." Alethia crossed the room and opened the shutter covering the single window.

"Aye, milady. Ye could have."

Alethia laughed at her sullen tone. "Let me bathe him first. I'll help you wash your hair once I've finished with the boy." She led the child to the bath and helped him in.

"I dinna mind waitin'."

"You sound like you're going to your death. It's only a bath."

"Humph."

Still laughing, she took up a scrap of linen and the soap. "Do you know his name?"

"Nay. I dinna know if anyone remembers, no' even the lad himself. He was still a bairn when he lost his hearing, and just beginning to talk, as I recall. Name him as you will, milady. 'Tis fitting he should have a new name along with his new life."

"How old is he?"

"Och, five, mayhap. I'm no' certain."

"I've been giving it some thought." She smiled into his eyes. He studied her face intently as she washed his scalp and scrubbed his face, neck and behind his ears. "I think I'll call him Hunter after my grandfather on my mother's side. It's a name that has been handed down from my mother's side of the family for as far back as anyone can remember."

"Hunter it is. 'Tis a good strong name, and one he'll grow into with time."

Alethia took a wooden bowl and rinsed his scalp, then touched his chest and signed his name to him. He watched, his features full of curiosity. He was smart as a whip and took everything in through those large gray eyes of his.

After scrubbing every inch of Hunter's skinny body, she lifted him out and stood him before the wooden bench to rub him dry. Pleased with her efforts, she slipped the altered peasant shirt over his head and tied the laces. He fingered the fabric. "I don't know how to do the wool. You'll have to teach me."

Beth pleated and wrapped the new wool around his body, fastening it with the belt Alethia handed her. They both stood back to admire their handiwork. Hunter felt the wool between his fingers. He looked up and gave them a heart-stopping grin.

How different he looked without the layers of grime. He had the face of an angel, and dimples appeared on each cheek when he smiled. His hair, what was left of it, was a soft golden brown. He'd break a few hearts for sure when he grew up. She sat him on the bench and signed for him to stay there.

"Your turn." She grinned at Beth.

Behind the screen that separated the two tubs, Beth faced her demons. Undressing with more complaints, she sank down into the water with a curse or two in Gaelic. Alethia set to work on her second charge. "Would you make sure someone replaces the water and stokes the fire? I'll want my own bath later this afternoon."

"Aye, milady. There are lads whose job it is to see it done."

Once they were in her room, Alethia led Hunter to the pine bed and signed that this was his place to sleep.

His eyes went large as he looked from the bed to her and back again. He pointed to himself and then placed a hand on the wooden frame.

She nodded and watched him examine it with a look of awe. He explored the rest of the room, picking up baskets and touching the gown that hung from its peg on the wall.

Alethia fetched the moccasins she'd made for him and tapped him on the shoulder to get his attention. He scrambled up to sit next to her on the bed. She signed that he was now in her care, though she knew he wouldn't yet have any idea what she was telling him. She slipped the moccasins onto his feet and watched with pleasure as he admired his new footwear.

She was curious to see if she could sense what Hunter was feeling. Her abilities seemed amplified in this place and time. Maybe it was due to the lack of technology, or maybe it had something to do with the untapped depths Giselle had mentioned. Whatever it was, lately she'd gotten more from people than simply truth or lie.

Focusing her mind, she directed her senses toward him. She gasped when her effort was met with his energy coming toward her in a tingling rush. His face mirrored the shock and surprise she felt. Hunter scrambled up to his knees and hurled himself into her arms, clinging to her as if his very life depended upon it.

She held him tight as wave after wave of the loneliness, isolation and fear he'd lived with since the day his grandmother had died washed through him. His tears soaked her shoulder, and the palpable force of his relief nearly bowled her over. She sent him love and reassurance. He was not alone any longer.

Neither was she.

CHAPTER SIX

I yield, Malcolm!" James thrust the point of his claymore into the ground. "You've the devil in you this day."

"You're growing soft, James. We've only been at it since Prime." The moment Lady Alethia had come to the lists, Malcolm had felt her presence. He meant to show her his prowess with the sword and couldn't help but be pleased with the results. He took his shirt off and used it to wipe the sweat from his brow, glancing to where she stood with the lad at her skirts. Aye, she watched his every move.

Malcolm flexed his muscles and stretched to show them to their best advantage. "Hie yourself to the keep, James, and break your fast. I'm ready for a new challenge." He grinned at his opponent with smug satisfaction.

James laughed. "I believe your lady awaits."

Malcolm walked over to her, eager for praise. "Good morn to you, Lady True." He gave her his most charming smile.

She frowned. "Lady True?"

"'Tis a fitting sobriquet."

"I prefer my own name."

"Aye, but 'twill help our clan to accept you if we give you a name of our own devising." He smiled, smug in his position of authority. "What brings you to the lists?"

"You said if I needed anything, I should come to you."

"I did. What is it you need?" She'd taken his words to heart, and it filled him with gladness.

"I need a dagger." She folded her hands before her and returned his smile.

He frowned. "You've no need for a dagger. You are well protected within the curtain wall."

"I'd feel better if I had one." Still she smiled, though it seemed forced.

"You are under my protection. Every man at my command would come to your aid should you need it."

Her smile disappeared altogether. "I appreciate the protection." She took a breath. "However, I'd also like to feel that I can defend myself if I need to. How about a bow and arrows? I'm an excellent archer."

"I dinna doubt your skills. You've no need to arm yourself, and no need to hunt. You will be provided for. I must think of everyone else's safety."

Her eyes grew large, and her mouth fell open. "Are you implying you won't arm me to protect everyone else *from* me?"

"'Twas you who broke Hugh's nose. Do you forget bringing me to my knees in hand-to-hand combat? You drew blood that day. You're dangerous enough without a blade to hand."

"You *do* mean that!"

"I have said you are under my protection, and that should suffice. No harm shall come to you." What was wrong with the woman? She was supposed to tell him how manly he was. She was supposed to praise his prowess with the sword and admire his well-formed body.

"What about the little daggers everyone uses to eat? Can I at least have one of those?"

"God's blood, you're obstinate. You have asked, and I have said nay."

Her eyes flashed, and her arms crossed over her chest. "If you won't get them for me, I'll find another way."

"I forbid it," he snapped.

"You're not the boss of me."

"Do you mean to provoke me, Alethia? God's truth, your company is far more pleasing when you say naught." The second the words left his mouth he wished to call them back. He reached for her, thought better of it and raked his hand through his hair. Her eyes met his just long enough for him to glimpse the hurt. She stomped away with the lad in her wake. Why did she always make him feel so twisted up inside?

"'Tis a novel approach," Liam said, coming to stand by his side.

"What?" Malcolm kicked a stone through the dirt, sending up a cloud of dust.

"Winning the lass's heart with harsh words." Liam chuckled and placed his hand on Malcolm's shoulder. "'Twill be interesting to see how this new strategy fares."

"She vexed me."

"Did she? How so?"

"She wishes to arm herself with dirk and bow. Next she'll be asking for a claymore."

"A dirk? Every female in our clan carries one hidden somewhere upon her person, and you refused her? Why, Malcolm?"

"'Tis a long story. I have no' told you all there is to tell."

"Ah, I see." Liam chuckled. "Well, you dinna have time to tell me now. While you ply your lady with insults, others take a more conventional approach." He nodded toward the keep.

Malcolm growled low in his throat and pulled his shirt back on. Alethia stood poised upon the bottom step to the great hall, a young swain with a handful of wildflowers before her. 'Twas an effort to refrain from running. Even so, his strides ate up the distance between them.

"Do you no' have some duty to perform?" Malcolm snapped at the weaver's oldest son.

"I was only giving milady—"

"Now be on your way." Snatching the bouquet from the man, Malcolm scowled at her. "You will no' accept flowers from any other man."

"They aren't flowers." She grabbed the plants from his hand and shook them under his nose, dislodging a shower of dirt to rain down upon his chest. "These are the plants I need to make the medicine for the weaver's youngest child." Pausing, she studied the late blooms in her hand. "OK, some of this is floral, but not in the way you're thinking." Another shower of dirt hit him. "I have news for you. I will accept flowers from anyone I want. In case you didn't hear me before, listen carefully now. *You* are not the boss of me."

What is a bossamee? A final layer of grit had settled over him. Why, in the middle of being vexed beyond reason, did he feel like laughing? He fought the urge to kiss her silent. "Och, woman. I dinna want to bicker."

"No? What do you want?"

"Faith, lass." He brushed some of the soil from his shirt. "I would have your faith that I am able to keep you safe." Stepping closer, he asked, "What need have you for a wee dagger when you have me to protect you?"

"Oh, Malcolm." She rolled her eyes. "I know you can protect me. I saw how good you are with that sword, but you can't be with me every minute of every day."

"Nay? The notion holds great appeal." Malcolm placed his hands on her shoulders and stared into her eyes. Her lips parted slightly, as if opening for him. Desire pulsed through his veins. His line of vision narrowed to the rise and fall of her breasts as her breathing grew more rapid. She wanted him. He was sure of it.

He drew her close and kissed her. She moaned and put her arms around his neck, pressing her soft curves against him. Malcolm's blood caught fire and rushed straight to his groin. He deepened the kiss, forgetting all but the way she fit so perfectly in his arms and the sweetness of her lips.

Kissing Lady Alethia could easily become his favorite pastime. Aye, that and goading her until her lovely cheeks bloomed with color. He tightened his hold and concentrated on coaxing her mouth open with his tongue.

Lord, the man could kiss. Afraid her knees would buckle, Alethia put her arms around Malcolm's neck. Seeing him half naked and glistening with sweat certainly hadn't helped matters. He was definitely a feast for the eyes. She couldn't press herself close enough to him. Her insides filled with delicious heat when he thrust his tongue inside her mouth, and she forgot where she was and why he'd ticked her off so badly.

Lost in sweet sensation, it took several seconds before she became aware of a small body inserting itself between them. Hunter pushed to separate her from Malcolm's embrace. She broke the kiss and tried to slow her breathing back to normal. Remembering where they were, her face heated.

Several people had stopped what they were doing to watch. Women were staring at her and whispering to one another behind their hands. Mortified, she muttered, "You can't just hold and kiss me like this right here in the middle of the bailey."

"Nay?" Malcolm leaned in and whispered back, "Where might I hold and kiss you like this then?"

His wicked smile scrambled her insides. She fought to gain control over her raging hormones. She couldn't fall for Malcolm. He was from a different century, and who knew how long she'd be here? Straightening her spine, she replied, "You know what I mean." She took Hunter's hand and headed up the stairs to the door of the keep. "You're such a Neanderthal."

"I heard that, True."

"I certainly hope so, Malcolm." The notion that he had no idea what it meant tickled her.

She worked up a good head of steam on the way to the ladies' solar. Malcolm was so overbearing and controlling it drove her crazy. The way he manhandled her and kissed her senseless made her even angrier. He didn't fight fair.

"Good morning, Elaine, Lydia," Alethia greeted them, and Hunter signed as they entered the solar. She took her customary place on the seat opposite Elaine. Hunter fetched the book she'd made for him and settled himself against her knees. She had illustrated animals and the signs that went with each. Elaine had given her the vellum, ink and quills. She also taught her how to trim the ends of the long goose feathers when needed.

Alethia tried to work on the gown she'd cut from the bolt of the muted plaid the weaver had given her. Agitated and distracted, she tossed it down and rose to pace around the room.

Lydia set her sewing aside. "What ails you, child?"

"Your son. No offense, Lydia, but his head is as thick as these castle walls."

Elaine giggled, and some of the tension left Alethia's shoulders. She shot her friend a quick grin.

"Aye, he gets that from his father." Lydia sighed. "Pray, tell us. What has my thickheaded son done now?"

"Do you know about what happened with Hugh?" She settled on the edge of one of the window seats.

"My husband told me. It must have been terrible for you. Had we known what sort of character he possessed, we would have sent him on his way much sooner."

"I asked Malcolm for a dagger or a bow and arrows. I know I'm safe here, but because of what happened, I don't *feel* safe. Anywhere. Do you know what I mean?"

"Of course we do," Elaine said. "My brother will get them for you."

"No. That's the problem. He won't. He said I have no need to arm myself because I'm under his protection." She shot up and paced again. "He can't be with me twenty-four/seven. I need to feel safe when he's not around."

"Twenty-four and seven?" Lydia asked. Mother and daughter shared a puzzled look.

"Twenty-four hours a day, seven days a week," she clarified. "Can you see why I'm upset?"

"Is this what you have in mind?" Elaine raised the hem of her gown to reveal a sheathed dagger strapped to her calf.

"Yes!"

Lydia raised her gown to reveal a jewel-handled dagger. "'Twas a gift from my husband upon Malcolm's birth."

"Why won't Malcolm let me have one?" She turned to Lydia. "He even implied my being armed would be a danger to everyone else. He was rude to the weaver's oldest son, and he had the gall to . . ." She'd been about to say he'd kissed her breathless, but thought better of it. Lydia was his mother, after all.

"What else did he do?" Lydia asked, her eyes twinkling with amusement.

"Oh, he just ticked me off." She sat down with a huff.

"Ticked you off? We dinna know what that means. Your speech is passing strange." Elaine laughed.

"He *vexed* me."

"I see no reason why you canna have a dirk and a bow if you wish. We'll go to the village to see the smith and the cooper," Elaine said. "Our cooper is a fair hand at making a good bow."

"Malcolm has forbidden me to go beyond the curtain wall." Both women looked stunned by her words.

Lydia's brow furrowed. "Mayhap he fears some harm might befall you. My husband told me how you came to us. They don't know whether it was your father's enemies or his allies who sent you away. Though he might go about it the wrong way, I'm sure Malcolm only wishes to keep you safe."

"Wouldn't I be safer if I had a weapon or two?"

"Of course. We often visit the village. 'Tis nothing out of the ordinary and only natural we should bring you with us." Lydia nodded firmly. "Leave Malcolm to me."

"Where is Lady Rosemary?" Alethia noticed her absence for the first time.

"She and my Uncle Robert left for home this morn. They've much to do before their journey to London."

"Oh. They don't live here?"

"This is only one of several MacKintosh holdings," Lydia replied.

"Oh. I had no idea." Alethia tucked her sewing back into her basket and retrieved the plants she'd dropped on the floor. "I really need to find Beth. I have the medicine to make for the weaver's son."

"Go. Hunter can stay here with us." Elaine smiled fondly at him and rubbed the stubble on his head.

Alethia strained the medicinal tea she'd made into an earthenware pitcher and added the dried cranberries. Fragrant steam rose in a cloud as she stirred some honey into the mix. She inhaled deeply before covering the container with a piece of cheesecloth the cook had given her. "Beth, tell the family he should drink this tea as often as he can. If they give him any other fluids, make sure they boil them for at least two minutes first."

"Aye, milady. I'll tell them."

"Oh, and he can eat the berries I added. They'll help." She handed the pitcher to Beth before thanking the cook. That chore done, she headed for her room for some much-needed solitude. Hunter returned at exactly the same moment, as if he'd known Alethia would be there. With all the activity surrounding the laird's trip to London, and the weaver's son needing tending, they hadn't had any time for just the two of them. She gave him a quick hug and opened their door.

She sank down onto the bed, and he scrambled up to sit beside her. She sent him pictures from her mind, teaching him the signs to go with them. Hunter learned very quickly, and his questions came fast. Like any small child, he was consumed with curiosity. Besides "I'm hungry," which seemed to be all the time, "Why?" and "What is it?" made up the bulk of his conversational signing.

Opening herself to the pictures Hunter sent back filled her with joy. She'd never met another person she could do this with. He sent her the image of a baby being nursed in his mother's arms, and signed the inevitable question.

"*What?*"

"*Mother and child,*" she signed back.

He sent her the image of a young woman with sad gray eyes. She had Hunter's golden brown hair and similar features. A wave of aching loneliness permeated his entire being, and Alethia knew the image belonged to the beloved mother he'd lost.

"*I lost my mother and father too,*" she signed and sent him pictures of her parents. "*I'll take care of you now. We can take care of each other,*" she signed. Hunter climbed into her lap and curled himself against her with a sigh. Eyes stinging, she scooped him into a hug. A knock on the door interrupted the moment. Hastily wiping the tears from her eyes, she called, "Come in."

Elaine swept into the room, a gown in her arms. "My father and the Douglas men are leaving for London two days hence. There is to be a feast and dancing tonight. You are to play."

She signed what Elaine had told her to Hunter.

"What do such gestures mean?" Elaine asked, sitting at the foot of the bed.

"We're talking," she answered.

"Show me."

Hunter scrambled over to Elaine and signed his name to her.

"He's telling you his name is Hunter. Here's how you spell your name." She showed her.

Elaine signed her name, then tweaked Hunter's nose once she'd finished. "Can you say everything this way?"

"Yes, it's a complete language."

"Do Malcolm and my father know of this? 'Twould be quite valuable to be able to communicate without sound, I should think."

"I haven't spoken to either of them about signing, other than to say I would teach Hunter."

"Mayhap you should. Och, but I've come for another reason. I wondered if you might be able to use this gown. 'Tis too short for me and might suit you." She held it up.

The gown was a sumptuous dark-green velvet. "It's lovely, Elaine. You're a terrible liar though." She flipped the hem to reveal the crease where the old hem had been before her friend had taken it up.

Elaine laughed. "'Tis not my fault you have the gift of a truth-sayer. I mean for you to have it just the same. The color is perfect for you. Wear it tonight," she said as she rose to leave, "and wear your hair down."

The great hall was full to bursting as Malcolm's clan danced to the music Alethia made with her wee instrument. Robley and Liam accompanied her with bodhran and bagpipes. Malcolm leaned against the wall by the hearth, content to watch. She was a vision in the green velvet gown. It clung to her curves and brought out the chestnut in her hair.

"Malcolm, I would have a word."

"Mother." He smiled and moved from the wall. "You look lovely this eve."

"My thanks. Walk with me outside for a breath of air." She took his arm. "That's a good lad."

It never failed to amuse him. He towered over her and hadn't been a lad for a long while. Yet she continued to treat him as if he were still a child of eight. Putting his arm around her slender shoulders, he steered her through the crowd and outside. "What is it you wish to discuss?"

"Alethia was quite upset with you earlier today. Is it true you won't allow her to carry a weapon of any kind?"

"Aye."

"To what end?" She looked up at him, her head tilted in a way he knew well. She'd made up her mind, and he was in for a battle of wills.

"There is much you dinna know. There are things I have told no one."

"You will tell me."

He chuckled. "Aye, I will. I ask that you keep it to yourself until such time I am certain any danger has passed." He waited until she nodded her agreement. "The fortune-teller who sent her to us is the same fortune-teller I saw as a youth. She told me 'truth' would save my life, and referred to truth as a 'her.' Aleth is Greek for truth. I am certain Alethia is the one the old woman referred to."

"How can you be certain?"

"True called the gypsy by name, Madame Giselle. 'Tis the same woman." Malcolm shook his head. "I canna allow her to put herself in harm's way for my sake. If she is no' armed, she will be less likely to jump into the fray should the need arise."

"We're calling her *True* now?"

Malcolm shrugged. "'Tis fitting."

"Is this why you will no' allow her outside the curtain wall?"

"There are men I trust looking after her within the confines of the bailey and keep."

"What if harm should find its way to her within our walls? Hugh managed."

"Aye, and he is gone. Until I know what the threat is, she will remain inside or within my sight. She *will* be safe."

"What if saving your life has naught to do with 'jumping into the fray,' as you put it?" Lydia argued. "Alethia has already proven herself an able healer. The weaver's son lives because of her. Mayhap you will fall ill, and she will nurse you back to health."

The notion had not occurred to him. He groaned in helpless frustration and gripped the hilt of the dagger at his belt. An enemy he could face was one he could fight, but an illness? How could he keep Alethia safe from harm if he were laid low? "Then I shall have to see to it that I don't fall ill."

"Oh, Malcolm," she chortled. "Have you told your father?"

"Told him what?"

"That you've chosen your bride." She patted his arm.

"Nay, I . . . What makes you say such a thing?" Had he chosen? There was no denying the attraction, and he did find her pleasing in many ways. Still, she was obstinate and far too independent in her thinking for his tastes. What did he really know about her?

"We've all seen the way you look at her. The signs are unmistakable. You're both twisted into knots around each other." She arched an eyebrow at him. "The clan gossips tell me you canna keep yourself from kissing the lass whenever she's within reach." She chuckled at his chagrin.

"She has naught to bring to a union between us. Father would never agree to the match."

"Aye, but she's the daughter of a king. 'Tis certain your father will object at first, but he'll soon see the soundness in your decision. You have my blessing, such as it is. She's a braw lass and a match for you in wits and will. She'll give me fine, strong grandchildren."

"Dinna speak of grandchildren just yet, Mother. I scarcely know the lass, and she may return to her own people ere long."

"As you say." Lydia folded her hands before her with a knowing smile lighting her features. "Elaine and I wish to take her to the village on the morrow. I would have your permission. If you deem it necessary, send a guard with us. We need to introduce her to our people. The sooner our clan comes to know her the better."

It went against the grain, and his gut told him to keep her on the island. Yet his mother was right. "Aye. You may take her. I'll send Robley, mayhap Galen as well. Come." Malcolm took his mother's arm. "Let us return to the hall."

Alethia tightened her bow, tuned her violin and glanced at Liam and Robley, who accompanied her. The hall had grown warm and stuffy from the sheer press of bodies packed inside, and both of their brows were beaded with sweat. The two brothers were accomplished musicians able to follow her with ease. The three of them had not practiced together before tonight, yet they jammed along with the jigs and reels she played as if they'd known them all their lives. Maybe they had.

Beth caught her eye, and they exchanged a smile. Her friend had never been without a dance partner. Her hair, shiny and clean, fell around her shoulders in golden waves. Beth's cheeks glowed with color, and she sparkled with happiness.

Seeing Beth this way made sharing her limited supply of shampoo and soap well worth the sacrifice. If she remained in this time for much longer, she'd apply herself to learning how to concoct something just as good. After all, all good bath stuff included some kind of plant life. Elaine and Lydia certainly glowed with cleanliness. They'd teach her.

"Lady Alethia, 'tis past time for a respite. A young woman such as yourself must long to dance, aye?" William said, approaching the dais where they played. "Let my nephews continue to play whilst you take a turn on the dance floor."

"I'm fine, Laird."

Elaine made her way through the crowd to stand next to her father. "Surely there are dances from your own land you'd be willing to share with us."

Alethia glanced at the expectant faces surrounding her. Should she show them the way she and her friends danced when they went clubbing in New York? She smiled to herself. These good people would be entirely shocked by what was considered acceptable in the twenty-first century. Nope. Best keep it a cultural exchange, something she could share with pride.

"All right. If I could borrow a shawl from someone, I could show you a dance our women do." A ripple passed through the crowd as a shawl was handed to her. She held it up to examine. Wool, with fringed edges, it would do nicely.

"Robley—there is a particular rhythm I need on the drum. You can play anything you want on the pipes, Liam." She tapped out the beat of a powwow drum for Robley until satisfied he had it. She stepped down from the dais. "I need space. All of our dances are done in a circle."

The crowd formed a wide ring, and Robley played the beat she'd shown him, improvising and adding more between the main rhythm. Half step, half step, back step, twist. Alethia extended her arms so the shawl resembled the wings of a large bird, a crane. Spin, step, step, dip. The bagpipes picked up the beat, adding melody. Spin, back step, twist, spin. She danced as the women of her nation had since the beginning of time, moving clockwise in a circle around the hall to the beat of the drum, the heartbeat of Mother Earth.

Intricate steps and spins came as naturally as breathing. Memories of contest powwows, of friends teasing and gossiping about the young men watching from the stands came to her in a rush. Soon, the faces surrounding her in the great hall changed to the faces of her family. Her mother and father, Gran, cousins and aunties, uncles and childhood friends all shadow-danced with her around the circle.

Joy turned to anguish as she realized the faces passing before her mind's eye might be lost to her forever if she couldn't get back to her own time. Homesickness and grief tore at her. She tried to swallow the lump forming in her throat and searched through the crowd of faces for Malcolm.

The moment she stopped dancing, bodies pressed close. She couldn't see through them, and she couldn't catch her breath. Where was Malcolm?

CHAPTER SEVEN

Malcolm returned to the great hall just as Alethia began to dance. She moved with provocative grace, drawing him like a moth to flame. Dark, silken tresses fanned out around her as she spun. He longed to run his fingers through her hair to feel its softness against his bare skin. Her exotic beauty charmed his senses and filled him with masculine pride.

Had he chosen Alethia as his bride? He hadn't given it any serious thought until his mother put the matter to words. He let the notion take root, and a feeling of rightness settled over him. Watching her weave a spell over everyone in the hall, his body tightened with desire. Adjusting his sporran, he noticed he was not the only man to do so. His jaw clenched, and he reached instinctively for the dagger at his waist.

"Malcolm."

"James." Malcolm spared his friend a brief glance.

"I have heard it said you do double time in the lists. Do you expect trouble in your father's absence?"

"I always expect trouble. 'Tis why I'm still standing."

"Shall we train together on the morrow?"

"Without a doubt."

"I would like to suggest a wager." James's eyes were fixed on Alethia.

"What prize do you hope to gain?" Malcolm hoped his friend heeded the warning in his tone.

"If you win the best two out of three bouts, you keep my favorite stallion. If I win, I take yon maid off your hands."

"Nay," Malcolm snapped.

"Do you fear losing?" James challenged.

"I fear doing you real harm at the end of my sword. 'Twould displease both our fathers."

"Ah, like that is it?"

"Aye." Malcolm frowned. Alethia's expression changed from joy to anguish as she danced. He needed to get to her. The music stopped, and she was swallowed up by the press of his clan. He worked his way through the tangle to the center. Alethia's face had gone pale, and her eyes were huge and bright. "The lady needs air. Give way."

Her relief at seeing him was plain to see. Taking her hand in his, he led her to the doors of the great hall and out into the fresh, cool night. "Come. Walk with me to the loch."

She spoke not a word as he guided her through the portcullis. He heard her sniff a few times, and she swiped at her eyes. He took her to the place where he'd rescued her from Hugh. Settling himself on a large, flat boulder, he drew her down beside him. "Tell me what has upset you."

She took a breath and let it out slowly. "I'm suffering from homesickness, I guess." She gave him a forlorn look. "I might never see my family or my home again."

"Och, lass. They search for you, aye?" He patted her back awkwardly.

"Of course they're searching, but they won't find me."

"Could you no' come to see this as your home?"

"What? You mean *inside* the curtain wall?" She sniffed.

Her tone made him smile. "'Twill not always be thus. Harvest will begin in a se'nnight. I'll take you to the fair in Inverness once the crops are in. Will that please you, *mo cridhe*?"

"Sure. Don't get me wrong, it's great here, but it's not the place that makes a home." She shrugged. "It's the people."

"I take your meaning well. When I was a young man—"

"You're still a young man."

"As I was saying," he said as he put an arm around her shoulders, "when first I earned my spurs, such a restless energy filled me that I set out the very next week to see the world with a group of like-minded young knights."

"Where did you go?" Her body relaxed, and she leaned against him.

"To France, Italy, Spain . . . wherever my fancy took me. I fought against the *Sassenach* with the French, won my fortune in contests of strength and saw the wonders each place had to offer. Liam and Robley were with me. We were all eager to test our mettle and make our fortunes."

She shifted against him. Her floral scent filled his senses, and he savored her pleasing softness and warmth beside him. The feel of her silken hair draped over the bare skin on his forearm robbed him of coherent thought.

"Go on." She jabbed him in the ribs with her elbow. "Keep talking. It's helping."

"You are a fierce little thing, aren't you?" He rubbed his ribs in mock hurt, pleased when she giggled. "I grew more restless with every passing day. We all missed our families, so we came home."

"When did all of this happen? How long have you been back?"

"Four years have passed since our return."

"Did the restlessness go away once you were home again?" she asked in a small voice.

Her face was luminous in the moonlight. He ran a lock of her hair through his fingers. "Nay. It plagued me still. Funny . . ."

"What is?"

"I dinna feel restless now." He dipped his head and brushed his lips against hers, thrilled that she didn't pull away.

"I'm happy for you." She glanced at him. "I wonder what made it go away?"

Malcolm tightened his arm around her. He had no doubts about the source of his newfound contentment, and when the time was right, he'd explain it to her. Now was the time to have some of his questions answered. "I wish to discuss another matter with you, something I've meant to ask since the day you spoke of Madame Giselle. Can you describe her?"

"She's small, about my height, and she looks old and frail, but that's not what I read from her at all." She shuddered and put her hands over his as she spoke. "She didn't feel *true*."

Malcolm twined their fingers together and forced himself to pay attention to her words.

"Her eyes are sharp and dark, like she misses nothing. She holds magic. I could feel it."

"Did she tell your fortune?"

Alethia shot him a glance and quickly looked away. "I don't want to talk about this. It's upsetting."

"Aye, but I do. You *will* answer my questions."

"Has anyone ever mentioned how overbearing you are?"

"No one dares."

She snorted. "Only because you work so hard at being intimidating."

"Alethia."

"No, she didn't tell my fortune." She shook her head. "She went on and on about someone being in grave danger, and she said she'd do anything to help."

"What else did she tell you?" He felt her stiffen. "Tell me."

"You're not the boss of me," she muttered under her breath.

"Aye, so you've said, but I am a nee-an-der-thal." He raised one eyebrow and gave her a stern look. Her laughter sent ripples of gladness through his soul. "You will tell me, so we can put this behind us."

She brought her thumb to her mouth and chewed on the nail as she thought the matter over. He took the hand from her mouth and held it, smiling at her disgruntled look. Everything about her pleased him, even her obstinate willfulness. Since finding Alethia, he hadn't suffered a moment's restlessness. Aye, he suffered other things in its place—lust, an aching need to claim her and a compelling desire to keep her safe. 'Twas a small price to pay.

"Giselle said she'd been watching me for a long, long time, but the fair was the first time we'd ever met." Her brow furrowed. "She also said I had untapped depths."

"Did she give you anything?"

"Yes," she snapped. "She placed a pendant around my neck before sending me here. Why are you asking all these questions?"

He fished in his sporran for the ring the old crone had given him the day she told his fortune. Holding it to the moonlight for her to see, he asked, "Does the charm she gave you resemble this one?"

"Oh crap," she cried. Reaching for the ring, she took it from his hand to study. "What does this mean?"

"You recognize it? What else did she say?"

She turned stricken eyes to him and handed the ring back as if it burned her hand. "She didn't tell me anything else. Madame Giselle mumbled something about destiny and sent me here without a single freaking clue." She rose abruptly. "I have to go back to the keep. I have things to do."

"At this hour?" He rose to follow.

"I have a lot to think about." Lifting the hem of her gown, she turned and fled back to the keep.

Malcolm let her go. He had much to think about as well. The moon hung full and low over the horizon, as if in ripe promise of the coming harvest. He watched the play of light and shadow upon the loch, while his mind puzzled over their discussion. Each question led to more.

What peril was Alethia to protect him from, and how could he prevent it? She had not told him everything. They would talk again on the morrow, and the day after that, until she confessed all of her fears. Only then could he conquer them and unravel the mystery plaguing them both.

The vision of Alethia dancing in the hall replayed in his mind's eye. He committed it to memory while pondering her odd mix of vulnerability and defiant independence. How was it one wee lass could have such a powerful hold upon his heart in such a short time? He laughed and gave one more passing glance to the moon before starting back to the keep.

Alethia pulled the bedcovers up to her chin and stared at the ceiling while mulling over what she'd learned from Malcolm. Giselle had given him the matching ring to her pendant. Which meant what? Had the fortune-teller given them both the matching pieces to provide a clue to solve the puzzle? If so, then Malcolm's life was in danger.

Or did the pendant and ring contain some kind of magic for keeping track of their whereabouts? How could she possibly know? In her efforts to get home, she'd tried every conceivable method she could think of to release any magic the jewelry might contain. She hadn't even caught an echo of power from the stupid thing. No. They were pieces to a puzzle and nothing more. She was sure of it.

Hunter got up and used the chamber pot she kept placed near his bed. Small boy, small bladder. She scooted over to make room for him as his small feet padded toward her in the darkness. It was the same every night. He started out in his own bed and ended snuggled up in hers.

Lifting the covers for him to climb in, she turned on her side and pulled his warm, sleepy body close. His own unique little-boy scent made her heart ache. Her life was becoming way too complicated. She belonged in the twenty-first century, yet she couldn't bear the thought of being taken from Hunter. He'd already suffered so much loss in his life, to lose her now might be the beginning of the end for him.

Having lost her own parents at a young age, she knew from personal experience that kind of hurt never went away. She understood what he was going through, and bonding with him had been automatic. Their connection stemmed from shared experience and a common need. In many ways, they were both outsiders here.

She lay awake until the birds heralded the approaching dawn. Damn that old fortune-teller. A single tear slid down her cheek. Kissing the top of Hunter's head, she felt torn. She walked in two worlds and always had. Not all native, and not all white, she'd never fit fully into either culture. Now, half her heart resided in the future, and half lived in the past.

Her thoughts shifted to Malcolm, causing a fluttery feeling in the pit of her stomach. What if she tried to save him and failed? No, better not think like that. Giselle had chosen her for a reason. She would not fail.

Someone patted Alethia's cheeks. She woke to find Hunter's face mere inches from hers.

"*I'm hungry,*" he signed.

"*You're always hungry.*" Digging her fingers into his ribs, she tickled him until he rolled into a ball and giggled. The sound filled the room with music far sweeter than any she could ever make with her violin. "*Today we go to the village. I'm going to buy you a bow. It's time you started earning your keep,*" she teased.

Hunter hopped around the room. "*And a sword?*" he signed, eyes bright with eagerness.

"*No. You're too young. In a few years, maybe.*"

Her refusal did little to dampen his spirits. He tugged her covers off. "*I'm hungry.*"

"*Wash.*" While Hunter washed and brushed his teeth with the torn twig as she'd taught him, Alethia opened the trunk and fished around for the velvet bag holding her jewelry. Dumping the contents on the bed, she surveyed the contents. The pearl earrings and gold bangle bracelets had belonged to her mother. No way would she trade them away for daggers and a bow.

Helplessness and despair flooded through her in a deluge as she lifted the pendant Giselle had foisted upon her. That damn witch had robbed her of any control she had over her own life and forced her into an impossible situation. Her despair turned to resentment, and the choice to trade the pendant away overwhelmed her. She wanted nothing more than to be rid of it and the memories it evoked of Giselle's betrayal.

Once they were ready, she took Hunter's hand and led him to the great hall. Elaine, Robley, and Malcolm sat at the long table before the hearth. Hunter broke free and ran to them. Jumping up on the bench to stand eye level with Malcolm, he signed a quick greeting to Robley and Elaine, and tugged on Malcolm's shirt.

She knew hero worship when she saw it, and her insides warmed. Malcolm rubbed Hunter's head and gave him his undivided attention, as Hunter told him his name and asked for his.

"Good morn, Lady True. The lad wants something, aye?" Malcolm asked.

"He's telling you his name is Hunter," Elaine said before Alethia had a chance to reply. "He asks for your name." Elaine showed Malcolm how to spell his name.

"Impressive, Elaine." Alethia filled two bowls with oatmeal from the large cauldron by the hearth. She added honey and thick cream from pewter pitchers on the table and fixed Hunter a piece of dark bread and butter. "You've been reading the alphabet book I made for him."

Hunter patted Malcolm on the shoulder and signed to him. Malcolm turned to her and asked, "What does he say?"

Alethia touched Hunter on the shoulder and asked him to repeat himself. "Oh." She frowned. "He's asking you to teach him how to fight with a sword. It seems to be his latest obsession." She signed for him to sit and placed his food in front of him. "He's too little."

"He's no' too little for a wooden sword. 'Tis time he started training." Malcolm gave Hunter a manly pat on the back. Hunter beamed.

"Elaine has been telling us about the language you're teaching the lad. I would ask a favor of you." Malcolm stood to offer her a place beside him.

"OK." Alethia sat down to her breakfast.

"What is the meaning of *oh-kay*?" Elaine asked.

"It means yes, or all right, depending on how it's used, two letters." She signed the letters in the air. "OK."

"OK." Elaine smiled as she tried the word out.

"I want you to teach some of the men in our garrison the signs." Malcolm continued. "I wish to learn as well."

"I'd be happy to teach anyone interested in learning. It would be helpful for Hunter to have more people to talk to."

"Good. 'Tis settled. We will begin our lessons after my father's departure." Malcolm rose from his place. "I have much to do. Robley will accompany you to the village today. Galen is already there and will join you."

Once Malcolm had gone, Robley turned to her. "Elaine explained your dilemma. I know what you seek from the blacksmith and the cooper." He grinned and winked. "I vow to protect all of you with my life, and I'll turn a blind eye to your doings. I dinna agree with my cousin on this. Every woman should carry a weapon. 'Tis foolhardy no' to be prepared for trouble."

"Malcolm will have a fit if he finds out," she warned.

"Aye." He grinned. "I'm counting on it."

Alethia studied the village during the ferry ride to the mainland. Several thatched cottages hugged the shore, and a large stable stood a distance away from the other buildings. Along with a number of unpleasant smells associated with habitation, the scent of something fermenting filled the air, indicating a brewery.

The sky was overcast, and the temperature had dropped. Winter wasn't far off. She pulled her woolen shawl closer. Movement caught her eye, and she turned to watch a single rider climb the hill. "Isn't that Liam riding off by himself?"

"Aye," Robley said.

"Where's he going?"

"I dinna know, and he will no' say. I suspect his many mysterious trips have something to do with a lass." He smiled at her and wagged his eyebrows. "Lady True, what do you think of our home?"

"You too? My name is Alethia. Why does Malcolm insist on calling me True?"

"Och, lass. He means it as a compliment. He sees you as *nas fìor*, which does no' mean the same as truth in the way *aleth* does in Greek. *Fìor* is a word that means true-hearted, genuine, just and upright. We all know how you healed the weaver's son." He smiled and took her hands in his. "Look upon your young lad. Hunter has put on weight and thrives in your care. You did no' have to accept him on as your ward, yet you did. True-hearted is what you are. Malcolm honors your character with the name."

"Oh." She swallowed. "I thought he was teasing me about being a truth-sayer. He does enjoy annoying me."

"Aye, that he does." He chuckled. "You rise to the challenge, match him wit for wit, and it pleases him. Malcolm would move heaven and earth to see you safe, lass. Dinna doubt it."

"Why? I'm nothing to him."

"Are you no'?" Robley winked.

"He sees me as his responsibility, that's all." She frowned and turned back to watch Liam disappear over the crest of the hill.

"'Tis certain that he sees you as his responsibility, lass, but no' in the way you think."

She liked that Malcolm thought of her as true-hearted. *True.* The nickname had a nice ring to it. She puzzled over what Robley meant when he said Malcolm saw her as his responsibility, but not in the way she thought.

Everything about Malcolm confused her, but then what did she know about men? Nothing. Being a music geek her whole life hadn't exactly led to hordes of boys lining up at her door for dates. She hadn't even gone to her high school prom.

The ferry landed, and they disembarked with Galen's help. Hunter ran in a circle around them, unable to contain his glee. Every now and then he'd return to her, clutch her gown or grasp her hand for a second's reassurance. Then he'd bounce off again. She couldn't help but laugh. His antics touched a tender place in her heart.

"Come, True. We're to the cooper first." Lydia nodded a greeting to Galen. She took Alethia's arm, and Elaine walked on her other side. The two women exchanged greetings with the villagers and stopped occasionally to introduce her.

At the cooper's workshop, Alethia explained what she wanted. He measured her with twine from the ground to her shoulder and from the tips of the fingers of one hand to the other with her arms outstretched. He did the same with Hunter. Alethia handed him the gold chain from the pendant Giselle had given her. The cooper studied it and said something in rapid Gaelic to Lydia.

"The cooper says it is too much. True, you needn't part with your jewelry. We'll take care of the cost," Lydia admonished.

"I want to pay my own way."

"You have more than earned your keep. It is we who owe you. Were you a minstrel in residence, we'd pay you with coin," Elaine persisted.

"Next time, maybe. I want to take care of this myself."

Elaine hooked her arm through Alethia's as Lydia explained to the cooper what she'd said. He shook his head but dropped the chain into his sporran.

"Come," Elaine said. "We're to the smithy."

Set back from the main road, the blacksmith's workshop was an imposing stone structure with a slate roof and heavy double doors of oak and iron. Tools hung from the rafters. Two strapping apprentices worked with anvils behind a large fire pit. The sound of hammers striking metal reverberated through the air, and heat from the fire wafted over Alethia from her place at the threshold. A large, beefy man with thick, muscled arms approached.

"Lady Lydia, Elaine." He bowed. "Good day to you."

He spoke English, surprising Alethia.

"Thomas is *Sassenach*, which is what we call the English," Elaine whispered into her ear. "He's Beth's father. 'Tis why she speaks the language so well."

"Good day to you, Thomas," Lydia said. "This is Lady Alethia. She is a guest at Moigh Hall and has need of your skills."

"Aye?" His curious gaze settled upon her. "What do you seek, milady?"

"I would like a couple of daggers with sheaths like the ones the women wear hidden under their skirts. One for Hunter and one for myself." She gestured toward the child. His eyes reminded her of a baby owl's, they'd grown so large with wonder. "I also need two eating knives, and a few dozen arrowheads to be delivered to the cooper." She pulled the pendant Giselle had given her from her pocket. "I wish to use this as payment if you will accept it."

The blacksmith took the charm from her and moved to the door to study it in the light. "Milady, you could arm the MacKintosh garrison with the emerald alone. I cannot accept this."

"I want to be rid of it." She took a step back when he reached out to return it to her.

"True, you cannot mean it." Elaine took the golden effigy from the smithy. She handed it to her mother. "Let us pay Thomas. Keep the piece. 'Tis quite valuable."

"No. Will you take it or not?"

"Aye, I'll take it."

Snatching the dreaded reminder of Giselle's manipulation from Lydia, she placed it back into the hand of the blacksmith.

Malcolm rode into the village, glad to be home at last. The past two days had been busy, and he still had much to do. He'd ridden several leagues with his father's party before turning back toward home. He glanced at the sun. 'Twas past the hour of Sext. He dismounted at the stable and turned his mount over to one of the stable lads.

As he approached the ferry, he caught a glimpse of the blacksmith chatting with the ferry master. The two sat companionably on the bench next to the landing, sharing a flagon of ale. "Thomas, Arlen, good day to you both."

"My lord," Thomas said, rising from his place and removing his cap. "I've been waiting to speak with ye." He glanced at the ferry master and back at Malcolm.

"Come. Walk with me, Thomas."

"Aye." Thomas gripped and twisted the cap in his hands as they walked, and his tension set Malcolm on edge. "What is it?"

"My lord, your mother and sister were by to see me and the cooper yesterday. They brought the outlander with them."

"Aye. Young Galen and Robley accompanied them, did they no'?"

Thomas nodded. "Lady Alethia placed an order for a number of weapons."

Malcolm stopped walking. "Did you fill the order?"

"Aye, with what I had to hand, and I promised to have the rest delivered. The cooper is crafting a bow for her and one for the lad in her care." He turned to face Malcolm. "Were we wrong to do so?"

"Nay." Malcolm placed his hand on the smith's shoulder. "I did no' think to tell you otherwise."

"Her order is no' what I wish to talk with ye about." He reached into the pouch at his waist. "She paid us with these. Connor and I both told the lass 'twas too much, but she insisted we take them."

Malcolm took the chain and pendant from the blacksmith's hand. The knotted crane was the mate to his ring. He'd expected as much, yet seeing it sent a chill down his spine.

"The lady said she wished to be rid of it."

"Mmm." Malcolm studied the necklace in his hand as if doing so would reveal its secrets. "What do I owe you and Connor for the weapons?" While the blacksmith named the price he and the cooper had agreed to, Malcolm's mind reeled with this new piece to the puzzle. Why would she wish to be rid of it? "I'll have the coin sent to you both once I reach the keep. My thanks." He grasped the smith's forearm and shook his hand. "I am glad you both came forward with this. Lesser men would have kept the goods without a word. You are both a credit to our clan, Thomas. Tell Connor I said so."

"I will. My thanks, my lord." Thomas bobbed his head and took his leave.

Anger at Alethia's disobedience and worry for her safety grew beyond reason on the ferry ride to the island. He took the ring and pendant from his sporran, opened the clasp of the chain and slipped them onto it before tucking them safely away.

He couldn't wait for the ferry to land and leaped to the beach. Striding toward the keep, he scanned the bailey for any sign of Robley. Though he could not be angry with the villagers, he *had* spoken to his cousin about his concerns. Robley knew better than to cross him. Pushing wide the doors to the great hall, he spied Beth coming down the stairs. "Where is Lady True?"

"Milady is in your mother's solar." She took one look at his face and scurried away.

Climbing the stairs three at a time, he ate up the distance to the solar with his strides. He shoved the door open so hard, a resounding crack echoed through the room as it hit the wall. "Alethia."

"Oh crap." She looked up at him, the guilt plain on her face.

"Oh *crap* is right. Mother, Elaine, I would like to have a word with Alethia in private."

They fled, glancing sympathetically her way as they passed.

"Give them to me," he commanded.

She shook her head. "Nope."

"You will."

"I *won't*."

In two strides he was before her, lifting her skirts in search of the contraband.

"Stop it!" She shoved his hands away and jumped from her place, putting the chair between them. "You know what you are?" she shouted. "You're a walking, talking oxymoron!"

Malcolm opened his mouth to retort, only to be interrupted.

"That's right." She stomped her foot. "An overbearing, arrogant, bellowing contradiction." Her breathing had grown rapid, and her eyes were wide with fear. She looked ready to flee at the slightest provocation.

Alethia feared *him*.

In an instant, all of Malcolm's anger dissipated. He couldn't bear to have her fear him. "What do you mean, lass?"

"You demand I answer your questions, but you ignore mine. You declare you want me to be safe, but you won't let me feel safe. Hugh would have raped me if you hadn't intervened. I haven't gotten over that. It's just a stupid dagger." She retrieved the small knife from the sheath strapped to her calf. "Don't you get it? Carrying this makes me feel better." She sucked in a huge gulp of air.

"You say I'm not a prisoner here, but you won't let me have any freedom. You demand I have faith in you, and you have none in me." Her voice quavered.

Her shoulders slumped. She looked defeated. He was responsible, and the knowledge laid him low. She spoke the truth. He shoved the chair separating them aside and took her into his arms. Holding her close, he bent to touch her forehead with his. "Woman, were you but a wee bit smaller, I would tuck you away in my sporran for safekeeping."

He kissed her before she could cause him more grief with her words. Twining his hands in her hair, he slanted her head to gain better access and ravished the velvety sweetness of her mouth with his tongue.

Her dagger dropped to the floor with a thud. She wrapped her arms around his waist. Alethia pressed against him, and he could feel the tension leave her on a sigh. Lifting her into his arms, he crossed the room and laid her on the cushioned bench, lowering himself to cover her. Her soft moans incited his passion to a fever pitch. If he wasn't careful, he would take her right here in his mother's solar.

Moving to her neck, he inhaled her irresistible sweet scent. He kissed his way up to her delicate ear and cupped one of her breasts through her gown. She arched into him and groaned. Hard and aching, he pressed his mouth against the swell of her breast where skin met gown.

"Malcolm," she whispered, drawing his face back to hers, kissing him with a passion equal to his own.

Frantic with desire, he undid the laces of her gown, tugging it down her shoulders. His breath caught in his throat at the sight of the dusky rose of her nipples against the exotic light brown of her flawless skin. Malcolm bent to her, taking one delectable bud into his mouth. His body tightened beyond endurance as she writhed with pleasure and pressed into him, tangling her fingers in his hair.

Switching to lavish her other breast with equal attention, he found the hem of her gown and ran his hand up the soft velvet curve of her calf, coming up to caress her thigh. She gasped and jerked at the contact. He'd explode if he didn't take her.

No. This was not how he wanted their first time to be. He wanted a wedding night for them, a memory they would both savor as they grew old together. Alethia deserved honor and respect, and here he was behaving like a rutting stag. It took all of his will to rein himself back.

Raising himself, Malcolm devoured her with his eyes and traced a finger from her forehead down her fine, straight nose to her full lips. "We need to talk."

"Now?" she groaned. "You wanna . . . talk?" She pushed herself up to sitting and attempted to put herself back together with fingers that fumbled and trembled slightly.

Her labored breathing did naught to help him calm his raging lust. He took a deep breath and let it out slowly, focusing on more important issues needing his attention. "Aye, lest we do something we might both regret."

"Right." She shot him a disgruntled look. "You started it."

He chuckled. "Aye, I'll no' deny my culpability. Here, let me help." He reached out to retie her gown. Settling her beside him, he reveled in her tousled appearance.

Her lips were swollen from his kisses, and her expression betrayed the passion he'd aroused. He chuckled. "Aye, True. We will talk. Everything you said must be laid to rest. I will answer your questions, and you may keep your weapons."

"And I can go freely wherever I wish?"

"Nay. You will stay within the walls until such time any danger to either of us has passed." She started to protest. "Alethia, on this I must be firm."

"What makes you think *I'm* in danger? Why do you object so strongly to my having a few daggers? Giselle never said anything about my being in danger."

"Giselle told my fortune the summer I turned ten and three. She said *truth* would save my life, and she gave me the ring. My ring is the mate to your pendant." She showed no surprise at his words. "Even before I revealed it to you, I suspected you were the one the old woman spoke of. I'm a warrior. You are not. I mean to take the burden of saving my life from your shoulders. Without weapons to hand, you cannot enter into a battle for anyone's sake." He gave her a squeeze. "Battle is a way of life for me. It is not for you to protect me, but for me to protect you."

"There's no reason to assume saving your life means putting myself in danger or that any of it involves fighting." "There is no reason to assume it does no' mean exactly that, lass. Either way, I mean to prevent any event which will put us in harm's way."

She shook her head. "I don't think life works like that, Malcolm."

"Then I will make it work like that. I dinna wish you to feel like a prisoner here, but I have taken measures to keep you safe." He ran his thumb over the curve of her cheek. "You may keep your weapons with the understanding that you stay within the walls until we know what we face."

Alethia chewed on her thumbnail while pondering his words. He took both of her hands and held them, counting the seconds until she gave him the disgruntled look he knew would follow. He brushed her lips with his when she did.

"Not fair." She scowled at him. "Maybe this whole thing has more to do with some kind of information I'll give you. I am a truth-sayer. Or maybe I'll prevent an accident from happening."

Hunter burst into the room then. Beaming at them both, he rushed to the couch and hopped up to snuggle next to Alethia. Malcolm put his arm around him, pulling the lad closer so he could rub his head. "You've done wonders with the lad, True. You'll be a good mother one day." He watched the blush rise to her cheeks. "Wouldn't you like to have children of your own?"

"I want a large family." She studied her hands, and the color on her cheeks deepened. "I always wished I had brothers and sisters, especially after my parents died."

The breath he'd been holding came out in a rush. He'd give her a keep full of children. The thought of their wee sons and daughters filling his home thrilled him. Aye, and the thought of Alethia growing large with his bairn had the blood rushing to his groin again. "Can we come to an agreement, Alethia?"

"What sort of agreement?"

He smiled at her skeptical look. "The kind where you obey my every command and reveal every secret you carry."

She snorted. "You're not the—"

"Aye. As you have informed me more than once, I am no' the bossamee."

CHAPTER EIGHT

Alethia set her wooden pail down on the ground and stretched, placing her hands on the small of her aching back. Inhaling deeply, she savored the earthy scents of freshly cut rye. The wind shifted, bringing with it the tantalizing aromas of the stew simmering over the open fires near the lake. Her stomach rumbled. The clan had been taking their meals communally since harvest began, and they would continue to do so until all the crops were in.

Taking up the pail again, she moved toward a group of women bundling the cut crops for pickup. She handed a ladle of cool spring water to an older woman while her gaze drifted to Malcolm for the hundredth time.

He swung a scythe through the field with fluid strength. She could watch him all day. She *had* watched him all day. His powerful body made the backbreaking task look easy. Early on, she'd noticed other men set themselves to his pace. Very few kept up with him for long.

"Milady?"

"Huh?" Alethia turned to find the woman regarding her outstretched arm in amusement, the empty ladle held up in midair. "Oh. Would you like more?"

"Maybe if you spent less time staring at my brother and paid more attention to your task, there would be far fewer who thirst as they toil." Elaine nudged her.

"I'm not staring at anybody." The heat of a blush filled her cheeks.

"Nay? 'Tis a wonder your neck has no' gone stiff from all the looking you have no' done this week." Elaine laughed, and the women joined her.

"Go away." Alethia scowled. "There are thirsty people in the fields calling your name."

"Really? 'Tis your name I hear most oft called." Still chuckling, Elaine moved away to offer water elsewhere.

Quick movement caught Alethia's eye. She turned to see Hunter streaking toward her through a field of oats. He slammed into her knees to stop himself, and water sloshed over the sides of the bucket onto her gown. Hunter scurried behind her, burrowing himself into the backs of her legs. She tried to dislodge him by turning. He stayed put.

She searched the fields, looking for whatever it was that had frightened him. Malcolm strode their way with a boy in tow. The child held his hands up to his nose to stanch the flow of blood. She put her bucket down and reached back to drag Hunter out from behind her.

"True, I have need of your aid," Malcolm said once they'd reached her. "This is Tieren." He gave the boy a small shake. "I would have you sign to Hunter what is being said."

Tieren glared at Hunter. She pulled a scrap of linen from her pocket, wet it with the ladle from her bucket and handed it to him. She watched as he smeared the blood from his nose over the lower half of his face. "Of course," she replied.

"'Tis unbefitting for a MacKintosh to hide behind a woman's skirts when his own foolishness lands him in trouble." Malcolm frowned at Hunter, who stood dejectedly before him. "You will each tell your side before I render judgment." Malcolm turned to Tieren and spoke to him in Gaelic, while she signed as simply as she could for Hunter to understand.

Only a few of Malcolm's words were familiar to her, but when the boy answered, she knew he wasn't telling the truth. "He's lying."

"Aye, I dinna doubt it," Malcolm replied. "He says Hunter attacked without provocation." Malcolm placed a hand on Hunter's shoulder. "Ask him to tell his side."

Alethia touched Hunter, whose gaze was fixed on Malcolm. She signed the question, and he sent her pictures and signed as best he could. "A group of boys taunt him," she began. "This one is their leader. As long as Hunter faces them, or can see where they are, he can protect himself, even though he's much smaller." At this point, Hunter lifted his chin and gave Malcolm a small, boastful grin. "But they wait until his back is turned and . . ."

She gasped, and her eyes flashed to Malcolm's. "They've been throwing stones at him!" She had to swallow hard and fight to keep from throttling the child in Malcolm's grasp. "Tieren believed Hunter wouldn't be able to tell his side." She forced the words out around the lump in her throat.

Malcolm turned Hunter and lifted his shirt. His scrawny back was covered with fresh, angry welts. More marked the backs of his legs. Malcolm spoke harshly in Gaelic to Tieren, who hung his head. She watched Malcolm's face tighten as he stepped away. The muscle in his jaw twitched, and his hands were clenched at his sides. Several tense moments passed before he turned back to them.

"What did you say to Tieren?"

"His actions are those of a coward and a bully. I let him know of my displeasure. Such behavior is unacceptable to our clan." Motioning to the boys, he took up the bucket of water resting at Alethia's feet. "Explain to Hunter the two of them are to share the job of bringing water to those who sweat in the fields, so that we all have food to eat during the long winter months. He and Tieren will share this task until harvest is complete down to the last turnip."

Alethia signed to Hunter while Malcolm spoke to the other boy in low tones. It was clear to her more was being said than the description of their punishment. Tieren's face fell, and she sensed the deep shame and the remorse he felt.

Without looking at each other, the two boys lifted the bucket between them and walked away. The disparity in their height caused water to slosh onto their spindly legs. "Do you think this will be the end of it?"

"Nay." Malcolm wiped the sweat from his brow with his sleeve and watched their progress.

"You reminded me of my father just now. He was a great leader and a good man."

"'Tis high praise indeed." His eyes twinkled as he smiled at her.

"It's meant to be. I remember a similar penance he gave three boys in our village. They ran wild and caused trouble everywhere they went. The three of them harassed an elderly woman and vandalized her property. She was a widow and alone. My father sentenced the boys to be her guardians for a year. They had to cut wood for her, shovel snow from her door and make sure she had food to eat, that sort of thing."

She smiled at him. "By the end of the year, one of the boys had grown so close to her, he adopted her as his *nokomis*. That's the word for grandmother in my language. My father managed to kill two birds with one stone. The elder was no longer alone, and the boys got the attention they needed."

"You miss him."

"Every day." She sighed. "He gave me my violin, and my mother was the first to teach me how to play. I think . . ." Suddenly feeling shy, she turned away from Malcolm to track the two boys.

"What is it, True?"

"I think my parents would have liked you." She spotted Hunter and Tieren straying from their path. They put the bucket down and moved into the tall rushes growing near the lake. Hunter faced Tieren with his chest thrown out and his hands held up in fists. Tieren swung at him, and Hunter ducked the blow and sprang up to head-butt Tieren in the stomach. They both went down on the ground, rolling, kicking and punching. "Oh! They're fighting." She took a step, intending to rush to Hunter's aid.

Malcolm's arm came around her waist. "You canna fight the lad's battles for him. No' if he is to grow into the kind of man we would have him become."

"Tieren is so much bigger."

"Aye, but Hunter is twice as canny. 'Tis a fair fight. Watch."

Hunter managed to free himself from Tieren's grasp, and both boys were on their feet again. Hunter grinned at Tieren, who threw wild punches that never connected. Hunter darted in, met his mark and darted away before the bigger boy could catch him. He soon triumphed, and Tieren lay on the ground in defeat. Alethia's heart swelled with pride as Hunter extended his hand to help Tieren up.

A rumble from deep in Malcolm's chest reverberated through her as he chuckled behind her. "Hunter is a fine lad, and he will grow to be a good man. The two have much in common. Neither has a father to guide him." He moved his hands to her shoulders. "I predict the two will become fast friends. 'Twould be good to include Tieren while you teach the signs to the men."

Admiration for Malcolm's skill as a leader filled her. Sure, he was domineering, but his actions revealed a deep caring for his people, thoughtfulness and an honorable character. The way he dealt with Hunter warmed her heart. No wonder she was falling for him.

Falling for him?

"Oh crap!" She pushed Malcolm's hands from her shoulders and started to pace. She was a talented violinist with a bright future in the twenty-first century, not the Middle Ages. Only the best were accepted into Juilliard, and she was one of the best. Her plans didn't include falling in love with a fifteenth-century, overbearing, controlling warrior. "This is all your fault, Malcolm," she accused with a glare.

"What is my fault?"

She covered her burning cheeks with her hands. "What do I do now?"

"About what, lass?"

"How could I have let this happen?" she muttered under her breath.

"Cease your pacing, woman. 'Tis making me dizzy." He stepped in front of her and took hold of her shoulders to keep her still. Lifting her chin until she had to look into his eyes, he studied her intently. Could he see what she was feeling?

"What ails you?"

Her heart skipped a beat, and she lost the ability to speak, or think. "I . . . I . . ."

"Aye?"

"The boys are doing my job. What should I do now?" *So lame!*

He gave her that wicked smile of his, the one that made her weak in the knees. Malcolm took her by the hand and pulled her behind a large oak. His hands encircled her waist as he pressed her up against the trunk of the tree and kissed her. A thrilling sensation flooded her body, and her heart raced. His kiss claimed her. He plundered her mouth with his tongue, inciting a rush of desire.

Did he feel the same, or was it only lust?

She tuned into him, opening herself to the truth his heart would reveal. What came back was a tangle she could not unravel. Lust, definitely, protectiveness and other feelings she didn't know how to interpret. Alethia ran her fingers through his thick hair and melted into his strength with helpless abandon.

Several seconds passed before she recalled where they were. Flushed and breathless, she ended the kiss and tried to take a step away. He tightened his hold.

"I should help with supper." She pushed at his chest.

"I must get back to my own task as well." Malcolm released her, running his hands up and down her arms. As if he regretted letting her go, he drew her back and kissed her again. "A few more days and the harvest will be done," he whispered against her lips, causing electricity to run straight through her. "I've a surprise for you, *mo cridhe.* 'Twill please you, I think."

"Oh?" She didn't think she could handle another surprise.

With a quick kiss, Malcolm left her and returned to the fields. Her mind reeled. No matter what happened or how everything played out, she was in for heartbreak. Either she'd lose her family for all time, or she'd lose Malcolm, Hunter and everyone else she'd come to care for in this time and place.

She watched Malcolm walk back to the fields, memorizing the way he moved, the breadth of his shoulders, his strength and the confident way he carried the authority he'd been born to. She blinked several times to ease the sting in her eyes.

Damn that old witch.

Dazed, Alethia wandered down to the lake and offered to help with supper. After dropping the ladle into the stew twice and nearly setting herself on fire, the cook sent her away with a disdainful snort. She sat down on a bench to brood by herself.

"What ails you, True?" Elaine took a seat next to her, placing freshly baked bread and two steaming bowls of lamb stew in front of them. "You have been staring at naught by air for a good while."

"Tired, I guess."

"Is that all? You look as though you've seen a ghost. Has my lout of a brother been ticking you off again?"

She shook herself out of her blue mood to smile at Elaine's use of twenty-first-century vernacular. "No. I'm fine."

"You dinna look or sound *fine.*"

"I used to spend most of every day playing my violin." She sighed. "I haven't even touched it for days."

"This concerns you?" Elaine dipped a piece of bread into her stew and took a bite, all the while eyeing her intently.

"Yes. No. I don't know." Alethia put her elbows on the table and rested her chin on her fists. "It's just that things have . . . changed, become more complicated." She glanced at Elaine.

"Aye, being in love will do that to a lass."

She covered her face with her hands and groaned. "Is it so obvious?"

"You think no one notices when Malcolm pulls you behind a tree to steal a kiss?" She nudged her. "Or when you put your arms around his neck and kiss him back? Today's kiss is no' the first. He stole another in the bailey, aye? Our people do love to gossip."

"What am I going to do?" she mumbled into her hands.

"What is there to do? 'Tis a good thing."

"It's not that simple." She raised her head to look at her friend. "This isn't my home, or my . . ." She pressed her lips together, and for the first time she longed to tell someone the whole story.

"Dinna vex yourself." Elaine gave her arm a squeeze. "It pleases everyone to see my brother so content. He canna keep his eyes off you, or his hands." She laughed at the expression of shock Alethia gave her.

"Elaine, can you keep a secret?"

"Of course." Her expression serious, Elaine studied her.

"I know your brother and father believe I was drugged and sent here by ship, but that's not what happened at all." She tried to read Elaine's reaction and detected only curiosity and concern. "I never ate or drank anything when I was in Giselle's tent. Things happened that I can't explain. One minute I was in my own land, and the next I was here. She used magic."

Elaine's eyes widened, and several seconds passed before she replied. "It matters no' how you came to us. We are a clan steeped in tales of such happenings. This land is ancient, peopled first by beings capable of doing great magic. Mayhap Giselle harks back to that ancient race."

"You believe me?" Relief washed through her. Until that moment, she hadn't realized how much she needed to tell someone what had really happened.

"Aye. I believe you." Elaine reached for Alethia's hand and gave it a reassuring squeeze. "You dinna strike me as one to tell falsehoods. It must have been frightening."

"To say the least. If Giselle could send me here without my consent, she can also send me back."

"Malcolm would never allow her to take you from us," Elaine huffed.

"How can he prevent it? Giselle isn't what she seems to be at all. I don't even think she's human. What can Malcolm do to prevent magic?" She played with the bread in front of her. "Nothing can come of what I feel for your brother. Giselle sent me here for a specific reason, and once I've completed the task, I'm sure she'll send me back." She struggled to keep from crying. "Besides, what Malcolm feels for me is only lust and a misguided sense of responsibility."

"You dinna know him as I do," Elaine admonished.

"Nothing can come of it." Alethia shook her head, trying to convince herself. She couldn't very well take Malcolm home with her to her own time. He wouldn't know how to fit into the twenty-first century. His time was now. He'd been born to lead, and his clan needed him.

"What is this task you speak of?" Elaine asked.

"I'm supposed to save Malcolm's life."

"True," Elaine exclaimed, "you could no' have been sent here to save the man you love only to be ripped from his side once the task is finished. 'Twould be a cruel joke indeed."

"No more cruel than being ripped from my own home and family. Am I never to see them again? I've had no choice in any of this. There is no reason to believe I will have any choice in the future."

"'Tis a quandary, for certes. You must speak to Malcolm about this."

"I can't do that. Are you nuts? Can you imagine what he'd be like? As it is, he won't let me leave the inner bailey."

Elaine's brow furrowed. "He'd lock you away in a turret and hide the key to keep Giselle from you, and to keep you from harm. Aye. Eat, True. You're naught but skin and bones. There's no use worrying yourself sick. All will be well."

Malcolm surveyed the caravan he would lead to Inverness. He'd handpicked men to accompany the traveling party. Liam had been eager to go, and Robley had volunteered to stay behind with the rest of the garrison. Satisfied with the arrangement, he knew his home to be in capable hands.

Leading the mare he meant to give to True, Malcolm sought her in the milling crowd. He'd raised the horse from a filly, taking the time to train her himself. His favorite stallion, an Andalusian he'd won in Spain, crossed with one of their sturdy palfreys had produced this intelligent, sweet-tempered mare. Her dark chestnut coat reminded Malcolm of True's silken locks the night she'd danced in the great hall. A smile of anticipation lit his face. She would be pleased.

Hunter had become his shadow, and even now the lad trailed behind him. Malcolm realized wedding True meant accepting Hunter as his foster son. The notion did not displease him. Hunter would grow to be an asset to their clan. Hunter was canny and brave, and he had a goodness about him that pleased Malcolm.

Just as Hunter put his small hand in his, Malcolm spotted True. Lifting the lad to sit in the saddle he'd had made for True, he led them through the crowd to her side. "True, I have something for you." Malcolm swung Hunter to the ground and placed the mare's reins in her hand. "She is yours." He watched her with expectation.

"Ah . . . she's lovely. *Mi-gwetch*, thank you." She looked helplessly at the gift. "Malcolm," she whispered, leaning close.

"Aye?" He leaned down to hear her.

"I don't know thing one about horses."

Incredulous, he straightened. "You jest."

"No. I don't know how to ride. The day you found me was the first time I've ever been on a horse. We don't have them in my country." That much she could say in truth. Horses had not yet reached North America in 1423.

"No horses?" Elaine asked, riding up to them on her own palfrey. "How can that be?"

"Do you know what an elephant is?" True reached out a hand to touch the horse's velvety nose.

Elaine nodded. "Aye, we've seen drawings of such."

"Are there any in Scotland?"

"Humph. I see your point." Malcolm guided her to the horse's left side. "'Tis time you learned to ride, lass." He hoisted her onto the mare's back and put the reins in her hands. "Unless you wish to walk to Inverness." He winked at her and put her foot in the stirrup. Coming around to the other side, he did the same with her other foot. "She's a good-natured mount and no' likely to bolt. Stick close by Elaine's side. Once we're under way, I'll come back to instruct you."

"Malcolm, she's lovely. Thank you."

Her shy smile stole his breath, and joy welled up inside him. He cleared his throat, touched Hunter on the shoulder and signed, "*You ride with me.*" Hunter threw out his chest and grinned from ear to ear. Malcolm chuckled as he and his wee shadow set out for the head of the procession and his own waiting mount.

Alethia gasped as she watched Malcolm and Hunter walk away. Hunter imitated Malcolm's swagger, every minute gesture and nuance of his hero's movements. "Oh, look, Elaine." She started to laugh, and Elaine soon joined her. When Malcolm stopped to give last-minute instructions to his men, Hunter put his hands on his hips and tilted his head exactly as Malcolm did. More people took notice as Malcolm and his mimic moved on to speak to the smithy's family.

As the laughter grew in volume, Malcolm turned their way. Hunter did the same in perfect synchronization, setting everyone off in fresh peals of mirth. Malcolm and Hunter both wore befuddled expressions. The two walked back to Alethia as if their movements had been choreographed. Hunter matched Malcolm's strides, leading with the same foot, holding himself exactly the same way.

"What is it?" Malcolm asked, his face clouded with confusion. Hunter's perplexed expression matched it to a tee. It was all she could do to stay on the horse. Helpless to control her giggles, she implored Elaine's help with a look.

"The lad idolizes you, Malcolm. 'Tis clear," Elaine answered, wiping a tear from her cheek.

Malcolm glanced down at Hunter, who gazed up at him with open admiration. Alethia could see the understanding dawn as Malcolm put his hand on Hunter's head. "Have I no' said he's a canny lad?"

CHAPTER NINE

With a toss of its head, the mare managed to wrest the reins from Alethia's hands again. The willful beast moseyed away from the caravan of travelers in pursuit of a tasty snack by the side of the trail. Alethia gripped her mane as if the horse were in full gallop. "You are not helping at all," she grumbled at Elaine, who laughed at her from her proper place in line.

"I canna help it. 'Tis quite funny."

"Aack!" Alethia jerked as her horse took a step and stretched its neck low to nibble on some grass.

"You must let the horse know who is master."

"Oh, I think it's obvious to the horse who's in charge." Her mare moved farther up the slope in search of greener fodder, the reins dangling along on either side. She already knew from experience she couldn't reach them on her own from her place in the saddle. "*You* are supposed to be teaching me."

"Aye, but this is so much more fun."

"I'm so telling your brother on you," she scolded. Elaine only laughed harder. She heard the sound of a horse approaching at a gallop from behind her. Relief poured through her as Malcolm rode to her horse's head and reached for the reins. Her relief turned to irritation when she saw the amusement in his eyes. Hunter giggled at her from his perch on Malcolm's lap.

"Your sister has been no help at all," she complained.

"How can you say such a thing?" Elaine cried. "Have I no' retrieved your reins at least a dozen times?"

"You're exaggerating." She scowled. "It's only been four times." Lifting her chin, she glanced at Malcolm. "I'd like to ride in one of the wagons now."

"Nay, lass." Malcolm grinned as he knotted the ends of the reins together. "You'll learn. 'Tis common enough for new riders to lose the reins. This should take care of the problem." He brought them back over the mare's neck and handed them to her. "She is trained to respond to your commands without them, should you wish it. Tighten your knees, and lean slightly in the direction you wish to go. Push slightly with the knee on the outside of the turn."

She did as he instructed and was pleasantly surprised to find herself heading back toward the road.

"Aye, that's it. Now give her a little kick with your heels."

The horse began to trot, and she bounced around on the hard saddle. "Malcolm!"

"I'm right beside you." He chuckled. "Relax. Pull lightly on the reins and lean back at the same time."

Her mare slowed to a walk, and he helped her to regain her place next to Elaine. For the first time since being placed on the mare's back, some of her tension melted away. She smiled at Hunter.

"*What will you call her?*" He gave her his most charming smile, the dimples on his cheeks in full view. She could tell he was in little-boy heaven riding with Malcolm at the head of the line.

"*I'm not sure. I'll think of something.*" Alethia winked at Hunter and turned her attention back to Malcolm. "Will there be furs and hides for sale at the fair?"

"Goods of all kinds will be available. Why do you ask?"

"Winter is almost here. I want to make boots and garments for Hunter and myself."

He grunted. "We have our own tanner. Did I no' tell you to come to me should you need anything? You and Hunter will be provided for."

"Thank you." Alethia concentrated on learning how to control her horse. She was becoming more accustomed to the mare's rhythm as they plodded along. "Why didn't Lydia come with us?" Malcolm and Elaine exchanged a knowing look, making her even more curious. "Tell me."

"Our mother is Father's second wife," Elaine began. "His first wife died in childbirth. We have an older sister, Helen, who is wed to the earl of Sutherland's heir. Father's first marriage united the MacKintosh and Chattan clans as one. 'Twas an arranged match."

When neither said another word, Alethia prodded. "That doesn't explain why Lydia didn't join us."

"She's terrified to travel, and for good reason." Elaine grinned. "Our parents met and fell in love before Father married his first wife. Mother was only ten and five at the time. Father was ten and nine. Of course, he did his duty and married the Chattan woman."

Elaine sighed. "Mother held valuable lands for her dowry, and there were many men who wished for her hand. She refused them all and swore she'd never marry. She vowed to run off and join a convent should her father force her to take a husband," Elaine added dramatically.

"Shortly after his wife passed, Father sought my mother's hand. Our grandsire was only too happy to agree, even though he'd never been overly fond of Father."

"Still doesn't explain the terror," Alethia muttered.

"I'm getting to that part." Elaine scowled. "Be patient. Mother traveled to Moigh Hall for the wedding with half a garrison to guard her. Even so, upon the way she was stolen by one of my father's rivals who thought to force her hand."

She gasped. "No."

"Aye." Elaine nodded. "My father nearly tore Scotia apart to get her back, and even offered part of her dowry as ransom. No real harm came to her, though she spent a good deal of time bound and blindfolded. The ordeal left her with little love of travel. Unless forced, she stays home. 'Tis because my father married for love the second time that he has granted Malcolm the privilege of choosing his own bride."

Elaine's expression became pensive as she shared that bit of information, and Alethia wondered what troubled her friend? Then she thought of Malcolm married to someone else. Jealousy pinched at her heart. Someone else would have his babies and share his life. She had no control over whether she stayed in this time or not, and either way it wasn't likely they could marry. Malcolm's father would not approve. Even though he had given Malcolm the right to choose his bride, she had nothing to offer in the way of a dowry or political gain.

What would her future be like if she couldn't get back to her own time? Options were few for a woman alone in the fifteenth century. Alethia blinked hard several times and forced herself to think about something else. "Will we camp while in Inverness?"

"Nay," Malcolm replied. "We will stay in Castle Inverness. 'Tis one of many we hold for our king. My father is the earl of Fife, as I will be one day."

She smiled at the pride in his tone. "Why would your king need someone else to hold his property for him?"

"King James has been held prisoner by the *Sassenach* for eighteen years. Even so, we are his subjects, and 'tis common for kings to grant the privilege to those nobles he favors, and we have taken care of Castle Inverness for three generations."

Alethia gave her horse a pat. "Who rules Scotland in James's absence?"

"The duke of Albany acts as regent," Malcolm said. "His father before him ruled as governor."

Elaine leaned toward her and lowered her voice. "Our King James had an older brother who should have been king. 'Tis rumored their uncle murdered him so he could take control of Scotland for himself."

Alethia looked at her in shock. "His uncle was the duke of Albany, I'm guessing?"

"Aye, Robert Stuart." Elaine raised her eyebrows and nodded. "James's brother David was locked away in a tower and starved to death. His uncle would have killed James too if he'd had the chance."

"No way!" Her brow shot up. "And the duke of Albany got away with the deed?"

"No one could prove it, and few dared to challenge him," Elaine replied. "Robert Stuart was a ruthless man and brutal. He's dead now. His son Murdoch has taken his place." Elaine's eyes widened. "Some say he's even more ruthless and greedy than his sire."

Malcolm shot Elaine a quelling look. "My sister has a flair for dramatics. James was sent to France for his protection and education when he was but a lad. The English captured him en route, and he's been held there ever since." Malcolm turned to her. "Father is in London now negotiating the release of our king. He and a contingency of Scotland's nobles will bring James home to take his rightful place upon the throne. By this coming spring, we shall once again be governed by our rightful king."

"And I thought our politics were a tangled mess," Alethia muttered. "This place is a regular soap opera."

Alethia surveyed their camp from the top of a small rise. Tents and wagons hugged the banks of the river they followed. She stretched aching muscles and started to walk, eager to take advantage of the freedom to explore.

"Lady True," Beth called.

She turned and waited as Tieren pulled Beth along by the hand.

"The lad has a question he wants to ask ye."

Tieren spoke rapidly in Gaelic to Beth, signing at the same time.

"He wants to know what this sign means."

Puzzled, Alethia frowned. "*Sign it again.*" He did, and she smiled at the silliness of young boys. "It means horse poop." As Beth translated, Tieren's expression changed rapidly from disbelief to outrage. He ran off. "What do you suppose that was about?"

"Och, no tellin'. Do ye want me to accompany ye on yer walk?"

"No. I just need to stretch my legs." She waved her off and walked toward the hills. It would be good to have a few moments alone to think about everything she'd learned today. She let her mind go, relishing the coolness of the air against her skin and the ground beneath her feet.

She was on the crest of her second hill when she saw Liam on the far side. Preoccupied, he surveyed the surrounding area. As she approached, she couldn't help but pick up on the strong emotions emanating from him. His feelings of yearning, frustration and anger revolved around a woman, that much she could tell. He turned at the sound of her footsteps.

"Good eve, Lady True." Liam smiled, but it didn't reach his eyes.

"Why are you troubled, Liam? Will she be there?"

His body tensed, and he looked away from her. "Is who going to be where?"

"The woman occupying your thoughts, will she be at the fair? Would you like to talk about her?" His eyes searched hers, and she sensed his overwhelming turmoil.

"Mayhap you are the only one I can talk to about this." He let out a long sigh and looked out over the expanse of wilderness. "I must ask you to keep my secret to yourself."

"Of course, but it can't be as bad as you think."

"Aye, it can." He glanced at her. "I love the daughter of our most bitter enemy. I want to make her mine, but I dinna dare. She will be at the fair, and it pains me we must pretend we are strangers." His hand went to the hilt of the dirk at his belt. "What I feel for her is honorable. I have pledged my heart. Yet we must meet in secret, sneaking behind everyone's backs to steal a few moments together." Bitterness and anger filled his tone. He held himself as if ready to do battle. "If her father should discover our secret, I fear to think what would become of her. He is a cruel man and has beaten her for far less."

"Have you considered eloping? Isn't there somewhere you could take her?"

"I have considered every possibility. There is no place we could go. Should we be discovered, 'twould lead to bloodshed." Liam raked a hand through his hair. "The enmity between our two clans runs deep and harks back to the days of Robert the Bruce." He plowed his fingers through his hair. "Highland clans have long memories, lass. The Comyn laird is my lady's father. He's a ruthless tyrant, and he sees his daughter as naught but a pawn to be used for his own gain. 'Twill no' be long before he's arranged a marriage for her. That I canna bear."

Liam's anguish tugged at her heart, and Alethia reached out to touch his arm. "I'm sorry. Does Malcolm know?"

"Nay. I have told no one."

She brought her thumbnail to her mouth and thought about his situation for a few moments. William and Lydia's story still fresh in her mind led her to believe something could be done. Malcolm would fix it. He could do anything. "I think you should tell him. No one can hold a woman responsible for what her father does. We can figure something out. Don't give up."

"You dinna know our ways, lass." Liam shrugged.

She turned at the sound of footsteps to see Malcolm striding up the hill toward them.

He nodded a greeting. "Hunter and Tieren are at it again, lass. There is need for you in camp, and 'tis almost time to take our evening meal."

"What have the lads done now?" Liam asked. "I vowed to Tieren's mother I would be responsible for him on our journey. Am I needed as well?"

"Nay, Liam. What they both need is a bath." Malcolm grinned. "Hunter has given Tieren a sobriquet that does not please him."

"What might that be?" She cringed.

"Och, lass, he's been calling him *horse poop*. Tieren took umbrage and decided the best way to retaliate was to fling fresh dung at Hunter." Malcolm shrugged. "Hunter flung it back. The two resemble mounds of the stuff, and none will go near them."

Liam burst out laughing.

She glared at him. "If you laugh, you get to bathe them." He stopped immediately. Alethia sighed as Malcolm took her hand to lead her back to camp. "What about Beth? Can't she help?"

"She's nowhere to be found. Elaine seems to have disappeared as well."

Alethia walked between the two men back to their camp by the river, where she found the boys, who did indeed resemble mounds of manure. It clung to their clothes and matted their hair. They glared at each other, and Galen stood behind them to ensure they didn't flee. Alethia didn't know whether to laugh or to cry, so she sent them both a stern look.

"*He started it.*" Hunter's small chin jutted out as he signed.

Tieren gasped. "*Did not!*" He shoved Hunter's shoulder.

Hunter shoved back. "*Did too!*"

"*Enough.*" Malcolm intervened.

Tieren took on a dramatic expression, playing the innocent victim. "*He called me a name.*"

Alethia had to fight the urge to laugh, and she wondered if Tieren noticed how automatically he used signing when dealing with Hunter. "*So I've heard.*"

She caught the grin Hunter tried to hide, and squelched it. "*You will apologize.*" She sensed the rebellion growing within him. "*Or you will not ride with Malcolm tomorrow.*" She raised a single eyebrow and glared at him. His rebellious posture deflated.

Hunter sighed audibly and turned to Tieren with a contrite expression. "*I'm sorry, Horse Poop.*"

Tieren lunged, Hunter let out a triumphant whoop, and the two were rolling on the ground, arms and legs flying before she could do anything about it. "Fast friends?" She turned to Malcolm.

He grabbed each of the boys by their upper arms and held them apart. "Give it time."

Other than the lack of Porta Potties and plumbing, the fair in Inverness bore a remarkable likeness to Renaissance fairs in the twenty-first century. Jugglers, magicians, musicians and vendors created a cacophony of sight and sound. The tempting scents of roasting meat, bread, ale and mulled wine permeated the fairgrounds, making her stomach rumble.

Alethia spied Beth and another young woman in MacKintosh plaid flirting with a group of men from another clan. Everywhere she turned, she saw a multitude of plaids in all tints and hues. And men. The fifteenth-century warriors were huge and well muscled. She linked her arm through Elaine's. "Look at all the eye candy."

Elaine giggled. "I never tire of the entertainment your odd speech affords me, True. What do you mean by aye candy?"

"Look around you. The place is overflowing with gorgeous men with hot bodies—a feast for the eyes—eye candy."

Elaine laughed again. "Ah, I take your meaning."

"Oh look, Elaine. A group of them is heading our way." She nodded toward the herd of hunks weaving through the crowd toward them. "The one leading them is breathtaking, like a Scottish Adonis," she whispered. Elaine stiffened beside her and grabbed her hand. Puzzled, Alethia glanced at her. Elaine's face had turned scarlet. She had no time to question her friend. They were quickly surrounded. Alethia moved closer to Elaine, who still held her hand with bone-crushing force.

"Lady Elaine," the blond Adonis said as he bowed. "'Tis a pleasure to see you. I did so hope . . ." Taking her free hand in his, he brushed a kiss across her knuckles and stared at Elaine with such intensity, Althia was forced to lower her gaze. If she hadn't, she would've missed seeing the man press a note into Elaine's palm. Elaine tucked it away with a furtive gesture.

"Dylan, 'tis good to see you as well. May I introduce my friend?" She gripped Alethia's arm. "Lady Alethia Goodsky is a guest at Moigh Hall. We call her True. This is Dylan of clan Sutherland. He is my half sister's brother-in-law, and the earl of Sutherland's youngest son."

"'Tis a pleasure to meet a friend of my lady's." He bowed and introduced the men with him. "May we accompany you? Might we tempt you into sharing refreshments with us?"

Dylan took Elaine's hand and tucked it through his arm before either of them could respond. Were all Scottish males as arrogant as Malcolm and Dylan? Surrounded by Dylan and his men, they were ushered along the path, stopping now and then to take in the sights. Alethia focused on Elaine to get a sense of her feelings. Longing and intense emotions flowed between her and Dylan.

"This place is a regular *Days of Our Lives* prequel," she murmured under her breath.

"Did you say something, my lady?" the young man at her elbow asked.

"No, just thinking out loud." She glanced at him. "You're a Sutherland?" The simple question provided all the encouragement he needed to boast about his clan, his skills and his future prospects.

He moved closer to her side, offered his arm and let her know he was interested.

Taking his arm, she pretended to listen.

"Malcolm," Galen said, nudging his arm, "Lady True and your sister are three-deep in Sutherlands."

Galen stood by his elbow as Malcolm saw to bartering their surplus produce and grains for needed commodities. He turned in the direction Galen indicated and growled deep in his throat. Sutherlands were allies. The women were not in any danger. Still, he did not like seeing True surrounded by men, and she looked to be enjoying herself far too much for his liking.

He sought Liam in the crowd, not at all surprised to find him missing again. His cousin had been acting strangely since they'd arrived, often disappearing for hours at a time.

For the moment he could do nothing. "Aye, Galen. I see them. She and my sister are safe enough. 'Tis only Dylan and his men. Join their party, and make sure no mischief ensues."

Galen smirked. "Whom am I guarding from mischief, your sister or True?"

"Both. Now go." Malcolm scowled and turned back to his negotiations.

The morning wore on slowly, and his frustration increased with each passing hour. Every time he caught a glimpse of True, she was deep in conversation with one man or another. Her laughter, and the smiles she gave away so freely, wreaked havoc on his peace of mind.

Once free of duty, he still had one errand he wished to see to before he could remove True from her growing circle of admirers. The sound of male laughter drew his attention. Five men—Sutherlands he did not recognize—hung upon True's every word. They stood too close to her. His sister spoke with Dylan and Galen off to the side. Galen caught his eye, shrugged and gave him a wry smile. Malcolm groaned.

His errand could wait.

Shoving two of the men aside, Malcolm reached True and rested his hand on her shoulder. "Come with me, lass."

"What for, Malcolm?"

Her smug smile undid him. He leaned close and spoke loud enough for all to hear. "I have no' yet kissed you today, and I wish to do so now." He straightened, gratified by her gasp and the blush rising to her cheeks. "Come, unless you wish me to remedy the situation right here." He raised an eyebrow in challenge.

"Neanderthal," she muttered, her eyes flashing.

Tucking her against his side, he staked his claim for all to see and glared at any who dared hope for anything more with her than a few brief words. Malcolm guided her through the group of men bristling at his challenge. His mood lightened in anticipation of a good fight. "The MacKintosh will be in the lists at dawn on the morrow. I welcome you to join us." He let the words settle over the Sutherlands and gave them his back.

"What was that all about?"

"I did not like the way they looked at you."

"Really?" She sighed. "Well, I certainly did."

"You will not let any other men look at you." Even to his own ears, the command sounded ridiculous. How could she control how men looked at her? Her laughter, and having her next to him, soothed his ruffled feathers. He grinned. "I know what you are going to say. You may save your breath."

"I will refrain from commenting about your absurd directive."

"You just did, lass." True glanced up at him through her thick lashes, her beguiling smile tempting him to make good his promise to kiss her right there in the middle of the fairgrounds. "I came for you because I wish to show you something. Look, True. Over there by the jugglers."

He pointed to the circle of spectators surrounding the performers. There, amidst the crowd, Hunter and Tieren watched the show side by side, each with an arm slung casually around the other's shoulders. His lady's quick intake of breath, and her hand reaching for his, made all his frustration disappear. Malcolm brushed a kiss across her forehead, content for the first time that day.

CHAPTER TEN

Alethia perched on the edge of the huge bed in the chamber she shared with Elaine in Castle Inverness. She'd suffered through the afternoon at the fairgrounds and through supper. Her curiosity had eaten away at her until she couldn't enjoy anything. Finally, she and Elaine had the privacy needed for a full confession. "Spill, Elaine."

"Whatever do you mean, True?" Elaine sat before the hearth, braiding her hair for bed.

She raised her eyebrows and stared at her. "You know what I mean. I saw the way you reacted to Dylan, and I saw the letter he passed to you."

"Oh." Elaine put her hands in her lap, her eyes filling with tears. "What a coil all of this is."

"Aren't the Sutherlands on good terms with the MacKintosh? I thought you said your sister married Dylan's brother."

"This has nothing to do with clan or kinship." Elaine joined her to sit on the bed. "Dylan fostered with us until he earned his spurs. We . . . I . . ." Elaine stood up, wrung her hands and heaved a loud sigh. "I love him." Her eyes filled with anguish. "With all my heart, and he loves me. A year past he asked for my hand. Father refused him because Dylan will no' inherit a title."

Alethia frowned. "Let me get this straight. Your father is letting Malcolm choose his bride, but you can't choose your husband? How unfair."

"Aye, 'tis unfair." She nodded as she paced. "My dowry includes land, and Dylan has a holding of his own. I would be content being the wife of a laird. My father, of course, seeks an alliance with another earl of his choosing. Since my half sister has already allied our clan to the Sutherlands, he will no' agree to his only remaining daughter marrying into the same clan. There's naught to be gained by it. What care I for titles when my heart is already given?"

"What will you do? Are you going to run off to a convent? Surely the irony would not be lost on your father."

"I dinna know what I will do." Her shoulders slumped in defeat, and she came to a stop in front of Alethia. "In the missive you saw him slip to me, Dylan asks me to elope with him. I have no' yet given him my answer. Such an act would surely cause my father to disown me. I dinna think I could bear never seeing my family again. But I canna imagine sharing my life with any other than Dylan."

"I know how you feel."

Elaine reached for her hand and gave it a squeeze. "I am sorry, True. 'Tis selfish to tell you of my troubles when you have enough of your own."

"It's all right. I wanted to know." She squeezed back. "I can't imagine your father would disown you over this. You said yourself he tore Scotia apart for Lydia. He understands what it's like to be in love."

"Aye, but Father did his duty first, and duty and honor are foremost in his mind. I dinna know how it is in your land, but here in Scotia, daughters are seen as a commodity. We are traded for political gain, wealth or land." She shrugged her shoulders. "'Tis the way of things, and I am his only unwed daughter."

"How soon does Dylan want an answer?"

"His father is in London with mine. I must send my answer by the New Year, a little more than two months hence. If I say to him nay, he says he will be out of my life forever."

"Men." Alethia flopped back to lie on the bed. "They cause most of our suffering."

"Aye." Elaine joined her. "They break our hearts one way or the other."

"Let me know if there's anything I can do." Alethia turned to face her.

"You have already, and I am grateful for your sympathy and friendship." Elaine wiped her eyes and sat up. "I am to sleep. This has been a trying day. Are you coming to bed?"

"I don't think I can right now. I'm restless." She went to fetch her woolen cloak. "Maybe a walk in the inner bailey will help."

"All the attention you attracted today has made my brother edgy. Dinna let him catch you outside the walls," Elaine warned, "or surely he will tick you off again."

After seeing to his people's welfare, Malcolm returned to the keep, looking forward to an ale and a long-overdue conversation with Liam before retiring. He intended to confront his cousin about his strange behavior. He would have answers. As he walked through the inner bailey, his gaze was drawn to a lone figure standing upon the catwalk. He recognized her immediately. True, wrapped in his colors, stared out beyond the curtain wall toward the river. He could tell by the way she held herself that her thoughts were troubled. He turned from his path and climbed the stairs to her side.

"What troubles you, *mo cridhe*?" Her sigh was loud and laced with melancholy. What else could he do but wrap her in the safety of his arms. "You should be in bed, lass."

"I couldn't sleep." She lifted her head from his shoulder. "How's Hunter?"

"He's having a grand time. He and Tieren are with the men. Dinna worry."

"Scotland seems like such a tragic place."

"Hmm, does it?"

"Yes. I haven't heard a single story that ends with 'and they lived happily ever after.' Everything seems to end in violence and heartbreak."

He refrained from pointing out that his parents' own story had ended well. "Mayhap the secrets you carry for others make it seem thus, aye?"

She laid her forehead on his shoulder and took a shuddering breath. He brushed his chin over the crown of her head and tightened his hold. "Would it help to share the secrets you carry? My shoulders are broad enough to bear your burdens."

"Friendship is not a burden; it's a blessing. Besides, I've been sworn to secrecy."

"Were it within my power, I would grant Dylan and my sister permission to marry, and gladly so." He ran his hands up and down her back in a gesture he hoped would soothe her. "Think you I have no' tried to sway our father to see things her way?"

"How did you know?"

True raised sad eyes to his, and his heart turned over. "Elaine spent the day with Dylan. The hurt is fresh in her mind. You are her friend, and 'tis only natural she would confide in you."

"It's not fair."

"Nay, 'tis no', and what of Liam? Has he also sworn you to secrecy?"

"You're way too clever." She smiled.

Malcolm drew her tighter into his arms and leaned to whisper in her ear, "Who holds your secrets, *mo anam*? Will you share them with me? I swear to keep them safe." As he knew she would, she gave no reply other than another sigh. The warmth of her breath against his neck turned him inside out. "There is still the matter I spoke of earlier today."

"What matter?" She gazed at him in question.

"I have not yet kissed you today." With that, his mouth found hers. When her arms came up to circle his neck, and the soft feminine sounds coming from deep within her spilled into his mouth, he knew he'd met his aim to distract her. Content just to hold her in his arms, Malcolm broke the kiss, stroked her hair and rested his chin on top of her head. "Alethia—"

She groaned. "You're going to ruin this perfect moment, aren't you?"

He chuckled, pleased that she found his kisses perfect. "What makes you say such a thing?"

"Whenever you have something serious to say, you call me Alethia."

"Aye." He brushed a kiss across the frown line on her forehead. "The last time we spoke of Madame Giselle, you said you were afraid. I would know what it is you fear, so I can lay those fears to rest."

True moved away from him to gaze beyond the walls. Moments passed, and he felt certain she would not tell him. Still, he waited and hoped.

"I am afraid of the *what-ifs*," she whispered.

"I dinna take your meaning. *What-ifs*?" He moved to stand behind her, drawing her back against his chest.

She nodded. "The what-ifs. What if I never see my family or my home again? What if Giselle sends me back home, and I never see you, Elaine, Lydia and everyone else again? What if I fail to save your life? Because of your own stubborn interference," she added, frowning up at him over her shoulder. "What if Hunter is taken from me? The what-ifs are endless and confront me at every turn." She placed her small hands on his forearm where it crossed her shoulders.

For the first time since he'd found her, he gained some measure of understanding how much her life had been thrown into turmoil by Giselle's actions. While his own life had improved immeasurably, hers had become frightening and uncertain. Now, Liam and Elaine had added their secrets to her list of worries.

His heart ached for her. She carried so much upon her delicate shoulders and never complained. Her strength humbled him, and he felt helpless—not a pleasant feeling for one such as he. "Och, lass, what can I do to ease the what-ifs you face?"

Malcolm turned her from the wall and wiped the tears from her cheeks with the pads of his thumbs. He cradled her head against his shoulder and silently railed at the forces at work he felt powerless to control.

"I want to go home, Malcolm," she whispered into his plaid.

His heart stopped beating.

"I've had enough of the fair, and Lydia must be terribly lonesome without us."

The breath he held left him in a whoosh of sound, and his heart started up again.

Life settled into a pattern, and Alethia welcomed the routine that being back at Moigh Hall afforded her. She practiced her violin in the early morning hours. Not jigs and reels, but Mendelssohn, Vivaldi and Satie. Determined not to let her skill diminish, she also played in the evenings after supper for any who cared to listen.

Signing lessons continued, as did her own lessons in Gaelic. Whenever a few spare hours presented themselves, Alethia taught Hunter to use his bow while honing her own skill. Malcolm had given Hunter and Tieren wooden swords. The boys could often be found in the lists imitating the adults or engaged in endless mock battles with each other.

And, of course, there were riding lessons. Sometimes she, Malcolm and Elaine rode together. Other times, Lydia, Liam or Robley came along. Hunter often joined them, and Alethia passed on what she learned, even letting him take the reins for short periods of time.

Today, she and Malcolm would ride alone, and he'd promised to show her his favorite boyhood haunt. Thinking about it sent a thrill of anticipation through her. Drawing her cloak closer against the chill, she waited on the steps in front of the keep and looked forward to the exhilaration a good canter through the hills and glens would bring. Traveling through the wilderness surrounding the lake reminded her of hours spent in the bush with her relatives, gathering maple syrup in the early spring, checking their trap lines, hunting and exploring with her cousins.

"Are you ready, lass? The ferry awaits," Malcolm said behind her.

She jumped at the sound of his voice behind her. "You do that on purpose."

"Do what?"

His expression of feigned innocence made her laugh. "Sneak up on me like that. I've been watching for your return from the lists."

"I came in through the kitchen." He held up a burlap sack. "In case we get hungry during our ride. Come, the day is short, and we've leagues to explore."

The stable master had their horses saddled and waiting by the ferry landing on the mainland. Malcolm helped her to mount, then swung up into his saddle in a single fluid motion that never failed to take her breath. "How do you do that? Can you teach me?"

"To become a knight a man must be able to mount his steed in a single motion. The feat takes years to master and requires a great deal of strength. If your mare were moving, you might be able to swing up. I dinna think it could be accomplished otherwise. Have you decided what to call her?" He reached over to pat the mare's neck as they rode out of the village.

"I've narrowed it down to *Onizhishiikwe* or *Wiishkobiikwe*. In Anishinaabe, that's Pretty Lady or Sweet Lady."

"Ah, Lady it shall be." He gave her a wry smile. "Am I correct in surmising the *Ikwe* part of the name is lady?"

"Loosely translated. There isn't really a word for 'lady' in my language. *Ikwe* means woman, and can be used for lady."

"How is your name said in your language, True?"

"In my culture a person has more than one name. We have a common name known to all, and then another which is more spiritual in nature, having to do with our character, who we are. Those names are given to us by our holy men and are not shared with everyone. Mine is *Madweweshigewiin*, 'She Makes Music.'" His gaze met and held hers with such intensity, her heart took flight.

"'Tis fitting, and it suits you," he said, his voice husky. "Are you up for a good run? Remember to grip with your knees, and hold on to Ikwe's mane should you feel the need."

They allowed the horses to stretch out, galloping to the edge of a forest bordered on either side by hills. Malcolm slowed his mount, coming to a stop at the beginning of a trail. He dismounted and helped her down. "We'll continue on foot. We are nearly there, and the way is narrow and sometimes steep and overgrown."

The path led them under a canopy of foliage at the peak of autumn glory. The red berries on the rowans stood out against the pale green-gold of their leaves. The deep russet of the oaks contrasted nicely with the pines, hemlocks and spruce. The trail wound a crooked path through moss-covered stone outcroppings, leading down into a grove of cedars growing on the banks of a small stream. Alethia took a deep breath, relishing the tang of the evergreens mixed with the loamy smell of the woods.

Malcolm tied his gelding's reins over a low-hanging branch and secured her mare nearby. Taking her hand in his, he led her on a narrow path between two ancient cedars into a clearing. He did not speak, and once she entered the clearing, she understood why.

A spring bubbled up to trickle over stone steps forming a low fountain. Ancient cedars stood like sentinels in each of the cardinal directions around the clearing. Oak and rowans, like foot soldiers, took up their positions of protection behind the evergreens.

A deep stillness and peace permeated the place. Sunlight and shadow played tug-of-war at the edges of the circle, casting patches of gold and hues of the deepest green and indigo. She strained to catch the echoes of timeless magic and spells cast by mystics long-gone from this world. Soft, inviting moss covered the gently rising slopes surrounding the spring, beckoning her to take a moment's rest against the pillowy green velvet.

"This is a sacred place." She spoke in a hushed voice and looked around her in awe. "There is magic here. I can feel it. If I had tobacco, I would lay some down as an offering to the spirits who dwell within this circle."

"Aye. This spring has been here since the beginning of time. 'Tis said those who followed the old religion considered it a holy place. I dinna know what tobacco is, but I take your meaning. Come. Drink from the spring with me. The water is the sweetest and most refreshing you will ever taste."

Malcolm knelt by the spring and cupped his hands under the steady trickle of clear water. He bent low to sip, and when she joined him, he offered his hands as a cup for her to drink from. Alethia placed her own hands under his and drank the water from his palms.

Time stopped, as if the moment were a ritual, something spiritual and pure. The grove took on a golden hue, and for a moment, she felt a bone-deep sense of rightness. A chilly breeze caressed her cheek, breaking the spell.

"What did you do here as a boy?" She searched Malcolm's vivid blue eyes, his beloved face, and had to swallow hard as love for him welled up. Such a beautiful man, inside and out. How could she face leaving him? Her own soul would be ripped right out of her. She studied their surroundings to hide her turmoil.

"I'll show you." Malcolm took a woolen blanket from the sack he'd brought and spread it out on the moss. He lay down on his back, folded his arms under his head and crossed one leg over the other.

She laughed. "And what is it you are doing exactly?"

"See for yourself." He patted the blanket next to him.

Malcolm waited with bated breath as she settled herself beside him. "Now, look up and let your mind go. Watch the clouds and daydream." He winked at her, pleased he'd managed to maneuver her down to the blanket.

"Tell me." She turned on her side and propped herself up on an elbow. "What does a young Scottish boy daydream about?"

He took a deep breath and let it out slowly. "I dreamed of becoming a great knight and of winning battles single-handed with naught but my claymore and the strength in my body." He grinned at her. "I dreamed of what I would do differently than my father once I was laird and earl. Especially when I was in trouble for some mischief or other."

"You hid here when you were in trouble." She laughed.

"Aye." He winked at her. "Here I plotted how I would make my fortune." He turned on his side to face her. "I dreamed all manner of things." *I dreamed of finding you.*

"And you grew to be an extraordinary man."

What he saw shining from her ocean eyes when she looked at him caused his heart to leap in his chest. "Nay, lass, no' extraordinary. I am but an ordinary man with extraordinary responsibilities." He traced her lips with a finger. "I have neither the ambition nor the ruthlessness to become a great man. My needs are simple. I am content with my lot in life. What I do possess is the will, the wit and the strength to hold what is mine and to keep it safe."

"I did not say a great man, Malcolm. I said an extraordinary man. There's a huge difference."

Her gentle smile, meant for him alone, melted his insides. He leaned toward her and captured her smile with a brief kiss. "We should eat."

He retrieved the sack and pulled out bread, cheese and apples. "Fill this with water from the spring." He handed her an earthenware bowl and started cutting cheese with the dagger he kept at his belt. Once they were settled, he would tell her about the legend of the spring.

Malcolm knew she cared for him. He'd seen the precise moment during the harvest when she'd realized it herself. But did she love him? Nothing less than her whole heart would do, for he feared a time would come when she would have to choose. Would she stay with him, share his life, bear his children, or would she return to her home an ocean away? The fear of losing her consumed him, and he would use any means to keep her by his side.

"This is a sacred spring." He handed her a share of their meal. "The water is said to have magical properties. Our people have been coming here for as long as anyone can remember." He gestured with one hand toward the spring. "The stones you see forming the fountain were placed there by Druid priests eons ago."

"Oh?" She turned to study the spring. Getting up from her place, she broke off tiny bits of her food and set them on the edge of one of the stones.

"What are you doing, lass?"

"Making an offering of thanks to the spirits who reside here. It's a common practice amongst my people."

"Aye, my people oft do the same." He waited until she returned to her place beside him to continue. "Legend has it, if a couple drinks together from the spring, they will fall in love. And if a couple already in love drinks from the spring, their love will remain as evergreen as the cedars that surround us." He nodded toward the trees.

"You're making that up." Her eyes grew large, and a blush rose to her cheeks.

"Nay," he protested, giving her a smug smile. He watched her intently, wondering how she would react.

Her thumbnail came up to her mouth as she pondered the matter. She frowned at him. "You didn't tell me this until *after* we drank together."

"Aye." He grinned at her, unrepentant. "The spring has one more boon to offer. If a couple is having difficulty conceiving a child, they come here, fast for a day and drink only water from the spring. Then they spend the night together within the circle of the cedars. If they do this, they'll soon have a bairn."

Her eyes searched his, focusing on him the way he'd noticed she did when listening for truth. He wished he could hear her thoughts and prayed his heart would say to her the words he feared to utter.

"Humph." She gave him a disgruntled look. "It's a lovely myth, nothing more."

"Mayhap you are right." Picking up the bowl she'd filled with spring water, he took a drink and handed it to her in challenge. "Drink. If, as you say, 'tis myth and nothing more, it matters not. Besides, you've already partaken." He watched the emotions play across her face as she considered his words. The moment she made up her mind, her countenance changed, and her chin raised a determined notch. Pleased, he smiled and placed the bowl into her outstretched hands.

She drank.

Malcolm took the bowl and placed it on the ground beyond their blanket with the remnants of their meal. Drawing her close, he cradled her body next to his and kissed her with all the love he felt for her. Only kisses. He would take only kisses, he promised himself.

True freed the shirt from his belt and ran her warm hands over his back and around to his chest. He groaned, his passion flaring as she pressed her soft, womanly curves against him. His tongue thrust into her mouth to taste her sweetness as he sought the laces of her gown. She helped him free her arms as he tugged the garment free. Malcolm raised himself to gaze upon her perfect breasts. Enchanted, he watched her nipples harden as he traced around one dusky bud. Only a touch, he promised himself. Aye, and mayhap a taste.

Nuzzling the soft skin on her neck where it curved to meet her shoulder, he inhaled her clean, floral scent and kissed a trail down to the swell of one breast. She sighed. He took it as encouragement. Cupping her breast, he ran his thumb over the nipple while tasting the other. The sharp intake of her breath, the way her body tensed and stilled in his arms, let him know he'd pleased her, and his own pleasure and desire heightened.

Malcolm's heart pounded; his whole body throbbed with need. He took the hardened nipple into his mouth and suckled, swirling his tongue around it until True writhed beneath him, arching her body into his. Her sighs and moans inflamed his senses. She twined her fingers in his hair and pulled him closer, offering an open invitation.

He took that as encouragement as well, and accepted.

Lifting his head, he beheld the vision in his arms. Long lashes fanned her delicate cheeks. Her brow furrowed in sensual concentration, and her lips, swollen from his kisses, were slightly opened as if ready to sigh his name. Something greater than passion flowed from his heart into his soul: the primal need to lay claim to his mate, to make her his, and the certain knowledge he'd walk through fire for this woman. His entire body tightened, and the promise to wait until they were wed went up in smoke.

"I want you, Alethia." He pressed against her. "More than anything I've ever wanted in my life. Let me touch you. I swear only to touch." He groaned into her neck, "I need to touch you." Her eyes opened. Full of trust and vulnerability, they met his and did not waver. His breath caught.

She whispered, "Yes."

A low groan came from somewhere deep inside him, and his mouth found hers in a crushing kiss. He plunged his tongue deep into the moist sweetness as his hand found the hem of her gown. His breath came fast and hard as he skimmed up the length of her bare leg, coming closer and closer to that secret feminine place that promised ecstasy. The silky, warm feel of her inner thighs as they opened for him drove him wild. His member, hard and throbbing, strained to follow.

She fumbled with his belt, finally getting it free. With a single tug, his plaid fell to a heap on the blanket. She gasped at the same time he did, as her hand came around his hardened length. She stroked him from tip to base, finally cupping his weight in her hand.

He lost his mind.

Frantic for the feel of her bare skin against his, Malcolm tugged and pulled the clothes from her body, laying her bare beneath him. In wonder, he could only stare, mesmerized by the sight of her beauty. "You are more lovely than the dawn, Alethia."

Tracing a single finger from her collarbone, through the valley between her breasts, to her navel and lower to the sable curls protecting her sex, he watched transfixed as goose bumps rose on her skin in the wake of his touch. Following the path his finger had traced with his mouth, he pressed kisses onto her warm, soft skin. The way she felt, her scent, her taste and the way she responded to him made him forget all of his self-control.

Today he would make her his, here amongst the cedars under the sky in this sacred place. Together they had partaken from the spring. Even after he told her of its significance, she drank with him. Their hearts were bound, their fates sealed as if they'd already said their vows before God. *Mine. Mine, now and forever.*

"I cannot wait until spring, True." He came up to kiss her, his voice raspy and hoarse with need. "I want you *now*. All of you." Crushing her to him, he moaned the words into her ear. "Do you understand what I am asking, love?" He leaned back to look into her face, needing to be certain she understood.

"Spring?" Her eyes, dilated and unfocused, looked at him in confusion. "What happens in the spring?"

"It matters not." He nuzzled her neck. "Do you know what I am asking?"

Her brow furrowed, and she raised herself onto her elbows. Her breasts, nipples like the buds of the loveliest roses, thrust out at him, as if chiding him for the interruption. "Something to do with . . . spring?" She canted her head and gazed at him.

Chuckling, he drew her back into his arms and pressed his forehead against hers. "Nay, lass. I'm asking to make love to you."

"Yes, Malcolm." Her voice came out a throaty whisper. "Yes." She drew his mouth back to hers and kissed him as she lay back down on the blanket, bringing him down with her.

He brought his hand up between her thighs and pressed against her mons. She tensed in his arms and moaned. Swearing he would be gentle, take things slow, Malcolm parted the folds of her femininity to find the bud of her sex. Stroking her gently with his thumb, he pushed a single finger inside her. She was hot, tight and slick with passion for him. Malcolm's heart pounded so hard he feared it would jump right out of his chest.

He increased the pressure of his strokes, and her hips moved against him as she sought release. He bent to suckle her breast as he brought her to a frenzy of heated need. True came apart in a rush, calling out his name as her body trembled in his arms. He whispered words of encouragement and praise, holding her until the shudders ceased.

Covering her body with his, Malcolm positioned himself between her thighs, the tip of his manhood pressed slightly against her opening as he struggled for control. He needed to go slow and to be gentle. This first time would cause her pain, and she would need time to adjust.

Two blasts from the village horn sounded in the distance. Malcolm froze, his body tense as he listened. Two tones. Who could be returning to Moigh Hall? Only his father's party had left, and they would not return until spring. Several seconds passed, and still he remained tense, listening.

"Two blasts means one of our own returns." True wiggled beneath him and tried to draw him back to her. "Three means danger. You said so yourself. Don't—"

In that instant, three warning blasts sounded from the village horn.

CHAPTER ELEVEN

Before Alethia's eyes, Malcolm changed from gentle lover to seasoned warrior. It took mere seconds for him to dress and gather their things. Her own mind refused to function. Hovering between fear of what the horn meant and passion, she couldn't seem to move.

Malcolm lifted her to her feet, snatched her chemise from the ground, and tugged it over her head, repeating the process with her gown. "Quick, lass. Do your laces."

She complied, feeling near tears.

"Can you stay your horse at a full gallop?"

"I don't know," she whispered.

"You'll ride with me then. The mare will follow." He took her hand and led her down the path. Hoisting her onto his gelding's back, he freed her mare and swung up behind her.

"I'm sorry, Alethia," he murmured in her ear, his arm coming around her waist.

She couldn't speak and didn't want to think. Swallowing the lump in her throat, she gripped the gelding's mane as they cleared the forest. Malcolm spurred his horse into a dead run. Her mare matched the gelding's pace, galloping beside them.

In no time they reached the village. Malcolm let out a shrill whistle and pulled up hard on the reins in front of the stable. Two youths came out in a rush, and one immediately caught the mare's bridle. Malcolm barked orders as he leaped from his horse, turning to help her down. Not even sparing a moment to ask the boys what had happened, he took her hand and pulled her to the ferry landing at a jog. Still she couldn't speak.

A small crowd waited to be taken to the safety of the curtain wall. They all watched the ferry return from the island, and she wondered how many trips had already been made. She withdrew, going deep inside herself, as if doing so could erase the fear and the icy dread filling her heart. Madame Giselle's words echoed in her mind. Whatever situation had caused the warning tones to be sounded, it could lead to Malcolm's peril.

Slightly more than two months had gone by since she'd come back to this time and place, and the specter of the task she'd been given had hung over her like a dark cloud. At times, she almost forgot. The warning brought it all back.

Her hands hung at her sides, and she stared at nothing. Malcolm twined his fingers with hers behind the folds of her gown. She gripped his hand tight.

"Once we land, go to my mother's solar." Malcolm put his hands on her waist and lifted her to the ferry. Taking his place beside her, he bent to whisper into her ear. "Dinna even think to argue. Once I know what is going on, and I've seen to our people's safety, I will come for you."

All she could do was nod, grateful he continued to hold her hand. More than anything, she needed to feel connected to him. With so many strong emotions emanating from all directions, she couldn't hold a thought of her own or stem the rising panic. The ferry landed, and Malcolm lifted her to shore. His strides were long and fast, and she had to run to keep up with him through the portcullis.

The inner bailey teemed with villagers and warriors armed and on full alert. Malcolm headed up the steps to the doors of the keep, stopping at the top to face the bailey. Scanning the courtyard and the ramparts, he shouted orders in Gaelic to those milling about. His voice acted like a catalyst, galvanizing everyone. Suddenly, every man, woman and child moved with purpose and direction.

Chaos reigned inside the great hall. A single man, his clothing and hair singed and sooty, his face and hands bloody, sat on a bench before the hearth, surrounded by angry men and women all shouting at once. Alethia spotted Hunter and Tieren in the mob, their eyes wide with fright. She caught Hunter's eye and signed for them to come to her. Malcolm took command, ending the chaos and issuing orders. The sound of his booming voice echoed behind her as she led the boys toward the stairs.

Around a corner, Beth leaned against a wall as if she'd been waiting for her. She pressed a finger to her lips, grabbed Alethia's wrist and pulled her along to the narrow back stairway, the same one Alethia had used when sneaking to the lake to bathe so many weeks ago. They ascended to the first landing and turned into a short, narrow hall ending at an opened door of oak. Again Beth cautioned them to be quiet, and they slipped silently through the entrance.

There, in the minstrels' gallery, Elaine and Lydia, along with several other women, sat huddled on the floor with their backs against the balcony wall overlooking the great hall. All eyes turned to her as she entered. Elaine motioned to a spot next to her, and the others scooted over to make room for the boys. Alethia took her place and reached for Elaine's hand. Hunter climbed into her lap, and Tieren pressed himself close to her side.

From their place they could hear everything being said. Malcolm ordered the women out of the hall and called for Robley, Liam, Angus and Galen. He sent someone for ale and food for the messenger, and told him to wait until those he'd summoned arrived before telling his tale. He spoke in Gaelic, but Alethia caught the gist of what was said.

The sounds of people coming and going continued until all were assembled, and Malcolm bid the messenger to speak. The bloodied man told his tale in a loud voice for the benefit of all, and the women surrounding her gasped in shock.

"The Comyns have taken Meikle Geddes," Elaine whispered in her ear. "Uncle Robert and Aunt Rosemary reside there. 'Tis one of many MacKintosh holdings." She gripped Alethia's hand as the conversation continued below. "Several of our clansmen are dead, and their cottages have been burned to the ground. Our people have driven the livestock into the surrounding forest, and they hide there now. Those who are able will come here in the cover of night. Those who are not will continue to hide in the forest. A number of men will stay to protect them and to care for the animals."

Elaine looked at her in shock. "He says Black Hugh of clan Fraser rides with the Comyns against us. We fostered him as a child," she huffed in outrage. "He became a knight under my father's tutelage. That treacherous viper."

Hugh. Had he joined the enemy out of revenge? She leaned her head back against the stones. Dread filled her. Her destiny, the reason she'd been sent back in time, seemed to be unfolding before her as Malcolm and his men discussed the insult done to them by the Comyn clan. Their voices raised in anger, the men spoke too rapidly for her to understand. "What will happen? What are they saying?"

"Malcolm commanded a watch be set upon the hills surrounding Loch Moigh. He's ordering the villagers to the island by nightfall. All but one of the boats are to remain here on the island. One will be hidden in the forest to be used by the men rotating on watch and to transport those who come from Meikle Geddes." She paused, listening for a time, and then continued. "The messenger says only a score or so of Comyn's men remain within the keep; the rest of have ridden off. He knows not where they've gone."

She sucked in a breath and gripped Alethia's arm. "Liam has volunteered to gather information. He claims to have a spy in Castle Rait. That's the Comyns' keep. Malcolm has bid him go with all haste. He's traveling alone. 'Tis very dangerous."

The conversation below became hushed, and they could no longer hear what was being said. Lydia was the first to leave the gallery, motioning the rest to follow. Like ducks in a row, the eavesdroppers traipsed after her to the solar.

Once the door closed behind them, everyone spoke at once, and the conversation flowed around her. While she waited for Malcolm, her thoughts went back to their time together at the spring. He'd apologized. For what? Had he been sorry things had gone as far as they had? Lord, what had she been thinking? All those lessons about safe sex flew right out the window when it came to Malcolm. It couldn't happen again. The possibility of pregnancy terrified her. Life in the fifteenth century already held all the complications she could handle.

Thinking about the way she'd come apart in his arms made her blush. The memory of his powerful body covering hers, the way he'd made her feel, she'd never forget. His touch had been so tender. He'd driven her crazy with desire and love. Surely Malcolm felt the same. Why else take her to drink from the sacred spring with him if he didn't care? No, she knew he cared. But was it love? Whenever she tried to read him, what came back was a tangle, strong complex emotions all wound together into an indecipherable mass. "What will happen?"

"We'll take Meikle Geddes back, of course," Lydia said.

"Oh." The comment brought her back to the present. She hadn't meant to voice her thoughts out loud. "Will the Comyns attack Moigh Hall?"

"No one has ever laid siege to our island fortress." Elaine's tone was tinged with pride. "The loch makes it impossible."

"So Malcolm will lead men into battle." This was it. She had to go with him, had to be there to save his life. "When do you think they'll leave?"

"Not until our people have arrived safely from Meikle Geddes and are settled. He'll wait for Liam's return. Within a se'nnight, no doubt."

Alethia waited all afternoon, through supper and late into the evening for Malcolm to return. Her thoughts went from one worst-case scenario to the next until exhaustion numbed her brain. She'd finally handed Tieren off to his mother, reined Hunter in and made her way to her chamber. Elaine joined her in the corridor, taking her arm as they walked.

"Once our people arrive, you and Hunter are to share my chamber," Elaine told her as they reached Alethia's door. "Every corner of the keep will be full." When she didn't respond, Elaine looked at her with concern. "You are upset."

"Of course I'm upset." She opened her door, and Elaine followed her in. "*Wash and get ready for bed,*" she told Hunter. "Malcolm will lead men into battle. Aren't you worried?"

"Not overmuch." Elaine shrugged a slender shoulder. "Only a score of men remain to hold Meikle Geddes. Malcolm is a seasoned warrior and quite skilled, as are all the men he will take with him." Elaine sat on the bed as Alethia helped Hunter. "Have faith in my brother."

She tucked Hunter in and leaned down to kiss him on the forehead. His arms came around her neck in a fierce hug, and she sensed how frightened he was by all he'd witnessed. Like her, he'd been inundated by the strong emotions emanating from everyone around him. She held him tight and sent him reassurance that all would be well. Disentangling herself, she signed that she would explain everything tomorrow, kissed him again, and rose to join Elaine on the bed. "Have you forgotten why Giselle sent me here?"

"Nay. If you are here to save Malcolm's life, then you shall do so. Giselle gave you no hint what is to be done?"

"None."

"I canna say why, but I feel it in my bones." She patted Alethia's shoulder. "All will be well."

The day had been eventful in more than one way, and the upcoming battle was not the only thing on her mind. For a few moments, her thoughts returned to her interlude with Malcolm. "Elaine, can I ask you a personal question?"

"Aye, are we no' the best of friends?"

"You and Dylan love each other, right?" Elaine nodded. "Have you and he ever . . . um . . . have you two—?"

Elaine gasped. "True, are you asking if he and I have . . . lain together?"

"Well, have you?"

"Nay, of course no'. Such a thing must no' happen until after a woman is wed." She looked indignant for a moment, then blushed and stared at her lap with an expression of contrition. "We've come perilously close," she muttered. "Have you and Malcolm . . . ? Nay, dinna tell me." She put her hands on her ears and made a face. "He's my *brother*."

For the first time that day, her spirits lifted enough to laugh. Elaine looked thoroughly disgusted by the thought of her brother having sex. She reached over and pulled Elaine's hands away from her ears. "No, but we've come perilously close. Where I come from, being a virgin is not that big a deal."

"Big . . . a deal? You're no' a . . . ?"

Elaine looked utterly perplexed, but Alethia's train of thought had left the tracks, and she couldn't seem to find the brakes. "Yes, I am. I haven't had much experience with men. I've always been too wrapped up in my music to become involved with anyone." She sighed. "I don't know what to do. You know my situation. I can't let what I feel for Malcolm go any further. What would happen if—"

"Malcolm has feelings for you. Dinna doubt it, True. He's an honorable man, and he'll no' let Giselle take you from us."

"I'm sure he'd *try* to prevent Giselle from taking me; I'm not sure he'd succeed. What if I carried Malcolm's child and she returned me to my home? What if I had no way to get back here? Even if I could return, what if your father wouldn't approve of a marriage between us?" She put her elbows on her knees, her chin in her hands, and groaned. "This just gets worse and worse. I am so screwed."

"Screwed?" Elaine's expression clouded.

"Yes. Screwed. Every which way from here to there."

Malcolm seethed. Hugh had informed the Comyns that Malcolm's father and uncle were away with a good number of their warriors. Of that he was certain. If they thought him unable to strike back, they would soon learn otherwise. In the meantime, organizing the refugees from Meikle Geddes, guard duty and planning the strategy to retake their holding had occupied every minute for the past several days.

It preyed on his mind that he'd not spoken to True since they'd left the sacred spring. He could well imagine the new *what-ifs* plaguing her thoughts.

His sentries had signaled Liam's return, and Malcolm paced back and forth at the ferry landing, awaiting the final bit of information before putting their plans to action. From the corner of his eye, he saw his cousin Robley approach from the direction of the garrison. He met him halfway. "Robley, gather the men and have them meet us in the great hall."

"Aye, Malcolm. I came to tell you our provisions are secured, and we've moved them to the mainland. The men are ready to ride at a moment's notice."

"Good." With Robley on his way with orders, Malcolm returned to the landing and resumed pacing. Once Liam disembarked, he joined him on his way to the keep. "You are well?" Malcolm asked, scrutinizing his cousin.

"Aye. I have much to tell."

"Wait until we reach the keep. I've sent Robley on ahead with orders to fetch the men. Liam, I would have you remain at Moigh Hall to take command in my absence." Malcolm didn't miss the slight ease in tension at his request. What secret did Liam keep? Why did he not share it with him, rather than True? He did not doubt Liam's loyalty to clan and family, yet he couldn't help but wonder who in the Comyn keep his cousin went to for information.

A lass, no doubt. Mayhap his mysterious trips and long absences were for assignations with a Comyn lass. If that be the case, he did not envy his cousin. For such a match would be ill-fated indeed.

All were assembled around the table by the time he and Liam arrived. Malcolm took his place and accepted an ale. He heard a sneeze from the minstrels' gallery, followed by shushing noises. At once he realized the value of True's signs. He knew the women listened from above. As a lad, he'd oft joined them and done the same.

He signaled for attention. "*Keep your voices low.*" He pointed to the gallery above their heads. "*The women listen, and I'll not have our plans known to them just yet.*" They nodded their understanding and put their heads together to speak in quiet tones.

"The men who took Meikle Geddes are high in the Comyn command," Liam began. "A score of warriors remain in the keep, Black Hugh among them." He gave Malcolm a meaningful look. "Hugh had a hand in this, make no mistake. In exchange for a place in their garrison, he gave them information. The rest of their men have ridden on to Nairn, where they'll remain. The laird resides at Rait, and did no' ride with the party. Though he commanded the attack, his nephew led the raid and leads the party for Nairn." He met the eyes of each man around the circle. "They believe themselves out of our reach there. To the Comyn laird's credit, they've left Black Hugh behind to suffer our wrath."

They argued long into the afternoon. Would they take Meikle Geddes first and then travel on to Nairn? Or travel first to Nairn, taking back Meikle Geddes on their return trip. Malcolm let the argument flow around him and counted down the hours before his reckoning with True.

Malcolm ended the discussion with a raised hand. He'd come to a decision and let his men know what their course would be. "We dine this eve in the great hall with our people. Our women will want reassurance, and our presence is required for such." He gave them all a stern look. "Dinna speak of our plans to anyone—not to wives, nor to lovers, not to brothers, sisters or parents. Dinna even tell your horse."

"Why such secrecy, Malcolm?" Angus frowned. "Ye've no' required such in past."

Robley grinned. "He's no' had a certain lady hell-bent to be his savior in past."

"Och, I ken your concern, lad. 'Twill vex my wife. And 'tis certain this night will be . . . quite chilly, as no doubt I'll be sleeping outside." Angus grimaced and reached over to clasp Malcolm's shoulder. "Not a word will I utter on the subject, upon my honor."

All his men gave nods of agreement, their faces grim.

Sitting upon the dais next to True, Malcolm wanted nothing more than for the meal to end. The few times their gazes had met, the uncertainty and what-ifs swirling behind her anxious eyes tugged at his heart. He'd reached for her hand under the table, only to have her pull away.

"Walk with me this eve," he whispered in her ear. "I understand you're upset. 'Twas no' my intent to leave you as I have for days without word." He watched her swallow hard a few times as she stared at the trencher before her. She'd hardly touched her food. Malcolm reached for her hand again, this time keeping a firm grip until she nodded her assent. The sooner he had his arms around her the better.

When finally he led True through the doors of the keep, the sun had set and they walked in darkness lit only by the waning crescent moon. She held tight to her woolen wrap with both hands, walking stiff and silent beside him. With his own hands clasped behind his back, he steered them out of the inner bailey, toward the portcullis and onto the path toward the loch. "'Twill be Samhain soon," he said to break the silence.

She made no response, and Malcolm knew a storm brewed beside him. He shored up his resolve and all the wiles he possessed to weather the squall.

Their path led them to the same spot where he'd held her against the sorrow of homesickness. This place was theirs, and each new memory they created together made it more so. He took a seat on the same boulder and waited patiently as True paced back and forth in front of him. Best to let her begin, so he kept quiet and let his mind drift to the day he'd found her. He smiled at the picture of defiance she'd presented and at the vision she'd made walking out of the forest with her glorious hair falling about her shoulders. He was a man besotted, and happily so.

True stopped in front of him with her hands folded in front of her, and her chin lifted. "There are a few things we need to discuss."

"Aye?"

"Yes. What happened at the spring, for one thing." Her voice faltered.

"What happened at the spring—"

"Cannot happen again," she interrupted. "We were playing with fire, Malcolm. I'm not blaming you." Her words came out in a rush. "I'm equally responsible. Surely you agree we can't let things go so far again."

"Nay, I dinna agree." She was within reach. "'Tis certain to happen again." Malcolm placed his hands around her tiny waist and brought her to sit next to him. "Often, if I have my way."

"But you apologized." Her eyes were wide. "I thought you regretted—"

"I apologized, aye. Not for what happened between us, lass, only for having to leave things . . . unfinished."

She blushed and covered her embarrassment with her hands. "We can't do that. You know what could happen," she muttered between her fingers.

Best to let the matter rest. He put his arms around her and kissed her forehead. "You said a few things. What else must we discuss?"

"You're going to retake Meikle Geddes?"

"Of course. Uncle Robert and Aunt Rosemary would be most displeased with me should they return from London to find their home in the hands of our enemies." He could see her working herself up to respond. "Give me a kiss before we discuss the matter further."

"Didn't I just say we can't go down that road again?"

"I am not asking you to disrobe, woman. I seek only a kiss." He feigned injured pride and gave her a crestfallen look, gratified by her smile.

"I know how *that* works." She shook her head, even as she grinned. "Only a kiss, only a taste, just a touch you promise, and poof, before you know it, I'm beneath you, sans clothing, and you're muttering something about spring."

His laughter filled the air as he lifted her onto his lap. "Och, 'tis no easy task seducing a truth-sayer." He cradled her face in his hands and took her mouth with his. Several minutes of blissful silence ensued as he feasted on her sweetness, reveling in the soft noises she made in response. Her small hands pushed at his chest, and he lifted his head to gaze into her eyes, losing himself in their depths.

"When do we leave?" she asked.

"There is no *we* in this matter, Alethia. You will remain here within the safety of the curtain wall while *I* am away."

"Don't be stubborn about this, Malcolm. I have to be with you if I'm to save your life. I can't bear the thought of not being there when you need me the most." She'd worked her fingers into the wool of his plaid, twisting the fabric in her distress as she stared at his chest.

"Alethia." He raised her chin with a finger until she met his eyes. "Dinna worry so. I promise no harm shall come to me. I know why you were sent, and the warning alone is enough. You will no' leave this island in my absence."

"Greater men than you have said the same, with disastrous results. I'm going with you. I'm supposed to save your life." She lifted her chin and met his eyes. "I mean to do so."

She scowled most fiercely, and he fought the smile threatening to ruin his stern countenance.

"Don't bother," she snapped.

"What?"

"Don't bother trying to hide what you feel. I can sense your amusement. It's condescending and extremely irritating." She stood up. "This is serious. I'm serious. At least promise me you'll think about it?"

"Aye, I promise to consider your words most carefully."

"And we'll discuss it again before you leave?"

He rose from his place and encircled her waist with his hands. Bringing her snug against him, he kissed her, ravishing her mouth with his tongue, caressing her with his hands.

Pushing him away, she whispered, "We'll talk about this again tomorrow."

Alethia woke with a start. Disoriented, she sat up and looked toward the window. Not yet dawn, the sky gave no hint of light. Her pounding heart set off alarms in every cell. Dread premonition, an oppressive force, swept the cobwebs of slumber away as she sought its source. With a gasp, sudden insight propelled her out of bed. Careful not to wake Elaine and Hunter, she groped her way around the dark room in search of clothes.

"True?"

"Go back to sleep, Elaine. I just have to use the garderobe." Finding her garments—or were they Elaine's?—she tugged them on as she went. Slipping out of the room, she ran down the shadowed corridor and down the stairs to the great hall.

Remnants of a hasty meal were strewn over the trestle table. Candles still burned in their holders in the midst of emptied dishes and pewter mugs. Embers glowed red in the hearth. Those who had shared the meal were long gone. She came to a dead stop at the sight. Disbelief, rage and fear held her fast as the truth crashed over her in waves. He'd left without her. He'd left her without a word.

Frantic, she ran out of the hall to the ferry landing. If she hurried, maybe she could catch him. Maybe they still loaded the ferry with supplies and hadn't yet crossed the lake. Not a soul stirred in the darkness of the bailey, dampening her hopes. She ran through the portcullis toward the landing.

In dismay, she stared at the spot where the ferry should be. She'd missed them. Grief and a piercing fear tore her heart in two. He'd deceived her, led her to believe they'd talk again before he left. Fury welled, choking out rational thought like a pernicious weed.

At that moment, when she thought all was lost, Alethia noticed the boats—fishing boats from the mainland, six in a row, pulled onto the shore and turned upside down. She'd borrow one, get to the mainland, take her mare and follow their trail. Then she'd force Malcolm to see reason, and he'd have to take her with him.

She took a step toward the boats, and someone grasped her arm.

"Dinna even think it, lass."

Startled, she jerked as she turned to see who held her. "Liam."

The compassion radiating from him was her unraveling. A horrible keening sound escaped through her lips. Liam drew her under his arm, just as the dam gave way to the flood of tears.

"Dinna worry, True. Malcolm will return to us unharmed."

"No, Liam." She turned anguished eyes to his. "No. He won't."

CHAPTER TWELVE

Alethia knew by the set of Liam's jaw she'd have no chance of leaving the island. Keeping a firm grip on her upper arm, he led her back to the keep. "Liam, Malcolm told you why I was sent here, didn't he?"

"He did." He gave her a grim look. "Robley and Galen will protect Malcolm, and I will see to it you remain safe."

"How can I convince you to take me to him?"

"You canna. I would do exactly as Malcolm has done. A battleground is no place for a lass, and your presence would only make him more vulnerable." His tone softened. "I know what you are going through. Rest easy. The men with Malcolm are all seasoned warriors, and they have fought together many times. Robley and Galen will guard him well."

"How long will they be gone?"

"A month, mayhap longer. Malcolm will want to set things aright at Meikle Geddes before returning."

They'd reached the keep, and utter defeat swamped her. Her plans thwarted, she wanted nothing more than to get back into bed and pull the covers over her head. Maybe she'd stay there until Malcolm returned.

If he returned.

Without a backward glance, she left Liam in the great hall and dragged herself up the stairs and back to Elaine's chamber. She crept back to the bed they shared, slipped out of her gown and slipped between the sheets.

"Are you ill?" Elaine whispered.

"No."

"You were a long time in the garderobe." Alethia felt the mattress shift as Elaine raised herself to study her in the half-light of dawn. "What is it, True?"

"Malcolm is gone. He and the men left before dawn." Alethia turned her back to Elaine and curled up into a fetal position, pulling the covers over her head.

The feeling of dread and premonition hadn't left her since she'd awakened. Defenseless against such an onslaught, sleep seemed her only escape. It had been her refuge against the agony of losing her parents so many years ago. She'd slept months of her life away until the pain of loss became a dull, bearable ache.

Fear, and the wrenching pain the thought of losing Malcolm caused, stirred up the hurt she'd suffered when her parents died. The faces of her uncles, cousins and aunts passed through her mind, and finally, her grandmother's image. They were lost to her. Somehow, deep in her heart, she knew the rest of her days would be spent in fifteenth-century Scotland. So much loss. Alethia closed her eyes and willed herself away.

She would have been better off keeping her heart to herself. It was time she started thinking about her future and finding a way to make her own way. She had skills, and she had no doubts she could be a productive, contributing member of this community. She had her music, rudimentary healing skills and twenty-first-century knowledge. Yep. She could carve out a life for herself, but not today.

"My dear, 'tis time you left this chamber." Lydia reached out to give Alethia a shake. "Are you ill, child?"

She tried to turn away from the voice disturbing her, but it wouldn't let her be. She tried to cover her head with the blankets, only to have Lydia tug them out of her hands and away from her face. "Leave me alone," she muttered.

"Nay. 'Tis not fitting. You dishonor Malcolm."

Alethia scowled.

"Aye, 'tis a dishonor to the MacKintosh clan to show such a lack of confidence in our ability to protect our own. You have been in this bed for two days," Lydia scolded. "Hunter is beside himself with worry. Enough. Get up."

She sat up.

"Your time would be much better spent preparing for their return. Mayhap there will be wounded to care for."

"Wounded?" Alethia saw Hunter hovering uncertainly by the door. His worry caused a wrenching sensation in her chest. She held her arms out to him. Relief danced across his face as he bounded across the room to climb up onto the bed. He settled himself on her lap, took her face in his small hands and studied her intently. She knew he looked for fever. His whole world had shattered when his mother and grandmother died. Guilt swamped her. "*I'm fine, Hunter. Not sick, only sad.*"

He nodded, his far-too-old eyes reflecting complete understanding. She pulled him into a tight hug, resting her cheek on the top of his head. He smelled like the outdoors, little boy and peat smoke. His warmth gave her comfort and drew her back from the black void.

"A bath awaits, True." Lydia patted her knee. "Then you will eat something and join us in my solar."

"Lydia." Tears pooled in her eyes. "Malcolm left without saying good-bye."

"Of course he did. He knew you would try to follow. If his attention were divided between keeping you safe and fighting, he'd be more likely to come to harm. MacKintosh men protect their women."

"Something bad is going to happen to him because I'm not there to prevent it," Alethia sobbed.

"Is this something you have seen in a vision?"

She shook her head. "No. I've never had a vision. It's just something I feel."

"Mayhap what you feel comes from words said to you by the woman who sent you to us, and no' from premonition at all." Lydia reached over to clasp her hand. "My dear, I dinna doubt the reasons you came to be here. I only question your conviction, and Malcolm's as well, that the deed has aught to do with warfare and bloodshed. A life can be in peril for many reasons, aye?" With a final pat to her hand, Lydia rose to leave.

"Thank you, Lydia. You've given me a lot to think about." Hadn't she said the very same thing to Malcolm herself? It could be that she'd nurse him back to health, or prevent some catastrophe. She hoped to God that was the case. Throwing the blankets off, she swung her legs over the side of the bed and set Hunter on the floor. "I'm sorry. I didn't mean to dishonor the MacKintosh."

"I ken our ways are foreign to you, True. There is naught to apologize for."

A week had gone by without any news from Malcolm and his men. Alethia had joined the other women as they prepared clean linen strips for bandages. She'd sterilized her needles, threaded them with strands of silk she'd teased from skeins of embroidery thread, and packed it all away for use when the time came.

It had been tricky finding time alone to transfer Neosporin from her emergency kit to the basket holding her supplies. She'd tucked the tube under the linen bandages in her basket. In the great hall, men prepared plank-and-barrel tables for the wounded. She scrubbed down all the surfaces with vinegar every night, just in case.

"Beth, is there something to drink stronger than wine or ale?" Alethia fixed breakfast for Hunter and herself and took her usual place at the trestle table.

"Och, aye. *Uisge beatha.* What would ye be wantin' it for?"

"For the men who will return from Meikle Geddes."

"Mean ye to give it to the wounded to dull the pain?"

"Yes, and to bathe their wounds. It drives out the spirits that cause fever."

"I'll get some for ye anon, though I dinna think they're likely to return for another fortnight at the very least." She rose from the table. "And ye ken there might no' be any wounded at all. This *is* Malcolm and our own MacKintosh warriors we speak of."

"I know." Alethia smiled at Beth's faith in her clan and Malcolm's prowess. "I just want everything ready and in one place. There's something else I need to talk to you about. I have to get to the mainland. There are plants I want to gather for medicines."

Red willow grew on the mainland near the shore. She'd seen the bright crimson stems standing out against the brown and tan. The spongy inner bark made a good anti-inflammatory and pain reliever when brewed into a tea. She'd spent countless hours with her aunts, peeling the crimson outer bark to get to the soft, light-green inner bark. She'd also been studying her herbal book for plants that aided healing or acted as antibiotics and antiseptics.

The time had come for her to stop being a guest and to start taking steps toward providing for herself and Hunter. Plump from a long season of feasting on nature's rich bounty, animals would be wearing their thickest furs. She intended to hunt and snare. "Liam won't let me leave the island."

"Aye, so I've heard."

"Any suggestions?"

Beth gave her a suspicious look. "Do ye intend to set out after Malcolm?"

"No. I wouldn't know where to go, and I don't have the supplies needed for such an undertaking." Her frustration boiled over. "I want to gather some plants for medicinal purposes and do a little hunting. That's all."

"I'll speak with Ian. He has a boat. Ye must avoid the ferry and the landing. Liam will be watching."

She thanked her and went in search of Elaine, the only other person with whom she'd share her plans and her whereabouts. The room they shared stood empty, so she set out for the solar. Elaine sat with her mother by the peat fire burning in the hearth. She worked with a spindle to turn the wool in her lap into yarn. "Elaine, come out to the bailey for a walk with me."

"Nay. The day is cold and damp, True," she said without taking her eyes from her task.

"Elaine." Alethia shifted from foot to foot, willing her friend to look at her. Oblivious, Elaine's focus remained on the yarn she twisted, but Lydia noticed and took the cue.

"I've been meaning to speak with the cook," Lydia said, rising from her place. "If you two will excuse me."

Finally Elaine looked her way. "Oh." She looked from her mother to Alethia. "What is it?"

Taking the place Lydia had vacated, Alethia thought about how best to broach what weighed on her mind. "I need your help. I want to get some things to set up a hunting camp. Beth is going to borrow Ian's boat for me. I need a kettle, and a half-barrel from the cooper."

"Malcolm said he would—"

"He's not here, Elaine."

"I'll take you to the tanner, and Malcolm will cover the cost when he returns."

"No." She let her breath out slowly. "I can't go on like this forever."

"Like what, True?" Elaine put her wool down.

The concern in her friend's eyes made it hard to continue. "Elaine, I think . . ." She swallowed the lump in her throat. "I think it's time I thought about my future. I can't be a guest forever. I need to start making a living for myself and Hunter. I want to be useful to the clan."

"Malcolm—"

"Malcolm has been very generous, and I'm grateful. But if he does not return, whose guest will I be then?"

"Mine." Elaine reached for her hands.

"And when you marry, will you take me with you to your husband's keep?" Alethia shook her head. "I need to find a way to take care of myself. I've been thinking about this a lot. Maybe in the spring I can hook up with other musicians, become part of a traveling minstrels' group. Or something."

"Oh no, True. Dinna even think such a thing. Malcolm will return soon. You'll see."

She nodded, unwilling to argue any longer. Whether or not he returned changed nothing. "In the meantime, will you help me get the things I need?"

"I will, though I dinna approve." She frowned.

Dressed in brown wool from head to toe to blend into the background, Alethia woke Hunter in the predawn hours of the morning and urged him to hurry getting dressed. She was anxious to check the snares she'd set the day before, and she wanted to be in the blind she'd prepared by the deer path before sunrise. If all went according to plan, she'd have a brace of coneys or fresh venison to share with the clan this evening.

It had taken a week to set up camp next to a stream feeding the lake. She kept her tools and weapons there, along with a pair of jeans, a long-sleeved tee, and wool jackets she'd made for herself and Hunter. She'd built a wooden rack for drying meat and frames for stretching hides.

She and Hunter crept out of the keep through the kitchen, taking up the oatcakes left for them as they went. They ate their breakfast as they walked along the path through the kitchen garden to the postern gate in the inner curtain wall. She took Hunter's hand and led him to the boat Ian had loaned them, careful to keep to the shadows along the way.

Once on shore, they hid the boat in the brush and followed the stream to the small clearing where their camp was located. Alethia had made a small lean-to under a large oak where she kept her things. She quickly changed into her street clothes and folded her gown and chemise, stowing them away. It wouldn't do to return with bloodstains on her gown, and jeans made everything so much easier to maneuver. Tapping Hunter, she gave directions. "*Stay by me. Do not wander. Watch what I do, and I'll teach you as we go.*" Taking him by the hand again, she set out to check her snares, following the signs she'd left to mark the way.

They passed a thicket of wild roses, and she made a mental note to bring a basket to gather the rose hips. The vitamin C from rose hip tea would be needed during the long winter months ahead. She looked for other useful plants along the way, her eyes searching the ground and brush they passed through.

By midmorning, she'd gutted and skinned six fat hares. They hung from a branch on the oak while she worked to scrape the fat and flesh from their hides. Her kettle of water hung over the fire from the tripod she'd made from green wood. Hunter's job was to keep the fire fed, and he scurried through the forest to collect wood.

She felt good for the first time in days. Her efforts would contribute to the well-being of her tribe—or clan. Tonight the people she cared about would eat a stew made from the hares she'd snared. She had six furs to tan, a good start toward preparing for winter. All her snares were reset, and if they were successful, she'd have six more tomorrow.

Venison could wait. This week, hares and other small animals were the furs du jour.

Work kept her mind off her fear for Malcolm. She didn't let the thought that he might not come back enter her thoughts. When dark feelings threatened, she forced herself to think of other things.

By late afternoon she could do no more. She and Hunter cleaned up and packed everything away for the day. She washed her hands and arms in the warm water she'd kept heated and changed back into her gown. She smothered the fire and gathered the hares. They were bound in pairs by the feet so Hunter could carry his share. "*You were a great help today. Tomorrow we'll come back and check the snares again.*"

"*Tomorrow I get to skin them?*"

Boys and gore. She smiled at him and ruffled his short hair. "*I'll let you try. It looks easier than it is. I've had many years of practice.*" She couldn't help but be pleased. Hunter had shown himself to be an apt student and very eager to learn. Gathering up her share of their burden, she took his hand and started down the path to the boat.

A twig snapped behind her, and she froze. Turning slowly, she probed the shadows surrounding their camp. Hunter tugged on her hand. "*What is it?*" he asked.

"*Probably an animal attracted by the smell of our kills.*" She gave their surroundings one more look. Turning again toward the path, Alethia headed back to the island.

Liam stepped out of the forest into the clearing as True disappeared down the trail, Galen beside him. He looked about him at her handiwork with a mixture of frustration and admiration. "What the devil is she up to?"

"Does she no' realize we can see the smoke from her fire, Liam?"

"Nay, it did no' occur to her." They'd known it couldn't be an enemy's fire. Still, the men on guard duty were puzzled by the smoke rising from the forest. None of the villagers would be out knowing they were on alert for an attack by the Comyns. Relief that they'd come to him rather than investigate on their own washed through him. "You did well to come to me, Galen."

"Aye, I knew it could only be one of our own. We would have seen if there were strangers on our land. What was Lady True wearing? I've never seen the like on a lass." Galen walked around her camp, examining everything.

"I dinna ken." He'd averted his eyes when she'd changed back into her gown and saw to it Galen did as well. 'Twould surely send Malcolm into fits to learn any of his men had watched her disrobe thus. "They must be a garment the men of her country wear. Why does she carry such a garment with her?"

"I dinna ken." Galen shook his head.

Liam walked over to the furs stretched inside their wooden frames. He could scarce believe it. Aye, ladies hunted, but they did not often butcher or skin their kills, nor did they tan the hides. Their clan had a tanner for such. He shook his head. "'Tis obvious she's skilled at what she's about, though I dinna ken the why of it. All she need do is ask for what she needs."

"Would you?" Galen asked.

"Would I what?"

Galen rubbed the back of his neck before he spoke. "If ye were snatched from Scotia, transported to a foreign land far across the ocean, and were taken in by people you did no' ken, would you ask for the things you need?"

"Humph, nay. I'd be anxious to prove myself an asset." Walking over to the lean-to, he reached out to touch the faded indigo fabric of her strange trews. Heavy and coarse, he'd never felt anything like it. Their Lady True held secrets and depths he could only guess at. "Think you our Lady True seeks to prove something here?"

"Mayhap." Galen shrugged. "She's a woman. What do I ken about how a woman reasons?"

Liam grunted. "What do any of us ken about how a woman reasons?" He'd been charged with keeping her safe, and he would. How to do so had been left up to him. "Galen, mayhap 'twould be best to let her continue to hunt. Malcolm wants her to remain on the island behind the curtain wall, but I see no harm being done here. Being occupied thus will keep her mind off worrying about him."

"Malcolm will be displeased."

"Aye." He grinned. "He will. Certainly he would prefer she hunt than to make herself ill pining away for him in her chamber." Besides, Liam admired her skill, and he enjoyed a good coney stew. 'Twas good she kept busy. He'd been concerned when she'd taken to her bed for two days and nights. This seemed the perfect solution.

With a constant guard in the hills surrounding their village, they would have fair warning if an enemy approached. It would be a simple matter to get True back to her boat and to the island now that he knew her exact location. Curiosity overwhelmed him. "What will she hunt next, do you think? Wild boar?" He laughed aloud at the picture in his mind.

"I hope not." Galen shot him a look of alarm. "Malcolm will have our testicles for it if we let her risk such a thing."

"Yours maybe." He grinned at Galen. "I've always been able to outrun him. We'll post a guard, only men we trust. See to it, Galen, and instruct them to keep their distance. We canna have any of them see her disrobe. Form a perimeter of safety unobtrusively. I'll take a turn when I can get away from my duties." He looked around the neat, efficient hunting camp one more time, bid Galen follow and walked back into the shadows of the forest. Shaking his head again, he wondered how Malcolm would react to all of this. Liam looked forward to finding out.

CHAPTER THIRTEEN

In the fortnight since he'd discovered True's hunting camp, Liam had been surprised to learn that everyone working in the keep knew what she was up to. They also knew Malcolm had forbidden her to leave the confines of the curtain wall. And yet, not one of them had come forward to tell him of her daily forays to the mainland.

She had their loyalty.

Their cook, Molly, even went so far as to leave breakfast out each morn for her and Hunter. Even more amusing, they all blamed Malcolm, referring to True as the "puir lass," whom he'd left without first providing for her needs. Putting the last tally down on his inventory, he shook his head and smiled as he left the buttery. The whole situation had become ludicrous.

Entering the great hall from the rear of the keep, Liam heard True's name mentioned. He recognized the voice of Angus's wife, Alice, and stopped to listen.

"You ken what we must do, Margaret," Alice said.

"Aye. There's nothing for it but to find our Lady True a proper husband. I had thought Malcolm would claim her. Though she has no dowry, he certainly seemed inclined."

"Margaret," Alice scolded. "He's the one who caused her to labor as she has in the first place. Nay, to my way o' thinkin', young Robley's our man. My Angus told me he declared for her the day our clan found her."

"Humph, he's a womanizing rapscallion, that one. I say Liam is the best choice for our Lady True. He's always been the more responsible of Robert's two lads. A finer man you couldna find. And comely as well."

"Mayhap, but Robley is willing."

"Ye've a point there," Margaret conceded.

Liam ran his hand over his face and backed away. His amusement turned to dismay. No doubt his little brother would embrace their plan with fervent enthusiasm. Even if he wasn't serious, he'd go along with it to goad Malcolm.

For certes, Liam was in a bind. If *he* procured furs and hides for True, putting an end to her need to hunt, the keep would be rife with speculation he wanted her for himself. And it would make no difference that he claimed to do so on Malcolm's behalf. His people loved to gossip. In their minds, such a scenario would surely lead to an entertaining confrontation between him and Malcolm for True's hand—more fodder for their wagging tongues.

Pretending that he didn't know where True went every morning put him under an enormous strain. No one said a word about the fresh venison and coneys they ate each night for supper. Even his Aunt Lydia turned a blind eye.

Liam left the keep through the kitchen, avoiding the curious looks sent his way by Molly and her assistants. He hoped Malcolm would return soon. He hadn't seen his own Lady Mairen in over a month, and he longed to lose himself in her sweet embrace.

Thoughts of his love turned his mind to the Comyn clan. Now more than ever he and Mairen would have to take care not to be discovered. Once the Comyn laird learned of Malcolm's retribution in Nairn, he'd know for certain he harbored a spy within his holding.

Fearing for Mairen's safety, Liam had taken steps months ago to plant someone he trusted in the Comyn keep to watch over her. And even though Mairen had not been the source of Liam's information, the Comyn laird would take his frustration out on his only daughter. Just as he'd done with Mairen's mother, until the day she died. He'd killed his own wife, and none would convict him. 'Twas a beating gone too far, one too many times.

The setting sun sent golden beams of light through the trees surrounding her clearing, alerting Alethia it was time to pack it up for the day and return to the island. She and Hunter were loading the boat when the warning horn sounded in the village. Two tones.

It *had* to be Malcolm and his men!

Alethia threw their things in a heap on the bottom of the dingy, helped Hunter in and shoved the boat off the shore in a rush. Only two tones had sounded. Did that mean there were no wounded? She rowed for all she was worth, aiming the small boat like a missile for the island. Once there, she dragged it into the brush, grabbed what she could carry and started for the keep, confident that Hunter would follow with whatever he could manage. She'd return later for the rest.

The moment she entered the kitchen, all eyes turned to her. The concern emanating from them nearly bowled her over. "What is it?"

"It's Malcolm, lass." Molly walked over and took the bundles Alethia held.

"Where is he?" Her heart hammered against her ribcage, and her mouth went dry. She'd known. All along she'd known something would happen, and now it had. She tried to swallow past the lump and couldn't.

"In the great hall being tended by his men. He's been hurt. I'm boiling water as ye said to if there be wounded." Molly gestured to the cauldron in the hearth. "What would ye have me do with it, my lady?"

"*Fetch my basket for healing and bring it to the great hall. You know which one I mean?*" she signed to Hunter. He nodded and was off in a flash. Alethia ran. As she reached the great hall, the sight before her froze her to the spot. Angus approached Malcolm's bloodied body lying prone on one of the plank tables, a knife glowing red hot in his hand. Alethia gasped in horror. "*Stop!* Don't you *dare* touch him with that!"

Angus froze, startled by her shout, and Liam took her by the arms, turning her away from Malcolm. "True, we must stop the bleeding. His wound is deep, and he's lost too much blood already. 'Tis certain to cause fever if not cauterized. This would have been done in the field if Malcolm hadn't insisted he be brought home first."

"It must be done quickly." Angus moved toward the table.

She jerked herself free of Liam's hold and placed herself between Malcolm and the glowing blade. "I want to see him." Cautiously she moved closer. Malcolm was deathly pale, his clothing soaked in blood. His eyes found hers. She swallowed the sob threatening to escape and bent to examine him just as his eyes rolled back in his head and his body went limp.

His wound had been unwrapped to sear. He'd been cut open from his left clavicle to the bend in his elbow. Alethia could see exposed bone at his shoulder, and the deep cut through the bicep oozed blood. "If you sear him with that blade, his arm will be damaged forever."

"If I dinna, he could die from blood loss or fever, lass. Give way." Angus took her forearm to move her from her place. For the first time, she noticed the others in the hall. Lydia and Elaine stood frozen in place as Alethia stood firm. "Lydia?" Alethia met her eyes.

"He's your son. Will you let me try to help him?" Lydia nodded, and relief washed through her.

"Beth, get me hot water from the kitchen." Hunter ran to her side with her basket. "I need light."

Elaine responded immediately, bringing lit candles close and placing them on the table. Alethia's hands trembled as she rolled up the sleeves of her chemise. What did she know about stitching flesh? Nothing. She only knew the wound needed to be cleaned and disinfected to prevent fever, or worse, gangrene. This was Malcolm. She couldn't fail him. Surely this was the moment for which she'd been brought to this time and place.

Beth returned with hot water, and Alethia washed her shaking hands and arms with the soap she'd tucked away. As she began the daunting task of cleaning Malcolm's wound, thoughts of tetanus from a rusted blade flitted through her mind. Dear God, so much could go wrong. She fought the urge to retch, and inhaled deeply several times and forced the fear out of her mind. Stitching skin together couldn't be that difficult. Certainly not any more difficult than sewing deer hide.

Except this was the man she loved lying before her so pale and still.

If she had been with him, could she have prevented him from being wounded? Anger and frustration at being left behind flooded her—and her hands steadied. Glad for the moment he was out cold, she doused the wound with the whiskey.

Alethia hovered, threaded needle in hand, unsure how to proceed. What stitch should she use? Holding her breath, she made the first stitch near the bend in his elbow, wanting to get to the deepest part of the cut first. She concentrated fully on closing the wound and worked silently for what seemed like hours. Her back ached from bending over him. A hand came to rest on her shoulder, and Alethia glanced up for a second to see Lydia by her side.

"He'll live, True. He's lost quite a bit of blood, and he will be weak for a se'nnight at least, but 'tis no' a mortal wound if he's no' taken with a fever."

Alethia nodded, turning back to her task. When had the tears started? Malcolm's breathing seemed too shallow, and his skin felt cold and clammy. "Beth," she called.

"Aye, Lady True?" She was at her side in seconds.

"Can you get blankets to cover him? And please ask Molly to prepare a hot broth of beef or venison. He'll need fluids."

"Besides the wound, he took a nasty blow to the head." Robley stood at her elbow. "We were ambushed not a league from home. 'Twas Hugh and the remaining Comyns we routed from Meikle Geddes."

"And what of Hugh?" Elaine asked the question that burned in Alethia's mind.

"Once he knew he couldn't win, he fled like the coward he is," Robley said, his tone flat.

"And you did no' pursue him?" Lydia asked.

"Nay. We had Malcolm to tend, and he wished to come home."

"Hugh's day will come," Angus added grimly. "Malcolm will want the privilege himself, aye?"

Once she finished stitching him back together, Liam and Angus came to carry him to his chamber. She followed, anxious to remain by his side.

Lydia stopped her. "My dear, you are needed in the hall. There are other wounds to tend. Malcolm's chamber is no place for you right now. Once he's taken care of, then you may go to his side with Elaine in attendance."

"But—"

"Liam and Angus will see he's bathed and put to bed." Lydia turned her by the shoulders and gave her a gentle push away from the stairs.

She watched Liam and Angus as they carried Malcolm away from her, turning reluctantly to help with the many injuries the other men had sustained. She urged Elaine and Lydia to wash the wounds with soap and to douse them with whiskey. After each wound had been tended, she liberally applied her Neosporin.

"My lady, here's the broth ye asked for." Molly came into the great hall, carrying a steaming earthenware bowl on a wooden tray.

Alethia took it from her, glad to have a reason to go to Malcolm. "Thank you, Molly. Elaine, do you know where Hunter is?"

"Aye, he finished unloading your . . . er . . . he finished a chore for you, and I sent him to the kitchen to be fed, and then he's to go on to bed."

Their eyes met for a brief instant of understanding. She nodded. "Lydia, may we go to Malcolm now?"

"Aye, go. I will finish here."

Malcolm awoke to the sound of snoring. Disoriented, he struggled to recall where he was and what had happened. The left side of his body burned like the devil, and his head throbbed with each pulse of his heart. A single candle in a stand next to his bed illuminated his surroundings. He lay in his own chamber. Vague recollections came back to him. He remembered being roused, held up to sitting while True poured broth down his throat. "God's blood, I'm thirsty," he croaked.

Who gripped his hand?

He turned his head slightly, seeking the source of the snoring. His heart melted at the sight. True sat in a chair by his bed, holding onto his hand with both of her own. She'd fallen forward, her head on the mattress and her neck at an awkward angle. 'Twould pain her on the morrow. He smiled. His woman snored.

Malcolm knew he should wake her and send her off to her chamber to rest. 'Twas not proper for her to be here in the middle of the night, but he hadn't the will to part with her.

Bare beneath the covers, he wondered who had removed his garments. He'd been bathed as well. Had True cared for him as a wife would her husband? He imagined her washing his battered body with tender care.

Another vague recollection came to him. He'd fought to remain awake until he'd seen her worried face hovering above him in his own keep. Once he knew True stood by his side, he'd succumbed to the blackness, certain all would be well.

Malcolm lifted his head to glance down at his injured arm. He couldn't help the snort of amusement from escaping. Checking to see she'd not been disturbed by the sound, he put his head back on the pillow and grinned into the candlelit shadows. The stitched skin now resembled his lady's most recent embroidery project. Crimson, white, and the darkest green threads formed a feathery pattern down the length of the wound. MacKintosh colors. God's blood, 'twas good to be home.

Nay. He would not wake her. Disentangling his hand from her grip, Malcolm pushed himself up to a sitting position, going still until the dizziness and nausea passed. He swung his feet to the floor and looked about his chamber. Spying two covered bowls on the table near his bed, thirst overcame him. He reached for the nearest, finding it held more of the broth True had fed him earlier. He drank it all and reached for the next. He inhaled. 'Twas a tea made from rose hips, chamomile and other herbs he did not recognize, and sweetened with honey. He downed the entire bowl. His thirst slaked for the moment, Malcolm set himself to the task of transferring True to his bed.

He pushed himself to stand, fighting the pain and dizziness. Nausea assailed him again. Using his bedstead for support, he worked his way around to her side. He hoped to God she'd stitched him well, for what he was about to do might very well reopen the wound. Squatting next to her, Malcolm put his arms under her knees and eased her back until he could put one arm under her neck. Using his legs and the chair to aid him, he leveraged her onto the mattress. Sweat beaded his brow from the pain and effort, and he arranged her as comfortably as possible.

He breathed heavily from the exertion and leaned against a bedpost until he recovered. He reached for furs to cover her, then worked his way back to his side of the mattress, sliding gratefully back between the linens. With his good arm, he tucked her against his side. Content at last, his head fell back onto the pillow, and sleep took him far from the pain.

The sound of his chamber door opening woke him. Malcolm opened his eyes to glance first at the woman asleep beside him, and then to the shocked expressions worn by Liam and Robley. One of True's legs covered both of his just above his knees. Her arm had found its way around his waist, and her head rested upon his good shoulder. Possessively, he reached down to cover her exposed calf, and he scowled at his cousins, chagrined. What had seemed a good idea in the dark of night, in the light of day proved to be folly.

Liam cleared his throat. Robley stared openmouthed, and Malcolm nodded toward the door. Thankfully, Liam grasped his meaning, crossing the room to shut it. Malcolm gently shook his sleeping beauty. True stretched and yawned, opening her eyes in the process.

Malcolm could clearly see the confusion in her eyes as she sat up and looked down at him. "How did I come to be in your bed?"

"Och, lass. You canna seem to keep your hands off me." He grinned as her eyes grew wide. Robley coughed, no doubt in an effort to contain his laughter, drawing True's attention to the fact that they were not alone. Malcolm watched as a delightful blush colored her cheeks. Without speaking, she reached out to feel his forehead.

Removing her hand, she rose from the bed with dignity, straightened her gown and stood with her back straight.

"There is no fever," she proclaimed. "Please inform Malcolm that I am not speaking to him." She graced him with a glare. "He left without telling me." Lifting her chin, she stomped to the door, threw the latch and slammed it behind her.

He and his cousins stared after her in silence, shocked when she stormed back two seconds later. Circling his bed to the side where she'd sat, she lifted the basket she'd forgotten and left again without a word, refusing to look at any of them.

"True is not talking to you, Malcolm," Robley informed him through his laughter. "She'll share your bed, but dinna expect conversation."

Liam cleared his throat again. "Malcolm, I must ask. What do you intend to do about our Lady True?"

Malcolm closed his eyes and rested his aching head against his pillow. "I had intended that we would wed in the spring upon my father's return. 'Tis clear I canna wait until then. I'll send to Edinburgh for a priest, though 'tis unlikely we'll see him arrive before spring with winter fast upon us."

"Sweeten the offer with a generous tithe," Liam suggested. "Robley, would you see to dispatching the missive? I need a word with Malcolm in private."

Something in Liam's tone alarmed Malcolm. "Before you see to writing the request, have Molly send me a tray to break my fast," he told Robley. "And ale. Have her send ale. I've a powerful thirst."

Robley closed the door behind him, and Liam raked his hand through his hair, clearly unsure where to begin.

"Dinna waste your breath scolding me, Liam. In my present state, I could do naught but sleep. True's virtue is safe, and I trow neither you nor Robley will speak of this to anyone."

Liam shook his head. "That is the least of my worries. Since the day we found her, I've kent the two of you would marry."

"What vexes you then?"

"It started within the keep and has since spread throughout the clan."

"What has? Is there an illness amongst our people?"

"Nay, no illness." Liam glanced into his eyes then turned his gaze to the floor. "Our clan is determined to find a suitable husband for True."

"Aye, myself." Malcolm shrugged his good shoulder.

"Nay, Malcolm." Liam sent him a sheepish look and shook his head. "You are no' on the list the elders have compiled. No' even at the very end."

"I'm no' on what list? She is *mine*." Malcolm made to rise, but he gave it up as he listened, dumbstruck, to Liam's accounting of True's activities over the past month. He'd been blamed, and rightly so. She had asked him for hides and furs, and he'd neglected to provide them before leaving. Liam described in detail his clan's loyalty to the foreigner they now viewed as their own.

"How is it she left the island without your knowledge?" he asked once Liam had finished. "I specifically commanded she remain behind the curtain wall."

"She had help. The weaver's son lent her a small fishing boat. Cook left her breakfast each morn. Elaine secured needed equipage, and Lydia turned a blind eye, ignoring your wishes. By the time our sentries spied the smoke from her fire, she'd already been at it a se'nnight. I saw no harm in keeping her busy whilst you were away, and I posted guards to keep her safe. I did no' foresee . . . that is . . . I never imagined things would take the turn they have."

"Think you she'll go to the mainland today?" Malcolm's frustration with his own physical weakness sparked his temper.

"I dinna ken. 'Tis unlikely. Surely she's exhausted this morn."

"Liam—"

"I mean from tending the wounded." He grinned.

A knock sounded on his door. "Enter." His mother came in with a tray of food. The smell of freshly baked bread and meat made Malcolm's mouth water, and his stomach gave an audible growl. Mayhap he'd feel stronger after he ate.

"True spent the night in your chamber, my lad."

He groaned. Liam laughed, and Malcolm sent him a quelling glare. "You've things to attend to, aye?" Still snorting, his cousin left him to face his mother's accusations alone.

Malcolm rubbed his temples with both hands; his head throbbed. "True fell asleep. I only saw to her comfort."

"Rather than wake her and send her off to her own bed where she belonged, you mean?" Lydia raised an eyebrow. "Here, drink this." She handed him a mug from the tray she'd set on his lap. "True sent it up for your headache." She waited as he took a sip of the bitter brew. "I ken naught happened. All saw the state you were in. We sent True off to bed when it was clear she would soon drop from exhaustion. I suspected she'd make her way back to your chamber. As we tended the wounded, I watched her."

"She was up to something?" Malcolm swallowed more of the bitter tea and looked at his mother over the top of the mug.

"Och, aye. She bade us wash everyone's wounds with soap and then insisted we use perfectly good *uisge beatha* to bathe the wounds again. When she thought none were watching, she took something out of her basket, a salve of some kind, and smeared it over their injuries. I checked this morn. Not one of the injuries she treated thus has festered."

"Humph."

"Well, don't you see? For some unfathomable reason, she's hiding the concoction. True came back to your chamber late last night while you slept to put the salve on your arm."

Malcolm rubbed a finger across his skin near the stitches. It came away with a film of something greasy. He rubbed his finger and his thumb together and brought them to his nose. He could detect no scent. "She's no' speaking to me."

"No doubt. She was quite distressed to find you'd left without a word. Liam caught her just before she took one of the villager's skiffs to follow you. True took to her bed for two days, and it required a good deal of persuasion to roust her. I am certain her distress is why Liam allowed her . . . um . . . activities on the mainland to continue."

"I missed her." Malcolm had to swallow hard several times.

"I am certain you did, Malcolm. Eat. You must regain your strength quickly."

"Quickly?"

"Have you no' heard? You are no' even *on* the list of suitable husbands for our True." She laughed at the sour expression on his face.

"I've sent for a priest."

"'Tis unlikely we'll see one before spring, and the clan may have her handfasted ere long. Some treasures have naught to do with coin, jewels or land." His mother gave him an arch look. "Do you ken my meaning?"

"Of course I ken your meaning, Mother. Am I no' your son? Will she come see me, do you think?"

"Aye. Whilst you sleep. And only to put more salve on your wound."

"Send Beth to me." He tore into the meal on his lap.

"As you wish." His mother patted his knee and rose to leave. "Do put something on before she arrives." She fetched his robe from the peg where it hung and draped it over his bed.

Clothed and his hunger sated, Malcolm rested his head against his pillow and thought about everything he'd learned this morn. His head had ceased throbbing, no doubt due to the bitter tea his lady had sent. He smiled. She would not speak to him, yet still she saw to his care.

As soon as Beth fetched her for him, he'd beg her forgiveness, hold her close and kiss her sweet lips until she moaned into his mouth. He closed his eyes, allowing the fantasy to unfold behind his eyes.

"Milord, you wished to see me?" Beth opened his door a crack and peered in.

"Aye. Go to your lady and bid her come to me anon. I would speak with her."

"Aye, my lord."

She curtsied and shut the door, and he closed his eyes to take up the fantasy where he'd left off. All would be set right soon.

True took far too long responding to his summons. Malcolm became impatient, frustrated and wanted out of his sickbed. A knock sounded on his door. He blew out a breath, relieved she'd arrived at long last. "Enter."

Beth walked through the door, looking as if she feared the worst. "My lady said I'm to *quote* her exactly." She twisted her gown with her hands. "But I dinna ken the word's meaning, ye see."

Malcolm let his head fall to his pillow. "It means you are to say her words exactly as she said them."

"Oh." Beth's face smoothed. "Well then." She took a breath. "Lady True says to tell ye, '*He's no' the bossamee.*'" She nodded. "Do ye ken what it means?"

"Aye." He closed his eyes and massaged his throbbing temples. "I ken what it means."

CHAPTER FOURTEEN

Using the walls, his bed and anything else within reach for support, Malcolm walked slowly around his chamber to regain his strength. It had been three days since he and his men returned, and he'd had enough of his bed. Since the night True had slept in his arms, he'd not caught even a glimpse of her. Frustration at his weakness ate at him. Her refusal to obey his summons infuriated him, and restlessness, combined with everything else, had him feeling like a caged animal.

It should have been a simple thing—stay awake through the night and catch her when she came with her ointment. But his body betrayed him, and he'd slept through her ministrations to wake with the dawn knowing she'd been there. Her floral scent lingered—had she? Had she held his hand for a moment, or stroked his brow?

His arm itched like the devil. He knew it meant the injury healed well, still 'twas another torture to add to his growing list of complaints. Malcolm snatched his robe from the peg and struggled into it. He wanted a bath and a hearty meal. Both would do much to revive him. Then he intended to go after True and force her to reason.

A knock on his chamber door sent his heart racing. "Enter." Elaine walked in with a tray. He took a seat by the hearth, exhaling his disappointment on an audible sigh.

"I'm not who you hoped to see." Elaine smiled as she arranged his breakfast on the table. "Still, I need a word with you."

"Aye? What revelations will you share this morn, sister mine? I've had a belly full of late, and find I suffer indigestion."

"'Tis about True." She handed him a mug of the bitter tea for his pain. "There are things I should have told you ere now."

"If you mean to tell me about her hunting, or that the clan means to marry her off to Robley or Liam, you are too late." He scowled at her. "I've already been told."

"Nay, Malcolm. 'Tis something True told me during the harvest. She mentioned you and Father believe Giselle drugged her and sent her to Scotia by ship."

"Aye?" He ate his breakfast, curious where Elaine was going with this.

"She told me what really occurred with Madame Giselle. She was no' drugged or sent here by ship. 'Twas magic that brought her here. She had nothing to eat or drink in the woman's company."

"Elaine—"

"Dinna give me that look." She straightened with a scowl and placed her hands on her hips. "How oft have we heard of some person disappearing, only to return months later with fantastic tales of some foreign land they say they found themselves in?" Her eyes offered a challenge. "Their stories are always the same. They have no inkling how they got there or how they got back. Mayhap this Madame Giselle is fae. I have no reason to doubt True. There's no reason for her to concoct such a tale, and she seemed loath to share it. 'Twould be far simpler to hold to the version you and Father concocted."

Malcolm shook his head, considering the possibility. "I will no' argue. I concede, I've heard the stories you speak of."

"She's afraid Giselle will take her away from us the same way. True loves you, Malcolm. She fears giving her heart if she's to be plucked from your side at any moment."

"She told you this?" He sat up straighter at the first good news he'd heard since his return.

"Aye. She also told me she plans to leave us to become part of a traveling minstrels' group come spring if Giselle hasna returned her to her home by then."

"The devil you say." His brow rose. "Why would she do such a thing?"

"She is frightened of being taken from us and frightened by an uncertain future. Put yourself in her place. True feels she is only a guest here. She worries our hospitality will come to an end. She told me it is time for her to find a way to support herself and Hunter on her own."

"This is my fault."

"Aye, 'tis all your fault." She grinned at him. "Now set it aright."

"Send someone to fetch Liam for me. Have him meet me in the great hall by Sext."

"I will. 'Tis good to see you up and about, Malcolm. I'm glad you are home."

Malcolm reached for her hand, giving it a squeeze. "'Tis good to be home."

Robley grinned at Malcolm as he descended the stairs to the great hall. "Up and about, cousin? I've come in Liam's stead. He's on the mainland doing guard duty. I believe this is the day he guards our Lady True."

"Can you tell me where she is?"

"Aye. I take my turn guarding her camp. We all do." He chuckled. "True has no idea she is so well protected. There is no' a single MacKintosh here who does no' ken what she does each and every day, yet none speak of it."

"Take me to her."

"*I* am the clan's first choice to wed the lass."

"Robley, dinna push me." Malcolm's control was at an end. He glared at his cousin and stood his ground.

"Humph. Let us be off." Robley turned on his heel and headed to the ferry landing.

The day was uncharacteristically fair for this time of year, and Malcolm was glad for the sun warming him as the ferry took them across the loch. He surveyed the forest, now bare of leaves, and spied True's thin column of smoke. Had she no sense at all? He shook his head and frowned. 'Twas a good thing Liam had maintained the perimeter guard, for surely her camp would have been a beacon for brigands and worse. The thought of Black Hugh riding the hills crossed his mind, and a chill slipped down his spine.

"I ken what you're thinking, Malcolm." Robley met his gaze with a grave expression. "She's no' been raised in the Highlands or in the manner we have. It hasna occurred to her the smoke gives her away. She's no' had an easy time of it. Consider her tender feelings before you crush her further."

"Think you I dinna ken I'm to blame for this?" Malcolm scowled at his cousin. "You need no' worry about her tender feelings."

"Aye, but I do. If she refuses you, I *will* offer for her."

Malcolm had never before seen Robley so serious. "She will no' refuse me."

His cousin made no reply as the ferry landed.

Robley had described where her camp had been set, and Malcolm immediately knew the place of which his cousin spoke. 'Twas just around the next bend in the burn flowing toward the loch. Careful to keep quiet, he rounded the curve and came to a halt. The sight caused his eyes to widen and his jaw to drop. All thoughts for her tender feelings fled. He stomped into the clearing with every muscle in his body tense. "Alethia," he growled. "You will get dressed this instant."

She jerked around, a startled look on her face. "Oh crap."

"Oh *crap* indeed. What are you wearing?" He couldn't take his eyes from her. The blue trews she wore fit her like skin, showing every feminine curve right up to the juncture of her thighs. Her chemise was no better. Clinging to her as it did, he could see the contours of her breasts and the dark outline of her nipples right through the fabric. The thought of other men seeing her garbed thus enraged him—and this had been going on for weeks. "You are finished here," he ground out through his clenched jaw.

"No." She turned her back to him, arranging a hide over a tripod of branches.

"You insult my hospitality and think to defy me?" He took a step toward her. "I bade you remain behind the curtain wall until my return."

Facing him, she straightened and met his scowl with one of her own. "This has nothing to do with insulting your hospitality or defying your commands. In fact, this has nothing to do with you at all. You left me."

Her words were spoken without rancor, yet they fell across his skin like a lash, leaving behind an angry welt. "Nay, lass. I—"

"Yes, Malcolm. You *left* me." She fed the fire under the hide, her back to him once again. "I'm grateful, because it forced me to take stock of my situation."

Her calmness disturbed him, though he could not put his finger on why. "Your situation?"

"What would become of me if you hadn't returned? At what point do I cease being a guest and start pulling my own weight?" She lifted her chin. "It's time I make a place and a life for myself."

"Alethia . . ." The welt her words had opened became a gaping wound.

"In my world, I knew where I belonged. In your world, I have no place. Things aren't so different between your country and mine. A woman must be provided for and protected by a father, a brother, an uncle . . . a male relative . . ." *A husband.* She shrugged her shoulders. "Here I have no one. Don't you see? I must make my own way, earn my keep."

Her shrug nearly undid him. Her vulnerability was like salt in the wound her words had opened. Such a wee thing to be so all alone in an unfamiliar world. "'Tis all my fault." He stepped closer, taking her hands in his. She tried to tug them free. He held tight, examining them front and back. They were chapped, raw and callused. He swallowed hard. "Do you remember the day I found you?"

"Of course."

"I took note of your hands that day. They were so soft and smooth, with nary a callus to mar their perfection. I knew you were a gently bred lady."

She snatched her hands from his grasp. "Nothing is your fault, Malcolm. Don't you think I realize how fortunate I am that you took me in?" She shuddered and rubbed her arms. "What would have happened if someone like Hugh had found me first?"

"It *is* my fault. You're my responsibility." His words came out in a hoarse rasp.

"Where did you get that idea?" She snorted. "You're not obligated to me in any way. I'm not your responsibility just because Giselle left me on your path." Her chin lifted, but her eyes didn't meet his. "I am grateful for the roof over my head and the food I have eaten at your table. Now it's time I stopped acting like your guest and start repaying my debt."

This had naught to do with defying him and everything to do with her uncertainty. And her pride. He gazed around the camp, noting for the first time the neatly stacked furs and skins, the strips of meat drying over a second fire.

He'd failed her. He *had* left her—alone, frightened and uncertain about her future in a foreign land. The insight laid him low. He was the worst kind of churl. Not only had he neglected to see to her needs, he'd neglected to let her know her place in his life—and in his heart. He took their future together for granted while she had no inkling they even had a future. Overcome, he moved away from her, needing distance to gain control of his roiling emotions.

Did she still care for him? He certainly didn't deserve it if she did. Yet, every night she came to tend to his wound, and every day her tea eased his aches and pains, helping him to heal. He knew what he had to do, what he should have done from the very start.

His sister had said Alethia feared being taken from them at any time. Her pride and independence were important to her. It would be best to secure her future without her knowing what he intended. She'd object. Or worse, she'd bolt.

"Would you feel better if you were a MacKintosh, Alethia? 'Twould give you a measure of security, would it no'?" He returned to her side as she continued to work. "You'd have a place."

"You mean like being adopted into the clan?" She sat back on her heels and looked up at him. "My people have a ceremony like that. It's called 'relative by choice.' It's a very serious promise. Is that what you mean?"

"Something like that, aye." He watched as she brought a thumbnail to her mouth while thinking it over. God's blood, he longed to take her into his arms and hold her. This path had to be trod carefully. He did not want to frighten her into rebellion.

"It would be an honor to become a MacKintosh, but it wouldn't really change anything. I'd still earn my own way."

"I have your consent?"

"Yes, Malcolm." She nodded, her eyes large and grave.

The solemn look on her face tugged at his heart. "Get dressed, lass. I dinna want any of my men to see you thus." He took several steps away and turned toward the forest, acutely aware of her presence. The sounds of garments being removed and replaced caused his body to tighten and his blood to heat.

"Malcolm?"

"Aye, lass."

"Just because I become a MacKintosh, doesn't mean that you're—"

"Dinna say it," he growled.

"Don't say what?"

"Dinna say that I am no' a bossamee." The sound of her laughter healed the welt her words had left on his hide. He grinned into the forest. All would be well.

"It's three words, Malcolm. Boss. Of. Me. Boss refers to someone who has authority over a person."

"Authority, you say? And as you see it, I dinna have authority over you?"

"Nope. I am my own boss."

He grinned. "Hmmm. Once you become a MacKintosh, you will be under my authority. All the clan is, lass."

"That's different. I'm talking personal authority, and you're talking clan authority."

"Aye?" Glancing at her out of the corner of his eye, he saw she'd dressed once again in a proper gown. Giving a sharp whistle, he waited for his men to answer his summons. Robley and Liam were the first to appear. True's surprised expression amused him. Galen came forward next, along with his brother, Gareth. Angus took up the rear. Malcolm spoke to them in rapid Gaelic. Liam nodded and came forward. With his knife, he cut a strip from the end of Malcolm's *feileadh breacan.* The rest of his men formed a loose circle in the clearing.

"Alethia, come to me." Once she stood next to him, he reached for her right hand, taking hold of it around the wrist with his right hand. Liam wrapped the strip of plaid around their joined wrists several times, binding the ends together in a knot. "What is your whole name, *mo cridhe?*"

"Alethia Grace Goodsky."

"True Grace." He smiled into her eyes as his men murmured appreciation. "I will speak first. Then I will tell you what to say in response. 'Twill be spoken in Gàidhlig." She nodded, her eyes wide with trust. He spoke his vows quickly.

"I'll say the words for your response, and you repeat them." True nodded, and he began. He knew she strained to understand what she was saying. Her brow furrowed in concentration, her head tilted slightly as if doing so would help her hear the words more clearly.

"*Mo colann* means my body. What am I to do with my body, Malcolm?"

"We'll think of something, lass." His men chortled. Alethia's expression went from curious to suspicious in a trice. "Ah, you're pledging your fealty, Alethia. Many of our words have different meanings depending on how they're used."

She studied him for a moment, nodded and told him to proceed. 'Twas the truth, and he was certain she'd read it from him. Once she completed her vows, he leaned down and kissed her lightly.

"Galen, see that my wife's things are packed and taken to the island."

"What? Wait. *Wife?*" Alethia's eyes went around the circle of men, twice, before she could look at Malcolm. "What just happened here?"

"We handfasted."

"What does that mean?"

He leaned down close to her ear, and his warm breath sent a tingle down to her toes. "It means we've said our wedding vows before God and witnesses." He repeated the vows—in English this time: "I, Malcolm

William, son of William of clan MacKintosh, pledge my troth to thee, Alethia Grace Goodsky. With my hands, I shall provide for thee. With my body, I pledge to protect thee. With my heart, I shall cherish thee, and only thee, all the days of my life. As God is my witness, and before my clan, from this day forward, we are husband and wife."

He grinned. "You are my wife. I am your husband."

"I see no priest here." Alethia could hardly breathe; her heart beat a quick staccato in her chest.

"Priests are hard to come by in the Highlands, Cousin True." Robley gave her a brief hug, his usual grin absent. "Unions take place without the benefit of a priest's blessing because we are so far removed from society. Rather than have us all live in sin, the Church has sanctioned handfasting as legal and binding. A priest comes in the spring to bless all the handfasted couples and baptize their bairns."

Stars danced before her eyes, and the world spun. "No." She tugged at their bound wrists, her hand trembling as she tried to work the knot free with one hand. "You should have said. I can't . . . I can't go through . . . No, no, *no!*" She stomped her foot.

"Leave us," Malcolm commanded his men.

Her whole body trembled, and panic made her frantic to untie their bound wrists. "Why did you do this? You didn't ask. I can't go through that again. I can't."

Malcolm took one side of the knot and held it so she could work it free. He unwrapped the strip of wool and tucked it into his sporran. "You canna go through what again, Alethia?"

She tried to bring air into her lungs and couldn't get enough. No way did she want to have this conversation, but the devil drew her into his arms, and she was lost. His solid strength felt so damn good, so warm, safe. She burst into tears.

"Wheesht, love." His hand went up and down her back. "What is it that you canna go through again?"

"I can't sit around for a month waiting to hear that you're . . . you're . . ." She put her arms around his waist and sobbed into his chest. "I didn't think you would come back. I thought I'd lost you. I can't love you only to lose you." Placing her ear on his chest, she listened to the beat of his heart. God, she'd missed him. "Don't men here *ask* a woman first before marrying them?"

"I did ask."

"No you didn't."

"Aye, I did. I asked if being a MacKintosh would make you feel better. Now you're a MacKintosh."

"You didn't tell me becoming a MacKintosh involved getting married!" His smug tone lit the wick of her already frayed nerves. "This doesn't count. I need to go home. I have a future, a family . . . and . . . and . . . Juilliard."

"Who is this Juilliard you speak of?"

Malcolm's voice had gone hard, and her head started to throb. "Juilliard is a place, not a person. Everything that meant *anything* to me has been snatched away." She massaged her temples.

"Everything?"

The hurt in his voice penetrated the fog in her mind, and suddenly everything seemed too much to bear. "Your father will never approve. I have nothing to offer to this union." She closed her eyes against the conflict of emotions overwhelming her. She loved him. She loved her family. "Am I never to see my home and family again?"

"You said yourself the Norse have ventured to your land in the past. If they can make the journey, we can as well. What say you to that?" He leaned down to peer into her eyes. "If I were to take you home, would it ease your mind? Would it no' give your family peace to see you well settled?"

She looked at him through her tears. "You would do that for me?" Of course it couldn't happen, but still the offer melted her insides.

Her heart lurched. A life with Malcolm tempted her away from her fears—life without him seemed a far worse proposition.

"Aye. I mean to do all in my power to make you happy. Dinna vex yourself about my father. I am my own man and make my own choices. I care naught for more land. You bring yourself to our union, and 'tis more than enough for me."

Malcolm put his arms around her once again, and she swallowed the constriction lodged in her throat.

"You said you wanted a large family, aye?" He lifted her chin and brushed his lips against hers. "I want that as well. We can start right away. Tonight."

Her body shivered from his touch, and his words were a seductive promise. "What about Giselle? What will we do when she comes for me?"

"I willna let her take you." His tone carried a hard edge, like the blade of his claymore.

"You don't know . . . I haven't told you everything."

"It matters not. Giselle will no' take you. I vowed to protect you, and I will." His hold tightened. "Have faith in me, lass."

"Why, Malcolm? Why did you do this?" She longed to place her faith in him, to let go of the fear she lived with every day.

"I won't have you worry about the future another moment. As my wife your place is secure. Today is our wedding day, Alethia. I had intended that we would wed since the day I found you by the side of the road. 'Twas my wish to wait until spring and my father's return."

"Spring?" Her mind went back to their day in the forest. "When you said you couldn't wait until spring, that day we . . ."

"Aye, *mo céile*, and I've already sent for a priest. We may see one ere long. Will you agree to be my wife if we say our vows before a priest?"

His expression was so tender and hopeful her heart melted in her chest. She snuggled closer to his body. "*Now* you're asking?" She snorted against his shoulder. "What does *mo céile* mean anyway?"

"My wife."

"What's the word for husband?"

He took her earlobe between his teeth, sending a delicious shiver racing down her spine, and whispered into her ear.

"Boss."

"Ha! In your dreams." She burrowed her head into his shoulder to hide her smile. "Yes, Malcolm. I will agree to be your wife. Do you think . . . ?"

"The word for husband is the same as the word for wife. Do I think what, Alethia?"

"Is this what I was sent here to do?" She touched his wounded arm. "Has the danger passed?"

He put his finger under her chin, tilting her face up so their eyes met. "There will always be danger. 'Tis the way of things."

She nodded and let go of the final thread of resistance. Today was her wedding day, and Malcolm her husband. And if she stayed in his arms until the trembling stopped, maybe everything would be all right. Reality sank deep into her bones—her future lay here in the past. Her family, Gran—they'd be fine without her, and she'd keep them always in her heart. "Don't you *ever* do that again."

"You have my word. I willna leave without letting you know first, but I canna promise never to defend our people again." His eyes held hers until she nodded. "Where is Hunter?" he asked, releasing her from his arms. "'Tis time we return to the island."

Pointing to the oak, True moved to the trunk. "He's supposed to be my guard." She peered up into the tree where the trunk split. "The little traitor, he's asleep." She smiled. "About Hunter . . ."

Malcolm reached up and lifted him from his perch. "From this day forward, he is our son."

Hunter's eyes opened in confusion as Malcolm settled him against his chest. His eyes sought hers, and she told him the news. "*Malcolm and I are husband and wife. He is your foster father.*" She watched as

Hunter's expression turned to wonder. He leaned back to look into Malcolm's face for a moment, put his small arms around his new father's neck, his head on his shoulder, and smiled at her as if he knew all along this was how things would work out.

"We've a wedding feast to attend. Are you recovered enough for my men to return?"

"Malcolm, about your men—"

"They've been guarding your camp since the first day you lit a fire, True. The smoke gave you away."

"Oh." Why hadn't she thought of that? "Why didn't Liam say anything?"

Malcolm gave her the smile that always made her weak in the knees. "Aye, well . . . he likes a good coney stew."

CHAPTER FIFTEEN

From her place in Elaine's chamber, Alethia could hear the sounds of the pipes and bodhran from the great hall below. "Beth," she said, glancing at the young woman over her shoulder. "You should be downstairs dancing."

"Aye, Lady True. I will be ere long." She smiled. "After I've seen ye ready for your wedding night."

Color flooded her cheeks. It wasn't that she didn't know what to expect, and it wasn't prudishness that made her cheeks heat up. Everyone in the keep—no, make that everyone on the entire island—would know that she and Malcolm were consummating their vows tonight. The notion sent mortification burning straight through her.

Beth pulled the brush through her hair as Alethia sat by the hearth. Her meager belongings had already been moved to Malcolm's room. She'd seen to it herself to ensure that no one fished around in her duffel. Bathed, petted and pampered before attending the hastily thrown together wedding feast, she'd not had a single moment by herself to think about all that had happened. Funny how drastically one's life could change in a single day.

Even though their wedding celebration had been a last-minute affair, the atmosphere had been festive and joyous, and the clan took the news of their handfasting with happy acceptance. She'd been humbled by all the well-wishers. Gifts of linens, wool, candles and small tokens had begun to pile up in the great hall all afternoon.

The refugees from Meikle Geddes planned to return to their homes tomorrow, led by Robley. He vowed to remain there to see that the Comyns didn't attempt another siege. Besides, someone needed to help repair the damage, and he claimed it should be him. But tonight everyone celebrated together, and for more than one reason.

Their enemies had been routed by Malcolm and a score of their clansmen, their land and holding restored with no more loss of life. The harvest this year had been plentiful, with enough to spare for luxuries traded for at the fair in Inverness. And now a wedding.

A knock on the door interrupted her thoughts, and Lydia swept into the room with a grinning Elaine behind her. "Thank you, Beth. You may take your leave. Elaine and I will see to my good daughter's needs."

Beth placed the brush on the table, curtsied and left, giving Alethia a wink at the door.

All afternoon she'd taken comfort in the warmth of Lydia's smiles and the welcome in her eyes as she celebrated her only son's union. Lydia and Elaine had attended her during her bath and had given her the embroidered night rail and robe she wore.

"We're truly sisters now." Elaine sat at the foot of her bed with a satisfied grin.

She smiled back, pleased, but unsure what to say.

"How old were you when you lost your mother, my dear?"

"I lost both my parents when I was ten."

"Then I shall act as your mother this night." Lydia took the chair opposite and reached out to pat her knee as if she were still ten. "This is your wedding night, and I would be remiss in my duty if I did not tell you what to expect . . . what happens between a man and a woman—"

"Oh. I already know about the birds and the bees, Lydia."

"The birds . . . and . . ." Lydia looked at her in confusion. "I dinna wish to speak of birds and bees, True. I came to speak about husbands and wives . . . and the marriage bed."

Now her face felt as if it would burst into flames. She looked to Elaine for help, only to find her smiling wickedly back at her. "Oh."

"Aye, ahem." Lydia smoothed the skirt of her gown, her own face rosy now. "You see, a man has certain needs," she began.

"What about women?" Elaine interrupted. "Do we no' have needs as well?"

"Um, aye, but we dinna speak of it," Lydia stammered.

"Lydia—" Alethia was desperate to get out of this awkward conversation.

"Men *and* women have certain needs," Lydia blurted. She held her hand up as if warding off further interruption. "If you are fortunate enough to have married a generous man, the marriage bed can be a blissful experience. And I certainly hope I have raised my son to be a generous man." Lydia fanned her face with one hand. "His father certainly is. I did my best to teach my son to care for others, to consider their feelings as well as his own. It is my hope that . . . that . . ."

"Lydia, I am sure everything will be fine," Alethia whispered.

"Well, most mothers would tell their daughters to lie still and simply endure what is to come. Those mothers do their daughters a grave disservice. Passion between a husband and wife can be a wonderful thing. 'Tis no secret you and Malcolm care deeply for one another." She reached for Alethia's hands. "I could no' be more pleased for Malcolm, my dear. You make him happy, and in the end, 'tis all we can hope for our children. Welcome to our family, Alethia."

Lydia rose and kissed her on both cheeks. Her eyes stung as she squeezed Lydia's hands. "Thank you. I am honored."

"Come, 'tis time to take you to your husband." Elaine left her perch and walked to the door. "Dinna worry about Hunter. I'll look after him. Tomorrow he can return to your old room; 'tis his chamber now."

Alethia nodded and let them lead her down the long hall. She took a deep breath and let it out slowly. It's not as if she'd never been alone with Malcolm before. They'd come close, so close that day by the spring. Even so, this felt different. So different. Before God and his clan they'd promised their lives to one another. Her heart raced with anticipation and something else much more profound. She loved him. She would always love him.

They stopped in front of the heavy oak door to Malcolm's chamber. Lydia and Elaine both gave her a fierce hug. Lydia opened the door and gently shoved her over the threshold, shutting the door behind her.

A fire blazed in the hearth, casting a soft, warm light to silhouette Malcolm where he stood. He wore a robe of midnight blue velvet. His hair shone golden about his shoulders. Backlit by the fire, it made him look like he had a halo. She smiled at the memories of their first meeting. *My love.*

"Alethia."

She sensed his nervousness and knew his heart raced with the same anticipation as hers. "Malcolm." She smiled from her place near the door, her hands clasped in front of her. Seconds went by, and still she stood, as if her feet had taken root in the wooden planks beneath them.

A loud, raucous cheer rose up from the great hall below. Lydia and Elaine must have announced she'd been delivered into her husband's keeping for the night. Her heart hammered against her ribs, embarrassed to the core. Everyone she'd come to know so well, even those she didn't, knew exactly what would transpire here tonight. She tried to speak but couldn't think of a single thing to say.

"Come warm yourself by the fire, lass." Malcolm grinned. "You look like one of your coneys—tempted by the bait, wary of the trap."

"I do not." She grinned back, the tension broken for the moment. She walked to the chair opposite his, concentrating hard so as not to trip over the long hem of the lovely silk night rail.

"May I pour you a glass of wine?"

"That would be nice." Gathering the billowing yards of cloth, she settled herself on the chair opposite his while he poured them each a goblet of wine.

"Mmph. I would have you nearer, *mo céile.*" Malcolm placed the goblets on the hearth, slid her chair closer and took his seat. "You've no need to be nervous. I'm the same man I was before we wed. Nothing has changed."

She accepted the wine he handed her and took a sip. "Everything has changed."

"Aye, for the better." He took the goblet he'd just placed in her hands and set it back on the hearth. "Come here to me, wife. I willna bite." He drew her from her chair and settled her on his lap, putting his feet up on her vacated spot. "Be at ease, *mo cridhe.*"

"You're as nervous as I am, Malcolm." She leaned into him and rested her head on his shoulder. Curly russet chest hair peeked out of his robe. She ran her fingers through it and splayed her hand over his chest. His heart raced beneath her fingertips. "Can you tell me our vows once more, so I can commit them to memory?"

Malcolm lifted her hand from his chest and kissed the tips of her fingers one at a time. She sighed with pleasure.

"I, Malcolm William, son of William of clan MacKintosh, pledge my troth to thee, Alethia Grace Goodsky—"

"Of clan Crane," she whispered.

"Aye, well, I neglected to say that this morn. 'Twill be said when we take our vows again this spring." He brushed a strand of hair behind her ear. "With my hands, I shall provide for thee. With my body, I pledge to protect thee. With my heart, I shall cherish thee, and only thee, all the days of my life. As God is my witness and before my clan, from this day forward, we are husband and wife."

He bent his head and kissed her. She loved the way he kissed, full, strong kisses with his whole being behind it. She put her arms around his neck and opened her mouth, inviting him in. His groan sent ripples of pleasure down her center, causing an answering dampness and throbbing sensation between her thighs.

"Wait." She straightened in his lap. "What about my vows? What did I say?" Malcolm's eyes had turned from sky to midnight blue with desire.

"I, Alethia Grace Goodsky . . . of clan Crane . . . pledge my troth to thee, Malcolm of clan MacKintosh. With my hands, I shall provide for thee. With my body, I shall succor thee. With my heart, I shall cherish thee, and only thee, all the days of my life," Malcolm recited.

He waited for her to repeat the words. She repeated each line, until she got to the part where with her body she offered succor. "With my body, I pledge to protect you as well as the succoring part." She raised her chin, firm in her resolve.

"Nay. 'Tis a man's duty to protect his family and a woman's duty to see to her husband's needs and provide him with the comforts of hearth and home."

"I can do that *and* protect you."

"Mayhap you can. 'Tis my hope the need will no' arise. Now say the rest."

"With my heart, I shall cherish thee—"

"And *only* me."

She giggled. "And *only* thee, all the days of my life. As God is my witness, and before our clan, from this day forward, we are wife and husband."

"Husband and wife."

"That's what I said." She glanced at him through her lashes and smiled as she went back to playing with his chest hair.

"I want you, Alethia. From the very first day I found you by the side of the road, I have thought of little else. You turn me inside out with worry and want."

"Worry?" She put her hands on either side of his face and placed a kiss on his furrowed brow. "Why worry, Malcolm?"

"I worry about your safety, our future. Dinna think for one moment I enjoy going off to do battle, for I dinna. I crave peace and wish only to raise our crops and kine so that none of my people go hungry. I want to raise my bairns—"

"*Our* bairns." She held one of his hands with both of hers.

He gave her a heart-stopping grin. "Aye, *our* bairns. Let us speak no more of worry. I've a deflowering to attend to."

"Malcolm," she gasped. "I cannot believe you said that."

He lifted her in his arms and moved to the bed, where he laid her down upon the furs and covered her body with his. Propping himself up on his elbows, he gazed down at her. "Unless you dinna wish . . ."

"Oh, I wish." She drew him down for a kiss, savoring the feeling of being enveloped by his large body. He rolled onto his unwounded side and held her close, ravishing the inside of her mouth while tugging and pulling at the fabric covering her body.

"Woman, where are you in all of this silk?" He managed to get her robe off, before getting tangled up in the gown.

She laughed, joy spilling out of her heart and into her voice. "Here, let me." She untangled herself and climbed down from the bed. Untying the ribbon holding the gown closed in the front, she let it slide slowly down her body, watching Malcolm's reaction as the heat of another blush rose to her cheeks. His quick intake of breath and the look of awe on his face pleased her and made her bold. "Now you."

She smiled as he leaped from the bed to comply. Standing before her, he untied the velvet robe and let it fall to the floor with a whoosh. Proudly he stood before her, his broad chest, taut muscled torso, and jutting manhood standing at attention. *Impressive.*

"Oh, Malcolm. You're so . . ."

"Virile?" He grinned.

"So . . ."

"Well formed? Comely?"

"You are all of those things." She reached out to touch his chest with one hand. "But none are what I was going to say." She bit her lower lip.

"What then?" His brow furrowed with uncertainty.

"You're so hairy," she whispered, tangling her fingers in the hair on his chest. "I love it." She sighed. Malcolm threw his head back and laughed as he brought her back into his embrace, and she could easily sense the joy spilling from his heart into his voice as well.

"Aye, well, remember you said that when it tickles you in the middle of the night. Sweet wife, give your husband a kiss."

Skin to warm skin, Alethia lifted her face. His tongue tasted every inch of the inside of her mouth and tangled with hers. A flood of love, desire and tenderness swept through her entire body. Pressing herself as close to him as she possibly could, Alethia tangled her fingers in his golden hair and let the pent up need for his touch overtake her senses in a heady rush. "Malcolm . . ."

Somehow he managed to maneuver them back onto the bed, his body covering hers. Alethia loved the feeling it gave her. In his arms she felt cherished, protected. Malcolm's hands, though large, scarred and callused, moved over her skin with exquisite tenderness. She ached for more.

He trailed kisses and licks down her neck to her shoulder. "I want to taste every delectable part of you." His mouth moved to her collarbone, while his thumbs stroked soft circles around her sensitive nipples, sending bolts of electricity down through the center of her body and taking her breath away.

Bending toward her, his mouth took over for his thumbs, his tongue circling around one nipple, then the other, while one hand sought the sensitive flesh between her thighs. Alethia nearly came up off the bed.

Malcolm stopped and turned himself onto his side. Her breathing came fast and heavy. Propping himself up on one elbow, his gaze moved slowly down her body from the top of her head down to her toes.

"Why did you stop? Malcolm, does your wound hurt? We can—"

"'Tis not my arm that pains me, lass." The desire in his eyes increased the throbbing sensation between her legs. Taking her hand in his, he brought it to his groin and placed it on his erection. "Here is where I ache for you, *mo cridhe.* I want this to be good for you. I . . . I need to slow down, or I'll lose control." He took a deep breath.

She wrapped her hand around him, reveling in the heat, the hardness and the velvet-soft skin. Rubbing her thumb over the tip, she stroked him to the base, then lower. He groaned, and his body tightened beside her. His hand returned to the place where she longed for his touch. "Please, Malcolm. I can't wait any longer." She opened her thighs wider. Desperate, her hips rose with every sweet stroke of his fingers against her aroused flesh.

His throaty chuckle in her ear almost sent her over the edge. "Soon," he whispered. Kissing and licking a trail from the tip of one erect nipple, down the center of her torso, past her navel, Malcolm opened her wider and looked his fill before lowering his head. The first touch of his tongue against the swollen bud of her sex sent her reeling. It took no time at all before she exploded in spasms of pleasure, crying Malcolm's name as she lost all thought.

Kissing a trail back up to her mouth, Malcolm settled himself between her thighs. Poised to enter, he held her face between his two large hands. "I dinna wish to hurt you, Alethia." The head of his member pushed against her opening, only to withdraw with the next breath.

"It's OK. I know what to expect, please . . ." He entered her, filling her another inch deeper. Her hips rose in an effort to bring him further in, frustrated when he once again withdrew. "Malcolm," she groaned. Again he pushed, this time coming all the way to the thin barrier of skin blocking his way. He rocked back and forth slightly, groaning against her neck. She couldn't take any more and brought his face to hers, kissing him with all the hunger in her body. "Now," she commanded.

Malcolm withdrew once more, making her want to scream, returning with a single powerful thrust. The tearing sensation stung, but only for a moment. She shifted beneath him, urging him to move within her, frustrated when he remained still.

"Are you all right?" he asked, his voice hoarse and raspy.

"Oh yes," she sighed, bringing his mouth back to hers. Malcolm moved slowly at first, as if he feared causing her discomfort. She met his thrusts with her own, and she knew the second his control snapped. A rumbling growl came from deep in his chest. His thrusts came faster and deeper, the pressure building within her once more, bringing her to a pinnacle of sensation. She came with a rush, just as she felt the hot flood of his climax erupting inside her. Words spilled out of his mouth in rapid Gaelic as he continued to move against her until completely spent.

Caressing her face from forehead to chin, finally taking her mouth in a sweet, lingering kiss that melted her heart, Malcolm whispered in her ear, "You are mine. Now and forever. I will no' let anyone take you from me. Dinna ever doubt it." He smoothed the hair from her face, traced her eyebrows with a fingertip and gazed deep into her eyes. "Have faith in me."

"I do."

Malcolm remained wide awake long after his wife had fallen asleep in his arms. Certain she would not wake, he rose to fetch a candle. Lighting it from the embers in the hearth, he returned to place it in the stand by their bed. She'd been on her side tucked next to him a moment ago, but now she lay sprawled on her back. Her glorious hair spread out over the bed linens, the covers down about her waist. Malcolm sat on the edge of the bed and watched her sleep.

His heart swelled. For certes he must be the luckiest man in Scotia, for the loveliest woman he'd ever beheld belonged to him. And so sweet a lover he could not have hoped for in his wildest dreams. Her passion matched his in every way. Generous and uninhibited, she'd thrilled him to the marrow.

Lifting a strand of her hair, Malcolm let it slide through his fingers. The sight of her perfect breasts, gilded by candlelight, caused his groin to tighten once again. Loving Alethia gave him a profound feeling of satisfaction and peace. Smiling, he remembered every detail of their wedding night and committed it to memory as she had their vows. The way she looked as she entered their room, like something out of a faerie tale, a vision in a cloud of soft silk, her glorious hair falling free down her back and over her delicate shoulders. Alethia was everything he'd hoped for—and more. He swallowed the lump in his throat and sent a prayer of thanks to the heavens.

He'd wanted the memory of this night to be something they could savor as they grew old together—and it had been. They'd made love until she could no longer keep her eyes open. The reality had far surpassed his fantasies.

He wished for a long, happy life, filled with the laughter of their bairns and grandchildren. But these were perilous times, and 'twas unlikely their enemies would comply. And what of Giselle?

He'd vowed not to let anyone take Alethia from him. What chance did he have against magic? Wracking his brain for some kind of plan, Malcolm took heart from the words the old crone had said to him so long ago. Giselle had bade him keep truth close to him all the days of his life if he would know contentment. Surely the old woman would not have said the words if she meant to take Alethia from him.

For the moment, his want had been satisfied—the worry, however, remained.

CHAPTER SIXTEEN

Malcolm stomped the mud from his boots outside the doors to the great hall. March brought the promise of spring to their clan, and along with spring came the mud. He'd returned from the lists flanked by his two shadows, Tieren and Hunter. He'd made the decision to train them in the ways of knighthood himself. Hunter was his foster son, after all, and he couldn't teach one without the other, for the boys were inseparable. Nor could he send Hunter to be fostered by another noble as was the custom. True wouldn't hear of it.

He smiled to himself at the thought of his wife. They'd been wed since the end of November, and still he could scarce believe his good fortune. Once inside, he removed the outer garment True had made him for Christmas. A *parka*, she called it—soft deer hide lined with thick wool and trimmed with rabbit fur. He found it exceedingly comfortable and warm. Hunter wore a smaller version identical to his. Malcolm's gift to her had been a ring made of gold set with sapphires, a wedding ring.

The boys, now deemed pages under his tutelage, rushed to prepare him a plate to break his fast as he took a seat at the table. The sound of feminine laughter floated down the stairs. True's laughter never ceased to cause his heart to flip. He reached to tousle Hunter's hair, and pointed toward the stairs just as True and Elaine made their entrance.

"I'm famished." True took a seat next to him as Hunter and Tieren tripped over themselves to serve the two women.

"'Tis a fair day. Would you and Elaine like to join me for a ride this afternoon?" The days grew longer with each passing week. Winter had always been Malcolm's favorite season. Fewer battles were fought, more leisure time to spend with friends and family, and this winter in particular, he'd spent a good deal more time in bed with his warm and willing wife.

"Oh yes." True smiled. "And while we're at it, you can show me places where maple trees grow. It's about time to gather the sap for syrup. Thomas has prepared the shunts and pails as I asked."

"Aye, I can."

"Good. Molly has a group of folks ready to help with the harvest. Just wait till you taste it, Malcolm." She gave his hand a squeeze and turned to Elaine. "Will you come with us for a ride?"

"Och, aye. I've seen enough of these gray walls." Elaine sipped the tea Hunter had placed before her. "'Twill be good to get some fresh air."

A single blast from the village horn interrupted their conversation. True looked at him with her brows raised in question. "Word from my father, most likely." He grabbed the remainder of the bread and cheese before him and rose from his place. "The ice is no' completely out yet. 'Twill take some time before our guest arrives." Bending down, he gave True a brief kiss before taking his leave with the boys on his heels. "We'll ride another day, lass."

Liam joined him on his way to the ferry landing. "Word from your father, no doubt."

"Aye. 'Tis time we heard something. I'm anxious to hear his response regarding Meikle Geddes, and he'll likely be sending word of his return." He put his hand on Liam's shoulder for an instant. "And news of our king."

"Think you the ferry will attempt the crossing?"

"Nay. 'Tis certain they'll send one of the skiffs." A crowd had gathered near the landing to watch the small boat make its way through the ice floes in a crooked path toward shore. One man sat in the prow, and the ferry master manned the oars. Malcolm moved closer to shore to pull the skiff up on the sand as it landed.

"Welcome," Malcolm said, offering his hand to the young man wearing the garb of a messenger. "I am Malcolm, son of William, the earl of Fife."

Muddy and travel worn, the messenger took the offered hand and climbed out of the boat. "My thanks, my lord. Edward of York be my name. I am the king's messenger and bring word from London."

Malcolm's eyes narrowed, and his heart raced. They'd heard naught since his father's departure, and he knew not what to expect. "King James or King Henry?" he asked mildly.

"Henry, though 'tis from James and your father that I bring tidings."

Satisfied, he gestured toward the portcullis. "Come to the keep. Refresh yourself and have something to eat before you tell us the news. It has been a long winter without word from my father. Is he well?"

"He is. Or at least he was when last I saw him. Your keep is only one of many I've visited these past three months. I bring an edict from your King James to all the clans."

"Aye? He gives us commands." Liam rubbed his hands together. "So he must be returning home this spring," he said, walking alongside the messenger.

"Liam," Malcolm said as he took his place on the other side of their guest. "Let us wait until Edward has caught his breath. Everyone will want to hear the news. Spread the word, and we'll gather in the great hall this eve. I will have Molly prepare food enough for all. Mayhap I can convince my wife to play her music for us."

"Thou art wed, my lord?" Edward's brow rose.

"I am. Why?"

"Ah . . . your father speaks of you often. 'Twas my understanding you were as yet . . . undeclared."

Liam laughed. "Aye, well, he was before his father left for London. Malcolm had planned to wait until William's return to take his vows with our Lady True, but the clan made other plans for her that did not include him. He had no choice but to take matters into his own hands. You'll understand once you've met the lady."

Liam took his leave as Malcolm and his guest entered the keep. He bid a servant to make ready a room and a bath for Edward, and led him to the table where his two pages prepared a plate for their visitor.

True rose from her place and came to his side, followed by his sister. "Edward, this is my wife, Lady Alethia. We call her True. And this is my sister, Lady Elaine. This is King Henry's messenger, Edward of York. He has brought us news from London."

"My pleasure." He bowed to the ladies and turned to Malcolm. "My lord, I was charged to see these missives safely into your hands, and I would do so before taking my ease." He reached into his leather satchel embossed with the king's seal and pulled out several vellum packets tied together in a neat bundle.

Malcolm took the letters, sorting through them as he sat. Two were for his mother, one in his father's hand, one in his aunt's. Two were addressed to him, one from his father, and one from his uncle. He broke the wax seal on the one from his father and began reading. "Mmph."

"What does he say, Malcolm?" Elaine asked.

"He returns home by the end of next month." He frowned over the letter.

"Something troubles you?" True rested her hand on his arm.

"'Tis nothing. Why don't you and Elaine take Mother's letters to her. Inform Molly we feed the clan this eve." He squeezed her hand and smiled. "I've told our guest you would play for us after we sup, if it would please you."

"I'd be happy to play tonight."

"Come, True." Elaine tugged at her sleeve. "Let us take these letters to my mother."

True looked from him to his sister and rose from the table. Malcolm watched them walk toward the kitchen, their heads bent close together in whispered conversation. He knew Elaine was telling his wife they would get the news from his mother much more easily. He grunted and read his father's letter again.

"Your wife is very lovely, my lord." Edward nodded in the direction the two women had gone. "Her accent is foreign. From whence does she come?"

"She is the daughter of a king. Her land lies across the ocean and is not well known to us."

"How does she come to be here in the Scottish Highlands?"

"Och, well, that is a long story and best saved for another time. I've much to see to before nightfall." He gestured to Tieren. "Lad, you will look after our guest and act as his page for the remainder of the day."

Malcolm glanced at the messenger's dirt-encrusted leather boots and mud-spattered leather jerkin. He wore an over-tunic proclaiming him to be a messenger so none would harm him in the execution of his duty. He'd see to it his garments were cleaned while here as well.

"Tieren," Malcolm continued his instructions. "Show him where the bathing room is once he's done eating, and then take him to his chamber." He spoke in Gaelic, and thought once again 'twas time to teach Tieren English and mayhap French. He would be Hunter's voice in this world, and he needed to learn to communicate with others not of their clan. "The lad will show you where you can bathe, and to the room prepared for you. Until this eve, make yourself at home."

Elaine took Alethia's arm as they walked to the kitchen to speak with Molly. "Whatever my father wrote to my brother he's also written to my mother. She's much more likely to share the news with us. Let us speak with Molly and then take the letters to Mother."

"You're right. Your father will be home in less than two months." How had his father reacted when he'd learned of his son's handfasting? Had William written something about it that caused Malcolm's tension?

"You're at it again, True." Elaine grinned at her as they entered the kitchen.

"At what again?"

"Worrying.

"I wasn't worrying." She frowned. "I was thinking."

"Aye. 'Tis the same thing where you're concerned."

After arranging things with Molly, they took the back stairs up to Lydia's solar, where they found her before the hearth with her embroidery.

"Mother, I've a letter for you from Father and one from Aunt Rosemary."

Lydia raised her head from her work with a welcoming smile. "Aye? I thought as much when I heard the signal from the village." She set her handiwork aside and took the vellum from Elaine, holding it to her heart for a moment. "Your father will be home soon."

Elaine sat on the edge of her chair. "Aye, and True is vexing about it."

"William will come to see things Malcolm's way, my dear. And the both of you have my support." She smiled and opened the letter from her husband as if she could hardly wait. "Och, they'll have words, to be sure. The two are a great deal alike, and both are as stubborn as oxen."

Lydia's attention shifted to her husband's letter, and Alethia sat next to Elaine to wait for her to finish. Lydia made small exclamations and murmurs as she read, bringing an answering smile to her own face. What must it be like to be separated from one's spouse for an entire winter? She hoped never to find out.

"Well, what does Father say?" Elaine asked, once her mother put the vellum in her lap.

"He'll be home at the end of next month." Lydia leveled a stare at her impatient daughter. "Our king and his new wife return at the same time. James has issued an edict to all the clans to cease fighting amongst ourselves. He says Scotland must become a united kingdom if we are to grow strong and prosper."

"That's a good thing, right?" Alethia asked. Lydia gave off the same disquiet Malcolm had after he'd read his father's letter.

"If all the clans will agree to it, aye, 'tis a very good thing, but also unlikely, especially here in the Highlands. Some of the clans have been feuding for centuries," Lydia said.

"Like with the Comyns and the MacKintosh?" she asked.

"Aye, exactly like that." Elaine nodded. "We will honor our king's command. That doesna mean the Comyns will. They've always been a treacherous lot. What else does he say, Mother?"

"Some of it is no' for your ears, daughter." Lydia grinned, her cheeks tinged with a blush.

Alethia could clearly see the clan's interest lay elsewhere as she played her third piece. All were anxious to hear the messenger speak, and their curious glances drifted to him again and again. She smiled, curtsied and quit. “It’s happened,” she remarked, settling into her place beside Malcolm with an exaggerated sigh.

“What has, True?” Malcolm covered her hand where it lay on the table.

“Our clan has tired of my music.”

He chuckled and drew her closer to his side with his arm around her waist. Content, she settled against him.

“Nay, our people will never tire of your music, *mo cridhe*. They canna wait any longer to hear what Edward has to tell us.”

“I vow, my lady, ’tis true,” Edward said from his place next to her. “I found your music truly captivating. I’ve never heard the like before.”

Alethia felt Elaine’s look and turned to find her friend raising a single eyebrow at her. She grinned and decided she’d been adequately compensated for the clan’s lack of interest. “Thank you, Edward.”

“We should probably get on with it,” Malcolm said. “’Tis time to introduce our guest.” He moved his chair back and stood facing his people. Taking his dagger from his belt, Malcolm pounded the hilt on the table three times to get everyone’s attention. The hall went quiet, and all eyes turned expectantly toward the dais. “Word has reached us from my father. He will be home at the end of April.” His voice carried to the far corners of the hall. “This is Edward, King Henry’s messenger. He brings tidings from our King James, and I bid you all to give him your attention.” Malcolm waited until Edward stood before taking his seat.

“I am sent here by your liege,” Edward began. “Your king sends his greetings and wants all of his subjects to know he is on his way home to take his place on the throne of Scotland.”

A raucous cheer and the stomping of feet interrupted his speech. “Long live King James!” someone from the rear of the hall shouted, and the echoed sentiment went on and on in a roar of sound. Edward appealed to Malcolm for his aid, and again her husband stood and pounded on the table until the noise ceased.

“That is no’ all,” he shouted. “Let him continue.”

Once again the hall quieted, with the exception of a startled toddler whose cries echoed off the walls as his mother shushed him.

Edward continued. "James travels to Scone Abbey in Perthshire, where his coronation will take place during the month of May, in the year of our Lord 1424. He will then continue on to Castle Hill in Stirling. I bring with me your king's first command as your liege." He held up a sheet of parchment with the crest of the house of Stuart affixed at the bottom for all to see. "He has issued an edict, which I pass along to his subjects as is his wish. Word has reached your king that his country is in chaos with clan fighting against clan. He is distressed by the news and seeks to remedy the situation. From this day forward let it be known: by order of your rightful king, James I, son of Robert III, all fighting amongst the clans of Scotia is forbidden. Furthermore, any insurrection will be punishable to the full extent of the law."

Stunned silence met his words, followed by exclamations of disbelief and skeptical grumbling. Edward took his seat as Malcolm rose again.

"'Tis our king's command." He spoke low, and soon all sound in the hall ceased as their people strained to hear what he had to say. "The MacKintosh are now, and always have been, true to king and country. Finally we will have our king home where he belongs. If King James desires that Scotland become one country united—so be it. His leadership can only strengthen us. We canna fall to an enemy from without so long as we are unified within. Long live King James." He lifted his goblet in a toast, sparking an echoing roar from everyone in the hall.

Alethia's heart swelled with love and pride. She'd married a natural leader, a good and honorable man—and she could not imagine a life without him.

A fire in the hearth cast warmth and light throughout their chamber. Alethia sat near the radiating warmth as she braided her hair for bed.

She watched Malcolm at his place across from her as he sharpened his sword with a whetstone and oil. All day she'd been dying to ask what his father had to say about their handfasting. "Malcolm?"

"Mmmm?"

"What did your father have to say in his letter about our handfasting?"

"He said naught about it."

Alethia stopped braiding and focused her attention on him. She sensed . . . discomfort. "Don't you think that's odd? His only son and heir gets married while he's away, and he has nothing to say?"

"I dinna find it odd at all."

A suspicion grew in her mind, making it difficult to swallow. "You haven't told him!"

With a resigned sigh, he stopped working on his sword and looked her in the eye. "I have no' told him."

"Why not? Are you ashamed of me?" She stared at him dumbfounded, feelings she couldn't name swirling through her.

"Nay, lass. I am no' ashamed of you. I havena told him because he has other things to deal with at present, and it can wait until his return."

"You wrote him about Meikle Geddes though, didn't you?" She rose from her place to stand before him. "We took our vows right after your return. I'll bet we'd done the deed before you sent your letter. Am I right?"

"Aye."

Stunned, she paced the chamber. "You regret it, don't you? William won't accept it. He'll pitch a fit when he finds out."

"That is enough, Alethia. I dinna regret anything. I am a man grown. Whom I wed and when has always been my decision. It matters no' how my father reacts."

"If that were true, surely you would have told him right away." She glared at him. "Send him a message tomorrow."

"I will do no such thing."

She gasped in disbelief. "See? I knew it. You're ashamed of me. That or you regret what you've done." She put her hands on her hips and glared. "Send him a message."

"Watch your tone. Do not presume to tell me what to do, woman." He growled as he rose from his place to loom over her. "There's little point now. Any rider we send will likely miss my father's party. He's on the road home as we speak."

She blinked rapidly to hide the hurt his ire caused. Watching him put his sword in its customary place near his side of their bed, she struggled to squelch the urge to scream. Far from offering reassurance, his words only confirmed her insecurity. She slipped her feet into her moccasins and began walking toward their door.

"Where do you think you are going?"

"I'm going somewhere else to sleep."

"You will no' leave this chamber, or there will be consequences."

"*Consequences?* How dare you talk to me as if I were a child. I'll give you consequences." She stomped to the door and made it to the hallway just as Malcolm lunged for her.

Tears filled her eyes, and she ran to Hunter's room, flattening herself against the wall by his door to listen. Malcolm hadn't pursued her, and her heart ached with misery.

She let herself into the chamber and peered at the outline of Hunter's small frame in the bed. She sighed, climbed in beside him and snuggled his warm body against her chest. Malcolm hadn't given her the reassurance she craved. Come to think of it, when had he ever said the words she longed so desperately to hear? He had never said he loved her. Tears slid down her cheeks, and her heart ached. Hoping he'd come and apologize, she waited for him until exhaustion took hold, and she fell into a fitful sleep.

Malcolm lay flat on his back in bed and glared into the darkness. True's accusations stung. How dare she order him about as if he were a mere lad. What he chose to tell or not to tell his father was completely at his discretion, and he could find no fault with his decision. His father had more important things to contend with at present than his son's marital state.

Still, he'd glimpsed the hurt in her eyes, and a pang of guilt followed by regret pushed his anger aside. Should he have gone after her? Nay. If he gave in, she'd have him always chasing after her. 'Twas best she learned early on who held the authority in their marriage. Firmness was needed in his dealings with her. Aye, firmness, and there would be a consequence for her defiance.

Smiling, he imagined all kinds of ways she could make it up to him. Without thought, he reached across the bed for her, only to be reminded of her absence. He growled. Let her sleep elsewhere. He was fine without her.

The night wore on, and still he could not sleep. He tossed and turned, feeling the emptiness of his wife's side of the bed acutely. Tangled in the bed linens, and aggravated with himself, he threw the covers off and lit the candle by his bed. There was no hope for him. He pulled on his robe and left the room. Sliding through the door to Hunter's chamber, Malcolm cursed his own weakness and stole to the side of his foster son's bed.

As expected, True slept soundly beside the lad. She looked as if their quarrel had not affected her in the least. His heart swelled with love and pride as he looked upon his little family asleep side by side. She and Hunter had filled the empty places inside him, and he'd do everything in his power to keep them safe and well.

Sighing, he lifted his wife without waking her, cradled her against his heart and made his way back to their chamber. Without her beside him, he could find no peace.

CHAPTER SEVENTEEN

A wave of nausea forced Alethia to sit down. She took the chair before the hearth in the chamber and took deep breaths until the urge to vomit diminished. As ill as she felt, she couldn't help smiling with secret joy as she reviewed the symptoms. Fatigue, nausea, tender breasts and she had to use the garderobe all the time. She counted back to her last period and figured it had been around the end of January, about seven weeks ago. Still, she wouldn't tell Malcolm until the critical first trimester had passed.

It had been two days since her argument with Malcolm, and they hadn't resolved anything. In his customary overbearing way, he'd ordered her never to sleep elsewhere ever again. She'd capitulated. Partly because she knew he was right about sending word to his father—William would be home before any letter reached him—and partly because she'd grown used to sleeping against his warmth.

A brief knock interrupted her thoughts, and Hunter entered. "*I'm hungry.*" He came to stand before her. Leaning against her knees, he plucked at her gown.

"*Me too. Did you wash?*" she signed.

Hunter rolled his eyes and kept his hands still.

"*Come to your room.*" She tied a strip of leather around the end of her braid. "*You will wash before we eat.*"

Hunter stomped beside her, a frown on his face. "*Do you make Da wash every day too?*"

"*I don't have to. He does it on his own.*" She laughed at the look of disbelief on his face. Tonight, Hunter would have a bath. Her stomach growled. Once the nausea left, mega-hunger took its place. Another symptom. In the past week, she'd even awakened in the middle of the night from hunger pangs. She'd see Molly about snacks to keep in the chamber—something to satisfy her hunger and perhaps help alleviate the morning sickness plaguing her.

Hunter, washed, brushed and disgusted by the whole unmanly process, ran ahead of her toward the stairs. Once she arrived in the great hall, she found him already seated and eating. He'd fixed her a bowl of porridge smothered in some of the newly made maple sugar, just the way she liked it, and set it at the place beside him. She took her seat. No one lingered in the hall. She'd been staying in bed longer and longer each day.

"*Shouldn't you be in the lists training with Tieren?*"

"*Already did.*" Hunter signed quickly between spoonfuls. "*Da sent me back to check on you.*"

That surprised her. Did he suspect? More likely he worried about her state of mind. Since their quarrel, she worried more than ever that he felt ambivalent about marrying her. Why else hadn't he told his father? A wave of unhappy insecurity washed through her. Of course, he denied any ambivalence, saying only that the decision was his alone. He claimed he had no concerns about his father's reaction. How was that even possible? His father was still the earl.

After breakfast she'd go through her sewing materials. The thought of making tiny garments for her very own baby sent a thrill of excitement through her. For a moment, her thoughts flew to her grandmother. Gran would have been beside herself with excitement at the news of becoming a great-grandmother.

"True." Elaine came in through the passageway leading from the kitchen. "Finally up? We all feared you would spend the day in your chamber."

"What time is it?"

"'Tis well past midmorn. Malcolm bid Molly leave the food for you until after the nooning hour. This is the second time Hunter has broken his fast this day." Elaine tousled Hunter's hair, and he grinned at her. "Are you . . . well, sister?"

Alethia couldn't ignore the speculative glint in Elaine's eyes. Did she know? "I'm fine. Just tired."

Hunter pushed his empty bowl away and shot out of the keep, presumably to find Malcolm and Tieren now that his task had been completed.

Alethia sighed and rose from her place. Searching the shadowy corners of the great hall to ensure they were alone, she took Elaine's arm and leaned her head close to her friend's. "I'm not going to be able to keep my secret from you, am I?"

Elaine's laughter echoed through the large room.

"Shush. Be quiet!"

"Oh, True." Elaine hugged Alethia's arm. "I only suspected. 'Tis you who canna keep this secret."

"Don't tell anyone, especially not Malcolm. I want to be certain all is well first."

"Not even my mother?"

"She'll know soon enough."

"How long has it been since you've bled?"

Before Alethia could answer, a single blast from the village horn rent the air. "Another message from your father, do you think?"

"No' likely. Come, let us go to the ferry landing. 'Tis a fine day, and the air will do you good."

By the time she and Elaine reached the beach, Malcolm, Liam and several other MacKintosh warriors were already there. Malcolm spared her a nod and a smile before facing the ferry. He tensed, and his expression hardened. Alethia followed his gaze to the lone man standing on the deck. Who could this visitor be to cause such tension? Normally when the ferry crossed the loch, the crowd anticipated the arrival of news and the pleasure of company. Now the mood seemed angry and fraught with wariness.

Elaine gasped.

"Who is it?" she whispered to her sister-in-law.

"'Tis John of clan Comyn. He's the laird's son." Elaine gripped her arm. "'Twas the Comyns who took Meikle Geddes."

"What on earth would he be doing here?" She watched the MacKintosh warriors as the ferry made its landing. None greeted the man. None offered a hand as he disembarked. All had their hands on their weapons, ready to draw them in an instant.

Malcolm stepped forward. "What business have you here?" His voice and stance carried authority and strength. He let it be known that any enemy would have to get through him first before they could reach the people under his protection. Alethia's heart swelled with pride.

"I come in peace bearing a message from my father. In proof, I give you my sword." John drew the sword from its scabbard and laid it on the ground.

"Indeed, you will give me every blade upon your person before you take a step farther onto our island." Malcolm's men murmured approval, watching their enemy for any sign of treachery.

"Done." John began to remove daggers from his belt and boots, laying them on the ground next to his sword. Liam stepped forward to gather the weapons. MacKintosh warriors surrounded the man, and the group moved in formation toward the keep.

"True." Malcolm reached for her hand and drew her next to him. "I would have you join us in the great hall," he whispered in her ear.

She nodded, aware that her abilities as a truth-sayer were finally needed for the safety of their clan. Her stomach churned with nervousness as she gripped Malcolm's hand, grateful for his steady strength.

Once all were situated in the great hall, Malcolm took his father's place in the center chair on the dais, flanked by Liam and Angus. Alethia stood behind him, her hand resting on his shoulder. The chairs were taken up by MacKintosh warriors, and the stern lot of them faced their unwelcome guest with grim expressions. Their placement forced John to face them alone and standing.

John reached into his sporran and pulled out a rolled parchment sealed with wax. Approaching the dais, he handed it to Malcolm. "Our two clans have been enemies since the days of Robert the Bruce. King James returns to take his place upon the throne, and it is his wish to unite the clans. I assume you have received the edict forbidding all clans from fighting amongst themselves?"

"We have," Malcolm replied. "'Tis no' the MacKintosh who keep the feud alive. Our actions have always and only been in retaliation for the treacherous aggression committed against us by *your* clan. Whatever message your father sends, 'tis unworthy of our notice. The word of a Comyn canna be trusted."

John reached for the sword no longer at his waist, and Alethia could feel the seething rage emanating from him.

"Much of the land your clan holds today was once ours." John spoke through gritted teeth. "Dinna speak to me of treachery."

"'Twas no' the MacKintosh who took your land, but the Bruce, and rightly so. Your clan chose unwisely, supporting a foreigner's claim to the throne of Scotland. To the victor go the spoils of war." Malcolm waved his hand in a dismissive gesture. "Enough. I've no stomach for a lengthy debate about ancient history. What is it you wish to say?"

Even before John spoke, she felt the malice emanating from him. Lies. Whatever he said would be lies. She squeezed Malcolm's shoulder to alert him.

"We wish to end the feud between our clans in compliance with our king's wishes. The missive you hold is an invitation from my father. In honor of our promise, you are invited to a feast of reconciliation."

The moment the words left John's mouth, a strange sensation flooded her entire being. Her peripheral vision began to darken. Stars appeared before her eyes, and her legs gave out from under her. Just as darkness took hold, she felt strong arms lift her. Then she left her body completely, to be dropped into a scene unfolding around her. It was as if she stood in the midst of a hologram or a three-dimensional film.

Inside a strange keep, MacKintosh clansmen sat beside men who were strangers to her. Men who wore kilts bearing the same colors as John's. None showed any awareness of her presence. Like a phantom, she moved around the room to stand before each warrior until she faced the dais. The MacKintosh men appeared to be inebriated, their speech slurred, their movements and coordination off.

Malcolm sat between John and a large, cruel-looking man with hair the color of silver-streaked copper. He could only be the Comyn laird, Ronald the Red. As she watched, servants brought out the head of a black boar on a large platter. As they set it down in front of their laird, he gave a signal, and servants rushed to fill everyone's goblet. The Comyn laird then raised his cup and waited for all assembled to do the same.

A toast. He was giving some kind of toast. But wait, why did he hold his goblet in his left hand when he'd clearly been eating with his right? With a sense of dread, she looked around the hall. All but a few of the Comyns did the same.

"*No!*" She rushed around the table toward Malcolm as she screamed.

No sound came out of her mouth as she frantically tried to warn him. "Malcolm, watch out!"

Even before his goblet was lowered, the Comyn laird rose up, a dagger in his right hand. She threw herself between the laird and her husband. The Comyn laird's arm went right through her as he slashed Malcolm's throat. She watched helplessly as blood gushed from the gaping wound through her formless fingers. Malcolm raised stunned eyes to his enemy, his mouth opening and closing as if trying to speak.

Horrified, she backed away from the table, only to find the same gruesome sight wherever she looked. Every MacKintosh present bled to death before her, their faces all wearing the same look of shocked disbelief. The floor turned a sticky, thick crimson as the Comyns laughed and congratulated themselves on their easy victory.

"*No!*" Alethia screamed and screamed, her heart breaking into a million shards like slivers of glass to splinter her soul.

True's hand slipped from his shoulder. Malcolm glanced at her just in time to see her swoon. He was out of his chair in a trice, catching her up before her head hit the dais. "You will excuse me." Malcolm lifted her close to his chest. "My wife has been ill of late. Liam, see our guest is settled into a comfortable chamber." He gave his cousin a pointed look, trusting Liam to post a guard at the door of said room. "We will speak again later."

"Of course," John replied, bowing slightly. "You must see to your lady's welfare."

Malcolm rushed up the stairs, met by his mother and sister in the corridor. "You were in the gallery?"

"Aye," Lydia said. She spoke over her shoulder to his sister. "Elaine, fetch a bowl of cool water and clean linen."

"Dinna worry, Malcolm. True is not ill. I'll come to your chamber anon." Elaine patted his arm on her way past.

His mother drew the bedclothes back so he could lay True down. The minute he let her go, she started to thrash about. He shook her gently to wake her, alarmed when she did not rouse. "Alethia," he spoke into her ear. "Wake up, lass." He shook her again, his heart freezing with fear. "Mother, what do I do? I canna wake her."

"*No!*" Alethia moaned from the bed, her body twisting and turning, her face a mask of terror. "Malcolm, watch out!"

Dropping to the bed, Malcolm gathered her into his arms and held her tight. "I'm here, love. All is well." He turned stricken eyes to his mother. "What do I do?"

"You are doing all you can, I think." Lydia put her hand on Alethia's forehead. "She's no' feverish. I dinna ken what is wrong with her."

Elaine entered the chamber, carrying a bowl of water with a square of linen folded over her arm. "Has she come to?"

"Nay." Malcolm looked into his wife's face, frightened by her pallor. "Alethia, wake up." He shook her again, harder this time—desperate. She remained gripped in horror, moaning and writhing in agony in his arms. His heart raced, and he couldn't get enough air into his lungs. Never had he felt so helpless.

"Lay her down. Let us tend to her. We'll call for you the moment she wakes." Elaine set the bowl of water down on the table beside his bed.

"Nay, I'll no' leave her." He tucked a blanket around her and smoothed her hair. Was it his imagination, or did she seem to be settling? Elaine laid the damp cloth on her brow, and Malcolm reached for True's hand. Her breathing steadied, becoming slow and regular.

"She sleeps, Malcolm. Whatever seized her seems to have passed." Lydia brushed a lock of True's hair behind her ear. "Stay with her if you will. Our guest will remain until you give him leave. Send for us when she wakes." Lydia took Elaine's arm and led her to the door.

"If you need anything, send Hunter for me," Elaine said.

Hunter. Malcolm hadn't given him a thought. The lad must be worried sick. Searching the room, he found him huddled into a corner, his eyes bright. "*Come, lad.*" Hunter sprinted across the room and climbed into his lap. He could feel his small body trembling. "*She sleeps. All will be well.*"

Hunter placed the palm of one hand on True's cheek. It seemed to Malcolm that he went completely still, as if listening for something. His small body relaxed, the trembling stopped, and Hunter swiped at his eyes in a furtive gesture. "*You will stay here and act as messenger. Once she awakens, I'll send you to fetch Lydia and Elaine.*"

Hunter nodded, still wiping at the tears running down his cheeks.

"*'Tis all right to cry, son. Even the strongest knight sheds tears.*" Malcolm cradled Hunter's head with his large hand for a moment. "*She'll be fine after a good rest.*"

He prayed it was so. He'd recognized all the signs of late—her fatigue, the nausea, and she hadn't bled for weeks. Though she'd said naught, he'd guessed. 'Twas the natural result of their lovemaking, after all.

Mayhap the bairn growing inside her had caused the swoon. His throat tightened, and he brought Alethia's hand to his mouth to kiss. Would they have a son or a daughter? He wondered when she would tell him.

Night had fallen when True finally stirred. Malcolm had not left her side for more than a few moments throughout the day. When she began to move about under the covers, he spoke into her ear. "Wake up, True." She turned toward his voice, a good sign. "Come, lass. 'Tis time you awoke."

"Malcolm?" She opened her eyes and tried to sit up.

Malcolm put his arm behind her back to support her. Relief washed through him in a rush. "I'm here, *mo cridhe*."

"I'm starving."

He pulled her into his arms and fought the urge to laugh out loud. "I'll send for food."

Hunter had fallen asleep next to her. He reached over her to give the lad a nudge. Hunter's eyes opened and sought his foster mother. "*Fetch Elaine and Lydia. Tell them to have a tray sent up. She's hungry.*"

Hunter's smile lit the room. He nodded and scrambled off the bed, bolting for the door. Malcolm's attention returned to his wife. "What happened?"

Her eyes filled with tears as she looked at him. "Oh, Malcolm, it was so horrible. Have the men come to us before I tell you. I don't want to repeat it more than once. I had a vision." Her voice shook as she reached for his hand. "I've never had one before, and hope never to have another."

"All will be well, love." Malcolm stroked her hair and held her to him. "As soon as Hunter returns, we'll send for them. Dinna vex yourself."

"John lied, Malcolm."

He snorted. "Of course he lied. He's a Comyn."

After a quick rap on the door, Beth entered carrying a tray, Hunter on her heels. She executed a quick curtsy toward Malcolm. "How do ye fare, milady?" She placed the tray on the table near the hearth and bent to stir the embers, adding bricks of peat, poking and prodding until they caught. "We've all been worried sick about ye. Come, Lady True. Sit here by the fire and eat."

"I'm fine, Beth. Thank you for bringing food. I'm so hungry I could eat an entire ox."

Beth glanced at Malcolm, her brows raised. He smiled over True's head before he helped her out of bed and over to the table. Concerned about her comfort, he'd removed her clothing hours ago, and managed to dress her in a night rail. He fetched True's robe, and then he signed to Hunter to gather his men. The lad once again ran out of their chamber.

"I've brought enough food for two." Beth grinned. "Or mayhap three. I know you have no' taken your evening meal yet as well, milord."

"My thanks." Malcolm helped True into her robe before settling her into a chair. He sat next to her, amused by her appetite as she tore into the meal. "Mayhap we'll have to send for more."

True stopped eating to frown at him, a blush rising to her cheeks. She swallowed the food in her mouth. "I'm sure we have enough."

He laughed, just as his mother and sister entered the chamber to take their places with True at the table. A short time later, Liam, Angus, Galen and Gareth arrived, and their chamber filled with the people he trusted most in this world. For an instant, Malcolm suffered Robley's absence acutely. He would send for his return on the morrow. "My wife has had a vision." Everyone turned, wide-eyed, to stare at True.

His wife pushed the tray of food away from her. "John lied. The invitation is a trap."

The chamber erupted with cries of outrage. "Cease," Malcolm commanded. "Let us hear what True has to say. Save your outrage for our retaliation."

"You cannot accept the invitation." She looked at him with wide eyes. "They plan to slaughter all who attend. When the head of a black boar is brought out, the Comyn laird will make a toast to the dead. Once the toast is finished, they all rise with daggers drawn and slit your throats." She shuddered and rubbed her hands up and down her arms. "Many of you were drunk. Part of their plan is to see that you all drink to excess." She raised her eyes to his, pleading.

"Don't accept the invitation. The Comyns will far outnumber the MacKintosh. You cannot go. I forbid it. In my vision you died before my eyes, Malcolm. I can't let it happen." She frowned and cocked her head as if trying to remember something.

"What is it, True?" He took her hand in his, alarmed by how cold it felt.

"I don't know. I feel like I've forgotten something important." She took her hand back and rubbed her temples with her hands, her eyes haunted and helpless as she looked to him for help.

Seeing her thus upset him beyond reason. His instincts to protect surged through him. "You've had enough excitement for one day." He stood abruptly and nodded to Liam. "Remove to my father's solar. I will meet all of you there once my wife is settled."

"We will see to her." Lydia crossed to True, putting her arm around her shoulders. "Go with your men."

Torn, Malcolm stood in the middle of the room with his hand on the dagger at his waist.

"Go," True said. "I can't believe I slept the afternoon away, and I'm still tired." She smiled. "I'll go back to bed. I'm fine, really."

Malcolm walked to the door. "Stay with her until my return?" His gaze went from his mother to his sister.

"Of course," Elaine said.

His mood as black as pitch, Malcolm made his way to the solar. There he found his men in the midst of a hot debate. All turned to him as he entered.

"So," Angus began. "We'll refuse the invitation, aye?"

"Nay, Angus." He took a seat at the table. "We'll accept."

CHAPTER EIGHTEEN

The bed shifted, and Alethia struggled to open her eyes to reach for Malcolm. They hadn't spoken since she'd shared her vision the night before, and she needed the reassurance of his arms around her. She tried to open her mouth, to call out for him before he left their chamber. No sound came out.

The harder she tried to wake, the odder she felt. The strange sensation from the day before overcame her, and once again her spirit left her body to be dropped into the Comyn keep in the middle of the same macabre scene. Only this time, the MacKintosh men had been warned of the impending treachery. When Ronald the Red gave the signal toast, Malcolm and his men rose from their places and drew their weapons.

The drama unfolded as Alethia moved among the warriors doing battle. Malcolm fought John, the laird's son. Though her husband seemed to have the upper hand, instinct told her she'd returned for a reason, and her eyes remained fixed upon the two.

John forced Malcolm into a retreat with a flurry of blows. Still, Malcolm defended himself easily. She cursed as she watched John's father come from behind Malcolm to trip him with his foot. Malcolm went down hard and tried to scramble away only to find himself up against a wall. She watched in horror as once again her husband was killed before her eyes.

Movement drew her attention. The Comyn laird took the stairs in quick strides, leaving his men to finish the fight without him. She ran to catch up and followed him to a chamber at the end of the corridor. Alethia slipped into the room behind him, only to freeze at the gruesome scene taking place inside.

A young woman was trying to escape through the window, her eyes large with fear and panic. The laird shouted at her as he grasped her skirts to prevent her escape. His rage was so great spittle flew from his mouth as he accused her of betraying him. He drew his sword, and the young woman shook her head in denial as she managed to free her gown from his hold. She gripped the window frame and tried to climb out. Alethia watched in disbelief as the laird raised his sword. The woman called him Father as she begged for her life.

Comprehension dawned just as Ronald the Red sent his own daughter crashing to her death on the stones below. What she'd forgotten had been revealed, and finally the pieces of the puzzle fell into place. "Liam!" Bolting upright, she threw off the covers. She rushed to dress, ignoring the nausea threatening to fell her.

"Milady?" Beth carried a bundle of clean clothing toward the stairs, nearly colliding with Alethia as she bolted through the great hall for the doors leading outside to the bailey.

"Can't talk now, Beth," she called over her shoulder as she pulled the heavy doors open.

"Where—"

She didn't stick around to hear Beth's question. Urgency propelled her toward the rear of the keep where the MacKintosh warriors practiced their battle skills. Breathless, she came around the corner and stopped. Surveying the lists, she located Malcolm surrounded by his men. They all crouched on the ground around him while he drew in the dirt with the tip of his dagger.

She located Liam in the group, caught his eye and approached. She didn't miss the subtle nudge Liam gave Malcolm, who raised his gaze to meet hers. He started to wipe the drawing away.

"Don't bother. I know the plan backward and forward." As she reached the group, the men drifted away until only Liam and Malcolm remained.

"You've had another vision?" Malcolm stayed where he was, crouched on the ground next to Liam in front of a clear diagram of Castle Rait.

"Liam, we have to *do* something. Her father is going to blame her. While you're all battling in the great hall, he's going to get to her." Alethia searched his eyes—the sadness she saw there overwhelmed her. He averted his gaze.

"Of whom does she speak?" Malcolm looked intently at his cousin.

Alethia ignored Malcolm's interruption. "She's going to try to escape through the window and won't make it." She wiped the tears streaking down her cheeks. "He's going to cut both of her hands off at the wrists. She's going to fall to her death while you fight for your life only a flight of stairs away." She turned to Malcolm. "We have to save her life. She's an innocent in all of this. Tell him, Liam."

"What is it you speak of? Of whom does she speak, Liam? Tell me."

"Mairen. She speaks of the Red Comyn's daughter, Mairen." Liam's gaze remained fixed on the ground before him, his voice tense, low. "Her father brutalizes her. He takes all of his frustrations out on his daughter because she canna defend herself against him." Liam thrust the point of his dagger into the dirt at his feet. "Just like he did with his wife—until she died at his hands."

"Aye? And what is Mairen to you?" Malcolm glared at him.

"She's . . . I love her." Liam's eyes filled with anguish. "She did no' choose who her father is. Aye, she's a Comyn, but she doesna have a mean or treacherous bone in her body." His gaze moved to Alethia. "I ken she's in danger. I've thought of nothing else since that bastard came with his cursed invitation. God's blood, I dinna ken what to do." He rubbed his face with both of his hands. "She and I have had no contact since we retook Meikle Geddes. Word has reached me her father keeps her locked away in her chamber. He suspects her of betraying him."

"You love the daughter of our most bitter enemy?" Malcolm scowled. "How did this come about? When?"

He swallowed hard several times. "I love her more than life." He finished his statement with a determined voice. "We met two years past at the fair in Inverness. You better than anyone must know we have no choice when we lose our hearts. I—"

"Wait." Alethia's attention had fixed upon the part about losing hearts. The past months replayed in her mind. "What do you mean, Liam, he better than anyone should know?" She studied his face before shifting her attention to Malcolm. "What does he mean by that?"

Had Malcolm married her even though his heart belonged to someone else? Yes, they'd handfasted, but when she'd asked him why, he'd said only that he didn't want her to worry about having a "place." Come to think of it, more than once he'd referred to her as his responsibility. And once again this realization brought her back to one fact: he'd never said he loved her.

No wonder he hadn't told his father. She'd been right all along—even though he treated her with affection, and she knew he cared about her, it wasn't love. She couldn't breathe, and her ears rang with the beating of her heart.

Who had he lost his heart to? Where was this woman now? Jealousy cut through her heart with a bitter blade. "I cannot believe you would marry me when your heart belongs to someone else."

"Alethia—"

"Don't you 'Alethia' me. And another thing. You were going to go through with this little plan of yours without so much as a word to me." As she stomped past him, she shoved his shoulder, sending him flat on his back in the dirt.

Blinking furiously against the angry tears falling down her cheeks, she didn't know which way to go. Malcolm didn't love her, had never loved her. Lust. That's all she was to him—a scratch for his itch. She had no desire to run into anyone and headed for the wooded path leading to shore.

"Och, Malcolm . . . you have no' told your wife what is in your heart?" Liam gave him an incredulous look.

"Nay." He stood up and brushed the dirt from his plaid. "I married her, didn't I? Is that no' enough?"

"You're an idiot, cousin." Liam shook his head.

"Nay, Liam. I'm an oxy moron." He gave his cousin a wry smile and followed True's path with his eyes.

"What have oxen to do with it?" Liam asked, his brow lowered in confusion.

"I dinna ken. True said it when we bickered about weapons." He shrugged a shoulder. "So it must be so."

"Aye, well you are covered with hair, and some might say you smell like an ox at times." Liam grinned. "How long do you think it will take her to work it out that she's the one you've lost your heart to?"

"She'll need some help, I expect." He grinned back, then sobered. "Liam, why did you no' come to me about Mairen?"

"I couldna see a way around it that didna lead to bloodshed. I still dinna, though now they've given us reason enough."

"We will see to it Mairen is removed from harm's way. None can blame a woman for the actions of her father." Liam's face tightened with suppressed emotion, and Malcolm embraced him briefly before taking off after his wife.

Women were known to be temperamental while breeding. Mayhap she would share the news with him this day. As overwrought as she was, 'twas not likely she'd return to the keep. Instinctively, he headed for the loch to their place—the spot by the shore where so much had transpired between them. He strode across the bailey, passing Angus on his way. "Have you seen my wife?"

"Aye," Angus replied. "She looked like a lass with a lot on her mind." He pointed toward shore. "She's on yon path. I'd think twice afore ye follow her, lad. Take it from a man who has been married a good long while. Wait until she's had time to settle her ruffled feathers a wee bit."

"My thanks." Malcolm nodded. Hurrying into the copse of cottonwoods, he caught sight of her and called out, "Alethia, stop."

"I'm not speaking to you," she shouted. Without sparing him a glance, she cut off the path and dashed into the trees.

Malcolm's blood quickened as he gave chase. He headed into the woods at an angle, coming out in front of her. She gave a startled yelp and changed direction. This tactic of hers he knew well. Scooping her up, Malcolm turned her around and draped her over his shoulder.

"Put. Me. Down."

"Nay."

"I am *not* a sack of grain you can haul around at will."

She struck at his back with her small fists and tried to lift herself up. He shifted her higher over his shoulder, dangling her lower down his back.

"Oh . . . this . . . is . . . not . . . good. Where . . . are . . . you . . . taking . . . me?"

She spoke in rhythm to his strides. He found it extremely amusing. "To our chamber. We need to talk."

"I'm . . . going . . . to . . . be . . . sick!"

Malcolm froze. Sliding her down to her feet, he peered into her face. If he'd made her ill, he'd never forgive himself. "Take deep breaths." Cradling her face between his palms, Malcolm studied her. "Are you going to cast up your morning meal, lass?"

"No." She swatted his hands away. "I haven't eaten anything. I wanted you to put me down, and you did." She sprinted away. "You're *so* easy."

He growled and went after her. Catching her about the waist, he lifted her off her feet and started for the keep. "What do you mean you have no' yet eaten? You will break your fast, and then it's back to bed with you."

"I'm not a child, so don't talk to me like one." She gasped in outrage.

"I dinna recall saying you were a child. These visions tire you. I will no' have you making yourself ill."

She gave him an angry scowl followed by a resigned sigh and remained mute as he carried her across the bailey, up the stairs and into the great hall.

His mother and sister sat at the table before the hearth. "Mother, would you please see to it something is put together for True to eat? She has no' yet broken her fast. Elaine, fetch a fresh pot of tea."

The moment Malcolm settled True on his lap, with the dark bread and slices of ham in front of them, she started to cry. Murmuring soothing nonsense, he fed her small bits of the meal.

"Whatever is the matter, dear?" Lydia asked, her brow furrowing with concern. "What have you done, Malcolm?"

"Nothing," Malcolm answered. "She's had another vision, there's no food in her belly, and she's no' had enough rest." True glared at him and opened her mouth to reply. He put more food into it.

"You must have done something." Lydia took True's hands, rubbing and patting them in sympathy.

His sweet wife nodded vehemently. Elaine returned from the kitchen with a fresh pot of tea. He could smell the chamomile and rose hips she'd prepared to soothe True's nerves. He continued to feed his crying wife, who chewed and swallowed between her tears—and glares. "Elaine, I think the tea would be best served once True is settled in bed. Will you have it sent up?"

"I'll bring it, Malcolm. Mayhap you have better things to do. I can see to her welfare." Elaine gave him a pointed look, one that pinned the blame for her friend's overwrought state squarely upon his shoulders. Aye, he would take the blame, and proudly. He was going to be a father.

He grinned at his sister. "Nay. I'll see to my wife. Bring the tea, or have it sent." Lifting True in his arms, he started for the stairs. The tears had ceased, and she yawned. Laying her head on his shoulder, her arms came around his neck. All he needed in this world to be happy rested right here in his arms. He bent his head and brushed a kiss across her brow.

"Not talking to you," she whispered through another yawn.

"Mmmm." He felt it best to refrain from comment. Once they entered their chamber, Malcolm set her on the bed. He moved to the hearth, where he stirred the few remaining embers to life and added a brick of peat. Beth came through the door with the tea and slices of toasted bread on a tray. "My thanks, Beth." She lingered, glancing at True and wringing her hands. He pointed to the door. "That will be all. Close the door as you leave."

Malcolm leaned against the wall and faced his distraught wife. He should have told her how he felt long ago—as he should have sent word to his father that he'd chosen the only woman he would ever take to wife. His neglect in these matters had hurt the woman he loved. She suffered needlessly because of him.

Why hadn't he told her? How oft did he put things off? 'Twas a flaw in his character. One he'd work to improve. "What has upset you so, Alethia?"

"If you don't know, I'm not going to tell you."

"You are the truth-sayer, *mo anam.* I am but a simple man and an oxy moron at that."

His wife's eyes were red-rimmed and puffy. She snorted at his words. Malcolm fetched a scrap of linen for her to wipe her tears, placing it into her hand before going to the table to pour her a cup of tea. "Alethia, if you dinna tell me what vexes you, how am I to make it right?"

"You *married* me."

"Aye?" He handed her the tea and took a seat beside her.

"You don't love me."

"Who told you this?"

"Liam. He said, you better than anyone should know you have no choice when your heart is given . . ."

"Aye. My heart is given." He nodded solemnly.

She burst into tears. "Why would you marry me when you love someone else?"

"I would no' do such a thing."

"You've never said you love *me.* So, it must be . . ." She blinked at him and looked genuinely confused.

He put his arm around her shoulders. "Drink your tea, lass."

She took a sip, opened her mouth to say something, and then shut it again.

"Do you no' ken the meaning of *mo anam*?"

"No." She shrugged her shoulders. "I assumed it meant 'my burden to bear' . . . or . . . or . . . my *responsibility.*"

"Nay. It means my soul, or the very air I breathe."

"Oh." She glanced at him.

"And *mo cridhe* means my heart."

"It does?"

"Alethia, with your powers to discern a man's intent, have you no' listened to what my heart and soul tell you every day?"

"I've *tried,*" she wailed. "What I get is a tangle. I have no idea what it means."

"Aye, well, what I feel for you is no' a simple thing. It goes deep, and it is tangled—with worry and desire. And there's the instinct to protect, possessiveness, and you do aggravate me at times, woman." Her eyes grew wide at his words.

"My heart beats only for you, Alethia. You are the very center of my world." He took her hand, twining their fingers together. "Now and forever." He brought her hand to his mouth and kissed her knuckles. "'Tis you I love, lass. And Liam spoke the truth. I had no choice in the matter. I lost my heart the very day I found you by the side of the road."

"*Oh.*"

She started to cry. Again. He took the tea from her and set it on the table by their bed. "Do you no' have something to tell me as well?"

"I . . . love you too," she sobbed, throwing her arms around his neck.

Malcolm lay back on the bed, bringing her with him, and tried to hide his smile. Tucking her body next to his, he rubbed her back until she yawned into his chest. "Is there anything else you wish to tell me?" He held his breath.

"Yes, Malcolm. I'm . . ."

He waited. "Aye?"

"I'm so very tired," she whispered.

"Humph. To bed with you, woman." He helped her out of her gown and tucked her in, stretching out beside her.

"Oh, Malcolm. I feel . . . another vision . . . coming." She turned to burrow closer into his side. "This is becoming a real pain in the ass."

And with that, she slipped from him, appearing as if asleep. Malcolm lay beside her and thought about her visions. Could it be the bairn causing them? She'd said once before she'd never had visions. Why now? Mayhap they came to her only when those she loved were in peril. If so, she was certainly a treasure to the well-being of his clan.

Poor lass. Extra precautions would have to be taken to see she took care of herself. Wrapping his arms tighter around her, he nuzzled the crown of her head and dreamed about his son, calculating when the lad would be born.

"It's a girl," Alethia murmured.

He drew back and looked at her in surprise. She gave no indication she was aware she'd spoken. He didn't doubt her words for a second. Och, well. There'd be plenty of time for sons. His thoughts drifted to the lass they'd have next fall. He smiled and played with a strand of his wife's silky hair while imagining his wee daughter with chestnut hair and eyes like the ocean.

"Malcolm, I'm just saying I know more about the Comyn keep than you do." Alethia rushed to keep up with his pace as he strode down the hall toward his father's solar. "I need to be there while you and your men plan. There are things you have not thought of. I can draw a diagram."

"You will no' be coming with us to Castle Rait, True."

"I haven't said anything about coming with you." She threw her hands up in exasperation.

He stopped and swiveled to face her. "Are you saying you'll agree to stay here where 'tis safe while I am away?" His gaze bored into her, and he gripped her upper arms.

"I haven't asked if I can come. I know it's pointless." She looked him square in the eye. It wasn't really a lie; she did know better than to ask. Besides, she knew their plans backward and forward, including the errors. She'd be there, all right. And she'd help them with the flaws, ensuring their success.

Studying her face for several tense moments, he finally grunted. "Mayhap you can be of help. You ken the keep, you say?"

"The last vision I had I made a point of getting to know the place. Remember I told your father I can commit to memory anything I study? Well, now's the time to put that talent to use." As the words left her mouth, Giselle's prophecy came back to her in a rush. Had the gypsy known this talent would be needed? She sucked in a breath. Had she also known she'd start having visions?

"What is it?"

"Giselle said I had hidden talents, and that I would need them all. Malcolm, this is what she sent me here to do. Don't you see? I can give you information that will save your life. Yours, Mairen's, and every MacKintosh warrior in your company."

"Come then."

Once all were settled around the large, rectangular table, she began to draw a map of the Comyn keep on a large square of vellum. "Their kitchen is not attached. It's a separate building, here." She sketched the building where it stood behind the castle. "This is the door they use to transfer food into the great hall. Mairen's chamber is here at the east end of this corridor." She pointed to the spot. "She'll be locked in, but not guarded. Liam." She paused to look into his attentive gaze. "Can you get word to her?"

"I'll find a way."

"Tell her to bar the door from within. You must somehow get a rope ladder to her, and instruct her to hide it well. The only way for her to escape will be through her window. The small gate built into the curtain wall lies not far from where she'll come down."

Alethia looked around the room at the men hanging on her every word. That she could aid them against the Comyn's murderous plot gave her a sense of purpose—it humbled and frightened her at the same time. She cared about these people, and more than one life hung in the balance. They'd come to be her family. All of them had a place in her heart.

"You need to know this—the villagers, bakers, blacksmith, craftsmen and shepherds—they know nothing of the planned treachery. They think the reconciliation is for real, and they welcome an end to the bloodshed. They must not be harmed."

"I agree." Malcolm nodded.

She smiled at him and continued. "Once the signal is given, one of you must see to it the doors to the great hall and the kitchen are locked. Only the men the Comyn has with him know what is to come. He planned it that way so they can claim it was you and your men who attacked them first."

A cry of outrage erupted in the small room.

"Let us hear the rest," Malcolm commanded, and the noise stopped.

"This is where Mairen comes in," she added, her eyes on Liam.

"I dinna ken your meaning," Liam said.

"Mairen knows her father's plan," she said. "That's why he keeps her locked in her chamber. He caught her listening as he discussed it with his men shortly after they received word of the edict from King James. He already suspects she has a lover within our ranks. And though he's not certain, he believes Mairen told us where to find the Comyns who rode on to Nairn after we retook Meikle Geddes."

"Aye, but that does no' explain—" Liam began.

She flashed him an exasperated look. "Liam, your king has issued an edict forbidding the clans from fighting amongst themselves. The Red Comyn's plan is very clever. Not only does he kill all of you, but he casts our entire clan as insurgents." She glanced at Malcolm. "Your father would have returned to find his only son and nephews slain and his clan disgraced."

"Och, I ken your meaning. Mairen will provide testimony to the contrary." Malcolm turned to Liam. "She'll prove her loyalty to you by doing so, which will ensure her acceptance by our people. How have you come by this information, True? Can we trust it, or are you speculating?"

"When I have a vision, it's like being a ghost." She smiled at the sudden flurry of movement as many of the men made the sign of the cross. "I seem to land in the future or the past as needed. I'm free to walk around, listen in on conversations, and explore the grounds.

Like Mairen, I gathered the information by listening in while they plotted." Alethia met each of their looks. None challenged her word. Satisfied, she went back to her diagram.

"Most of you will go through the main entrance. Liam and Galen, here's where you must enter. Liam, have your man—"

"His man?" Malcolm frowned.

"Yes. Liam planted someone he trusts inside the keep long ago to look out for Mairen and to carry messages between them." She glared at Malcolm for interrupting. "Liam, have him see to it the small door in the curtain wall is unlocked. And of course, he'll return here with us."

"You are no' coming, lass." Malcolm scowled.

"Of course not. I only got caught up in the plan." The heat of a blush rose to her cheeks at her inadvertent slip. "I meant with you," she muttered.

CHAPTER NINETEEN

"Wake, *mo céile*." Malcolm nudged her.

Alethia stretched and turned to him. "Is it time?"

"Aye."

She pushed the warm furs back and sat up. Swinging her legs slowly to the floor, she gave herself a few moments to adjust. She'd made Malcolm promise to wake her before he and his men left for the Comyn keep, a day's ride east of Loch Moigh.

"Go back to sleep, True. 'Tis no' yet dawn."

"No. I want to see you off." She stood up and accepted the robe he offered. Malcolm had already dressed. She stepped into his open arms. His broadsword hung down his back, and a multitude of daggers were hidden all over his body. "Please be careful."

"Always."

"Remember everything we talked about when we planned."

"I will."

"I love you, Malcolm. Remember that." She felt the rumble deep in his chest as he chuckled.

"How could I forget?" Lifting her chin, his mouth found hers in a lingering kiss. Stepping back, he ran a knuckle down her cheek. "Best leave now while I'm still able."

Clutching the front of her robe together, she watched as he walked out the door, waited several seconds to be sure he'd really left, and then rushed to her trunk. She pulled on a pair of jeans and a leather tunic and slipped into her moccasins. Next she gathered her bow and the quiver of arrows and retrieved the pouch full of supplies she'd hidden under the mattress.

Wrapped in her wool cloak, Alethia crossed to the door and stuck her head out cautiously. She stepped into the deserted corridor, ran to the garderobe and cursed under her breath about the constant need to visit that particular room.

Near the kitchen, she hid in the shadows, peered inside and waited until backs were turned to slip past and out the back door, taking cover where she could along the path toward shore.

It had been easy enough to secure Ian's skiff again. She had claimed she wanted to gather healing herbs on the mainland and explore the lake a little. No one had doubted or questioned her request. Her plans were a secret even from Hunter. If anyone had known, they would have stopped her. A pang of guilt sluiced through her for the worry she'd cause.

It was *her* job save Malcolm's life, even if it meant putting herself and their child at risk. She could not remain behind knowing what she knew. And trusting someone else to perform the deed was out of the question. *Only you can tip the scale, Alethia.* Giselle had said the words sealing her fate, and now the time had come. She swallowed her fear and prayed for courage.

When she reached the shore and the hidden skiff, she took deep breaths to slow her racing heart and watched as the ferry loaded with men crossed the lake. She knew where Liam and Galen would split off from the rest of the party. They would approach Castle Rait from the rear. She planned to stay far enough back to escape detection. She'd join them once it was too late to be sent back.

Malcolm would be furious, but he'd be alive. She could bear his fury—not his death.

The ferry landed, sparking a flurry of activity as the men left the village. As soon as they rode over the crest of the first hill, she launched the boat, tossing her things into a heap on the bottom.

Other than a few tense moments trying to avoid detection by the stable master, everything went according to plan. She led Ikwe to a mounting block and climbed onto her back. All she had to do was remain hidden, and everything would be OK. Keeping her mare close to the forest, she stuck to the shadowy regions off the main trail and hung well back.

Liam and Galen split off from the rest of the group near midday. Alethia continued to keep her distance from them for another hour or so, then urged her mare into a gallop to catch up. She came over a small rise and reined to a halt in a panic. The two men had disappeared.

She scanned the ground and the horizon for any sign of them. Her heart pounded in her chest, and her eyes stung with tears. No matter. If necessary, she'd get there on her own.

"Alethia Grace!"

Alethia jerked in the saddle at the sound behind her, and Ikwe sidestepped in agitation. She fought for control of her horse and turned in the saddle to see Liam emerge from behind the rise.

"What the devil do you think you are doing, lass?"

His tone, a mixture of anger and exasperation, grated on her already raw nerves. "I think I am saving my husband's life," she snapped.

Galen appeared from the other side of the trail and snatched her horse's bridle.

Liam stood beside her, his face a furious scowl. "God's blood, True, you must be mad." He put his sword back into its sheath. "Turn back. Now."

"I won't. Nothing you say or do will stop me. I'm going—with or without your help."

"I could tie you to yon tree." He nodded toward a single young oak growing nearby.

"You would risk having something happen to me while I'm tied? I'd be unable to defend myself against man or animal," she reasoned. "We don't have time to debate the issue. I'm coming with you, or I'm going alone."

"My lady," Galen pleaded. "Malcolm will feed my innards to the crows if we dinna stop ye. Please, turn back."

"No. I have to be there."

"Galen, you take her back. I'll continue on." Liam retrieved his horse from behind the hill.

"Nay, Liam. You ken as well as I 'twill take both of us to rescue your lass. Besides, 'tis our way to see that none go without another watching his back." Galen scowled at Liam. "We stick together."

"Aye, but we canna leave True here, and we canna take her with us. You must take her back to Moigh Hall," Liam commanded as he glared at her. "She willna return on her own."

She jerked Ikwe's head up and kicked her into a canter, breaking Galen's hold. Let them bicker; she hadn't the time to waste.

Both men wore fierce expressions as they rode up to flank her. Neither tried to stop her. They must have concluded she'd be safer in their company than by herself. Good. That's exactly what she'd counted on.

By late afternoon, the keep came into view. As far as castles went, the small stone edifice fell far short when compared to Moigh Hall's imposing size.

"Castle Rait is no' much in the way of a holding. The MacKintosh held this keep at one time. 'Twas long before my birth, or Malcolm's." Liam reached for her mare's bridle, bringing them to a halt. "From now on, we use only signing. You will remain with me and Galen until we return home, True."

"Liam, I must get to the minstrels' gallery inside the keep. I'll stay there until the fight is over." He started to protest, and she placed her hand on his arm. "I had the visions for a reason. I know the outcome. I can guarantee that if I am where I'm supposed to be, all will be well. If I am not, Malcolm will die today." She could see in his eyes the internal battle he fought. "Shall I tell you what happens? Will that convince you?"

She waited for his reply and watched as he came to a decision.

"Nay." With a nod, he kicked his horse into a canter.

She and Galen followed suit, and the three continued on in silence.

"*I will see you safe to the gallery,*" Liam signed.

"*She must remain with us,*" Galen argued.

"*I won't remain with you, no matter what. And you two must see to Mairen.*" She watched him struggle against her words, finally accepting what she knew to be inevitable.

They kept close to the brush near the surrounding forest and worked their way around to the rear of the castle. They hid, waited and learned the rhythm of the single guard walking the catwalk of the curtain wall facing them.

"*The door lies just beyond the rock formation, there.*" Alethia pointed. Liam and Galen nodded.

"*We are to wait until the sun meets the horizon,*" Liam signed.

Alethia reached into her pouch for pieces of venison jerky and handed each of the men a share of her cache. Liam passed her a skin full of water, and she drank her fill. Galen offered oatcakes, and the three shared their meal in silence.

Once the sun had reached the horizon, Liam turned to her. "*I must see to the guard. Galen, you and True meet me inside the door. I'll signal when it's safe.*" Galen nodded, and Liam left. Alethia's stomach knotted with fear. She took a deep breath and tried to calm herself. She knew what she had to do.

Galen tugged at her sleeve, nodding toward the catwalk. She saw Liam, just as he disappeared below the edge of the stone fortress. She and Galen crept toward the castle, moving in the shadows and scrambling around the rocks hiding the door. They reached it without incident and slipped through like shadows in the dusk.

Malcolm's skin prickled with unease as he and his men rode through the portcullis and into the inner bailey of their enemy's keep. His wife had said the villagers knew nothing of their laird's plan. He looked over the villagers crowding the courtyard. Their eyes were filled with a wary curiosity.

Malcolm caught the eye of a large man wearing the long leather apron of a smith, and he offered a smile. Was that hope flaring in the man's eyes? The smith nodded, a brief smile lighting his face. He lifted a young lad to his shoulders to watch their procession. Encouraged, Malcolm smiled and greeted any whose eyes caught his, signaling his men to follow suit.

What to do about these people had plagued him from the onset. Like him, most of them wanted nothing more than to live out their lives in peace.

Ronald the Red, the laird of clan Comyn, and his son, John, approached from the keep, surrounded by their men. Malcolm watched as father and son sauntered toward them. Both wore smug looks. Neither hid their disdain for him and his men.

"Welcome, Malcolm of clan MacKintosh." The laird spoke loudly for the benefit of his assembled people. "Today we end the feud between our two clans."

A cheer rose among the villagers. The Comyn's shrewd eyes

assessed their party as they dismounted, and several lads approached to take their horses. Malcolm held a hand up to stop them. "We will see to our horses ourselves. Your lads can lead the way to the stables," Malcolm said.

A few of their young warriors not yet blooded in battle had volunteered to come along for this purpose. Malcolm's young men gathered the reins as he spoke. They would see the horses were fed, watered and cared for before removing them to the agreed upon spot outside the curtain wall. "I'm sure you understand." Malcolm turned to challenge the Comyn. "'Twill take some time for trust to build."

The Comyn snorted derisively. "So be it. Come, let us enter. A feast has been prepared. We wish to offer our hospitality."

The laird's smile reminded Malcolm of a serpent before it swallowed its prey whole. His hackles rose. Flanked by Angus and Robley, he followed the snake into its lair. True's description of the great hall proved accurate. The large table, already laid for the feast, dominated one end of the hall. Stairs leading to a minstrels' gallery and the passage into the private living quarters lay to the left of the large hearth.

"As you can see, we are unarmed." The laird spread his arms, his hands empty. "In good faith, will you no' lay aside your weapons?"

The Comyn's request brought Malcolm's attention into sharp focus. "If, as you say, your intent to end the feud between our clans is sincere, we have no need of our weapons." A murmur of voices rang throughout the hall. "So it will make no difference whether or no' we are armed." Moving toward the dais, Malcolm studied the laird's reaction to his words. "We keep them."

"You insult our hospitality and our honor," John cried, as angry accusations flew through the air, polarizing the room into two distinct factions.

"Come, you canna expect us to trust the word of a Comyn blindly," Malcolm challenged Ronald. "We have been enemies for centuries. If you are honorable, it makes no difference whether or no' I have my claymore to hand. My sword will remain in its scabbard so long as no act of aggression occurs against me or mine. You have my word."

Again the Comyn's cunning eyes assessed him. Malcolm kept his expression neutral.

"It changes nothing," Ronald announced, gesturing to his men to take their places at the table.

That too proved to be exactly as True had described. The Comyn warriors took every other seat, separating him and his men. A chill crept down his spine as Malcolm imagined what it must have been like for his wife to watch as every MacKintosh man in the hall bled to death before her eyes. She had proven again and again to possess an inner strength and resourcefulness that humbled him and filled him with pride.

As soon as he'd taken his place on the dais between the laird and his son, servants came forward and filled their goblets with *uisge beatha*. Another point True had warned them about. Raising his cup in a toast, the Comyn bid them all drink to their truce. As agreed, he and his men did no more than to touch the liquid to their lips. Servants rushed forward bearing platters of food, as the Comyns made idle conversation and encouraged them to partake of the fine spirits they offered. 'Twas their best, they claimed, in honor of their reconciliation. Malcolm forced himself to relax and waited.

"*Wait.*" Liam pressed himself against the wall and watched both the kitchen and the door to the keep. Once clear, he grabbed Alethia's hand, pulled her inside and dashed for the stairs ahead.

At the top, Alethia took the lead. "*I know the way. There are no guards here at present. You must go back to help Mairen.*"

"*I said I would see you safely to the minstrels' gallery, and I shall.*"

Arguing with him would be a waste of valuable time. Instead, she led him the short distance down the dark corridor to the small door into the gallery. "*This is it. Return to Galen. Mairen waits for your signal.*"

She watched him leave as soundlessly as they had arrived. Holding her breath, she put pressure on the door and prayed the hinges were well oiled. It didn't budge. Frustrated and tense, she waited until noise from the great hall rose loud enough to cover any noise the door might make. It didn't take long before an argument broke out below. Sending them her silent thanks, she pushed with all her might. The door creaked open, and she slipped through.

The small gallery hadn't been used in a good long while. She covered her face with both hands to smother the sound of a sneeze, as each step sent up a cloud of dust. She crouched low and crept toward the half wall overlooking the hall below. Unfastening her cloak, she let it fall and slipped her bow out of the quiver slung on her back. She reached the railing and pressed herself up against the wall far enough back that any man happening to glance her way wouldn't see her.

She found the folded skin holding the bowstring in her pouch and drew it out. Her hands shaking, she fit the loop at the end of the string onto the notched end of the bow, stepped through it, and bent the wood over her leg to loop it over the top notch. Sweat beaded her forehead.

Cautiously, she peered over the railing at the scene below. It was not yet time for the toast. Notching an arrow, she listened. Her body thrummed with tension and dread. She forced herself to breathe deeply. It wouldn't help anyone if she couldn't shoot straight because of nerves. Closing her eyes, she leaned her head against the wall and again prayed for courage—courage and a good aim.

The laird gave the signal for slaughter. His voice rang loud through the hall, and her heart jumped to her throat.

"From this day forward, let there be peace between our two clans. Come, lift your cups and let us toast the dead."

Each MacKintosh warrior leaped from his place as the signal was given. Man-for-man they stood behind their Comyn foes as if the move had been choreographed. The sound of swords being drawn from their scabbards filled the air with a metallic twang, making her ears ring.

Angus crossed to the doors of the keep and lowered the beam of wood that would keep the innocent out of the impending fray.

Malcolm pressed the tip of his sword against the throat of the treacherous laird, staying well out of the man's reach. Everything went still. Tension filled the hall. She held her breath.

"Before we toast, raise up your right hand so that we might bear witness to your sincerity," Malcolm shouted.

The laird roared with rage and brought up the hand gripping a dagger. Every Comyn followed suit.

"So much for the word and the honor of a Comyn. Move and he dies," Malcolm proclaimed. "Unlike you, who would win a battle through cowardice and treachery, the MacKintosh will only fight fair. Let us end this once and for all." He stepped back, but remained poised to strike. "Gather your weapons."

The Comyn warriors scrambled for their swords and clubs where they rested against the opposite wall. The MacKintosh men kicked the trestle table over, sending the contents of their goblets and trenchers crashing to the rushes covering the floor. The smell of the spilled feast mingled with the scent of fear and sweat radiating off the men. The warriors faced each other from opposite ends of the hall, waiting for someone to make the first move. Then all hell broke loose with the crash of metal against metal and the sounds of men exerting themselves in a fight to the death.

Alethia readied her weapon and fixed her eyes on her husband. He fought John—just as her vision foretold. Without sparing a glance toward the others, she watched Malcolm and John. Her husband had the upper hand, but she'd witnessed this fight before and knew the outcome.

John forced Malcolm into a retreat with a flurry of blows. Malcolm fended them off easily enough, took one step back, then another. She pulled her bowstring taut, holding it in position until her muscles shook with the effort.

Another step, and the laird himself appeared behind Malcolm, tripping him with an outstretched leg. It took only an instant as Malcolm fell to the floor and tried to roll away. John struck, opening a gash in her husband's thigh. Malcolm shouted with rage as John lifted his broadsword to attack Malcolm while he was down. Pushing himself back with his legs, he attempted to scramble away, but his body met solid wall. He lifted his sword to deflect the blow, and John kicked viciously at his wrists, sending Malcolm's sword flying through the air to land out of reach.

The enemy stood poised to deliver the blow that would end her husband's life.

She aimed for the most vulnerable spot on John's body. Taking a deep breath, she held it and released the arrow. Time slowed. She watched without breathing as the arrow flew toward its target and pierced his neck. John dropped his sword, sending it clattering to the floor. Both of his hands clawed at the wooden shaft protruding from his throat. His mouth opened and closed, and blood spurted down his chest. He dropped to his knees and fell over. His body twitched, and his blood formed a crimson pool in the rushes beneath him.

Frozen to the spot, she turned her eyes to Malcolm. He'd followed the arrow's trajectory back to its source. Their eyes met—and held. Disbelief flashed across his face, followed by fury like she'd never seen before.

Gasping for breath, she pulled back. Her ordeal wasn't over. Bringing another arrow to her bow, she faced the door into the gallery. Ronald the Red had also followed the arrow's path back to her. She'd killed his son. He would be on his way with murderous intent—and this time, she had no vision to guide her.

CHAPTER TWENTY

The coppery scent of blood and death permeated the keep and wafted up to the minstrels' gallery where Alethia stood her ground. The groans of the dying and the occasional clang of swords from those few still fighting filled the air. Above it all, the sound of her own ragged breathing and her heart pounding in her chest filled her head. A single bead of sweat trickled down her temple. She sucked in her breath—and held it.

The door to the gallery slammed against the wall with a loud crack, sending a cloud of dust into the air as the laird burst through. "Bitch. I am going to kill you," he growled.

Her skin crawled, and her stomach roiled at the murderous rage aimed her way. The arrow she aimed at his heart was the only thing keeping him at bay. "Don't move. Not a muscle. *Help!*" she shouted, not taking her eyes off Ronald the Red. "I need help in the minstrels' gallery!" She shouted again, her entire body trembling. Weak from fatigue and the aftereffects of adrenaline pumping through her system, would her muscles obey the demands she made on them?

Killing someone threatening a loved one was one thing. Facing your own death—or killing a man while he looked you in the eye—was another thing altogether.

God, let one of the MacKintosh warriors get here in time. She caught a movement as the laird's right hand shifted. The glint of metal gave her a target, and instinct took over. Another arrow flew from her bow.

It pierced the palm of the laird's hand, and his dagger dropped to the floor with a thud. Ronald growled with pain, his face twisted in a mask of hatred. She notched another arrow and watched beads of sweat form on her enemy's forehead. He bit the end of the arrow to break the shaft behind the steel point and pulled it from his palm, never taking his eyes from her.

Another dagger appeared from his sleeve as he advanced. She knew he meant to get close enough to render her weapon useless, He meant to slit her throat.

"Don't move," she croaked, taking a step back. "Or the next arrow will go through your eye." Why hadn't any of their men come to help her? Had they lost the battle after all? Her legs and arms now felt like rubber bands. She wouldn't be able to stand for much longer, much less send an arrow with any force. And if she fell, she'd be defenseless, an easy kill. She drew her arrow back as taut as she could manage, resolved to kill him if she could. Ronald came at her. She released the arrow. It grazed his shoulder, hit the wall and came to land on the floor behind him. "No," she sobbed.

The sound of footsteps in the corridor distracted the laird. All the air left her lungs as Malcolm burst through the door and lunged at Ronald the Red. Alethia moved to the farthest corner, out of range of the wrestling men, and collapsed to her hands and knees. She vomited in the dust and watched through eyes blurred with tears as her wounded husband fought for their lives.

All was quiet when Malcolm lifted her to her feet; his strong arms came around her. She leaned against him and sobbed.

"We must away," he whispered into her ear.

She managed to nod. Her insides felt like Jell-O. It took great effort to put one foot in front of another. Malcolm lifted her over the laird's still body. MacKintosh warriors lined the hallway. Some were bloody, but all were standing. Every one of them put their hands on their hearts and inclined their heads to her as Malcolm set her down.

Fresh tears started at their gesture of fealty. Malcolm tugged her hand to get her moving. His men fell into formation, some taking up the front, and the rest guarding them from behind.

"You're wounded," she whispered.

"Only a scratch."

"I saw more than a scratch." She fought the building hysteria and swallowed the urge to laugh. In shock, dazed, she stared at her empty hands and stopped. "My bow . . . I . . . I . . . dropped it."

"We'll have a new one made."

Malcolm tried to get her moving again. She planted her feet. "I want *that* one. I want my bow." She knew she was being unreasonable, but she couldn't help it.

"God's blood, woman." He rubbed his face. "Angus," he called over his shoulder. "Retrieve my wife's bow."

In mere seconds, Angus returned with her bow unstrung. Instead of handing it to her, he tucked it into her quiver and gently wrapped her cloak around her shoulders. "Oh. Thank you, Angus. I forgot all about my cloak." She ran the thick fabric through her fingers. Her thinking had grown disjointed, as if her head had been stuffed with wool, and all she could think were fuzzy thoughts.

"*Now* may we proceed?" Malcolm's tone held an edge of impatience—and anger.

"Of course." She straightened her spine and took a step. Her legs buckled, and she sank to the floor. Malcolm scooped her up. "I'm sorry," she whispered into his stiff neck. "I'm sorry. I . . . can't seem to . . . walk."

Once out of the keep, they headed for the small gate where she, Liam and Galen had entered hours ago. Darkness had fallen, and they made no effort to hide their movements as they joined the rest of their party waiting to depart on the other side.

As soon as Malcolm set her feet on the ground, a petite woman hurled herself at her, throwing her arms around her shoulders. Alethia could feel Mairen's body tremble, and her tears dampened her tunic where they fell onto her shoulder.

"Thank you. Oh, thank you," Mairen murmured.

"You're welcome," Alethia whispered, patting her back.

Liam peeled her away. "We must take our leave." He helped Mairen to mount Alethia's mare.

She blinked, confused. "What am I—"

"You will ride with me," Malcolm snapped, reining his horse up beside her. Robley lifted her from behind into her husband's waiting arms. Malcolm signed his command, and the party departed with haste.

They were well on their way when she finally risked focusing on Malcolm. His emotions alternated with a rapidity that made her dizzy. Fury, relief, frustration, concern—then back to fury. Her nerves, frayed beyond repair, couldn't take much more.

"You placed yourself in danger," Malcolm snarled into her ear.

"You're *welcome*," she snarled back.

He gave her a shake. "You disobeyed me again."

"Ha! You never specifically ordered me not to follow, because I knew better than to *ask*."

"You could have died."

"I know." She scowled at him over her shoulder. "I also know you *would* have died for certain if I hadn't been there. I saw the whole thing happen in my visions."

"Damnation, woman. Do you think *you* are the only one among us who can draw a bow and shoot an arrow? You had only to tell me what was to be, and I would have put a man where you stood."

"No." She shook her head. "This is what I was sent here to do. I know you don't understand, but I *had* to be the one to save you. If it had been anyone else . . ." Her voice broke. "I couldn't leave it to chance."

Twisting around to face him, she pleaded, "Look, I know how much you enjoy giving me an ear beating. But can we let it go until tomorrow? I have bigger things to worry about, and saving your life has exhausted me." If she hadn't been so worn out, she might have been amused by Malcolm's stunned expression. Instead, she sank back against his chest and closed her eyes. Several moments of blissful silence ensued.

"What, pray tell, do you have to worry about now?"

"Ouch." His words, and the tone he used, stung. She didn't have the energy for this. A painful lump formed in her throat.

"Tell me." He gave her another little shake.

"Giselle said I had hidden talents. Hence the visions. She said my task was to right a wrong. Hence the Comyn laird's evil plot to do you all in. That's definitely a wrong. I have completed my task, and now Giselle will come for me. She'll send me back where I came from, and you won't be able to stop her." Her voice broke. "No one will be able to stop her."

Shutting her mouth tight, she fumed. She had saved his life, and it rankled him. Instead of thanking her, he scolded and lectured. Her actions had been a blow to his masculinity, and it was obvious he couldn't see beyond his wounded ego. *Stupid, stupid man and his stupid fifteenth-century male pride.*

"Let her come. She will no' take you." His hold around her waist tightened. "You have no faith in me," he accused.

"Ditto."

"Sleep, Alethia. 'Tis a long ride home."

Malcolm prayed never to experience that kind of fear again as long as he lived. He couldn't bear it when his wife placed herself in harm's way. When he'd seen her peering over the rail of the minstrels' gallery with bow in hand, his heart had stopped. When she'd called for help, he feared arriving too late. He'd aged a decade in the seconds it took to reach her.

"Does she sleep?" Robley asked as he brought his mount closer to his.

Malcolm checked. "Aye. She'll likely sleep the entire journey."

"There is something you should know." Robley spoke quietly beside him. "Giselle is in Inverness. She resides in a small cottage at the edge of the village."

"How do you come by this information?" Malcolm's protective instincts leaped within him. His hold on his wife tightened.

"I saw her with my own eyes when I went to Inverness for supplies for Meikle Geddes. I tell you, Malcolm, there is something uncanny odd about that old hag. 'Twas a decade ago she told your fortune, yet she has no' aged one bit. 'Tis unnatural." Robley pointed to True. "She is right to fear her. And you would do well to take heed. Has True no' proven herself to us many times over?" He gave Malcolm a hard look. "I think you are too hard on the lass. She deserves your gratitude, no' your wrath."

"I'll no' argue, Robley. I confess, I've never been so afraid as when I saw my wife in the keep of our enemies. I spoke harshly out of fear for her." Truth be told, he felt awful. It galled him. He should be protecting her, not the other way around. "I vow, the woman is going to be the death of me. 'Twas utter foolishness on her part." He leaned closer so none but Robley would hear him. "I canna bear the thought of losing her."

Robley grinned. "That is what you must tell her, Malcolm. I pray one day to find a woman as braw and canny as True. I am considering a journey to her land to see if there might be more like her there. I would gladly accept a worry such as the one you hold in your arms." He placed his hand on Malcolm's shoulder and gave it a shake. "Hold her close. Put your pride aside, man, and thank her."

"Humph." He'd have to work on his pride. Just once *he* wanted to be the one doing the rescuing.

Robley laughed and dropped back. Malcolm turned his thoughts to the fate of the villagers they'd left behind. A pang of regret shot through him. He spurred his horse ahead to ride alongside Liam and his lady. "Liam, will you introduce us?"

Malcolm saw her flinch at the sound of his voice, as if she expected recrimination, or worse. Even by the light of the half moon he could see the fading bruises on her face and neck, her split lip. His heart went out to her. She'd suffered brutality at the hands of the very man who should have protected and cherished her. Her hands trembled as she held the reins.

"Aye. I'm sorry we had no time to do so earlier." Liam reached to cover Mairen's hands with his for an instant. "Mairen, this is my cousin, Malcolm. Malcolm, may I present my betrothed, Mairen."

Mairen's voice quavered with emotion. "I owe you my life, my lord. My thanks to you and your lady wife. May God bless you both."

"My wife says you are well loved by your people. What will become of them?" Malcolm asked.

"I dinna ken their fate. They are good folk and had no knowledge of my father's treachery."

"But you did?" Malcolm asked.

"Aye, I did. And if he hadna been so certain of victory this eve, I would be dead now. 'Tis only because he wished to use me for his own gain that he let me live. Dinna blame my people for his black heart, for they had no hand in it."

"I bear them no ill will. 'Tis their future that concerns me now. They will discover their laird's death on the morrow. Your warriors died with their swords to hand. 'Twas a fair fight, though they did no' deserve fairness." Malcolm watched Mairen closely, gauging her reaction to his harsh words. She nodded and averted her gaze. He could see she felt shame on behalf of her clan.

Malcolm turned to his cousin. "I have been giving this some thought, Liam. What say you to the notion of joining those Comyns remaining at Castle Rait with our clan? There may be some who are willing."

"We can offer, Malcolm. Though 'tis unlikely. Our clans have been enemies for far too long."

"Aye, but when you and Mairen wed, there will be those amongst them who remain loyal to her. I suggest you hasten your union, handfast as soon as possible, and send word right away to Castle Rait of your marriage. That is, if you are willing."

Liam's eyes went to Mairen. "What say you, love? We can say our vows on the morrow and have the union blessed in a fortnight when the priest comes to Moigh Hall."

"I should be in mourning for my father and brother, but I feel nothing but relief. Is that a sin, Liam?" Her eyes, wide with worry and pain, filled with tears. "You ken I want to be your wife more than anything," she cried. "I—"

"'Tis no sin, lass. I ken it will take you some time to recover, but there's no reason we canna handfast." Liam reached for her hands again.

She nodded through her tears.

"Is there someone at Castle Rait you trust, Mairen?" Malcolm asked.

"Aye, our garrison commander is an honorable man. Father assigned him duty elsewhere during the feast. He knew Wallace would object, and Father feared a rebellion."

"Does he read?" Liam asked.

"He does." She nodded.

"Are you willing?" Malcolm prayed she'd prove herself worthy of Liam. "Will you tell the truth of your father's treachery to your people?"

"Aye, I will tell them the truth, and to our king as well. For surely we will be called upon for an accounting of today's events." Mairen's spine straightened.

"Liam, they will have need of someone to lead them. With you and Mairen wed, 'twould make sense for you to become laird of Castle Rait. If King James approves after he has heard all that has occurred, would you agree to it?"

"I dinna ken if they would accept a MacKintosh as laird."

"It's brilliant," Mairen whispered. "I canna think of a man better suited to lead us. Please, Liam, for my sake, and for the sake of my people, say you will."

Alethia awoke in her own bed to find herself draped in hot, naked Scot. Her eyes flew open to find the brilliant blue of her husband's gaze fixed upon her. Their conversation last night had ended in anger. She cast him a wary look and noticed something else. "I'm naked."

This elicited a low rumble from deep in Malcolm's chest. "Aye, that you are. I put you to bed last night and didna have the will to clothe you."

He moved his hips, and she could feel the hard length of his erection pressed against her thigh, causing a wave of answering heat and dampness to spread inside her. "Malcolm . . ." She pushed at his chest. "This will not fix things between us."

"I beg your forgiveness." He whispered into her ear and nuzzled her neck, leaving little kisses as he went. His large hands cradled her face as he looked deeply into her eyes. "I canna bear the thought of something happening to you. I vow I canna. My heart stopped beating when I saw you in the gallery. I won't live long if I must endure that kind of fear oft. I'm telling you, Alethia, I canna bear it." He brought his forehead to rest against hers. "I spoke out of fear for you, lass."

Holding each other tight, neither said a word for several moments. She had never been so grateful in her life. He felt so solid and warm against her, so alive. "I would have done anything to see you safe, Malcolm." Her throat tightened with emotion, and all she could manage was a raspy whisper. "I beg your forgiveness for putting you through so much. And I'm sorry, but I'd do it all over again if it meant I could hold you once more in my arms."

She put her arms around his neck. "Don't you get it? Don't you know I feel exactly the same way you do? I cannot bear the thought of something happening to you. My God, do you have any idea what it's been like for me these past few weeks? I saw you die over and over in my visions, and I couldn't do anything about it."

Malcolm nudged her thighs apart with one knee and moved to cradle his hips between them. Rocking slightly, he managed to work the tip of his erection between the folds of her already aroused flesh, to tease her with long, slow slides, gliding just so over the sensitive bud that now throbbed with urgency.

She sought his mouth with hers and kissed him with every ounce of feeling she held for him in her heart. Malcolm crushed her into the mattress with the force of his emotions. She welcomed the storm of passion, opening up to take him inside her body and her soul to a place that offered them both refuge against the uncertainty of a world filled with peril.

Later, their limbs still tangled, he gave her the ear beating she knew she deserved. Through it all, she smiled and kissed his face all over as he lectured her about safety, and explained all about how wives were supposed to obey their husbands. "Mmm-mm. OK. I've been properly chastised. Now I'm famished. Plus, Hunter, Lydia and Elaine will also want a piece of my hide for causing them worry."

Malcolm rose first, and she searched for the wound on his thigh. He'd spoken the truth. In the light of day, it appeared to be no more than a deep scratch. And it had already begun to heal.

She sat up slowly, waiting to see if she'd be able to get up without feeling nauseated. Malcolm handed her a piece of dry toast he snatched from the table by the hearth. She glanced up at him, surprised. "You know, don't you?"

He gave her a smug grin. "I share your bed every night, Alethia. Do you think I take no notice when your courses come, or when they fail to come? Think you I canna see the changes already taking place in your body?"

"What changes?" She glanced down at herself. She didn't see anything different.

"Your breasts have grown larger." His gaze slid over her body and came to rest on her breasts. "Your skin, when no' tinged green from nausea, fair glows. You want to sleep all the time, and you're always hungry."

"Oh."

"You spoke of it during one of your visions." He told her as he washed.

She gasped. "I did?"

"Aye. You said we are to have a wee lass. I've no reason to doubt you speak the truth."

He dressed as she nibbled the toast. "Cool." She smiled and covered her abdomen with one hand. "A little girl with golden hair and blue eyes." Suddenly feeling shy, she asked, "Are you pleased?"

"Aye." His smile took her breath. "I am pleased." He crossed the room to take her up in his arms. "How could I no' be, my love. I long to fill this keep with our bairns, to hear their laughter and watch them grow healthy and strong. You said you wanted a large family. Do you recall?" He brushed the hair from her face and kissed her brow.

"I remember everything," she whispered.

"I want to give you your heart's desire, *mo anam.* Your happiness brings me joy. However," he said as he smacked her bare bottom, "you're breeding. When you put your life at risk as you did at Castle Rait, you also risk our bairn. You *will* take more care in future, or there will be consequences. Now, get dressed, love. Liam and Mairen are to handfast this day."

"You're right, Malcolm. I will stay out of trouble." She crossed the chamber to wash. "I promise. I am so happy for them. Poor Liam has carried that burden for far too long. He didn't believe there could be a happy ending. Now, if only something could be done for Elaine." She stilled as the events from the previous day flooded her mind. "Malcolm, when will a priest come to Moigh Hall?"

"The middle of May. Why?"

"I . . . I . . . killed a man." Her emotions were swinging out of control, blissfully happy one moment and despairing the next. She didn't like it. "It's a mortal sin. I need to talk to a priest."

"Dinna think on it overmuch. There is no sin in protecting kith and kin. You did no wrong, Alethia." He drew her back into his arms and held her tight, rocking her back and forth in a gentle motion. "If I could take it from your mind I would, *mo céile.* Come, we've a handfasting to attend, and then a feast. Would you like to play your music this eve?"

She nodded against his shoulder and wondered if she should mention she hadn't really been sleeping when Robley told him about Giselle's whereabouts.

Alethia watched Mairen interact with Elaine and Lydia as they all sat in the solar. It had been eight days since they'd rescued the Comyn's daughter, and a week since Mairen and Liam had handfasted. She wanted to be close to Liam's new wife, and only one thing prevented her from feeling at ease.

Mairen's soft brown eyes gave no hint whether or not she knew Alethia had been the one who shot the arrow that killed her brother. She studied the woman. The evidence of her father's brutality had faded. Her lip had healed, and she no longer cringed when spoken to. Her bruises were yellowish smudges that would soon be gone altogether.

Everything about Mairen seemed soft—from her light golden-brown hair to her large brown eyes. She radiated goodness. How had such a warm and caring person come from such a cold, cruel father? She wondered what Mairen's mother must have been like. Had she willingly married the Red Comyn, or had she been given to him by an indifferent father?

They would remain in residence until negotiations were complete with the Comyns remaining at Castle Rait. Liam also wished to see his parents safely returned with William. Gathering her courage, Alethia prepared herself to broach the subject that had haunted her dreams. "Mairen, I need to talk to you about something."

"Nay, True. You dinna need to speak of it. I ken what troubles you." Mairen put her work in her lap and turned her attention to True. "Liam told me what occurred in the great hall at Rait."

"I killed your brother."

"You saved your husband's life, Liam's and mine." Mairen took her hand in both of hers. "My father and brother were two of a kind. John and I were ne'er close. What they intended shames me deeply. Do you no' ken I worry about how you must look upon me?"

"Oh, Mairen." Relief poured through her. "No one holds you responsible for your father's actions, or your brother's. Please, let's put this behind us."

"Aye, let's. We have much to look forward to. Laird William returns soon, and there is the birth of your bairn to anticipate. We are kin."

"Does everyone on the island know I am with child?" She glanced from Elaine to Lydia.

"Of course, dear." Lydia beamed.

A single tone sounded from the village horn. "Oh, brother. I'm really beginning to dislike that sound." Alethia folded the tiny sleep-sack she was making and rose to leave.

"Now you ken why I remain here when I hear it." Lydia smiled as she continued to work. "Word always reaches me soon enough."

"Elaine, Mairen, will you join me?" she asked. "I might be needed."

"I'll stay with Lydia." Mairen smiled.

Malcolm scanned the bailey for True. It seemed so long ago he'd insisted she stay inside the keep whenever the village horn sounded. She never had, of course, and he'd grown accustomed to having her by his side at the ferry landing. The shift in his thinking made him smile. She'd proven herself indispensable to the welfare of their clan. Robley had been correct—his people loved her.

True and his sister emerged from the keep at the same time, their arms linked, as they oft were, and their heads bent close to share their most intimate secrets or something they found amusing. The day would come, and soon, that Elaine would be given in marriage. 'Twould be a difficult time for his wife. He stepped into their path. "True, Elaine." He nodded to his sister. "Come, let us walk to the ferry together."

Taking True's hand, he tucked it into the crook of his elbow and studied her carefully. The worry she'd carried since they'd returned from Castle Rait had eased. She glowed with health, and he'd noticed a decline in the morning sickness. "How do you fare this morn, *mo céile*?"

"I'm great." She smiled. "I spoke with Mairen about her brother earlier, Malcolm, and everything is good between us."

Her voice faltered, and it became clear why her worry had eased. Bad dreams about taking the life of Mairen's brother troubled her oft in the past se'nnight. He'd soothed and comforted her every time until she fell back to sleep. Though she never said, he'd suspected part of her worry centered around Mairen. The issue had been resolved, and he hoped the dreams would cease to plague her. Such dreams could not be good for their bairn.

"Who do you think has arrived?" True tugged at his sleeve.

"'Tis most likely news from my father's party." He squeezed her hand. "He will return home shortly."

"Aye, True," Elaine added. "My father always sends word when he's been away for a time. He enjoys a bit of fanfare upon his return." Elaine exchanged a grin with her brother.

"Just so long as it's not another clan with an invitation to reconcile," she muttered.

Chuckling, he reassured her with a brief hug. They reached the landing as the ferry pulled to the shore. Another man wearing the garb of the king's messenger waited to disembark.

"I am Malcolm, son of William, the earl of Fife. Welcome," Malcolm greeted their guest.

The messenger bowed slightly once his feet were firmly planted on the beach. "My lord, I am Brian of York, King Henry's messenger. I bring you word from your father." Brian took a scroll of parchment from his satchel and handed it to him. "He bid me tell you he arrives one day hence," Brian said. "He plans to be here in time for the evening meal."

"Och, he'll expect a feast." Elaine clapped her hands together. "Come, True. We'll tell Mother and Molly. There will be music and dancing, of course."

"Do you need me?" she asked Malcolm.

"Nay, lass. Go with Elaine. I'll see our guest settled." Watching his wife walk back toward the keep, Malcolm vowed to tell his father of his wedded state immediately upon his arrival. And then he'd have to explain Mairen's presence—and the battle at Rait. "Does our king travel here with my father?"

"Nay, my lord. He travels on to Stirling," Brian told him as Malcolm guided him through the portcullis. "I travel with your father until his return, and then I'm off to spread the word throughout Scotia of your king's return."

Good, word of Castle Rait could not have reached them yet.

His mother's hand on his arm, and True and Elaine beside him, Malcolm watched as the ferry carried his father, uncle, aunt and their guardsmen across the loch. Their clan lined both sides of the path leading to the keep. The day could not have been more perfect, even if he'd ordered it thus. A few fat clouds drifted in the rare blue sky, and the air held the promise of the coming summer. The ripe scent of the earth ready for tilling and sowing permeated the island.

The ferry landed, and William's deep laughter filled the air. Malcolm went to him immediately, handing his mother into his father's waiting arms. 'Twas the same whenever the earl returned. The first thing he always did was seek his wife's long-missed affection. Malcolm moved forward to clasp his Uncle Robert's forearm. "'Tis good to see you home safe, Uncle Robert. Aunt Rosemary, welcome."

Soon the returning MacKintosh were surrounded with their clan, and Malcolm waited to take his place by his father's side so they could proceed to the keep.

William raised his hands in greeting and raised his voice so all could hear. "'Tis good to be home. I have much to share with you this eve, and I look forward to supping once again in the comfort of my own hall with my clansmen." A cheer rose, and the crowd parted, making a path for their laird and his family.

Taking his place by his father's side, Malcolm spoke quietly. "Father, if I could have a moment of your time before we sup, there are things we need to discuss."

"Can it no' wait until morning? I want nothing more than a bath, a hot meal and time alone with my lady wife."

"I would rather we—"

William stopped and put his hand on Malcolm's shoulder. "Lad, if whatever you have to say is so pressing, why did you no' send word of it before today?" He slapped his shoulder. "Come, 'twill keep one more day, aye?"

Why indeed? Mayhap it could wait. What harm, one more day? Seeking True in the crowd, he found her eyes on him, and he gave her a warm smile meant to reassure. She walked with Elaine and Mairen behind the returning members of their garrison. His mother had taken her place on his father's other side. Perhaps his mother would think to mention his handfasting sometime before the feast. No matter. His father would learn of it soon enough.

The MacKintosh clan filled the great hall to overflowing, and more plank-and-barrel tables had been set up in the bailey to accommodate the crowd attending the feast celebrating their laird's safe return. Malcolm reached for his wife's hand under the table. Giving it a squeeze, he smiled into her wide eyes. "'Tis a fine night, aye? After we eat, the tables and benches will be cleared from the hall for music and dancing."

"True," Robley said, leaning toward her. "If you dinna feel up to playing this eve, Liam and I will do the honors without you."

"I'm fine. I want to play." Her gaze went to the empty spots to Robley's right. "Where are Liam and Mairen, Robley?"

"They are with my father and mother and will be down shortly, I am certain. The feast will no' begin until all are present upon the dais." Robley winked at her.

Malcolm wondered how Liam fared with his parents. Movement on the stairs caught his eye, and he watched Liam and Mairen with Liam's parents descend into the hall. His uncle's face was grim, and he wondered which part of their tale had caused the look—the Comyn's treachery, or their son's union with the daughter of their enemy? True tugged on his sleeve.

"What is it? I can sense your tension."

He nodded toward the party coming down the stairs. "My uncle does no' look happy. I expect things will be somewhat strained this eve." Even as he spoke, Robert stopped at the bottom of the stairs, gestured to his father to join them, and then whispered in William's ear. Malcolm watched his father's face suffuse with color and his expression turned grim as well. Rosemary spoke rapidly, and his father nodded and visibly forced himself to calm down. Lydia had also spoken into his ear. William took Mairen's hand in his and bowed over it.

Malcolm did not envy his cousin. Liam had his arm protectively around Mairen, whose face looked pinched and pale.

They took their places, and the signal was given to begin the meal. Malcolm let the breath he'd been holding out slowly. All would be well. Tomorrow he'd tell his father the entire tale. For the moment, he'd enjoy a fine meal and the company of his family, who were once again safely reunited.

The table had been cleared, and mugs had been filled with ale and wine. All attention focused upon his father. The clan held their collective breath, waiting for news and the tale of his journey. William rose from his place and pounded the hilt of his dagger upon the wooden surface of the table, signaling his intent to speak.

"Long live King James." William raised his cup. The hall reverberated with cheers. William raised his hand for quiet, his gaze sweeping the hall to encompass all of them. "'Tis good to be home with kith and kin," he announced to the approving murmur of their clan. "I have much to tell, but before I begin, I have a surprise which concerns my son and the future of our clan."

His father turned to face him, and a prickle of unease raised the flesh on the back of Malcolm's neck. William once again raised his goblet as if to toast. Time stopped as Malcolm listened to the words his father spoke so that all could hear.

"As you all ken, 'tis well past time for Malcolm to take a wife and to give us an heir. I am happy to announce that I have contracted a marriage for him with the daughter of the earl of Mar, our neighbors to the north." With a satisfied look, he once again swept the hall with his gaze. "'Tis a good match, and 'twill strengthen our clan. She holds vast lands near our allies, the Sutherlands. She is a comely lass as well," he remarked with a smile. "She and her parents arrive at Moigh Hall within a se'nnight."

Not a sound came from the hall as all sat in stunned silence, their mouths agape, their eyes riveted upon the drama playing out upon the dais.

Malcolm watched the color leave his wife's face. Her hand covered their bairn in a protective gesture, and her eyes fixed upon the table in front of her. He didn't need the skills of a truth-sayer to sense her hurt and humiliation. His gut ached. He had caused this. Never again would he leave to chance anything so affecting to the feelings of those he cared for.

"I am sorry, Father, but it canna be."

CHAPTER TWENTY-ONE

"What, Malcolm? Do you defy me in this?" Malcolm's father faced him with an incredulous look.

"I am already wed." Malcolm placed his arm around True's stiff shoulders. "Lady Alethia and I took our vows before God and our clan almost six months past in November. We are handfasted."

Malcolm watched his father's jaw clench. His mother accused him with a look, and True's eyes remained fixed on the trencher in front of her. He ran his hand over his face and wished he could turn back time.

"Come, Malcolm." His father left the dais abruptly. "To my solar."

He followed his father and tried to compose himself. 'Twould do no good to lose his temper. As soon as the door shut behind them, his father took his seat and turned to face him, his expression somber.

"*When* exactly did this handfasting occur?" William gritted out through his clenched jaw.

"Shortly after we retook Meikle Geddes." So many decisions concerning their clan had taken place in this room, with his father sitting in that very same chair. How many times had he dreamed of the day the chair and the decisions would be his? Malcolm took a deep breath. "And you have no' yet heard what has transpired between our clan and the Comyns since."

"Liam told Robert, who has spoken to me briefly about it. Dinna change the subject. Was your letter regarding Meikle Geddes sent to me before or after you wed?"

"After."

William slammed his fist down on the table, causing an inkwell to bounce and spill. "And you did no' think to include this bit of news? You did no' think to tell me? God's blood, you have put me in an awkward position."

"Nay, Father. You did that on your own. I never asked you to arrange a marriage for me, nor did I give you my consent. I am a man grown—"

"Your union has no' yet been blessed by a priest." William rose from his place and began to pace. "A couple can decide to walk away from a handfasting."

The intensity of his father's glare made him feel like he was once again a lad of eight caught in some mischief. "It makes no difference." He widened his stance, folding his arms over his chest. He knew his father's thoughts and wanted to head them off. "Our union will be blessed within a fortnight."

His father scowled at him. "Or you can keep the woman as your leman, and marry the earl of Mar's daughter as your laird and father bids you."

Malcolm's temper slipped. "*The woman* has a name. She is Lady Alethia Goodsky, the daughter of a king, and she is my wife. I will have no other."

William waved his comment away like he would swat at a fly. "Have you taken leave of your senses? You found the lass by the side of the road. She brings nothing to the union, and she's no' even a Scot. I granted you the privilege of choosing your bride with the stipulation that it be an advantageous union." William leaned toward him across the table. "As my heir, you have a duty to your clan and to the earldom. Keep Alethia, but give Scotia heirs who will join two powerful clans and mayhap one day the earldoms of Fife and Mar. 'Tis an acceptable solution. Wed a Scot, lad. The match I have arranged pleases James, and it pleases me."

"It does not please me. I will no' have you dishonor my wife." Guilt weighed heavy upon him. Had he sent word to his father of his handfasting back in November, they would not be at odds now. Yet, his father bore an equal share of the blame. He had sent no word of his plans either.

"Och, man. The earl of Mar and his daughter are on their way." William took his seat again and rubbed his hands over his face. "This does no' bode well. We canna renege on the contract. 'Twill cause bad blood between our clans at a time when we can ill afford it. King James will hear of Red Comyn's death—and his son's. I dinna ken what he will make of it."

"Mairen will bear witness to her father's perfidy. Send a messenger to intercept the earl's party. You didna ken I'd already wed. I'm sure there are many who would gladly wed the lass. No harm has been done."

"Nay. Things will go forward as I have planned. How will we look to King James? We have destroyed our neighbors to the east, and now we break our word to our neighbors to the north? Talk to Alethia, Malcolm. She's a canny lass. She'll come to terms with the arrangement. 'Tis best for all."

"I am sorry, Father." Malcolm could think of only one solution. He straightened himself to his full height and faced William with determination. "We are at an impasse, for I will no' break the vows I made to Alethia. I would rather renounce my inheritance. I'll take my wife across the ocean where we will live with her people. I will no' forsake her. She is my wife." He glared at his father. "I will have no other."

Alethia had followed Malcolm and his father, determined to eavesdrop on their conversation. She covered her mouth to stifle the sob threatening to break free as she heard Malcolm swear to give up his future for her. She heard a gasp from across the corridor. Peering around the corner toward the stairs, she caught Elaine's eye. Her friend motioned for quiet and held out her hand. She hurried to take it. Elaine hustled her along the hall to her chamber and pushed her through the door, slamming it behind them.

Numb, she stood frozen in place as her friend paced.

"My brother is willing to sacrifice all for love."

"I can't let him do it, Elaine."

"Would that I had such courage." Elaine stopped on her frenetic path to face her. "He will take you home. The two of you will live with your people." Elaine took her hands briefly, seeming to look right through her.

"I won't let him throw his future away, Elaine. We cannot return to my home. It isn't possible."

"You must ken by now the answer I sent to Dylan's proposal to elope." Elaine paced again, wringing her hands. "I'll never love another. I . . . I have made a grave mistake." Her eyes stark, she sank down to sit on her bed. "Nothing is more important than love. Not land, or titles—not my father's approval or his permission. And now, Dylan is gone from my life forever." She put her face in her hands, a sob breaking free. "My brother has it aright, True. Malcolm will no' forsake you as I have forsaken Dylan. I did no' deserve him, and now he is lost to me."

"Oh, Elaine." She had no words to offer. Her own world was crumbling beneath her feet. This was not her time or her place. Her coming had been both a blessing and a curse. And tonight—she'd been proven right. No matter how things turned out, hearts were breaking—her own for certain.

A knock sounded behind her. Malcolm entered. Nodding briefly at his sister, he turned to her. "Come, *mo céile*. I find I am in need of your company."

She gave Elaine a hug and whispered in her ear, "Don't give up. You deserve happiness."

Malcolm took her arm and urged her out the door. "Come, lass. We must talk."

"How did you know I was here?"

"This has been a most trying evening. I knew you would seek my sister's company. She is your friend."

"Do you want to walk to the lake?" she asked.

"Nay, too many people celebrate my father's return this eve, and the ale and wine are flowing too freely. We'll go to our chamber."

Once inside the privacy of their room, Malcolm removed his weapons and began to disrobe.

"You said you wanted to talk, Malcolm."

"I do. Later. Right now I want you in my arms." He started undoing the laces of her gown. "I need to feel your skin next to mine."

She didn't want to talk either—or to think. Alethia stepped out of her clothing and into Malcolm's arms. He had the right idea after all. Lost in his kiss and moved by his touch, she could forget the decisions facing her.

Enveloped in Malcolm's heat, she reveled in the sensation. She ran her hands over his muscled body, memorizing each dip, each and every contour. His masculine scent, tinged with the outdoors and peat smoke, surrounded her. She took it deep into her lungs to savor. "Malcolm, did you resolve things with your father?"

"You've naught to worry about."

Shivers danced over her skin as he kissed his way down the center of her torso. His hands ran over her rib cage to cradle her hips. "Yes, but did you resolve your differences?" She held her breath. Would he tell her of his decision to give up his birthright?

"Alethia." He raised his head look at her. "I've no wish to speak of my father at present." He placed several kisses where their babe grew inside her. "Can you no' see I'm busy?"

As dire as things were, she couldn't help but smile. She tangled her fingers in his hair. "I can see that you are," she whispered, and let the magic of his touch take her far from the problems facing her.

Later, she lay snuggled next to his side with her hand over his heart to feel its steady beat. What were her choices? If she stayed and became his mistress, his wife would surely hate her and see her as a threat. Their daughter would be illegitimate. Not a good thing in the fifteenth century—she'd have no future to speak of. And if something happened to Malcolm, what would become of them? It was all moot anyway. She could not bear his being married to someone else.

"Alethia, in a fortnight the priest will arrive. Our marriage will be blessed, and immediately after we shall make preparations to travel to the land of your people."

"For a visit, you mean?" She raised herself up to look at him, holding her breath. Would he tell her about his argument with his father?

"Mayhap we'll stay for a time. That would please you, aye?"

She nodded. She couldn't allow him to throw his future or his birthright away. It was not a choice. "I love you, Malcolm. Never forget that I love you."

He rolled her over, pinning her beneath him. Nudging her thighs apart with his knees, he entered her again. His forehead came to rest on hers, and his breathing fanned her face with warmth. Love and loss welled up inside her, and she closed her eyes against the threat of tears.

"And I love you, *mo anam*. Never doubt it."

Again he brought her to the pinnacle of pleasure, only this time it was bittersweet. This time was the last time she would ever hold him in her arms. And once he fell asleep beside her, she let the tears come. She had to leave, and the sooner the better. Malcolm would be all right. Hearts healed. He would go on, marry, and fulfill his destiny without her.

But what about Hunter? Should she take him with her? For that matter, she wasn't certain Giselle would or could send her back to her own time. She hadn't come for her after the battle at Castle Rait as she'd expected. She only knew she must confront the old witch. And if she took Hunter with her, perhaps something could be done about his hearing. He was young enough to adapt, and so bright. She had no doubt he'd thrive in the twenty-first century.

Didn't Giselle's presence in Inverness mean the time had come for her to go home? Surely Giselle knew she'd completed the task she'd been given. She'd saved Malcolm's life more than once, and Mairen's. Her hidden talent, the visions, had all come at precisely the right time, and she hadn't had a single one since. Wasn't that proof?

Covering her womb with her hands, a fierce love for her child filled her. She could not allow her to suffer the stigma of being a bastard. Their daughter deserved more, and she would see that she got it. This baby girl would be all she had of Malcolm once she returned to the twenty-first century. She was certain her uncles and aunties, her cousins and Gran would welcome her child with open arms.

Unable to sleep, she slipped out of bed and tiptoed to the window. Lifting the latch to the hinged pane of glass, she swung it open to breathe the cool night air. Her eyes turned toward the sky. She'd never seen stars like she saw them here in Scotland—like diamonds against black velvet. If she tried hard enough, maybe she could find the answers she sought somewhere in that blueprint to the universe.

She was responsible for the rift between Malcolm and his father. She'd been dropped into a place and time not her own and had no right to stay. She prayed her leaving would restore things to the way they were meant to be—except her heart. That would never be the same. She would leave tomorrow, and take Hunter with her.

"*Where are we going?*" Hunter asked from the back of his sturdy little pony.

Alethia had fastened her duffel bag to the back of his saddle, and her violin she tied to the back of her own. "*We are going to Inverness.*"

"*Without Da?*"

"*Yes, without him.*" The words made her heart ache.

"*I don't think we should.*" Hunter stopped his pony on the back side of the first hill. His face wore the expression of a child whose hand is caught in a cookie jar.

"*I must. There is someone there I have to talk to.*"

"*Ask Da. He'll come with us.*"

"*Hunter, if you do not want to come with me, turn back. I won't force you.*"

He regarded her for several moments, shook his head, and reached around for the quiver holding his bow and arrows. He strung the bow and draped it over his shoulder. Straightening in the saddle, he firmed his little chin. "*I will ride with you. But this is foolish.*"

As heartbroken as she was, she couldn't help smiling. Her little man saw himself as her protector. Her own bow hung down her back, and her dirk was within easy reach strapped to her calf. She wore her plain brown gown and no jewelry. It was unlikely they would encounter any travelers until they were closer to Inverness.

They'd only ridden a short while, and already she had a raging headache. Hunter had kept up a constant stream of admonitions—turn back, this is not a good idea, Da wouldn't like it. Maybe bringing him had been a mistake. She stopped Ikwe on the trail and rubbed her temples. They had come to the same forest that held the sacred spring. The road narrowed to a darkened path cutting through it. A new feeling took hold. Unease.

She urged her mare forward and scanned the shadows near the trail. Something about this stretch of road sent prickles of anxiety down her spine. There were too many places to hide—the path too narrow, and escape routes too few. Even her mare tossed her head and sidestepped.

"*Please, let's turn back. I don't like it here.*" Hunter's eyes had grown large with fear. Whatever lurked ahead, he felt it too.

Hunter's constant harangue had eroded her certainty, replacing it with doubt and fear. What had seemed like the right thing to do now felt foolish and dangerous. Defeat weighed heavy on her shoulders. She would have to regroup. They would return to Moigh Hall. Maybe she could bribe a few MacKintosh warriors to go with her the next time. "*All right. We'll turn back.*"

Just as they turned their horses around, two figures on horseback emerged from the forest to block their way. Tension squeezed the breath from her lungs, and her mouth dried to dust. She turned her horse's head around to run in the opposite direction. Two more men emerged to cut off their escape, one of them all too familiar.

Her heart lodged in her throat—Black Hugh faced her from his horse, evil intent pulsing from him in waves that made her ill.

CHAPTER TWENTY-TWO

Hugh dismounted and moved toward her. "When first I cast my net this day, I did not think to catch so fine a fish." He sneered. "And we were going to abandon our plan if another day passed without sight of our quarry. 'Tis fortuitous indeed you happened by."

The malice radiating from him raised goose bumps all over. She reached down to get the dirk strapped to her calf. Hugh gripped her wrist and a handful of her hair and dragged her from her horse. She struggled to break his hold. He wrenched her arm painfully up behind her. Her eyes stinging with tears, she stopped struggling and instead fought to maintain her wits.

Hunter's terror was clear as he surveyed the men surrounding them. She willed him to look her way. Forcing everything else out of her mind, she sent her energy to him. Thank God, he felt it and turned to look at her. She sent him images of Moigh Hall, and images of her signing to him. "*Go. Get help. Go back the way we came. Hurry.*"

Hunter gave her a slight nod, and the fear left his face to be replaced with determination. He kicked the sides of his pony, heading into the cover of the forest before the men could stop him.

"Damnation. Go after him, Fergus," Hugh snapped at one of

the men. "I dinna care what becomes of the lad, but there may be valuables in the pack."

The man set out after Hunter, and a wave of dread and grief swamped her. Had she sent Hunter to his death? Hugh had a tight hold on her hair, almost ripping it from her scalp. He released her arm to reach down to yank her dirk from its sheath and used it to cut the quiver from her back.

"Tie her hands behind her, Rupert," Hugh ordered another of his men.

Her arms were pulled roughly behind her and tied so tightly the pain brought tears to her eyes.

"Ye will share this delectable morsel, Hugh. Equal portions, that's what ye said."

"Of course. After I am through with her, you and the others are welcome to my leavings." Hugh laughed again.

"Do you remember what Malcolm told you?" Alethia hissed. "He said if you touch me, it will be the last thing you do. You are on MacKintosh land. Malcolm is my husband, and he is only a short distance behind me on the road."

"Let us hope so," Hugh smirked.

The sound of a horse screaming with pain pierced the air, and Hugh looked uncertain for a second. She bit her lip to keep from crying out and prayed Hunter was OK. Hugh growled, tossed her mare's reins to his man, and dragged her into the woods.

"To camp," he ordered.

As they made their way along a narrow trail, Hugh shook her. "If what you say is true, he'd no' let you out of his sight. You are the perfect bait for my little trap."

She swallowed hard. After all that had happened, she could very well be the cause of Malcolm's death. She could not bear such a thing.

It wasn't long before they reached a clearing where a rough camp had been set up. Hugh shoved her hard. Without the use of her hands to break her fall, she landed on her side and slid across the ground. Her face scraped over protruding roots and stones embedded in the dirt. It stung, and her hip ached where she'd landed on it.

The men laughed. Hugh took great pleasure in looming over his unexpected prize where she lay sprawled on the ground. Mayhap things had taken a turn in his favor at last. He'd hoped to catch Malcolm out for a ride and unguarded. Catching Malcolm's woman was even better.

"I owe Malcolm for his many insults against me." He nudged her with his boot. "'Tis the reason I have camped so near Loch Moigh for the past fortnight. Though I had hoped to catch him, you will suffer my vengeance in his stead." He leered at her. "'Twill be a far sweeter endeavor, I think. And when he comes, he'll see what has befallen you at my hands before I plunge a sword through his heart."

Just then the fourth man broke through the brush, breathing hard as if he'd been running. "The little rotter put an arrow in me horse and got away. Give me your horse, Hugh, and I'll go after 'im."

"Nay," Hugh said. "Our plans have changed. Let him lead Malcolm to us. The lad saw only the four of us, and Malcolm is arrogant. He'll bring only a few men, certain he can take us. Hie yourself to the others and bring them back here. Set up a guard, and let me know the moment you see Malcolm and his men approach." Hugh dragged his catch to a tree and tied her to it. "In the meantime, I will no' be disturbed." He glared at the men. "No' even by you."

He grabbed his crotch and eyed the little bitch from the top of her head to her feet. He watched the repulsion rise in her eyes, but not fear. It angered him. He reached to grope her breasts, giving them a vicious squeeze, and waited for the fear. He grew hard waiting for it. He needed it, and stepped closer in anticipation.

She spit in his eye. "Bitch!" He swiped at his eyes, and her knee came up hard against his groin. His first blow caught her left eye. She turned her head to lessen the impact, and rage washed through him. His second blow caught the bottom of her chin, sending her head back with a loud, satisfying crack against the tree.

She slumped against the trunk, unconscious.

"Damnation." Hugh bent over in pain.

"Can we have a go at her, Hugh?"

"Nay, Rupert," he growled. "I want the bitch wide awake when I take her, and I will have her first." He straightened and turned to face his men. "Did you no' understand my orders? I want two men here with me, the rest hiding in the forest. Be off."

Malcolm returned to the keep from the lists plagued by unease. Hunter had not appeared to train, and the great hall felt bloody empty as he strode through it to take the stairs two at a time. He rapped his knuckles against the door of his mother's solar and entered. The room stood empty. He made straight for his chamber, cursing under his breath. Throwing the door wide, he scanned the room. Alethia's gowns hung from their pegs as they always did. He let out the breath he'd been holding.

Then he noticed the quiver holding her bow and arrows missing from their customary place. A closer look sent a chill down his spine. Where was her violin? Striding over to her trunk, he flipped it open and found it empty.

She'd left. Bloody hell. He should have anticipated this. He knew how his wife's mind worked. She couldn't have gotten too far. The hour was still early, and she'd still been abed when he'd risen.

He ran for the ferry landing, the bad feeling in the pit of his stomach increasing the closer he got. The ferry approached, and

Malcolm could see Hunter aboard—without True. The lad looked agitated, and he could not stand still. Malcolm's prickle of alarm grew to an all-consuming dread.

As soon as Hunter saw him, the lad began to sign wildly. Malcolm couldn't make any sense of his gestures. Hunter strained forward, as if he could make the ferry move faster by doing so. Once the ferry was within range, he backed up, took a running start and leaped the distance to shore.

Malcolm rushed forward, his heart in his throat. Catching Hunter in mid-leap, he swung him up to the shore and knelt in front of him. "*What has happened, lad?*"

Hunter's face screwed up, and tears filled his eyes. His gestures were frantic. "*Bad men have Mother. I told her to turn back. I told her, Da!*"

"*Who? What bad men have her?*"

Hunter breathed hard as he tried to think. "*The man.*" His eyes seemed to beg Malcolm to understand. "*The one who used to live here. Mother broke his nose.*" Hunter looked desperate—his eyes pleaded with him to make it all better.

Malcolm's blood turned to ice. Black Hugh had his wife. Rising from his crouch, he shouted at the top of his lungs, a call to arms. The war cry reverberated throughout the island. Warriors came, rushing from all directions, their weapons to hand. Malcolm sought those he trusted, Galen, Gareth, Robley and Liam.

"What is it?" Robley reached his side first.

"Hugh has Alethia." Cries of outrage sounded all around him as his attention went once again to Hunter. "*Do you ken which way they went? Can you lead us to her?*"

Hunter nodded. "*To Inverness.*"

"*How many men?*"

Hunter held up four fingers. Turning to the men around him, Malcolm gave orders. "There is no time to waste. We ride now. Robley, Galen, Gareth, come with me. The rest of you, set up a guard in the hills. Liam, inform my father what has occurred, and tell him we are on the road toward Inverness."

God, let me get to her in time. He and his men boarded the ferry, Hunter in tow. How dare she put herself and their bairn in such danger. "Arlen," Malcolm urged the ferry master, "make haste."

"Aye, my lord. Have the lads take up the poles to aid me."

Malcolm nodded to his men, and they took up the task, hastening the vessel toward shore. He lifted Hunter and gave him a fierce hug, then set him down at arm's length. "*You were very brave to get away, son. I am counting on you to lead us back.*"

Hunter nodded and swiped the tears from his cheeks. The trip across the loch took interminably long. Once there, Malcolm lifted Hunter to his shoulders and ran for the stables.

Ikwe's empty stall stopped him dead in his tracks. Hunter's pony, wet with sweat, was being rubbed down by one of the lads, and his wife's pack rested in the corner. "*How far?*" He turned to Hunter.

"*Not far. I rode slow on the way out.*" He shrugged. "*I did not want to go, but Ma said there is somebody in Inverness she needs to talk to.*"

"Giselle." Malcolm ran a shaking hand through his hair. He turned to one of the stable hands. "See my wife's things are taken back to the keep, lad."

"Aye, milord." He nodded.

"She must no' have been asleep when we spoke of Giselle, Malcolm. Makes you wonder what else she might have heard, does it no'?" Robley gave him a shove to get him started. "Come, we've no' a moment to waste."

They rode hard. Malcolm's horse was covered with froth, and its sides heaved when Hunter grabbed his hands. Reining in, he signed to his men to stop. Turning his son in the saddle to face him, he waited.

"*The forest around the next bend is where we were stopped,*" Hunter signed. "*The men will be watching.*"

Nodding, Malcolm dismounted. "*We go on foot from here. Gareth, guard the horses beyond the rise there.*" He pointed to a hill to their east. "*From here on in, we use sign only. Hunter, stay to help Gareth.*" He squeezed his shoulder.

Lifting his nose to the wind, he sniffed and caught the faint scent of an old campfire. Malcolm pointed to the left side of the forest. "*Hugh will have posted his men to guard their camp. Find them. Hugh is mine. Once the other three are dispatched, we'll meet at their camp.*"

"*Wait,*" Robley signed. "*This may be a trap. Mayhap there are more than the four Hunter saw.*"

"Aye," Malcolm whispered. "Why would Hugh camp on MacKintosh land? He will expect us to ride right into it. Use stealth, and take care." He knelt once more before his foster son. "*Can you watch the horses by yourself? It is a very big responsibility.*"

A look of determination came into Hunter's eyes. He nodded. Malcolm and his men led their mounts over the rise and secured them, leaving Hunter with his bow strung and an arrow notched at the ready.

"*Gareth, join the others,*" Malcolm signed. With that, Galen, Robley and Gareth melted into the trees, fanning out in search of their enemies.

Hugh and his men had left an easy trail of broken brush. Malcolm crept along, careful to keep to the shadows, careful not even to snap a twig, alert for any sign of Hugh's men. Soon, he heard movement. Edging closer, he remained hidden—until the sound of ripping fabric snapped his control.

Drawing his sword, he broke through the brush. The sight before him turned his vision red with rage. Alethia had been staked to the ground, spread-eagle. Hugh, his back to him, stood above her with a dagger in hand, slitting her garments from bodice to hem.

Malcolm grabbed him by the back of his shirt and hurled him across the clearing. "Your life is forfeit, Hugh. Pick up your sword." Two men leaped into the clearing and came at him. He cursed as he noted the Comyn plaid they wore. Hugh hung back—the coward counted on others to do his dirty work. The men he fought were ragged and hungry, fueled by desperation.

Out of the corner of his eye, he saw Hugh sneaking around the perimeter of the clearing, edging closer and closer to True, with his sword drawn and a dirk in his other hand. Malcolm gave a shrill whistle, a signal for anyone close to come to his aid. The sound distracted his opponents enough to give him the upper hand.

Malcolm plunged his sword into one man and kicked the other in the chest to buy some time. He took the dagger from his belt, flipped it in the air to catch it by the blade, and whipped it straight for Hugh's heart. He spared only a second to watch the stunned look come over Hugh's face before he fell.

Malcolm drew his sword from the corpse on the ground and spun in time to see two more Comyns come at him, Robley right behind them.

"Malcolm, there are a score of men or more surrounding us." Robley huffed as he met his enemy's ax with his sword.

"You'll not be so fortunate this day, MacKintosh," the man fighting him spat out.

"Aye, a score or more you say?" Malcolm could feel the fatigue creeping over him. He had worked his way over to stand protectively near True. Robley had done the same to flank her other side. "Four have fallen here," Malcolm said as he deflected a blow. "How many have our lads taken, Robley?"

Robley had done battle with him countless times and knew his mind. He meant to intimidate these leaderless men into fleeing. Another man appeared from the forest. Malcolm was beginning to worry. He delivered the killing blow to the enemy before him and turned to meet his new adversary.

"I took three before I reached this clearing, and Galen and Gareth have at least that many each."

"That does no' bode well for them, eh?" Malcolm continued to banter with Robley, praying his strategy would work. His new opponent came at him with a war club and sword. The sound of other struggles going on in the shadows of the forest came to him. Worried for his men, and for True, Malcolm feared he wouldn't last much longer.

He heard the thunder of horses on the trail, and his heart skipped a beat. They'd not survive this day. He'd failed True.

A familiar war cry rent the air, a MacKintosh promise of victory. His father had come. And by the sounds of it, half their garrison as well. He gave them a shrill whistle to guide them, and the noise of warriors crashing through the brush sent the Comyns fleeing just as Malcolm buckled to his knees.

"Cover True. The men will be here in a trice," Robley hissed.

Malcolm pushed himself up with the aid of his sword and reached for her cloak lying at the base of a tree. He'd just made it back to her when his father broke through to the clearing. He covered her nakedness first and then bent to cut her free.

"God's blood." William froze at the edge of the clearing to survey the scene. "This is my fault."

"Nay, Father. The fault lies with me." Malcolm's voice broke as he slid his arms under True's head and knees to lift her.

"Does she . . . is she . . . ?"

"She lives." Malcolm found he could not manage lifting her, and so he settled her against his chest and sat to catch his breath. He swallowed hard several times and blinked to clear his vision. Sweat must have gotten into his eyes during the battle.

"Uncle William, these woods are infested with vermin." Robley wiped his sword on the plaid of his enemy. "I suggest we be about the task of ridding ourselves of the infestation."

"Aye. Let us be about it."

Malcolm watched his father direct their men to fan out in search of any remaining Comyns, and suddenly, he was left alone with his wife in his arms and his heart breaking asunder in his chest.

Alethia came to and became aware of two things. Malcolm's scent—and pain, all-encompassing and pervasive. Her arms and hands felt as if they were crawling with fire ants as blood worked its way back into them. Her head throbbed, and her face burned. One of her eyes was swollen shut, and her right hip ached. She struggled to remember where she was and how she'd come to be in such a state.

She strained to see with her good eye and caught a glimpse of Malcolm's face. She could hardly draw breath, and she trembled. Oh God, Malcolm was pissed. She stared into the furious blue of her husband's icy gaze and tried to sit up. "Malcolm, I—"

"Dinna speak, woman."

She closed her mouth and looked around her at the death and destruction everywhere. Her eyes fixed on something not far from where she'd been tied. "Ohhh, oh no." She crawled out of Malcolm's lap toward the tree. There beneath it lay her violin—broken into bits.

Dazed, she picked up one piece after another of the beloved gift from her father. "No." Tears of anger and sorrow coursed down her cheeks. Helpless tears, and tears of regret.

Gentle hands lifted her. Malcolm replaced the cloak around her shoulders, drawing it tight to cover her exposed front. "W-why did he want to hurt me? What d-did I ever do to him?" she sobbed.

"He didna want to hurt you; he wanted to hurt me."

"Yeah? Well I don't see any bruises on *your* face."

Malcolm held her battered face in his large hands—his eyes desolate. "You were leaving me. You said you loved me, Alethia. Why were you leaving?"

"I do love you, Malcolm, more than my life." Her insides crumbled. "I heard you arguing with your father. I heard you tell him you would renounce your inheritance and your future rather than break your vows to me."

"Aye. We can begin anew in your land. I look forward to it. I thought 'twould please you to see your family again. Did I no' tell you I care naught for titles?"

"You've never asked me when my birthday is!" She grasped the front of his plaid and shook him, or tried to. He was immovable, a solid wall beneath her fists. She loved him—loved him enough to leave if it meant his life would be what it was meant to be.

"Och, you make no sense, Alethia. Are you saying you'd leave me because I dinna ken the date of your birth?" Malcolm shook her by the shoulders.

"I was born in the twentieth century, Malcolm. Giselle didn't just take me from my country to yours. She sent me back more than five hundred years in the past, from the twenty-first century. We can't go back to my country to live with my people." She tried to shake him again. "They haven't been born yet!" she shouted. "I can't let you throw your life away for me." She let her forehead fall against his chest. "I . . . I can't let you do that. I love you too much."

He put his arms around her and rocked her back and forth. "Och, lass. You've been through a terrible ordeal. You are talking out of your head."

"Oh, Malcolm. You don't believe me? I have proof. Why would I make up such a thing?" She pushed herself away from him to make a sweeping gesture encompassing the clearing strewn with bodies. "My God. Life is nothing like this in the twenty-first century. Stuff like this only happens in the movies.

"We have washers and dryers . . . and tampons. And . . . and . . . electricity. All I have to do is flip a switch and I have light and heat. Men have walked on the moon. Astronauts live for months at a time on an international space station." She hugged herself, trying to stop the shaking. "And I have news for you—the earth is *round.* Round, dammit—like a *ball*!"

She took a deep breath. "I've gone through more hell in the past eight months than I've gone through in the entire twenty-two years I've been alive. I can't do this anymore. I can't go through it anymore. I've had it." She swiped at her eyes. "I need a freaking vacation. And do you know what really pisses me off?" She glared at him. "When your life was in danger, I got one damned vision after another. But when my life is in danger—I get nada, zilch, nothing." She sniffed. "What the hell is up with that?"

"Let us leave this place and start for home. We'll sort it all out on the morrow."

"Home?" She started to cry again. "Your father doesn't want me there. I heard him. He suggested I become your whore while he marries you off to some bimbo with a dowry. I don't want to see that man ever again." She turned away. The sight of all the bodies made her gag.

Robley slipped quietly into camp. "I had no idea you had such a rich and varied vocabulary, Cousin True." He chuckled. "You dinna look so good, lass."

"I know." Her legs gave out, and she collapsed to the ground in a heap, clutching her cloak around her. "I don't feel so good either."

Malcolm lifted his wife into his arms as Galen joined them in the clearing. He knew his men well and had no doubt they'd done what they'd set out to do. "Come, let us return to the horses. Hunter must be worried sick by now, and we need to get home."

"Is your lady well enough to travel?" Galen peered at True's swollen and abraded face. "Mayhap 'twould be better to camp and return on the morrow. Half the garrison is here with your father, and we'd be safe. 'Twould be best to let her rest a bit."

"Nay, Galen. I have no healing teas or salves with me to ease her pain. The sooner we are home the better." He tried to communicate his thoughts to Galen without speaking. True's eyes were shut, but this was another of her tricks he'd learned well. Nodding his head toward her violin, he looked at it, then gave Galen a long look. Thankfully, Galen caught on and quietly began to retrieve the pieces, putting them back into the case. He would see if one of their craftsmen could repair it, or use what was left as a model to make her a new one.

"I believe her, Malcolm." Robley cleaned the blade of his sword against another Comyn and put it back into its scabbard.

"You overheard our conversation?" Malcolm pinned him with a look.

"Aye. I thought it prudent to stay nearby lest our enemies circle back to have another go at you."

Malcolm snorted. "She says men have walked on the moon, Robley. 'Tis no' possible. She's suffered a blow and talks out of her head."

"Hmm, I wonder. If the son of God could be born to a virgin, die on the cross, and rise from the dead three days later, surely anything under the heavens is possible." He grinned at him.

"Mmm. I dinna—"

"Think, man. You believed her visions well enough, did you no'?"

"Aye." Malcolm gave him a skeptical look.

"She traveled through time to see things that had already happened, and to the future to see things that had no' yet occurred. 'Tis but a small step to believe the rest. I wonder what electricity is, or an astronaut?" Robley's gaze went to True.

"I dinna ken. I only caught a portion of what she spoke of."

"And tamp-ons, I do hope she has some of those to show us . . . and move ease," Robley continued. "Wonders from the future, what think you of that, Malcolm?"

"She says she has proof. I will see it before my mind is made up."

"I do have proof," she muttered with her eyes still closed. "And thank you, Robley. Malcolm should listen to you more often."

"I'll no' argue the point." Robley raised a brow and switched to sign. "*True left because she could not bear to see you give up your place in our clan, Malcolm. Her feelings will not have changed on the matter.*" Robley grinned at him. "*You will have a fight on your hands, cousin.*"

Malcolm smiled back. The fear for his wife's life and his anger toward her for leaving had left him. His braw lass had the heart of a lion, and she loved him. Nothing else mattered. They would find their way together. "Aye, I expect I will. My feelings have no' changed on the matter. If my father continues to dishonor my wife, we will leave. If Alethia's home and family lie in the future, then we will confront Giselle together. I will take my family to the twenty-first century."

CHAPTER TWENTY-THREE

Alethia's entire body ached. She stretched each limb to assess the damage, and realized she was once again in her own bed. She touched her face gingerly. The skin around her left eye was tender and swollen. The abrasions on her right cheek had begun to scab. Hunger and thirst added to her misery, and she felt the presence of others in the chamber with her.

"Oh, my dear," Lydia cried. "We have been worried sick."

A cool, wet cloth came to rest against her eye. "Where is Malcolm?"

A man's throat being cleared caused her to open her good eye. William stood at the foot of the bed. Alethia didn't want him there, and she struggled to gain control of her emotions.

"My son has gone to fetch something for you to eat, lass." William came to stand beside Lydia.

She turned her face away and closed her lips tight. She heard the rustling of Lydia's gown and watched with dismay as her beloved mother-in-law left the room. She wanted to burrow under the covers.

"My wife lays the blame for all that has befallen you at my feet," William said. "My people tell me, were it no' for you, we would have ceased to exist as a clan. They say I have you to thank for my son's life many times over, and for the lives of my nephews and several of our best men as well."

William took her hand. She yanked it away.

"Good daughter, I have come to beg your pardon."

His words took her by surprise, and anger loosened her resolve not to speak to the man. "I heard you and my *husband* arguing. Malcolm said he would renounce his inheritance for my sake. I cannot let that happen."

"Nor can I, Alethia."

"I heard how you spoke about me. You do not know me or my people. I know who I am, William, and where I come from. I will never forget it." She couldn't control the emotions causing her voice to break. "If my father were alive, you would have to answer to him for suggesting I play the part of Malcolm's whore so you can marry him off to someone you find more worthy." She raised herself to sitting so she could glare at him.

"I have wronged you." William took the seat by the bed. "It seems I dinna ken my own children."

For the first time, she noticed how haggard he looked. "I know you only want what's best for your clan. I couldn't let Malcolm throw away his future. That's why I left."

"It seems I no longer have any idea what is best for my family or my clan. I'm afraid ambition clouded my vision. I dinna suppose you ken where Elaine has gone off to?"

"She's not here?" Her mind raced through the possibilities and came up with the only logical solution to Elaine's whereabouts.

"Nay, she disappeared without word the same day you did."

"I might know." She played with the edge of the linen sheet. "She said Dylan of clan Sutherland asked for her hand a while back, and you refused to grant them permission to wed. They love each other very much, William. Their feelings endured even though they rarely saw each other. We met Dylan at the fair in Inverness last fall.

He asked Elaine to elope with him." Once again, she glared at her father-in-law. "She refused him out of fear you'd disown her. I think maybe she changed her mind."

"I pray it is so and that no harm has come to her. I would no' forgive myself if anything were to happen to my lass."

"I'm sure you'll hear from her soon." Their conversation had worn her out. She lay back down and covered her eyes with her arm. "I'm tired."

The door to their chamber opened, and Malcolm entered with a tray. The smell of food made her stomach growl. Hunter rushed in behind him and climbed up on the bed beside her.

"*I did what you told me.*" He beamed with pride. "*I shot the bad man's horse and came here and got my Da. And then I guarded the horses all by myself.*"

"*You did? I'm proud of you, Hunter. You saved my life.*"

His little face went solemn. "*I told you we shouldn't have left without Da.*"

"*You were right.*" She hugged him to her and glanced at Malcolm. His back was to her as he fixed a cup of tea at the table by the hearth. "I haven't thanked you, Malcolm. You saved my life. It's the fourth time you've done so, and I'm grateful."

He straightened and tilted his head as if recounting the past eight months. With a smile that took her breath, he came to her side with the mug of steaming tea.

"Have I saved your life that many times?" He leaned over and kissed her forehead, placing the tea into her hands.

"Yes, you have. The first time was when you found me, then the first time you rescued me from Hugh. There was the time Hugh trapped me in the lake, and again when the Comyn laird had me trapped in the gallery, and yesterday."

"Yesterday makes it five times, *mo céile*. And here I thought 'twas you who did all the rescuing." Malcolm gave her another chaste kiss on her forehead.

"Do I have your forgiveness, Alethia? And yours, Malcolm?" William rose from his place by the bed. "There will be no peace for me unless I set things aright."

"Aye, so long as there is no more talk of my wedding any other than my own sweet wife." Malcolm tilted her chin up to examine her battered face, and his eyes were full of tenderness and concern. "Did Mother tell you Alethia carries our bairn?"

"Aye. 'Tis happy news indeed." William placed his hand on his son's shoulder. "I will leave you. I expect you have much to talk about."

The door shut behind William, and Alethia waited for the lecture she had coming.

"Alethia, you have no faith in me."

"Malcolm, I—"

"Nay. Harken to me. You *will* hear what I have to say this day. 'Twas easier for you to leave with my heart like a thief in the night than to place your faith and our future into my keeping. And what of my daughter? You had no right to take her from me, nor to place her life and yours in danger."

For the first time she sensed how badly she'd hurt him, and she cringed. She started to respond, only to have the intensity of his glare stop her.

"No' once have you come to me with what troubles you. No' once! Why did you no' tell me from the first Giselle sent you here from the future? You never came to me with Liam's secret or Elaine's. And you kept things from me about the battle at Rait, placing your life and the life of our bairn at risk rather than to have faith in me. You made up your mind to leave me, rather than to tell me what you overheard." He ran both hands over his face. "It must change. We canna go on as we have, lass. I willna have it."

The sadness and hurt in his eyes broke her heart. From his place in her lap, Hunter's gaze went anxiously from one adult to the other. She hugged him to her. She couldn't deny the truth. "I . . . I didn't tell you I was from the future because I didn't want to be burned at the stake for a witch."

"The MacKintosh have never done such a thing."

"Well," she muttered, "I didn't want to be the first. I'm sorry, Malcolm. What you say is true. I've been frightened of everything since I arrived here. At first my only thought was to perform the task Giselle thrust upon me so she'd return me to my own time. It was never my intent to fall in love with you, but then I did. I think, maybe I haven't relied on you out of fear she'd take me from your side." She swallowed hard. "Since my parents died, I haven't relied on anyone but myself, not even my grandmother. I've kept a part of me from you because—"

"I ken your reasons." His voice sounded weary, exasperated. He tipped her face up to look at him. "It changes today."

"Giselle—"

"Will no' take you and our bairn from me. This I vow. I ken I have your heart, *mo céile*, now I will have your faith."

Alethia nodded, unable to speak through her tears. The knot of fear that had taken up residence in her heart since the day she'd walked into Giselle's tent melted away to be replaced with trust. Malcolm would keep her safe by his side. No matter what.

"Giselle remains in Inverness for the time being. We will confront her together, lass. 'Tis the only way we can remove the threat she poses to us once and for all. 'Twill be on my terms, and the time will be of my choosing." He brushed a tender kiss across her lips. "Are we in accord on this?"

She nodded through her tears again, her heart swelling with love for the fifteenth-century nobleman who had stolen her heart.

"Now, I would see this proof from the future you spoke of." Malcolm sat on the edge of the bed. Taking her hand in his, he brought it to his mouth to place tender kisses in the center of her palm.

"I want to eat and bathe first. Let's share it with the whole family at the same time, Malcolm. I've tried to turn my laptop on every week to keep the battery in good shape, but even with the solar recharger, I'm not sure how long it will last."

"I dinna understand a thing you just said." He grinned. "Except the eating and bathing part. 'Twould be my pleasure to see to both."

William, Lydia, Malcolm, Robley, Liam, Mairen and Hunter sat around the table in the laird's solar as Alethia passed around her driver's license and money from the twenty-first century. "DOB means date of birth." She pointed to her license as William studied it. "I was born in the twentieth century." She giggled. "I married a man more than five hundred years older than me."

Robley held the cash she'd earned working at Renaissance fairs. "You say this is currency from your time, True?"

She nodded.

"And Giselle sent you to us. We must talk about this future, cousin. Mayhap I'll ask Giselle to send me there one day. 'Twould be the adventure of a lifetime, aye?" He grinned. "Are all the lasses from your time as canny and braw as you?"

"Women in the twenty-first century are as varied as they are in this century, Robley. Most are very independent. Some choose careers rather than marriage and a family. We have more choices." She opened her laptop and turned the power on. The tone it emitted startled those sitting around her. "It's OK. This is just a tool to use. It cannot harm anyone. Have you thought about what you want to see, Malcolm?" She opened her photos library.

"Aye. You said you can show us our planet as it looks from out amongst the stars. I would see it for myself, and the space station you spoke of." Malcolm moved behind her place to look over her shoulder.

She clicked on the file of pictures she'd saved to use as wallpaper from the NASA Web site. The screen filled with the images he'd requested. Everyone assembled gasped.

Lydia reached out a tentative finger to touch the picture. "Och, you say this is truly our world?" she asked, her voice filled with awe. "'Tis quite beautiful."

"Humph," William grunted. "You said you had images of your parents to show us, True. I would see this father of yours now."

Alethia brought up her favorite picture from her parents' wedding. Her mother had chosen a full, white traditional wedding gown with a long train. Seeded with tiny pearls and rhinestones, it glittered richly. She wore a tiara and veil over the long golden locks curling over her shoulders. Her mother's image smiled out at her, while her father's gaze remained fixed upon his new bride. The adoration he felt for her mother came through very clearly.

Her father wore a black tux with long tails. Across his chest he wore a beaded bandolier bag as testimony to the pride he felt for his heritage. He also wore a traditional beaded black felt and beaver pelt hat. Alethia could not help but be proud. They looked every bit the royal couple.

"Oh, my dear. Your parents were quite handsome. Your mother looks as if she could have been from Scotia. She's so fair and bonny." Lydia sighed.

"She was Scottish, a MacConnell. In the twenty-first century, there are more Scots living on the North American continent than in Scotland." She grinned.

"The devil you say." William moved closer to the screen.

"I don't know what to do with all this stuff. It's from a different time, and it wouldn't be good if—"

"I agree." Malcolm placed both hands on her shoulder. This shall remain between us, aye?" He waited until everyone nodded their assent. "Mayhap we should destroy these things, or bury them where they can never be found."

"Eventually." Alethia glanced up at him. "I'm not quite ready to part with them." A lump rose to close her throat. "This is all I have left of my life and family. I have no way of printing the pictures I have on my hard drive."

"Hard drive?" Robley leaned closer. "I agree with Cousin True. Let's not be so hasty to dispose of these wonders."

"Dinna even think it, lad." William huffed out a laugh. "My brother would never forgive me if you were to disappear to the future."

Alethia caught Robley's eye, and he winked at her.

"Of course no', Uncle William."

Alethia shook her head, knowing whatever was to come was out of their hands, exactly like her arrival had been completely out of hers. She let her gaze fall on each member of her new family. Her heart filled with love, and she placed her hand gently on her growing baby bump. "Here, I'll show you the space station."

June 1424

"I still dinna ken why my daughter and her husband insisted we must travel to Inverness to see them," Lydia complained from her place in the caravan traveling to the spring fair in Inverness.

"I think despite William's letter giving them his blessing for their union, they are nervous about seeing him and wish their first meeting to be on neutral ground," Alethia answered from atop Ikwe's place beside her mother-in-law. "Elaine knows how much you dislike traveling, Lydia. It will mean so much to her that you made the trip."

"I should think so," she snapped. "You should no' be undertaking such a journey in your condition, True."

"I'm fine." She placed her hand over the swell of her growing child. "We're fine. Besides, nothing could have prevented me from seeing Elaine." She glanced to the head of their party. William and Malcolm led them, with Hunter in his place of honor in Malcolm's lap. She sighed with contentment. She and Malcolm had discussed the possibility that Giselle could still be in Inverness. Together they decided to confront her if they had the chance. Both knew it was necessary if they were ever to put all fears of her behind them.

Alethia fixed a wary eye on the fortune-teller's green-and-white-striped tent, and gripped her husband's arm. "Malcolm," she whispered, pointing with her chin toward the dreaded tent.

"I see it, *mo anam.*" He gave her hand a reassuring pat.

Hunter, sensing their sudden tension, clutched her gown with one hand and Malcolm's plaid with the other. Alethia took a deep breath and raised her chin. "Let's get this over with."

As they approached, she felt the same sensation prickling down her neck she'd experienced the first time she entered the fortune-teller's tent. Giselle appeared in the entrance as if she'd been expecting them. Hunter balked, stopping in his tracks.

"Welcome, Alethia." Giselle beckoned them to come inside. "Malcolm."

"Madame Giselle, we have some questions for you." Her heart pounding, Alethia forced herself to move forward. The old woman chortled, sending goose bumps skittering over her skin. She nudged Malcolm, who hadn't said a word.

"Aye, we have questions. I would have your assurance my family is safe to enter yon tent."

Malcolm had his hand on the dagger at his waist, and she held her breath.

"You have naught to fear from me, lad. Enter. I will answer your questions as best I can."

Hunter wouldn't budge. Sending Malcolm a look, Alethia beseeched him for help, and he lifted his son and ducked as he entered the tent. She followed. Giselle had three chairs set around her table. She had been expecting them. Alethia arranged her gown and sat in one. Malcolm took his place beside her, and Hunter clung to him with his face pressed into his foster father's neck.

"First, I want to know why you never came for me after I saved Malcolm's life," she began. "Did you always intend for me to stay?"

"Malcolm's life? Humph. 'Twas not his life you were sent here to save, child." Giselle snorted.

"Whose then?" Fear that her ordeal was not yet over gripped her.

"There sits the lad whose life hung in the balance." Giselle pointed to Hunter.

Hunter glanced at the old woman over his shoulder, his eyes wide with fear.

"I don't understand." Alethia frowned. "Why did you give me the pendant? You said I'd know my destiny when I found its mate." She looked at her husband. "He had the ring."

"Aye, I gave Malcolm the ring so you'd know you were in the right place." She cackled with glee. "I do enjoy a bit o' matchmaking. Do you still have the necklace?"

Giselle looked at her as if she knew very well what had happened to the pendant.

"No."

Beside her, Malcolm reached into his sporran and drew out the necklace with the ring on its chain. Alethia jumped to her feet. "You've had that damned thing all this time and never told me?"

"Be at ease. Neither piece holds any magic whatsoever," Giselle commanded. Her voice had changed. No longer did she sound like the old woman she appeared to be. "They are a gift to you both. My husband had them made for me as a wedding present eons ago."

"Who are you, Giselle? Do you pose a threat to me and mine?" Malcolm demanded as he too rose from his place.

"Nay, I am no threat to you and yours. Sit, both of you."

As Alethia watched, Giselle changed before her eyes. The visage of the old gypsy gave way for a brief instant to reveal a being so ethereal and beautiful it hurt to look at her. Hair the color of moonlight hung about her shoulders and fell all the way to her ankles, huge eyes an impossible iridescent blue set wide in a perfect oval face regarded them with an expression she could not interpret.

She sat as ordered. Malcolm did the same beside her.

Just like that, the image disappeared, and they faced Giselle once again. "Did you see what I saw, Malcolm?" she whispered.

"Aye, I saw."

"My name is Áine. I am of the race called *Tuatha Dé Danann*. Some call us faerie folk, though we do not name ourselves thus. Only once in my long life did I wed, and he was a mortal—a braw warrior and the founder of clan MacConnell. I gave him seven sons and one daughter. Hunter is my grandson many generations removed. The blood of the *Tuatha Dé Danann* also runs through your veins, Alethia. 'Tis why you have the gifts that you do. It took me some time to find one such as yourself. My husband's clan intermingled freely with my people. Their giftedness was highly revered by all. You are both MacConnells."

"Wait. Time out!" Alethia cried. "I'm part faerie?"

"Aye." Giselle laughed, and it sounded like a running brook. "I am a time traveler. I like to visit my progeny from time to time. It gives me pleasure to do so.

"Shortly after Hunter was born, I came to see him. As I left, his father got caught up in my wake and was taken to the future with me. He died before I could return him to his home. Time travel is not an exact science, you see. One cannot always predict—"

"So that left Hunter without his father, which led his mother to return to our village, which in turn led to the illness that took his mother and his hearing," Malcolm surmised.

"That is so." Giselle nodded. "If I had not sent Alethia when I did, my grandson would have perished over the winter."

"Humph. You chose my wife because you knew the two would have an affinity?"

"Yes. Hunter needed her, and only she could save him."

"What about the visions, Giselle? When the Comyns threatened the MacKintosh, I had visions. Are they part of my hidden talents?" she asked.

"Yes and no. I cannot be certain. You carry a daughter who has gifts of her own. It may be her power mingles with yours, and that is why the visions were possible. It may also be that in times of trouble you will receive visions to guide you." Giselle smiled. "I have no control over such things."

"I have another question, if you dinna mind my asking." Malcolm looked at Alethia as he spoke.

"What is it you wish to know, warrior?"

"My wife has told me about the wonders of her century. She has shared with me many of the miracles healers from her time can perform. I fear for her life when the time comes to deliver our babe. So many women perish during childbirth . . ."

"Malcolm, you've never said anything about this to me." Alethia grabbed his hand, sensing what he would say next and wishing to stop him. "I'll be all right."

"I canna bear the thought of losing you, True."

"What is it you wish to ask, Malcolm?" Giselle interrupted.

"Is it possible to send us to the future when my wife's time comes? Could anything be done about Hunter's hearing in the twenty-first century?"

Stunned, she realized he'd been giving this a great deal of thought. He'd intended to ask these questions since he'd learned the truth about her origins.

"Hmm, if it is his hearing that concerns you, give the lad to me." Giselle reached for Hunter, who took that as a signal to climb like a monkey up his foster father and cling to his back—as far from Giselle as he could possibly get without leaving his parents. Malcolm pried him loose and handed him to his grandmother—many times removed.

Hunter kept his eyes locked on Alethia and signed frantically, "*I don't like this. Please, Ma, I don't like her. She scares me.*"

Alethia leaned forward, intending to take him from Giselle, only to be stopped by a push of pure energy.

"I mean him no harm, child. This will take only a moment." Giselle blew into one of his ears, then the other. Then she placed her hands over both and closed her eyes for a moment. Satisfied, she handed him back to Alethia.

"What did you do?" she asked.

At the sound of her voice, Hunter covered his ears and made a sound of distress. He scrambled into her lap, and Alethia hugged him tight to her chest.

"He hears. It will take some time for him to adjust," Giselle answered. "As to your other question, Malcolm, no, I cannot send you to the future. It is forbidden. I had to set things right after taking Hunter's father from him. It is our law and the only reason I could bring Alethia here to you."

Giselle shook her head as Malcolm made to argue. "Do not fear. Though I cannot send you to the future, I can bestow upon you a blessing. The little family you protect is dear to me, warrior. I grant you this boon. Know that the two of you shall live a long and happy life together. You shall have six strong and healthy children, and all will survive. When you need help the most, help shall find you." She rose from her place and moved toward the back of her tent to draw something from a large old trunk.

Alethia's eyes went wide, and she leaned back in the chair. *Six children?* And all healthy. She would have the big family she'd always dreamed of after all—a family her gran, cousins, uncles and aunties would never meet. Regret stole her breath, and she glanced at her husband, grounding herself in his strength and presence.

He'd straightened in his chair and puffed out his chest. A dazed, happy expression suffused his features. His obvious pride at Giselle's revelation brought a smile to her face. Her future was here with him, and life in the twenty-first century would go on without her.

"This is for you, Alethia."

Giselle's voice brought her back to attention. She handed her a small lap harp, like the ones used by the bards in this era.

"I regret the loss of your violin. I know how important music is to you. You must continue with it."

Alethia ran her hand over the smooth polished wood. "It's lovely, thank you. Um . . . does it . . . is it . . . ?"

Giselle disappeared once more to reveal her true identity. Áine laughed softly as she stood before them. "The harp holds no magic, child. Go now, live your lives in peace." With that, she disappeared altogether.

"Let's get out of here, Malcolm."

"I'm right behind you, woman."

EPILOGUE

October 1424

The entire clan waited with bated breath as Malcolm's wife labored to give birth to their wee bairn. A collective sigh went up all over the island and across the loch in the village when the newborn's wail could be heard. News that mother and child were well traveled swiftly from the island to shore.

At least, that was how it seemed to Malcolm. He knew his thoughts were fanciful. No matter. He smiled down at Hunter pacing beside him.

They both waited outside his chamber door, Hunter imitating his foster father's actions right alongside him. His own mother had banned him from their chamber, and the midwife scolded him for upsetting True with his fretting. His heart had leaped with joy at the sound of his bairn's first cry. At least his mother had the courtesy to inform him that his wife and child were well.

"Are we invited in to see the babe yet, lad?" William beamed as he approached.

"Nay, no' yet. They are cleaning up first. I dinna think I can bear it much longer."

"Da, Ma is fine." Hunter tugged at his hand.

Malcolm tousled his hair. It still thrilled him to hear Hunter speak aloud. "I ken she is. Do you no' wish to see your new sister, lad?"

"Aye." Hunter grinned up at him.

Just then the door behind them opened. "You can come in now, but be quiet," Lydia bid them. "True is quite exhausted." She put her hand on Malcolm's arm. "Your wee lassie is beautiful, Malcolm. Perfect in every way." She opened the door wide for the MacKintosh men to enter.

Malcolm went to his wife's side; their daughter lay cradled in her arms. True never looked more beautiful to him than she did at that moment. He swallowed the lump in his throat. Gently he sank down on the bed beside her while Hunter climbed up the other side. His mother and father stood together by the foot of their bed.

"Let me see her," Malcolm said as he reached for his daughter. She made tiny noises as he unwrapped the swaddling blanket to see what their love had wrought. She had ten perfect toes, ten wee fingers, and dark downy hair covering her perfect little head. He couldn't get enough, couldn't take his eyes from her. Raising her up, he kissed her soft, warm head and cradled her next to his heart. Leaning over, he kissed his wife. Her expression was that of tired bliss. "What shall we call her?" he asked.

"I want to call her Sky, after my family name. You can choose the middle name."

"What think you of Elizabeth, after my mother?" Lydia asked. "It has a nice ring to it. Sky Elizabeth of clan MacKintosh."

"I like it." She smiled.

"Hunter, do you wish to hold her?" Malcolm asked.

"Aye, if you please."

"You must support her head, like this." Malcolm demonstrated before wrapping her back up and placing her in his foster son's waiting arms. He took True's hand in his as they both watched Hunter gaze with wonder at Sky.

"Give her back to me, Hunter," True said as Sky began to fuss. She held her arms out for her daughter, and Hunter scooted out of her reach, keeping a firm hold on his foster sister. "I'm going to marry her one day," he said, not taking his eyes off the baby in his lap.

Malcolm chuckled, taking the bairn from Hunter. "Mayhap you will, but not today, lad." He handed his wee daughter to True, his chest full to bursting as he beheld those most dear in this world, content to the very depths of his soul.

Read on for a sneak peek of Barbara Longley's next Novel of Loch Moigh.

Available Summer 2014 on Amazon.com

The Highlander's Bargain

Summer 1426

I agreed to pilfer this for you, and I have." Robley placed the gold-chased disk of silver on the table between them. "I've done my part."

"So you have." Madame Giselle turned the platter over and traced her finger reverently over the inlaid gold. "So you have."

"Now for your part of our bargain—"

"Impatient?" Giselle straightened and raised an eyebrow. "Very well then, mortal." She crossed the room and took a large wooden box from the floor, and returning with it, she set it upon the table and opened the lid. "Now, I'm sure I put them in here . . . ," she muttered while shifting around the objects inside. "Ah, here it is." Her eyes lit up, and she lifted a small leather pouch. "Listen carefully." Placing the pouch in his hand, she gestured for him to sit.

He pressed the leather between his palms, trying to ascertain its contents.

"This pouch holds two crystals, tokens for your passage to and from the future. Wherever your departure may be, that will be the very point of your return. Hold fast in your mind the time and place you wish to be, and spin one of one of the crystals like a child's toy."

"A toy?" His eyes widened.

"You'll know what I mean when you see the crystals."

He tugged the pouch open to take a look.

"Not now." Giselle covered his hands with hers. "Just listen. When you spin the crystal, you will see a change in the air above. Remember. Hold fast in your mind the time and place you wish to be and step into the disturbance. Time travel is not always exact," she warned. "More so on the journey. You will always return to the exact spot, but you must hold the time you mean to return to in your mind. It's crucial, or you may end up in a century not your own."

"I understand." He stood and opened his sporran, dropping the pouch inside. Much had to be done before he departed, and he had to decide when and where his journey would begin. Not knowing what to expect, he'd brought the currency True had given him, but now he wanted one more conversation with his cousin before he departed. He needed more details about the fair she'd been attending when she'd been taken. The Renaissance fair would be the perfect destination. Aye, it felt right. "My thanks, Madame Giselle."

"Don't thank me yet, lad. You've no idea whether or not the future will be to your liking." She stood as well, walking toward the door behind him. "Good luck to you. Journey well, and may you find what it is you seek."

Floating on a cloud of elation, he took his leave and set his course for Inverness Castle. Tomorrow he'd start out for home. He'd return to Loch Moigh with his fate held securely in a leather pouch within his sporran. Bloody hell! He'd just been to the realm of the fae. How many men could say that? Fetching the silver-chased disk had been easy, just as Giselle had said. Too easy.

For certes he'd gotten the better end of the bargain. Hadn't he? He stopped in his tracks, doubt clouding his mind. Giselle was fae, and he'd heard the stories his entire life. Rarely were things what they seemed with the fae.

He shook it off. She'd said his task would be simple, and it was.

That's all there was to it. She had familial ties with his clan, and he had naught to worry about. Excitement thrummed through his blood. Within a se'nnight, he'd begin the greatest adventure of his life.

Erin swiped at the perspiration wrecking her makeup and checked the ground at the base of the cottonwood. She didn't want to get anything on her Renaissance gown during her short break. Scanning the area for anthills, she set her bowl of "the Queen's Caramel Apples" down and settled herself on the grass.

She tugged off her veil and headpiece, tossing them to the ground. Leaning back on the rough bark, Erin closed her eyes against the mother of all headaches torturing her. The unseasonably hot day, constant blowing dust and the smell of fried food and stale beer sure didn't help. She massaged her temples, trying to stop the throbbing. If only she could ease her own pain the same way she did for her patients, but no. Her gift had never worked like that.

No doubt her headache was stress related, exacerbated by the heat and too many layers of heavy brocade and linen. Maybe if she pounded her head against the tree, she'd knock out the pain. Or not. She let out a long sigh, opened her eyes and stared up at the canopy of leaves.

What was she going to do? Almost finished with her master's program, so close to getting her midwife certification, and her roommate chose now to move out of their apartment without notice? "Just my luck."

She couldn't afford the rent on her own, no matter how much she loved her large old apartment with its oak floors and built-in buffet. Thinking about the daunting task of finding a cheaper place sent another throb pounding through her skull. Her plate was already way too full. Plus, only one more weekend before the Renaissance festival closed, and this little bit of extra income would come to an end. With classes and clinicals, she hardly had any time to pick up nursing shifts. She supposed she could give up sleeping. "Screwed. I'm so screwed."

She surveyed the back lot of the Renaissance fairgrounds. The grassy field held all the RVs, tents, trucks and trailers the seasonal workers brought with them for their weekends at the fair. The scent of horse manure drifted to her resting place, reminding her of the state of her life. "Crap."

Well, there wasn't anything she could do about it right this minute. She brought her treat to her lap, dipped an apple slice into the gooey caramel and took a big bite. The tartness coupled with the sweet caramel was so good she swore her mood lifted at least a few millimeters. Nothing like a bowl full of something sweet to bring her spirits up. She popped the remaining bit of apple in her mouth and sorted through her options.

Going to her mother for help was out. She and stepdad number four were going through another rough patch, and no doubt her mother would soon be single and impoverished once again. It was too late to take out a larger student loan for the semester. Did she have anything to pawn? Nope. She'd just have to float some bills and find a new roommate in a big fat hurry.

Dipping another apple slice into the dark golden sweetness, she caught movement from the corner of her eye and lifted her gaze, squinting a bit. About five yards from where she sat, heat waves shimmered and rose from the dirt like something you'd see radiating off a blacktop road, only way more defined. As she watched, the anomaly grew even stronger. "What the heck?"

She set her snack aside and pushed herself up to investigate. The moment she rose, the undulating waves took on color—pale pink and green. "Huh, a mini aurora borealis right here in the middle of the grass and on a bright sunlit day?"

She moved closer, glancing around to see if anyone else had noticed. Nope. All alone and standing an arm's length away, she fought the urge to reach out and see what would happen if she stuck her hand into the mirage. "Probably not a good idea," she muttered, mesmerized by the dancing light show.

Something changed. A form appeared behind the shimmer. A man? Erin gasped a second before the impact sent her flying. "*Ooph.*" Flat on her back with the wind knocked out of her, she found herself pinned by his weight. She stared into the bluest eyes she'd ever seen. Her mouth went dry, and her heart pummeled her rib cage. Frightened out of her wits, she blinked a few times, hoping he'd disappear and everything would go back to normal. Impossible! Gorgeous men do not just fall out of thin air.

ACKNOWLEDGMENTS

A special thanks goes out to Lindsay Guzzardo and the Montlake crew for giving this book of my heart a home. I also want to thank my wonderful agent, Nalini Akolekar, for believing in my work and for her constant support. And last, but certainly not least, a big thank-you to my readers. I love to hear from you. You can contact me through my website: www.barbaralongley.com. You can also follow me on Twitter @barbaralongley and on Facebook: www.facebook.com/pages/Barbara-Longley. Happy reading!